BOY ROBOT

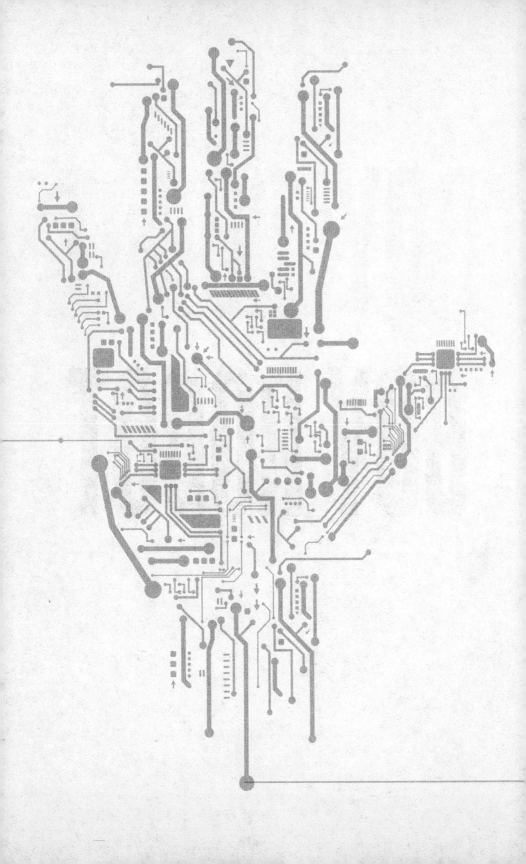

BOY ROBOT

SIMON CURTIS

SIMON PULSE
NEW YORK · LONDON · TORONTO · SYDNEY · NEW DELHI

SIMON PULSE

An imprint of Simon & Schuster Children's Publishing Division

1230 Avenue of the Americas, New York, New York 10020

First Simon Pulse hardcover edition October 2016

Text copyright © 2016 by Simon Curtis

Jacket illustration copyright © 2016 by Will Staehle

All rights reserved, including the right of reproduction in whole or in part in any form.

SIMON PULSE and colophon are registered trademarks of Simon & Schuster, Inc.

For information about special discounts for bulk purchases, please contact Simon & Schuster Special Sales at 1-866-506-1949 or business@simonandschuster.com.

The Simon & Schuster Speakers Bureau can bring authors to your live event. For more information or to book an event contact the Simon & Schuster Speakers Bureau at 1-866-248-3049 or visit our website at www.simonspeakers.com.

Jacket designed by Russell Gordon

Interior designed by Steve Scott

The text of this book was set in Melior.

Manufactured in the United States of America

1 2 3 4 5 6 7 8 9 10

This book has been cataloged with the Library of Congress.

ISBN 978-1-4814-5929-7 (hc)

ISBN 978-1-4814-5931-0 (eBook)

The blood in our veins
The stars in our eyes
The push of a seed
Toward the sun, till it dies
The unwhispered dreams
And hope in our lungs
We breathe it
And vibrate
The bell has been rung
Though who is to say
Who can, and can't hear
The sound of our souls
Crying out to closed ears
But once in a lifetime
One moment that matters
Shoots through the heart of the world
And then shatters
Every illusion
Every facade
Dispels the confusion, and
Clears the mirage
That we build in our heads,
In our hearts,
And our minds
That somehow we differ,
And vary in kinds
Fantasies held
So deep and so dear
Our fingers go numb
Clinging on to our fear
But once all is broken
And dust in the wind
It's time that we realize
Without and within
We all are no more
Than motes in the air
All beat with one heart
The pulse
We all share.

I wrote the dedication below in early 2016 and wanted to make sure it remained intact. However, after the massacre at Pulse nightclub in Orlando on June 12, it is necessary that I add forty-nine new names to the list of people whose lives this book is dedicated to.

||||||||||||||||||||||||||||||||||||||||||||||||||||||||||||||||||||||||||||||||||||||||||||||||||||||||||||||||||||||

One of my dearest friends was one of the first people to read this book. Halfway through, he told me he felt overwhelmed by how sad some of the stories were. He said he felt as though some of the characters' origins were almost too tragic, too gutting.

There is a story that has haunted me since I read about it in the news, just before I started drafting this book in earnest. It was a story of a girl who'd lived her entire life reaching out for acceptance, compassion, and understanding. Who needed, more than anything, just a bit of empathy, and love. She lived her life bearing the weight of a world that told her it didn't want her, and ultimately, it crushed her.

I thought of her often while writing this book, thought of the stories of people like her. People like myself: young gay kids, kicked out of their homes, as I was, for simply being who they are. I thought of so many others who have faced horrible, unfathomable things because they simply dared to be born differently.

I feel so incredibly lucky to be who I am today. To have found reconciliation, and genuine, true love in this world—with my family, my parents, and my loved ones. But so many others have not been so lucky. I've compiled a brief list below—a list that I'm sure only begins to scratch the surface—of names you can research and learn more about should it ever cross your mind that someone's origin story might be "too tragic, too gutting." Names of real people who lived, and died, bearing the weight of a world that told them it didn't want them.

This book is dedicated to Leelah Alcorn, Jess Shipps, and every single young soul who has ever been made to feel less than she is because of who she is. May you shine bright, stand tall, love proudly, and above all else, live.

—S. C.

Papi Edwards

Lamia Beard

Ty Underwood

Yazmin Vash Payne

Taja Gabrielle DeJesus

Penny Proud

Bri Golec

Kristina Infiniti

Keyshia Blige

London Chanel

Mercedes Williamson

Jasmine Collins

Ashton O'Hara

India Clarke

K.C. Haggard

Shade Schuler

Amber Monroe

Kandis Capri

Elisha Walker

Tamara Dominguez

Kiesha Jenkins

Zella Ziona

Eylul Cansin

Melonie Rose

Zander Mahaffey

Aubrey Mariko Shine

Ash Haffner

Sage David

Taylor Wells

Blake Brockington

Ezra Page

Taylor Alesana

Sam Taub

Rachel Bryk

Cameron Lagrell

Kyler Prescott

Sam Ehly

Skylar Marcus Lee

Ryley Courchene

Emmett Castle

Ashley Hallstrom

Stanley Almodovar III

Amanda Alvear

Oscar A. Aracena-Montero

Rodolfo Ayala-Ayala

Antonio Davon Brown

Darryl Roman Burt II

Angel L. Candelario-Padro

Juan Chevez-Martinez

Luis Daniel Conde

Cory James Connell

Tevin Eugene Crosby

Deonka Deidra Drayton

Leroy Valentin Fernandez

Simon Adrian Carrillo Fernandez

Mercedez Marisol Flores

Peter O. Gonzalez-Cruz

Juan Ramon Guerrero

Paul Terrell Henry

Frank Hernandez

Miguel Angel Honorato

Javier Jorge-Reyes

Jason Benjamin Josaphat

Eddie Jamoldroy Justice

Anthony Luis Laureanodisla

Christopher Andrew Leinonen

Alejandro Barrios Martinez

Brenda Lee Marquez McCool

Gilberto Ramon Silva Menendez

Kimberly Morris

Akyra Monet Murray

Luis Omar Ocasio-Capo

Geraldo A. Ortiz-Jimenez

Eric Ivan Ortiz-Rivera

Joel Rayon Paniagua

Jean Carlos Mendez Perez

Enrique L. Rios Jr.

Jean C. Nives Rodriguez

Xavier Emmanuel Serrano Rosado

Christopher Joseph Sanfeliz

Yilmary Rodriguez Solivan

Edward Sotomayor Jr.

Shane Evan Tomlinson

Martin Benitez Torres

Jonathan Antonio Camuy Vega

Franky Jimmy Dejesus Velazquez

Juan P. Rivera Velazquez

Luis S. Vielma

Luis Daniel Wilson-Leon

Jerald Arthur Wright

THE RUNNING GIRL

Run.

Her heart pounded in her ears. The muscles in her legs burned, but the adrenaline wouldn't let her mind acknowledge the pain. Her feet slammed into the pavement and her eyes frantically, instinctively, scanned for a way out. Any way out. The night air hung thick with the remnants of a scorchingly hot day, and the humidity was slowing her down. It wouldn't slow down the others though.

The others . . . It won't affect them, and they're all that matters. Don't let it affect you either. Run.

But they were closing in, the men dressed in black. No matter which turn she took, which alley she went down, the pursuing footsteps were always just behind. Unshakable. Relentless. She needed to get to the canal, with the people in the little boats, tourists seeing the city, and restaurants with the patios. People, people everywhere, enjoying their carefree summer evening. The men dressed in black wouldn't follow where there were so many people. Or would they? They were getting more ruthless and less careful in their efforts to be inconspicuous. But still, the men dressed in black wouldn't take her on in front of all of those people, especially not when she had three with her now. No. They couldn't.

The three of them ran just behind her, despite the fact that they could have easily outdistanced her. She was guiding them to safety. She'd led dozens, if not hundreds, to the Underground already. She was to be trusted, and had more than proven herself.

The youngest had just turned eighteen last night and was still weakened from the excruciating headache. She knew his brain felt like a balloon that had been filled triple, quadruple, a hundred times its normal capacity. It was hard for him to run; his reflexes weren't quite as sharp as the others yet.

And he was the first to go down. The whizzing sound of the single Taserifle shot was all she needed to hear to know time was running out and that they were about to be overtaken. She turned slightly and saw the men approach her fallen lamb, thrusting a thin metal shaft through his temple, right into his brain. He didn't even have time to scream. One by one, the cells in his body disintegrated, then exploded in a brilliant flash. How many times had she seen this same light from her periphery?

Another young life exploded as she fled.

A million little lights flared up behind her, floated into the sky and melted into oblivion. For just a moment they illuminated the street, revealing an alleyway just behind a brick building. She spun as quickly as she could and raced into the blackness.

Faster. Faster!

She couldn't feel her legs anymore. Her lungs ached, and sweat was beginning to sting her eyes. The men dressed in black were still closing in.

A shot from one of the Taserifles ricocheted off a dumpster beside her with a flurry of sparks.

Just a little farther. He's waiting on the next block. Just a little farther.

If the loss of the youngest one affected the other two, they didn't let it show. Neither spoke. They just ran. She'd picked up the girl in a town just outside of Dallas earlier that week. *Girl . . . She's only a few years younger than me.* But she herself didn't feel like a girl anymore. Ushering this lost soul of an early-twentysomething misfit from Nowhere, Texas, to a place where she would belong, while still somehow managing to evade the Sheriffs, made her feel more than a few years older despite their true ages.

She was pretty too, this girl, with strawberry-blond hair, bright cherry lips, and an impeccable, athletic frame. She was so shy, working in an old diner where she rarely had to see anyone she hadn't known since birth and most certainly never had to deal with any modern electronic devices like computers or cell phones. She was nice and quiet. Without even asking, she had known that this girl from just outside of Dallas had probably cried herself to sleep almost every night of her life, not understanding what she was, not understanding what was wrong with her, or why she existed in the first place.

It was the same with all of them: orphans, walking the world with nowhere to go and no one to confide in.

The girl hit the ground like a rag doll as the Tasershot hit the back of her neck, almost like it worked before making impact. She landed facedown on the pavement, red-gold silk strewn all about her shoulders.

Another flash of a million little lights floated up into the sky and melted into oblivion.

Run! Run!

The guy, the last still running, had been with them for a while now. She'd found him in Houston, living on the street and working as a prostitute and a drug dealer while somehow managing to avoid the Sheriffs. He was twenty-six. She had no idea how he'd managed so long. They almost never found any over the age of twenty-one who'd survived on their own and evaded the Sheriffs all that time, but here he was, running beside her, running for his life . . . and for hers.

She could see lights on the other side of the redbrick building now. They were close to safety.

They hurtled around the last corner and stopped.

Dead end.

There was no turning around. Footsteps were already rounding the corner behind them. The only escape was a tiny, rusted metal ladder scaling the side of the building to their left, but there was no way to climb it without giving the men ample time to take them down and kill them, just like they had the others.

Without a pause, the lost boy from Houston grabbed her hand and looked into her eyes. Knowing, and death and hope and gratitude, passed between them. He turned to face the Sheriffs coming down the alleyway, lowered his hands, and let the light start to glow within his eyes.

The air in the alley began to prickle, and the thick moisture that clung so deeply to her lungs seemed to wick itself right out of the atmosphere. Tiny red particles of light drew into his fingertips and gathered like fireflies in a jar. They rapidly swelled, then flared up into a blinding light. At the same moment, a giant wall of fire severed her from the boy and the men pursuing them. She could still make out his silhouette on the other side of the massive blaze—a solid wall that reached the roof of the buildings on either side—standing still, standing tall. Completely isolated behind the towering inferno and completely unable to help him face the men, she turned and raced up the rusty ladder.

A crack of lightning and a deep, drumming roll of thunder pealed across the sky.

Each rung was slick with her own sweat, and she could feel blisters forming. The muscles in her arms now burned just as much as those in her legs, and when she thrust herself onto the roof of the three-story brick building, she staggered backward, overcome. Every ounce of her fought to turn and look, to peer down into the alley and see if the boy was still alive, but she couldn't. One untrained twenty-six-year-old Unreclaimed versus two dozen Sheriffs?

She knew the outcome without looking.

She raced over the roof as the tiniest of raindrops began to pelt the earth, heading for a fire escape at the far corner, and hurtled down the steps until she slammed onto the street below.

There was the canal. There were the people eating, laughing, and walking. Some twangy song about losing love in a drunken stupor blared from a country singer's restaurant across the way. All were blissfully unaware of the storm that was coming.

She ripped off her hat and tossed it, letting her long black hair fall onto her sweaty face as she attempted to walk the length of the canal just fast enough so she wasn't quite running. Tornado sirens began to blare, and the loud crescendo of a thousand howling ghosts now echoed across the city. She just had to make it to the other end. Quickly.

She could see the car. He was waiting.

She bolted down the street, away from the people and the lights and the loud music, and scrambled inside the black Jeep just as the storm unleashed its deluge. The air-conditioning was instantly cool and dry to her pallid, sweat-soaked skin. Her body collapsed into the seat as her muscles relaxed. She closed her eyes and let out the long, deep breath she'd been holding all night.

"They didn't make it." It wasn't a question.

She looked out the window, back toward the people scrambling to find shelter. "Just go. We need to get out of here."

He put the car into drive and sped off into the night. They would have to leave the city tonight. The increasing presence of

Sheriffs in this part of the country was disconcerting enough, but this many in a city this size meant it would be that much harder from here on out.

They had to find more. They'd been tasked with a mission so important that only a few within the Underground even knew it existed, and they needed more in order to achieve it. How would it be possible if they were now being ferreted out and killed the day after their eighteenth birthdays? The Sheriffs were getting too good at this. Too efficient.

They would need a significant amount of help very soon, but they both knew that help would never come.

He didn't take his eyes off the road as he put his hand gently on her leg. "You did everything you could."

She squeezed his hand in reply as a heavy, single tear welled up in each of her eyes.

She closed her eyelids and tried to halt the gathering tears that had fallen for so many others before. Before the young boy, before the girl with the bright cherry lips, and before the young man with so much hope in his eyes who'd been so lost for so much of his life and never knew why. She tried to save them, tried to help them all, tried to bring them to a place where they could be safe and not hunted like wild beasts. So much weighed on her shoulders now. The fate of how many? Thousands? Tens of thousands? She didn't know.

She let the two teardrops fall and took a deep breath . . . and all she could see were a million little lights that floated up into the sky and melted into oblivion.

CHAPTER 1

ISAAK

Another running dream.

They happen more frequently these days. For a few moments I lie in bed, stare up at the ceiling, and try to grasp at the last remaining fragments. The more I try to recollect it all, the more it pours right out of me. Such is the way of dreams: enveloping your entire being through the most vulnerable parts of your unconsciousness, but attempt to illuminate the shadowy transpirings and even the most significant plot points become shapeless craters where mountains once stood.

I'm scrambling around the edge of one of those craters now. This time someone died. I can still feel the loss, like an explosion within me. My cheeks are still wet with tears.

I throw off my covers and step onto the thin brownish green carpet. The floorboards creak beneath my feet, the sound of another morning getting underway. Mary, Mother of God, watches from her plastic perch above my dresser as I open it and get dressed for the day. It's one of the many chintzy Catholic relics strewn about a room that isn't mine to redecorate. A gilded, bloody Jesus, who more closely resembles an oatsy, white, folk-music artist from the sixties, stares up toward the ceiling in a cry of perpetual agony. I spare a moment to read the words scrawled below him.

Pro Omnibus Hominibus.

That painting, hanging above the dresser, used to terrify me and keep me up at night as a child, but now I just find it bizarre.

Black jeans and a red hoodie will do—my standard uniform.

All these years spent in this house—all of my years, period—and I still feel like a guest. An unwelcome guest. It isn't that my parents don't love me, since I'm sure they do, but they've never *wanted* me. There is a difference.

I'm grateful to have a home in the first place, as they've made it clear that I'm on my own after graduation. It wasn't a surprise for me—I've been told I was nothing more than adopted since before I even knew what the word meant—but it's still left me feeling abandoned and alone.

In front of the bathroom mirror, I run my fingers through my hair, notice bags under my eyes, and wonder what the hell I'd been dreaming about. I just can't remember, but somehow it seems important.

I finish getting ready as quietly as I can, then head into the wood-paneled hallway. Dozens of faces fill old black-and-white photos that line the hall. Faces I've never been told much about, other than not-so-subtle reminders that I am not, in fact, related to any of them. I pass the kitchen, with its nearly ancient appliances and its linoleum floor with the looping ivy patterns. I go down the stairs past the kitchen, through the basement, and step into the garage, where the pungent smell of gasoline, oil, and mildew always chokes me a bit. I grab my rusted old bike, step through the side door, take a deep breath of the early mist, and push off.

The little red house sits near the top of a hill, right up against cave-filled woods, but here in the Ozarks there are a lot of hills and a lot of caves. Pacific, Missouri, is probably one of the tiniest towns to have ever been called a town at all. A relic of another America—one that had been built by trains and industry—the town now exists as a flicker on the way to St. Louis if you're going up I-44. Small, dilapidated houses line the streets, where grandchildren buy one of the dilapidated houses just down the street from their grandparents and reno-vate it to fill with children of their own. The population here never really grows; about five thousand people always seem to stick around. Maybe a new generation will have a spurt of children and push it up to 5,255 or so, but somehow just the right amount of people decide to leave or die and it always evens out around five thousand.

Chilled air from a cave pours down the hill behind me. I imagine it would be strange to feel that for the first time, the way a cave releases a constant stream of cool air. Like it's breathing. I feel it against my cheek, where the first rays of the late-springtime sun are now beaming.

At the bottom of the hill, I take a right on First Street and pedal off toward school.

At Walnut, I take a right and start up another big hill. I do this most every morning, except when it rains, and sometimes even when it does. The hill leading up to Blackburn Park is enough to get my blood pumping, and I think of it as the last step in my process of waking up. I have to get up a little earlier to make the detour every morning, but the view at the top is worth it.

Once the hill crests, I take a path that leads to the towering flagpole at the edge of the limestone bluff. There, the town's giant American flag stirs in the morning air. Towns like these usually display flags this large in used-car lots, but Pacific has hers placed atop her highest hill.

I park my bike next to a picnic table and walk toward the chain-link fence, the only thing separating me from the two-hundred-foot drop down to the road below. I loop my fingers into the rough metal and inhale.

With the breath I take in the endless trees, the never-ending hills, the infinite sky, all of it. Standing up here on the cliff at Blackburn Park, the entire town beneath my feet, is almost what I imagine standing at the edge of the ocean would be like. I've never seen it myself, but I've seen it in movies and on TV, and from what everyone always says, standing next to the ocean is awe-inspiring. That the sheer scope of it can make humanity itself feel insignificant. I like that feeling, like there's something greater out there than the sum of my own existence.

Pacific, Missouri, Pacific Ocean . . . almost the same thing.

The sun bathes the entire valley in a golden orangey pink,

burning off the morning dew. Like clockwork, the cicadas begin their day-long, droning cacophony—the sound of summer's impending arrival. The buzz melds with my thoughts, striking a chord as just another layer of my morning, my being.

I drop my backpack to the ground and pull out my plain black leather journal and a pen, then sit atop a picnic table and look out onto my very own Pacific Ocean. I write

Morning comes again
Sometimes some things are simply inevitable
Some things that never will change
But change is itself inevitable
And yet here I sit, yearning for the inevitable
    change to pass me by
To lose track of time
Forgo my progression
Progress me down
Down the hill, down with all the others
All the others who do not take the time to climb
    the hill
And breathe in the morning
And contemplate change
The change that is inevitable
Sun, stop rising higher
Don't remind me, please
Another trip downhill awaits

Another day is here
Another try to test the fates
And somehow persevere

I've written poems and thoughts and whatever words came into my head since I was old enough to do so, but this one was especially emo. I laugh and draw a big *X* through the words, gather my things, and head off to school.

For real this time.

"How is she?" I ask.

The hallway buzzes, packed with students like a hive. Worker bees filing down the corridor in chaotic order, prepping for the day. The metallic rattle of dozens of combination locks being undone fills the air, and the scent of gas station coffee wafts over me from somewhere nearby.

I pull a world history book out from my locker as I go through another ritual with my best friend, my only friend, Jonathan.

"Fine. Seems to be taking to the new stuff they put her on." Jonathan's eyes linger, looking beyond the space of his locker.

"That's good."

We only talk about it like this—briefly mentioned, almost like an insignificant remark about homework before class. His mom is the only family he has, and I know how much she means to him. I don't want to pry. I just want to make sure my friend is okay.

Jonathan Conner is a good head taller than me, with sandy brown hair he keeps at a buzz, eyes to match, and shoulders broad enough to show how much more he's grown than the other kids already. He volunteers at the fire department, loves hockey and going to Blues games, and is probably one of those most likely to get that house for sale down the street from his mother's come his twenties. He's pretty good-looking too, though I'd never actually tell him that. We've always been polar opposites, but I think that's why we became friends in the first place. Spending time with someone who sees the world differently than you can be comforting. It can also be frustrating at times, but I think that's half the appeal. I know he will always have my back.

"So what're we doing tonight?" Jonathan asks, just as one of the varsity hockey players crashes into me accidentally. My books and papers fall to the floor and scatter as he and his buddies take their Neanderthal horseplay farther down the hall.

"What the fuck, dude?" Jonathan yells, immediately outraged. He shoots through the crowd, grabs the guy who collided into me by his collar, and slams him into the lockers.

"I know you think you're better than everyone else, but you're not." Jonathan boils with a deep rage as a crowd draws around.

His temper has always been bad, but he's had a hard time keeping a lid on anything these days, much less when provoked by the school's token asshole. Well, one of the school's token assholes.

"Dude, I didn't even mean—" the guy stammers as Jonathan slams the locker behind him, hard.

"I don't give a fuck what you meant," Jonathan sneers, even as he seems to realize what he's doing. He lets go of the stunned guy as more spectators gather.

I'm quick to follow him as he pushes his way out of the gathering crowd.

"What the hell, Jonathan? What was that?" My words stop him in his tracks, and he faces me.

"He has no right. Who the fuck does he think he is?"

"Who do you think *you* are, Jonathan? It was an accident, but you completely lost it."

His jaw clenches as he looks away.

"Look, I know you're going through a really hard time right now—"

"Fuck you, Isaak," Jonathan says as he walks away.

"Sorry, I just . . . I don't feel well." I know they're the worst possible words to say at that moment, but they slip out anyway.

Jonathan turns back around. "Happy birthday, dude."

And with that he's gone.

It's true though: I don't feel well. I can feel a buzz in the back of my head, like the beginning of a headache. One that's been building for days.

My head is throbbing by the time the last bell of the day rings. My head is an island on the verge of being swallowed by an ocean of pain—waves relentlessly crashing ashore, a tide pushing further and further inward. I wince at the light streaming into Mrs. Howard's class, lagging behind as everyone else is leaving. Maybe it's just a migraine.

"Are you all right, Isaak?" Mrs. Howard asks once the room has all but cleared.

Even sound has a dull pain to it.

"Yeah. I've just got a bad headache," I say. "I think it's a migraine." I collect my things and stand.

Mrs. Howard pulls her purse from her desk and seems to talk into it. "I'm not supposed to give you guys anything, but I'm not about to let you walk home in pain."

She hands me three pills, and I just look at them in my hand.

"Ibuprofen. Don't worry. I'm not giving you the hard stuff. I think I might save those for myself today." Her voice falters a bit, and I notice that her eyes are wet.

"I'm sorry, Isaak. You should probably go."

Another falter.

"I hope you feel better."

She can't stop the tears from flowing down her cheeks now.

"Thank you for the medicine, Mrs. Howard."

She nods. "You're welcome."

I make my way to the door.

"And, Isaak—"

I stop.

"It's Debbie."

She tries to give a faint smile through her tears, but it, too, falters.

I pocket the pills and leave Debbie Howard in her class-room, oblivious to the perfect day just outside the windows, the glaring smudge of red lipstick on her front tooth, and the fact that not a single one of her students had more than a passing shred of interest in trigonometry come sixth period.

It takes a tremendous amount of effort to get up the last part of the hill before reaching the little red house on Sand Street. I park my bike in the garage and make my way up the basement stairs and into the kitchen, which smells of lemon and bleach. My mom—standing over the sink, scrubbing dishes with her back toward me—doesn't bother to turn as I walk in.

"How was school?" she asks with a cool indifference.

"I'm not feeling too well, actually."

She turns to look at me, a suspicious glint in her eyes. "What's wrong? Do you need to take something?"

"No. Mrs. Howard gave me some ibuprofen already."

"A teacher gave you pills?" She takes her hands from the soapy water, dries them on the towel hanging below the sink, and turns fully toward me. "I don't like the sound of that. I find that alarming. Terrifying, actually."

"It wasn't that big of a deal," I say. "She was really upset about something and said she didn't want to see me in pain. It was totally innocent."

"Handing out pills to students is completely unacceptable. I won't tolerate some two-bit teacher drugging up *my* child."

She only claims ownership of me when it bolsters her

aptitude for getting offended. I've lost count of how many free meals we've received at restaurants after she just happened to find a hair in her food: "How do you expect me to let *my* child eat at such an unhygienic establishment? I think I may write to the Health Department!" I think the only thing she's ever enjoyed about having me around is the wide world of indignancies having a child gives access to.

"Really, Mom, it's okay. I just have a headache. Nothing to worry about."

She purses her lips in the way she does when something disgusts her. "You know how I feel about that word."

Mom. She means the word "mom."

"I'm sorry," I start, but before I can finish my sentence, it hits me. My knees buckle as one of the waves crashes ashore a little too hard. I fall forward and my forehead smashes against the corner of the counter. My head makes a loud crack on the floor when I hit the ground, and my mother shouts.

She rushes beside me and slips her fingers beneath my head, but her shouts quickly turn from those of a worried mother, *guardian,* to a scream of sheer terror, and everything goes dark.

Moments later, when I open my eyes, my mother is still screaming. But it isn't a scream of concern.

I shoot up, confused, bewildered. "Mom, what's wrong?"

She scrambles back from me, across the kitchen floor. Her eyes are wide and roiling in fear like a feral, cornered animal.

I touch a finger to my forehead and bring my hand down. It's scarlet red, dripping with blood.

She's praying now, almost inaudible, frantic mutterings, but I make out, "God save me; he's a monster."

"Mom, tell me what's wrong!"

She screams in terror. "Get away from me!"

"What're you talking about?" My hands tremble as panic takes hold of me.

She screams again and pulls a rosary from her pocket, holding it up as if to ward off a demon.

"Get out of my house! Get out! Now!"

"Mom!"

"I am not your mother!" Her entire body shakes as she bellows this toward me. Her face trembles in rage and fear and tiny flecks of spittle fly from the corners of her mouth.

I pick myself up off the floor and run to the bathroom, where I slam the door shut, silencing the sound of her gurgled prayers. After a moment's pause I look in the mirror and see it.

A huge chunk of skin on my forehead, a flap that's been sliced loose by my fall, is sealing itself before my eyes. The skin reattaches from the edges and works its way to the middle. Where it reseals, it's as if there never was a gash in the first place. Soon there's no trace of the giant bloody wound that was gaping across my forehead mere moments ago.

I stagger back against the wall, bracing myself so I don't fall again.

Footsteps race past the bathroom and down the hall to my

parents' bedroom. The door slams and the lock clicks tight.

Silently, I stare in horror and wonder at a face in the mirror I no longer recognize.

I stay in my room for what feels like hours, waiting for a sound, anything, from my mother. My black journal is in my hand, but I can't write. I just stare. There are no words.

The late-afternoon sun is turning orange when I hear my father come in from work. Almost instantly the door to their room clicks open and I hear her feet scurry down the hall past my door.

She is going to tell him.

After a few minutes that feel like days, my father calls for me. My stomach drops. I don't know what's coming, but my heart is pounding harder than my head, and my palms have gone clammy with sweat.

Why am I so nervous? I haven't done anything.

Each step down the green mile to the kitchen makes my heart pound faster. I walk in to find my parents sitting at the table, staring at its surface, refusing to look at me.

After a moment that feels like an eternity, he speaks. "Sit."

I take the chair across from them and wait.

"Your mother and I—"

A slight clearing of her throat interrupts him. Carl closes his eyes for a moment and takes a breath.

"Patricia and I don't know what you are, Isaak, and to be frank, we don't want to know."

My stomach falls away completely.

"We've cared for you, raised you as our own, did everything right by you, but we don't know what to do about this."

Her red, cried-out eyes are like two immovable boulders, firm and affixed to their spot on the table.

"Whatever you are, it's not right, not natural, and we don't want it around us."

Panic, tears, and a million bubbles of fear well up inside me. The blood rushes to my face, and my mouth goes dry. "But . . . I haven't done anything." My voice is barely more than a whisper.

"It's not about what you've done. It's about what you *are*."

"But I'm a good kid. I make perfect grades. I've never gotten into any trouble. I don't know what else—"

"You're an abomination!"

Her eyes now rage toward me. She trembles and shakes. Her bloodshot eyes lend her a startling appearance. This is a woman worn to the very edge.

"I wished for a baby." A trickle of clear snot drips from her nose. "I wanted nothing more my whole life. I prayed and prayed and prayed so hard that one day I would have a baby of my own to love. To give a better life than the one that I had. And then you came to us. The answer to my prayers."

Her breath catches.

"God had listened to me. My entire life spent praying and He finally listened to me, and answered." Her eyes lock with mine. "I see now that those prayers were in vain."

She takes the damp, crumpled tissue clenched in her hand and finally wipes her nose and upper lip while I sit, bewildered, unable to process thought or emotion.

"You need to leave."

He can't look at me when he says it. For a moment he gives yet another look to Patricia, as if hoping she will find some last bit of mercy and change her mind. Her eyes remain firmly affixed on the table again as her answer. He sighs and continues the task he was ordered to execute.

"You're turning eighteen tomorrow, tonight, and we want you out by then. You're no longer welcome in this house. You need to leave."

It feels like I've been hit in the chest, with no air to breathe even if I could inhale.

With trembling legs I stand and find the courage to look directly at them, though they both refuse to look at me.

But there's nothing to say.

I back up from the table and, without thinking, open the screen door and walk out into the late-springtime evening.

Then I run.

The throbbing in my head dulls as the adrenaline pushes me up the hill toward Blackburn Park. I'm running and I can't stop, can't give my mind a moment to think about what just happened. I push and push and push. Finally I reach the top and violently inhale.

I'm panting and out of breath and completely unsure of

what to do next. I don't know whether to cry or laugh or scream. So many emotions are swirling in my head. Too many. The reality hasn't even begun to hit me yet.

Where am I supposed to go? What am I going to do?

Bile rises in my throat. My feet are on autopilot and take me toward my spot, to the bench under the flagpole. I need to sit down before I pass out again.

But someone is already there.

No one ever comes up to the park, no one I know at least, but in the pink light of the sunset the silhouette looks familiar. "Jonathan?" I manage to catch my breath on the walk over.

Jonathan turns and looks back to me. He has tears streaming down his face.

Instantly, my worries seem less substantial.

"She's gone, Isaak. She's gone."

I sit on the table and take his hand in mine. I never would've done something like that before, but stupid pretenses fade away in the wake of tragedy. He squeezes my hand and grips it with everything he has, then looks me in the eyes. His are bloodshot and his face, crumpled. Tears fill my eyes as I wait for him to speak again, but he doesn't have to. I know what happened.

"She's dead." He barely gets the words out before he collapses into me, sobbing.

Jonathan, for all of his strength and eagerness to prove it, has a mother who is fighting leukemia.

Had a mother who *was* fighting leukemia.

I hold him as he sobs. He cries and cries and his body shakes. His hands dig deep into my back, he clings so hard.

When he finally stops, he lets go of me and quietly apologizes.

We sit next to each other, hand in hand, and watch as the setting sun bathes the entire valley before us in a golden orangey pink. Almost like clockwork, the cicadas end their day-long, droning cacophony. We take in the endless trees, the never-ending hills, the infinite sky, all of it.

It's almost like standing at the edge of the ocean.

When I start back down the hill toward the house, it's already nighttime. Stars litter the sky, and the moon is heavy and large in the distance.

I didn't say anything to Jonathan about what brought me to the park. That I've been kicked out of my own house, that I don't know what to do and have nowhere to go. He needed me too much tonight. After all, what's worse: losing one parent who truly loved you or losing two who don't even want you?

I've almost forgotten the throb of my headache until I see my house, my *former* house, perched up among the trees on Sand Street. The living room lights are on. They're still awake.

I sneak up to the porch, the first of the year's fireflies blinking in and out of existence around me, and hear a voice from the kitchen. I duck down and, ashamed at feeling like a trespasser in my own home, I listen.

"I don't care about the money. The checks stop coming after he graduates next month anyway."

Silence.

"No, we're not going to wait for someone. We've already kicked him out. He's gone."

She's on the phone.

"He's an abomination is what he is, and he is not staying here any longer. You people knew exactly what was going on and you still . . . No, sir, there's no need to . . . Now you just wait a minute! We've raised him since he was two days old and we've done a damn good job of it. We always knew something was wrong with him, but you didn't tell us he was . . . Well, I don't know what he is! Now he's gone, and if you really were all that concerned for him you shouldn't have given him up in the first place!"

She slams the phone back into the receiver and stomps out of the kitchen.

My mind races.

Gave me up?

My head hurts so bad that my vision blurs. I have to get up to my room and just lie down, sleep this off. Sleep off the entire nightmare if I can. They're usually asleep by now. If I could get to my bed, I know they wouldn't notice just one more night.

My fingers jiggle the metal handle on the screen door, but it's locked.

Another twist of the knife.

I get up and creep around the side of the house, down the little slope to where the garage connects to the basement in the back.

A flicker of movement catches my eye in the trees across the way.

Just across the road behind the house is a little trail that makes its way up into the woods and into the caves. Memories come flooding into me of my childhood, playing in the mouth of the cave, convincing myself that the reason I wouldn't go all the way in was because I wasn't allowed and was afraid of getting caught. A little boy would never admit that he was just too scared of the giant, gaping maw in the earth to venture in. It was like a dark, ancient, abandoned cathedral, and something about the unending stream of cold air pouring out into the woods always seemed to frighten me.

I saw something now though, in the trees by the trail. Probably just a fox, or a homeless traveler, who sometimes hop off the myriad trains that come to a crawl through the town at night and make their way into the caves to find shelter.

I make my way down around the garage and up the other side of the house to where several small windows peer into the basement, right at ground level. I kneel down in the chalky white gravel of the driveway and brace my weight up against the window, trying to slide the rusty frame up.

Eventually, it gives.

I slide feetfirst into the basement, lowering myself down as best I can.

I drop to the floor, dust off my jeans, and come face-to-face with my father. Well, the man who used to be my father.

I can barely make out his face in the darkness, but the bright moon coming in through the windows and the tiny red glow of his cigarette reveal a tired man, exhausted to the very core.

I don't know whether to speak or to run.

"I'm sorry, Isaak. I told her to leave the door unlocked, but . . ." He doesn't finish the statement.

I watch him take a long drag from his smoke, the little red ember flaring up in the darkness. He hasn't smoked in the house since I was a little boy. Hasn't smoked at all in years that I could remember.

"I never meant for it to be like this. For things to turn out this way."

I can smell the alcohol now.

"It was never enough, just us. Just *me.*"

His eyes seem to glaze over, lost in his own thoughts.

"She wanted a baby, needed it, and I couldn't give that to her. I'd never prayed for anything, but you don't know how hard I prayed then, for her to get what she wanted, for us to be fixed, be happy again."

I can hear his voice trembling in the darkness.

"They went unanswered . . . all of them. All those years wasted just praying."

Stillness.

"So we made a deal with the devil, and we got ourselves a baby."

He cracks. One single sob. I've never before seen him shed so much as a single tear.

"You're a good kid. You don't deserve this. But we don't know . . . and I can't tell her . . ." He swallows. "I'm so sorry, Isaak, but you can't stay here."

He composes himself and wipes his face clean.

"You can sleep in your room tonight, but you have to leave by morning."

I take a step toward the stairs.

"Don't let her see you."

Reeling with questions I can't ask and a pain slowly eating me from the inside out, I make my way up the staircase and leave the crumpled man I used to call Father sitting in the dark, the glow of a cigarette in hand and empty bottle of whiskey at his feet as he tries in vain to stifle his tears.

I lie in my bed, tossing and turning. The moonlight streaming into my room is so bright it makes the walls glow blue. My head throbs and pulses. I am in agony.

It has to be close to midnight when I start to hear it.

Whispers, murmurs, and little buzzes seem to come from everywhere and nowhere all at once. They are trickling in at the moment, but I know it won't be long until the cracks shatter open and they consume me.

This all has to end.

I force my eyes shut, lost in the maelstrom in my head. The waves of pain are so intense that they rock me into nausea.

Whispers become shouts, the buzzing growing into a droning howl within. I hope that as long as I keep my eyes closed it will all go away soon.

Eventually I begin to succumb, and drift into the most restless sleep of my life.

I don't know how long I've slept, but something wakes me with a start. I'm instantly alert, holding the stillness of the entire night within my breath.

I hear the floorboards creak down the hall toward my room.

Someone is in the house.

My heart pounds. I don't know whether to jump out the window, or to lie as still as possible. A primal, human instinct tells me I'm in danger.

The footsteps draw closer.

Creak.

Creak.

I draw the blanket up over my head and press myself into the mattress as much as I can, a toddler's maneuver to make himself invisible. If I could laugh at myself for being so stupid I would, but I'm paralyzed with fear.

The metal of the doorknob clicks. My breath feels hot under the covers, reflecting back toward my face, and my heart is about to beat itself out of my chest.

Silence.

And silence still. Someone is standing in my room and watching me. I know it.

My panic mounts. I can't just lie here. It might be stupid, but I have to do something.

I jump up and rush toward the middle of the room, blankets and all, trying to tackle the intruder. With a muffled grunt, I'm briskly, deftly, thrown back onto the bed, tangled in my sheets, and pinned.

Two legs, strong and muscular, hold me firmly in place. Two solid arms hold my own. I am a helpless sack, subdued with barely any effort whatsoever.

I've never seen, much less been attacked by, someone so incredibly strong.

Wrapped in my blanket and completely bound, I know I'm about to be killed.

Slowly, my captor pulls the blanket down over my face.

The image before me is not what I expect.

A young woman—a girl just a few years older than me—straddles me. Boyishly short platinum-blond hair falls flat across her forehead. A pert mouth and big, wide gray eyes give her the appearance of a pixie. Her black cargo pants and form-fitting black track jacket, the clench of her jaw, and the look of pure fire within her demeanor indicate that this particular pixie can kick some serious ass. I know she could snap me in two with a mere flick of the wrist.

I have no idea how such a small form holds so much power, but here she is, this tiny girl on top of me, holding my life in her hands.

She claps a hand over my mouth before I can scream.

"I know you're frightened, and I'm sorry for coming to you like this," she whispers, "but there are people, very bad people, coming to get you tonight. To *kill* you. I refuse to let that happen."

I stop my attempts to escape and lock eyes with her. The liquid pools of slate, glowing faintly in the blue moonlight, are sincere. She's telling the truth . . . or some version of it, at least.

"Come with me if you want to live." She pushes off the bed with such ease it's like she floats, then holds her hand out to help me up. "Put your shoes on. You don't need anything else."

I stumble as I look for my hoodie from earlier, my head still reeling from pain and confusion.

"Now!"

The ferocity in her whisper is enough to get me moving. My shoes and hoodie are on in an instant, and then I'm standing in the hallway with the girl, all but silent.

She puts a hand on my chest, holding me back a pace as she leads me down the hall. My vision still blurs, and the pain in my head has gotten so bad that I almost can't bear it.

At the end of the hallway we step into the living room, and I catch the silhouette of a man, a big man, passing by the curtained windows.

They're already here.

In an instant she has me down the basement stairs. We reach the door that leads into the garage and try to open it silently, but the rusted metal creaks a bit.

As we tear through the garage and out into the moonlight,

I silently thank my father for always leaving the door open after running contraband whiskey bottles to the dumpster late at night.

We dart across the driveway, over the road, into the trees, and start up the tiny, overgrown path. She thrusts me into the thicket at the edge of the woods, crouches down with me, and turns to observe the house in the dark.

We're surrounded by poison ivy—I'd recognize it anywhere—but before I can open my mouth to say something, I see them.

People dressed in solid black seem to materialize out of the night and surround the house. They crawl over the roof, sneak into the windows, and make their way around the back to the garage. Masks cover their faces and they all have guns. Big guns.

A light goes on in a bedroom—*their* bedroom—-and almost as soon as it comes, it goes out with a crash and a blood-curdling scream. The sound is muffled not even a second later, and the night is quiet once more.

They're dead.

The knowledge barely sinks in before the girl pulls me up. The men are circling now, and one has spotted footprints leading into the woods. Leading to us.

"Run."

We turn and flee up the path behind us. Branches whip our faces, and the ground is littered with football-size chunks of limestone, but neither get in our way. We run.

The sky is clear and bright with stars, and shadows play all across the ground as we charge through the brush—tumbling over rocks, kicking up the white dust of the trail, trying to escape.

Then I see it. The mouth of the cave. A monolithic chamber of limestone gleaming white in the moonlight, hidden behind the house for so many years. It terrified and mesmerized me throughout my entire childhood, and now a nameless girl leads me into it, away from something that scares me so much more.

We climb over the boulders at the entrance and run down the slope of rocks until we hit cold, white sand. I stop to marvel at having not tumbled down the rocky slope just before a loud, whizzing *ping* ricochets off the ceiling above me.

"Hurry!" she yells.

They're shooting at us, and not with regular bullets.

We run to where the moonlight ends in the main space of the cave. Only jet-black emptiness is before us. She takes hold of my hand and barrels into the dark just as the sound of dozens of feet begin to echo at the entrance.

"Trust me," she whispers.

With my left hand firmly grasped in hers, she takes off into the nothingness just as fast as when I could see. I stumble and trip to keep up with her, yet somehow she is navigating us through the dark with perfect ease.

We run for what feels like an eternity. I know that if I stop, even for a moment, the pain throbbing in my head will take me down and leave me vomiting on the cavern floor. Adrenaline surges me forward. The sand turns to rock once again and slopes upward, while the sound of feet closing in on us still echoes behind. We push up the slope, and I see moonlight coming in again.

The exit is just above us, a tiny manhole about eight feet off the ground.

We are trapped. There is no way to scale the wall and no way to reach the exit so high above us without a foothold.

The echoes come closer. We are about to run out of time.

In a blink the girl leaps straight from the rocky floor to the exit. She throws her legs out of the hole and then slings her torso back down toward me.

"Grab hold."

She offers her hands to me and I grasp them. Without a hint of strain, she lifts me up and out.

I tumble over her into the moonlight, down about fifteen feet from an embankment overlooking Osage Street. I clamber down the rocky slope as quickly as I can without falling face-first.

My feet catch hold on the flat pavement of the road as I look up toward the top of the cliff and see the flagpole. We'd been chased through the hillside below Blackburn Park. I never even knew the cave went that far.

A train's horn peals in the distance, like a ghost howling in the night. It sounds like a death knell.

I turn and for a moment I panic, not sure where the girl has gone. My eyes scour the cliffside and the trees.

"Come on!" She tears across Osage and begins to race down Third Street.

The horn rings through the night once more, closer now.

"We probably have less than a minute before the vehicles arrive," she says while we run. "We have to get to the tracks."

We pass another intersection when headlights swing around the corner behind us, and the engines of two black SUVs roar down the street.

"Faster!"

I push myself harder than I thought physically possible. My legs flash beneath me, and my mind peels away everything but the instinct of *Left, right, left. . . .*

We cross St. Louis Street. The tracks are now just half a block in front of us, cutting over the road, east to west, as we run southward.

The approaching train rings out once more. It is close now.

The vehicles barrel down the street toward us, closing in.

Left, right, left, right, left . . .

A white-hot flash of pain shoots into the back of my neck as my legs give out. The motion in my body dissipates, leaving so abruptly it's like I never knew how to walk in the first place. I feel my knees take the brunt of the blow as they hit the pavement, and my face takes the remainder. As my skin slides away, tearing against the rough, dirty pavement, and my lifeless bones press into the ground, I hear the girl shout.

From my new position, I can see that we're right in front of the old nursing home parking lot, right by the tracks.

The horn blasts into my ears. The train is here.

The girl takes a firm stance before my paralyzed body,

between it and the two black SUVs that have stopped a few yards away.

They leave the headlights on as the doors open and the men climb out.

Guns fire all at once. But not normal guns. The shafts are significantly wider, and though I know practically nothing about firearms, I can see that these guns do not shoot bullets, but something much bigger. The sound of the fired shots isn't like a normal gun either. It's quieter. A buzz, almost, like an electric sound effect from a cartoon.

With a flick of the girl's wrist, a convex veil of translucent, electric-blue light springs forth between us and our pursuers. As each of the massive silvery bullets connects with the blue wall, the light fizzles and crackles and the bullets fall to the ground.

I can feel the train hurtling behind us, shaking everything as it roars past.

As the men reload, the girl turns to look back at me, and I see her eyes blazing with a bright blue light. The same color of the electric-blue shield she is wielding. In that brief moment, through the light, I also see regret, sorrow, and a pain welled up so deep within her that I know someday it will consume her. Something under her hairline flares with the blue light as well, but I can't fully make it out before she turns around and withdraws a tiny glass orb from one of the pockets on her cargo pants.

With a flash the veil before us dissolves, and she hurls the glass orb at one of the vehicles. It crashes into the windshield and cracks open. The orb is filled with a sticky, clear goo that clings to the window, letting off a soft purple glow.

Before I can process what is happening, she raises her hands and the veil of electric light appears once more, except this time as a dome around the men and their giant vehicles. Without warning, a massive explosion erupts from within the blue dome. A raging hellfire that barely rattles the ground below and makes no other sound or vibration besides. It is completely trapped inside the dome—a nightmarish snow globe filled with a churning fire.

The fire goes out almost as quickly as it erupted. The dome flicks out of existence, and the girl bends down to me. I can see that her eyes no longer glow as she almost effortlessly picks me up from the ground, slings me over her shoulder, and runs toward the train.

I feel my body leave the girl's shoulder and my back land on hard metal. Before I can make out what is happening, the girl is beside me, leaning up against a rusty wall behind her, face drenched in moonlight, hair whipping in the wind. I can see it clearly now: a patch of skin on her forehead, right at her hairline, that emits a faint blue color. A bioluminescent birthmark.

My eyes attempt to scan my new surroundings, but they won't move in their sockets, and my head won't lift. All I see is black metal and an open side panel where she sits.

For several moments she stares out into the night and

takes in the landscape flying by, lost in thought.

I can't even blink as I watch the mysterious girl who's taken me from my home and saved me from the men. Had she saved me? I saw what she did to the whole group of them. Who was really in danger back there?

As the adrenaline fades, the headache comes surging back. My head feels like it truly may burst. The voices flood into me, threaten to overwhelm me entirely.

I try to clear my mind and watch as Pacific, Missouri, flies past me in the night. I say my silent good-byes to my home and to my parents, but both had been neither, ultimately. This was not my home, and those were not my parents. I don't know who I am, or even what I am, and there is nothing left to hold me in this tiny town any longer.

I watch the trees and hills dance before me in the night as we zoom past and bid a silent farewell to everything and everyone I've ever known.

Everything is about to change.

She pulled her long black hair into a ponytail as she paced back and forth across the small hotel room. Motel, rather. She hated being stagnant, hated feeling useless, but right now they had no choice but to sit in this tiny, dumpy room in the middle of the country and wait. It was starting to get hot out—not the soothing dry heat like back in Vegas or LA, but the sticky, wet heat of the South and the Midwest. The cicadas droned on endlessly outside, but only the air conditioner and the old TV stuck on the news made any noise in the room. She hated it. All of it.

"Please relax for a minute. You're stressing me out."

She ignored him.

He seemed to be taking this odd limbo they'd found themselves in quite a bit better than she was. How could he, though? They needed to find her, and the other six as well. They desperately needed to find the other Gates in order to get to them, but after what had happened a few nights ago, they no longer had anyone to operate a Gate even if they did locate another one. They hadn't even figured out how to get them through the Gates alive yet.

Maybe I should go to him? Maybe I should tell them the truth about what they are—

No. The thought was shot down in her head almost immediately. That was simply not, and never would be, an option. If there was any hope for the Underground, for her mission, then that couldn't be an option. She couldn't go. They'd never take her back if they found out. They wouldn't believe her, and she would be ostracized. Then there truly would be no hope for her, or for any of them.

He got up from the bed, blocked her way midpace, and put his hands on her shoulders.

"We're not going to get anything done with you losing your mind like this. You have to relax."

Her eyes snapped back to him, back to the room around her.

"I'm sorry. I just hate this. I don't know what to do. I always know what to do," she said softly as she sat on the bed.

"Nobody ever *always* knows what to do." He sat beside her and held her hand. "If we're here for a few days, then clearly it's for a reason. This only gives us more time to think."

She held his hand in silence for moment, and her eyes drifted back out into the plane of her own thought.

"We need to send a Flare."

"You know we can't do that," he said, taken aback.

"We don't have a choice."

She was serious.

"They're not safe anymore. Sheriffs will be on us in seconds if they're anywhere within fifty miles of here. You know that."

"It's a risk we have to be willing to take."

"We can't get reckless. Not now." His eyes were locked with hers once more. "We've come too far. That could jeopardize everything. You know that."

Her eyes narrowed and her jaw clenched tight.

"Pack everything up, get the computer ready to go, and we'll find a place. Somewhere out in public, where we aren't backed into a corner. We'll send it out tonight, after midnight, and be ready to run if anything goes wrong. We have to find more of them." She stood and began to round up her things. It didn't take long for her to get ready to run.

She was always ready to run.

"Otherwise they're all going to die."

THE PUNCHING BAG

Help me.

Her panicked eyes scanned the hallway behind her attackers, but there was no one there. She was alone. She was always alone. Their fists pummeled into her as slurs rang in her ears, their breath hot and wet on her face. They punched again.

And again.

And again.

And again.

She winced as tears spilled from her eyes. She knew each drop was futile. They wanted to see her cry, wanted the satisfaction. She didn't want to give it to them, but she couldn't help it. She just wanted it to end. She wanted everything to end, really. At least by now she'd learned how to make herself go numb enough to stop from crying out loud.

This happened every week. She never knew when it was coming, but sure enough, it always did.

"Girls!" A voice echoed in the hallway behind them. "Jesus. Girls, get off of her!" The *click* of cheap heels coming toward them should've called off the onslaught, but the attackers kept going.

The woman pulled the two on the side off by their ponytails

and fell back into the lockers as the one in the middle continued her assault.

"Stop this now, goddammit!" the woman yelled as she tried to get back to her feet.

As the woman attempting to rescue her stumbled, the main attacker stopped, leaned in to her victim's ear, and whispered, "We're going to kill you."

The attacker jumped to her feet, grabbed her two accomplices, and ran down the hall.

The woman adjusted her brown tweed skirt as she finally found sure footing once again and hopelessly yelled down the hall for the girls to return. Then the woman cursed her freshly broken heel.

Dazed, she waited a brief moment for the woman to ask her if she was all right, to help her up. It never happened.

It was okay, though. She was used to it. She'd get up on her own.

She'd done it so many times before.

"We need to get you to the office to file a report with campus police," the woman said as she brought her finger to the side of her own mouth, checking for blood.

No. That will just make it worse tomorrow.

She pulled herself up to her feet and slung the straps of her fallen backpack back over her shoulders.

The woman finally looked at her. "Are you okay?"

No. Go away. Please. You'll get me killed.

She searched the floor. It had to be around here somewhere.

"Talk to me. Are you all right?"

She leaned down and grabbed her sketchbook, her prized possession. Her only possession.

"Sweetie, we need to file a report."

No.

She ran.

"Young lady, where are you going? Get back here!"

She heard the woman curse her broken heel again and knew she wouldn't be followed.

The orange double doors burst open and she fled down the steps at the front of the school. Her bag shook and rattled on her back, and she clutched the sketchbook tightly to her chest. She was running so hard she didn't even look to see if the girls were out there, waiting for her. She just ran.

The bus stop came into view. One of the long, jointed city buses was already there, doors open and people climbing in. The doors began closing as she approached.

Please. Please!

She made it just in time.

Finally, she made it up the stairs and put her key in the door. Slate-gray paint crackled all around the entryway, and a fine layer of black dust covered everything. Someone told her once that it was brake dust. That it's everywhere in this part of town, so close to the freeway. She pulled off an envelope that had been taped to the door and stepped into the tiny apartment. Slowly, she released a breath.

She walked past the flimsy kitchen table and saw her grandma there in the living room, wheelchair parked in front of the TV, sucking down oxygen through her plastic mask. The girl knew her grandma could hear her. Of the myriad ailments the older woman had, hearing loss was not one of them. But she didn't even look up.

The girl adjusted her backpack and opened the envelope.

An eviction notice.

Her stomach dropped as she fumbled with the piece of paper and walked toward the living room. "Grandma?"

There was no reaction.

"Grandma, this is an eviction notice."

Still nothing.

"Okay, I'm going to leave this here for you. Just, please, we have to take care of this."

The TV cut to a commercial.

"Let me know what I can do to help."

Her grandmother turned and locked eyes with her.

Nothing.

Sometimes she still caught a glimpse of something in there, but it was mostly disgust and, on the very rare occasion, hatred. She set the notice down on the coffee table and went to her room.

She slid the backpack she'd been toting off her shoulders and let it slump to the floor, then fell back onto her bed.

The world outside the window above her bed blurred and wobbled as tears tried to come again. She bit her lip and stifled them, shoving them back down into the empty pit where she'd learned to hide away everything over the years. Anger, sadness, fear, pain, and even joy all lived together down there, locked away deep inside.

She was alone. She was always alone.

It was times like these when she would've given anything in the world, anything at all, just to have a mother.

The next morning she woke to a buzz in the back of her head, like the beginning of a headache, one that had been building for days. She rubbed her temples and her bleary eyes and got up to face another day. There wasn't really ever a choice in the matter.

She got dressed, gathered her things for school, and quietly went to the door, checking for her grandmother. The bathroom door was closed. She'd be in there for at least an hour. It always took her a long time these days.

She closed the door, went to the little desk by her dresser, and carefully slid her hand behind the mirror.

There it was.

She didn't even need to pull it out. She just needed to feel it, to know that it wasn't a dream, and that it really was happening.

Last month she'd received her admissions letter to Columbia, and everything had changed. She had an escape. Another chance at life, a real life, and it was only a few months away. As long as she could touch this envelope, feel the thick folds of paper hidden away behind her mirror, then she knew she could survive another day. There was finally a light at the end of the tunnel.

She threw on her backpack, grabbed a banana from the kitchen, and headed out the door.

On the bus, she opened up her sketchbook and flipped through a few pages. This is where she kept her superheroes. She'd drawn ever since she could remember, and over the years had grown quite good at it. This was her escape. As long as she could create people with the power to shape their own destinies, then maybe one day she could do the same.

Her favorite was named V. Her hair was buzzed and her arms were covered in tattoos. No matter how many others she drew, she always came back to V. To draw V fighting new villains, overcoming some new obstacle, or just her, standing there, embodying everything she wished she could be. She was so badass.

Her newest sketch was nearly finished. V was ripping the ninth and final head off of a snapping, multi-headed Hydra. The beast's noxious poison dripped down her tatted arm as she squeezed the last bit of life out of it. It was vicious, and had fucked with V for the very last time. V always knew how to take care of things.

The bell rang for lunch and everyone piled into the hallway to get to the cafeteria. She went to the bathroom, washed her hands, and stopped to look at the scars inside her wrists. She rarely looked at them now, but sometimes, every so often, the thought of finding a razor and opening them up again crept into her head. The adrenaline had a way of clouding everything else out, and sometimes that was exactly what she needed.

That'd make for a happy birthday tomorrow, wouldn't it?

She pulled her sleeve back down and splashed cold water on her face.

Columbia. Just think about Columbia.

But the headache was still there, and it felt like it was getting worse.

She walked back out into the deserted hallway and headed away from the cafeteria, toward her locker at the other end of the building. She typically preferred to spend her lunches sketching in the courtyard instead of trying to vie for a seat at a table where she didn't feel wanted. She didn't mind, though. It made her feel productive.

She clicked the combination into the lock, her fingers on autopilot. The creak of a door echoed down the empty hall as she retrieved her sketchbook. She slammed the door shut and turned back the way she'd come. Then she saw them. The girls.

Her blood ran cold and her heart began to pound. Her locker was at the rear of a dead-end hallway, and the only way out was past the girls. The girls who told her yesterday that they wanted to kill her. Who she was sure *would* kill her if given the chance.

She stood, paralyzed in fear, as the girl in the middle smiled and began to saunter toward her.

She ran.

She tried to charge past them, but one grabbed her hair, one clotheslined her neck, and the third grasped her arm and twisted it behind her back. They dragged her into a bathroom as the middle girl clamped her hand over her mouth. Once inside, they slammed her up against the mirror so hard she thought it might shatter behind her head. It didn't.

"You almost got us in trouble yesterday, you little bitch."

The middle girl spit in her face as the other two held her back. Then they ripped the sketchbook from her grasp.

"Aw, look, her little drawings. She thinks she's so fucking special. Well, you know what I think?" The middle girl got in her face, so close she could see the small flecks of color in her irises and smell her cheap cotton-candy-scented perfume. "I think they're shit."

Her breath was hot and her eyes boiled as she spoke through a clenched jaw. "And I think you're shit. You're a little piece of fucking shit, and I'm tired of seeing your shitty face around here."

The girl opened the sketchbook and began ripping out the drawings, page by page. "You know what happens to pieces of shit like you? They get flushed and go away forever." The girl opened the door to a stall and began tossing the pages into the toilet.

The tears came to the surface again, but she pushed them down. Hopefully the numbness would take over soon.

"Oh, is the little piece of shit gonna cry now?" The girl

threw the entire book in and pulled down her pants.

No. Please no. I could still get them out.

She accidentally let one of the tears slide down her cheek as the girl began to relieve herself over years' and years' worth of drawings. They were her hopes and dreams and the only thing she ever had to call her own.

The girl finished, pulled up her pants, and approached her again.

"Now we gotta flush."

The girl pulled out a knife.

The door burst open. The woman from yesterday stood in the doorway with two overweight campus police officers.

"Oh my God! Oh my God!" the woman shouted at the sight as the officers rushed in and apprehended the girls. They fought and kicked and spit like feral cats, noosed by animal control. As they pulled the girls out of the bathroom, the middle one turned to look her in the eyes one last time.

The headache pounded into her right then, like a wave crashing ashore, and knocked her off her feet. She slid down the wall and gripped her head in agony.

She knew it wasn't over.

The principal offered to let her go home early after the attack, but she didn't feel like it. What sanctuary would she find there? She wanted to be around people right now.

On her way to fifth period, she saw the guys those girls hung out with—the gang-banger dudes. They'd never noticed her before. Never so much as even glanced at her. Now they were staring her down. All of them.

A chill went up her spine and she went to class.

I should've gone home when she told me to.

Eileen Carter, principal at Van Nuys High School, had seen her share of bullying, but she could not, for the life of her, understand what was happening to kids today. Over the course of the past ten years, the school had become a veritable war zone. It was all so baffling—the sex, the drugs, the way these kids treated one another now. They should've been children, but they weren't. Not anymore.

The bell signaling the end of the day was about to ring, but there was one more thing she had to do. She'd filled out the paperwork and gone over the story with campus police again and again. She didn't want to do it, but with a situation like this . . . She couldn't bend the rules for someone she didn't think deserved it. Hell, the real police were about to get involved now. There was no way around this, especially with the superintendent breathing down her neck and rumors of layoffs getting louder every day. Her ass was on the line, and she had to play by the rules.

The door opened and the girl walked in.

"Have a seat." She motioned to the chair before her and realized she spoke much harsher than she'd intended to. She had to do this the right way though and not let her emotions get the best of her.

"I think you know why you're here. . . ."

The girl looked at her, genuinely confused.

"I know you've been going through some difficult times, but there are certain things that we cannot tolerate at this school."

She spotted a bruise along the side of the girl's face and paused, momentarily unsure.

No, she had to do this.

"We received word this afternoon that your recent physical altercations have been linked to the dealing of drugs."

She saw the panic on the girl's face; her eyes welled with tears.

"Now, I didn't want to believe it myself at first, but campus police searched your locker last period and they found everything."

The girl just stared blankly ahead.

"This school has a zero-tolerance policy, and I'm sorry to say, but unfortunately, I'm going to have to expel you."

The girl's tears dissipated. Her eyes seemed to go dead right before her. Like she'd just blown the last flicker of a flame out from behind them.

"I'm sorry. I truly hope you get the help you need."

The girl got up silently, grabbed her backpack, and walked out.

It hadn't been that difficult after all. She hadn't even put up a fight or denied anything.

Eileen Carter could not, for the life of her, understand what was happening to kids today.

●–●–●

She walked into the apartment, barely able to process thought. The pain in her head was too immense. She leaned on the sink and tried to breathe.

"I got a call from your principal."

Her grandmother stood in the doorway, braced against the frame. Her lungs must've been having a good day.

She hobbled to her wheelchair in the corner and lowered herself into it, catching her breath and sputtering as they tried to speak again.

"Do you know"—she began to wheeze between the words—"that I begged your mother not to have you. I begged . . . and pleaded . . . to scramble you up and pull you out . . . before you ruined her life."

Her grandmother took a hit from the oxygen tank. "You were a disgrace to this family before you even popped out . . . and if I could change one thing in my life . . . I'd go back . . . and pull you out with my bare hands . . . before you were able to kill my baby girl." She heaved into the mask.

"You killed my baby . . . ruined what was left of my life . . . and I will never . . . forgive you." She gripped the wheels of her chair and began to scoot away. "I should've left you . . . in a dumpster."

Even with hardly any breath to support them, her words were more painful than any punch or stab could ever be.

In her bedroom she rocked herself to sleep, roiling in a pain that would not relent. She thought about the mother she never got to have, the college she would no longer be able to attend, and the love she so desperately wanted to feel, just once, in her life.

Finally, she thought about V—her hair, her tattoos, her power. She wondered what she would do and how she would handle the mess her life had become.

V always knew how to take care of things.

The next morning she woke in a pool of her own sweat. She'd barely slept. A buzzing migraine had kept her tossing and turning, screaming even, all night long. Though the pain had subsided, all the voices remained—a million voices in the night, filling her brain to the point where she thought she would die.

The alarm had gone off, but she wouldn't need it anymore now that she wasn't going to school. No school. No more Columbia.

What was she going to do?

Just breathe.

She reached over to hit snooze, and as she touched the clock she felt a tingle, like a gentle shock, pulse through her. She could feel the clock, feel the electricity within. It was like a new, foreign limb, an alien muscle. A muscle that she some-how knew she'd be able to flex.

She flexed, and watched in shock as she changed the screen. Electricity seemed to flow between her and the clock, and she could control it. All of it.

She pulled her hand back and severed the connection. She was dreaming, or hallucinating. She must've had some sort of a seizure during the headache last night. Maybe she'd had a small stroke. Whatever this was, it was wrong, and definitely not real. Panicked, she reached for her phone.

Again, it was like getting shocked, only she was the source. She was in control of the flow of electricity. Whom could she call? She instinctively thought of the only number she knew by heart.

At the same moment the phone in the kitchen began to ring.

She threw her phone across the room and shot out of bed. This was absurd. She was going insane. What the hell was this?

Before she even had time to think, the phone in the kitchen began to ring again.

She stared suspiciously at her phone lying on the floor.

The phone rang again and again.

You're being ridiculous.

She went to the kitchen and waited for the voice mail to pick up. Finally the ringing ended. After a few moments, the red light began to blink.

She walked to the machine and debated whether or not she should touch it. She darted her hand out and, before she could feel anything, clicked the play button.

She held her breath and listened.

"Hi, there. This is Eileen Carter, the principal over at Van Nuys High. I wanted to see if we could have a chat. It seems that a witness has come forward claiming to have seen a group of male students placing the drugs that were found in the locker and, well, in a case like this we'd like to make sure we've done the right thing. Anyway, it's looking like we very well may owe your entire family a huge apology. If you could give me a call back, or swing by my office later this afterno—"

She bolted to her room. Clothes flew in a whirlwind around her. The room would be a mess when she got home, but she didn't care. She was going to get her life back, get Columbia back. She left the apartment in such a hurry that she forgot her fears of a possible stroke last night. Who cares if she occasionally heard voices and felt a tingling sensation when she touched electronics now? She was alive again, and for once she felt like things were finally going her way.

She turned out from the courtyard, walked past the dumpster, and into the alley behind the building.

And there they were.

All of them—the girls and the boys, and even a few more besides—waiting for her.

A fear like nothing else gripped her heart and, without thinking, she ran. If they caught her, they would kill her. There would be no principal here to save her this time.

She ran behind the buildings as fast as her body would allow, frantically searching for a way out. Any way out. She rounded the corner at the end and stopped.

Dead end.

With her back to the wall, she watched as the entire crew pressed forward and closed in. Her hands began to tremble uncontrollably. The others sneered at her with a hatred she'd never seen in a human before. She was about to experience a long, painful death.

She cried for help just as the lead guy's hand grasped her throat and slammed her into the concrete wall. Stars broke out before her eyes. The wind was knocked out of her. He let go and she fell to ground, gasping for air.

The girl, the one who'd always been in the middle, stepped forward.

"Ready to get flushed, you piece of shit?"

The girl smiled, and it began.

Legs smashed into her. Fists pummeled deep into her flesh. Nails tore at her skin and hair. There was so much happening, so fast, she couldn't feel anything at all. More numbness. Only this time she knew there would be nothing after it subsided. Only death. A deep, eternal void.

They cursed at her, spit on her, and beat her until she could barely breathe. One of the guys came forward and stomped down as she gurgled and gasped for air. The snap of her clavicle echoed off the walls behind them.

She should've been dead by now, but she wasn't.

Let me die. Please.

The middle girl's boyfriend stepped forward, stooped over her body, and punched her so hard she coughed up blood. He punched again.

And again.

And again.

And—

Something was happening inside of her. With every punch, her body filled with an energy like the electric charge she'd felt earlier, but different. This new energy felt like it needed to get out. It wasn't a gentle flow she could control. It was a dam on the verge of bursting.

The guy punched again. It brought the energy close to the brim. All went silent in her head—the calm before the storm.

And again—

A blast of yellow light flared from her palms. The guy flew from her, shooting through the sky like a weightless toy. The sound of his shaved head cracking against the concrete wall on the other side of the alleyway was deafening. His body was a motionless heap on the ground now, his clothes and skin charred where the blast had hit him. He was dead.

She silently stood and watched the remaining crew shrink back in terror. She felt her body enveloped in a cloak of golden energy, and all her wounds closing and healing. A seemingly infinite number of electrical charges lit up her body—the fibers of her muscles felt activated, and her skin prickled with radiant energy unlike anything she'd ever known. The energy churned and pulsed through her with the fury of every blow she'd ever been dealt. She felt every punch, every kick, every setback, every name, every single nasty, horrible part of the sick joke her life had been for the past eighteen years, and let it fuel her. Revenge prickled in golden light at her fingertips.

And she wasn't going to let any of them get away.

She lifted her hand and took three of them down as they staggered back. The energy poured from her hands in a blazing torrent, ripping through their bodies with horrifying ease. The others quickly fled. She blasted one as he attempted to climb over the wall. He went through it instead. The three girls ran for their lives as the final guy charged her with a knife. The cold metal blade slid into her abdomen, but she felt no fear, no pain. She looked into his eyes, slowly pulled the knife from her gut, and put two fingers to his forehead. She let the energy blast forth.

He didn't have much of a head left after the flash subsided.

The three girls were getting away.

No.

She leaped the entire length of the alleyway in a glimmering, awesome burst of light, and landed in front of them. They weren't getting away today.

The girls blubbered and cried as she approached. A flash from both hands dismissed the two who always flanked the one in the middle. Their leader. Now only she stood there. The one who'd decided to make her life hell. The one who'd tried her best to ruin her completely. The one who'd tried to kill her.

The girl sobbed and muttered uncontrollably. Thick streams of black eyeliner poured down her face as she wailed and pleaded for her life.

It was a pathetic sight. Almost enough to snap her out of her frenzy.

Almost.

A long, satisfying blast of the yellow light pummeled the girl into the ground and pushed her all the way back to the dead end at the other side of the alley, her body digging a trench in the pavement from the strength of the force. Then the flow of golden energy stopped. It had been expended completely.

She looked around in horror and saw nine charred, mangled bodies strewn about the alley.

She'd done this. She was a murderer.

She took a step back, clasped a hand over her mouth to keep herself from screaming, and ran. Those nine faces would haunt her for the rest of her life.

She wished that they'd killed her instead.

That night she curled up under an overpass as far away from the city as she'd been able to get. Her old life, or whatever hell that had been, was over. There would be no Columbia, no graduation, no Grandma's apartment. Hell, no more Grandma at all. She wondered if her grandma would ever even wonder what had happened to her. Probably not.

The night chill crept in as the cars passed endlessly overhead. She lay on the concrete and shivered in the cold. Hunger pains cramped her stomach. She hadn't had food all day and desperately needed to eat. She couldn't remember ever feeling hunger like this. Hunger that threatened to consume her from the inside out.

She didn't know what to do, or where to go. She didn't even know what she was anymore. If she was still even human.

She was a murderer.

It resounded in her head over and over again like a never-ending death knell.

The tears welled up again, and she told herself this would be the last time she would ever cry. This one, though, this last one—this would be the cry of all cries. She curled up, clutched her aching stomach with her freezing arms, and sobbed so hard she shook against the concrete, wishing, hoping, and praying that she wouldn't wake up in the morning.

The lonely orphan girl, who only ever wanted a mother, finally fell asleep under the overpass and never woke up again.

CHAPTER 2

ISAAK

I wake up to the sound of the train's horn, cold metal under my back. My body feels like it's been run over, demolished, and put back together again. I'm sure the crick in my neck will be there for days. The sky outside is turning a milky shade of lilac, and my sweat-soaked skin breaks out into goose bumps as chilled morning air whips through the open freight car.

My eyes dart around, looking for her, looking for confirmation that I didn't dream the entire thing.

"How are you feeling?"

She's right behind me, sitting cross-legged, back to the wall. I scoot up onto an elbow so I can turn to face her. The girl's platinum-blond hair is the same color as her skin in the soft glow of the sunrise. The iridescent blue mark above her forehead is no longer visible. She looks hard and ferocious, but in this light she also looks rather beautiful and, as I noticed briefly last night, a bit sad. There's an unmistakable sorrow in her eyes, like she's lost something and knows she'll never get it back.

I wonder what it is.

"Hi."

I grimace and try to turn myself over. Metal freight train cars are not meant to be slept in, apparently. At least that's what my back is telling me.

"Are you all right?" She speaks sternly, as though she doesn't really want to ask it at all.

"I guess. The headache is gone. My back has been better, but I think I'll survive."

She takes no notice of my attempts at humor.

"You have a lot of questions, I'm sure, and you'll have many more in the coming days." She speaks like a military general. "The first thing we need to do is find a safe place for you to rest. The manifestation process has used up every ounce of energy your body had and then some, so you'll need sleep and food. Once the train stops, we'll make sure we aren't being followed and then find shelter. I can answer your questions then."

I take this in for a moment before speaking. "What's your name?" My question seems to throw her. She's in business mode and didn't expect a real conversation. I wonder if she's even had many real conversations.

"My name is Azure."

"I'm Isaak." I try to smile at her, but she isn't looking at me. "Thank you for saving me from . . . whoever they were." I'm pretty confident that she's saved me from more than just a group of men with guns, but I'm not about to get into that now.

"You should try to sleep a bit more," she says, deflecting. "We have about an hour until we make it into the city, and you're still giving off a hell of a charge. If there are any Sheriffs around, we'll need your pulse as low as possible to get you to a safe resting place undetected."

I take her orders and lie back down on the rigid steel, though I don't think I'll be able to fall back to sleep. But she obviously doesn't want to talk anymore.

The sun peeks over the horizon and the first beam of light feels warm on my face. It's a soothing ray of comfort that reminds me just how cold and uncomfortable I've been for the past several hours. I yawn, again feeling very tired—deeply fatigued, down to my bones. Maybe it won't be so difficult to fall asleep after all.

"Azure?" I'm already half unconscious. "What am I?"

She gazes out toward the molten orb of pink gold rising over her shoulder.

"Isaak, you're a Robot."

I hear the words, but they don't register. My eyes close of their own volition, and I instantly pass into another deep, troubled sleep.

Azure shakes my shoulder and tells me to get up as the train begins its slow grind to an eventual halt. I can see that we've arrived in a city. I wipe the sleep from my eyes and try to pop my neck. Nothing.

"Where are we?"

I try my neck from the other side.

"Tulsa. There used to be a big safe house here, but there was a raid. No one survived. To my knowledge it's been somewhat off-limits ever since, but I've been a bit . . . aloof as of late. I don't really know for sure."

Something tells me she is always aloof.

"I still know my way around though."

Downtown Tulsa comes into view as a tiny cluster of skyscrapers gleaming brilliantly in the early-morning sun. The train begins to pass dilapidated houses and brick buildings that press right up against the tracks. It reminds me of Pacific.

The air smells like humidity and pollen.

Without warning Azure pulls me up by my arm. "Get ready to jump."

I thought we were going to wait until we stopped, but I was wrong. The ringing of tinny train-crossing warning bells echoes over the heavy, metallic thunder of the train itself.

"When I say go," Azure says.

I hold my breath and brace myself as my pulse quickens. I don't know this girl, where I am, or what I'm doing here.

"Go."

We both jump from the car. I land firmly on my feet and my worries briefly dissipate as astonishment washes over me. The control I suddenly have over my body is incredible. Everything has been fine-tuned. My physical self is perfectly aligned with my thoughts, like I've been living my entire life in a thick fog that just lifted unexpectedly. The sensation is exhilarating.

"This way."

I snap back from my daze, and the concerns creep back into my head as I follow her.

We leave the train tracks and head south. To our right looms a giant dome of glass and steel. Its swirling, twisted exterior shines in the early sunlight.

"They designed it to look like a tornado," Azure says, nodding toward the arena. "Only a human would celebrate the very beast that would so eagerly destroy him."

Her eagerness to distinguish herself as something other than human is jarring. I suppose I'm not a human anymore either.

I wonder if I'd ever been.

We make our way toward the arena, keeping close to the buildings near us. Azure is alert, scanning the area at all times. She maintains a complete grasp on her surroundings with a still coolness that is truly impressive.

The only city I've seen in my life is St. Louis, and this place reminds me of it. Old brick buildings flank the outskirts of the city center and slowly grow, transitioning to a cluster of skyscrapers that feel more like melancholic monuments to former glory days than symbols of modern prosperity. I suspect all cities in the Midwest would evoke a similar feeling.

We're walking toward the skyscrapers near the center of downtown when a single car approaches from behind. Azure grabs my arm and yanks me into a parking garage on our left. Her fingers feel like they could crush steel. We press our backs to a column, away from the street, and wait for the car to arrive.

It passes.

I take a breath and follow Azure back out onto the sidewalk.

"We need to hurry. We're too exposed right now." She quickens her pace.

"It doesn't seem to be that busy," I reply as I check behind us for any more cars. It feels like there should be more people here to fill all of these big buildings.

"This city was the oil capital of the world once, but every kingdom has its fall. It's inevitable."

We cross a street, heads low and pace quickened. We pass a shuttered office building on our left, our reflections muddy in the dusty glass.

"When we arrive, try not to speak or even make eye contact with anyone."

My feet come to a halt on the sidewalk. "How do I know I can trust you?"

"We *have* to trust each other, Isaak." She stops abruptly and turns to face me. "Our kind doesn't have the luxury of operating any other way."

She pivots and takes off down the sidewalk, turning at the end and disappearing around a corner. I look up at the buildings all around me and start to feel dizzy.

Damn it.

I jog around the corner so I don't lose her.

When I round the building, I find her standing in front of a burgundy brick building about twenty stories tall. Large gray Roman-style columns stand along the base.

"If we don't trust each other, we die." She smooths her bangs down over her forehead and walks in.

When she said we needed to find a safe place to hide I envisioned a dumpster shared with a few rats in an abandoned rail yard, given last night. Instead, we walk into a grand parlor with black-and-white checkered floors and giant draperies hanging from the walls. A marble staircase sits near the far end, and the ceiling is heavy with ornate, wrought-iron chandeliers. I feel like I've stepped into a beautiful old film.

I follow as Azure makes her way to the reception desk. I wonder how we're going to get a room and how a luxury hotel could possibly be a safe place to hide from the men who want to kill us.

"Welcome to the Mayo Hotel. How may I help you?"

The receptionist is far too chipper for this early in the morning.

Azure casually slides her hand across the top of the woman's computer screen as she speaks.

"We're guests of the hotel. I need a new room key."

The woman gives a slightly puzzled look.

"I lost it," Azure adds dryly.

"Yes, of course, my apologies. What name was the room under?"

The woman is suspicious.

"Anna Gables," Azure replies, tapping her fingers lightly on the top of the marble reception desk.

Now I begin to doubt her myself.

"Okay, and just for verification purposes, do you have the credit card that you used to book the room?"

"Not with me. It's in the room."

The woman isn't buying it.

"But I can give you the number, if that helps," Azure says cockily.

"Of course. What is it?" the woman asks in a sweet, Southern manner that can only mean she is ready for an excuse to call security and have us escorted out.

I panic as Azure rattles off numbers. She's making it up. The police will be called and then those men will surely get me. They'll get us both. It'll serve her right, though, for being so reckless with our lives.

"Oh, all right, Miss Gables," the woman says with a visible mixture of surprise and a bit of disappointment. "Here is your new room key. Let us know if you need anything else at all."

Azure takes the plastic key card and smiles sarcastically. She turns on point and leaves the flustered woman behind her desk gaping. I can't help but let out a small smirk as I turn and follow. The elevator doors open as we approach, and close right behind us as we enter.

"So do I get to learn the magic tricks or what?"

The elevator doors open once again at the fifteenth floor.

"It isn't magic," she says as we walk down the hallway.

"Sorry, *Robot mind tricks.*"

She holds her hand over a lock. The light turns green and she opens the door. No key needed.

"They're not mind tricks, Isaak."

I step into the room, puzzled.

"Why did you even bother getting a key if we could've just walked in here and snagged any room we wanted? What was the point?"

She walks into the bathroom, turns on the sink, and begins splashing water onto her face.

"We needed a room, and we are going to need food. Yes, we could've just walked right in and taken any room we wanted, but we didn't know which rooms were occupied, or which were about to be occupied, and we would've still been stuck up here without anything at all to eat."

She grabs a towel and begins to dry off.

"In a single touch, I was able to connect to her computer and scan and alter any information I wanted, all before she even finished saying hello. I made it so that to her, or anyone else who might check, you and I are registered guests of this hotel, with a real reservation, a real room key, and a real credit card number with which we will pay for room service."

I take it all in. "And this isn't magic?"

"No," Azure says as she folds the towel and sets it back on the bathroom sink. "This is much more powerful."

I finish in the bathroom and come out to find Azure staring out the window. I can still hear the voices, the ones that made my head feel like it'd implode the night before. The pain left me in my sleep, but the voices still remain. Along with what might be an endless amount of questions.

"What are they? The voices?"

Her eyes don't leave the window as she surveys the road fifteen stories below. She is always watching.

"They're not voices, Isaak." She turns to face me. "They're waves."

I can't mask the puzzled look on my face.

"Wavelengths. Frequencies." She goes to sit in the chair by the window and motions for me to take a seat on the bed.

"This planet is covered in an ever-growing web of radio waves and frequencies—an entire world of invisible transmissions just floating through the air. We can tap into all of it. As Robots, we have a keen awareness of every frequency our body comes into contact with. Some can even manipulate it. The influx of new information during your cellular manifestation is extraordinarily painful, but once your body adapts, once you learn to harness it, it becomes an invaluable tool, and a powerful weapon."

"Weapon for what though?" I ask.

"For surviving."

I lie back on the bed, my head swimming. The voices, frequencies, or whatever they are, swirl with my thoughts. I can feel the exhaustion creeping back in. This is all so confusing.

"Who were those people last night?"

Azure keeps her gaze out the window. "Sheriffs." I watch her face as she studies the scene before her, eyes lost in thought. "The Synthetic Humanoid Reclamation Force, the SHRF, is a top-secret branch of the US military, created to 'reclaim' their property."

"So the army created us?" I ask.

"Not the army, per se, or any other publicly acknowledged branch of the military. The government saw the potential in a technology being developed by the CDC, stepped in, and took the project over under the guise of 'employing' the scientists who were working on it. Although I don't think any of them had much choice in accepting the position."

My mind is running wild. "But I can't be a Robot. I'm real. I bleed."

She looks back at me. "You are composed of synthetic cells—a wonder of biotechnology. The pinnacle of every scientific breakthrough achieved by man. Nanorobotic 'Master Cells,' as they're called, overtake the germ cell production in a human host, which then produce synthetic cells capable of fertilization, and subsequently, mitosis. The embryo, the fetus, every stage of a synthetic cell's development is nearly identical to that of a human being. The baby is born in a labor that almost always kills the mother, and grows into an unusually healthy child, peculiarly resilient to the disease and minor injuries that plague her human counterparts. Beyond that, she appears to be nothing more than human. A *real* human."

I note the emphasis. I must've struck a nerve.

"On the eve of her eighteenth birthday, however, the manifestation begins." Her eyes look past me, lost deep somewhere a million miles away. "The military's goal was not to eliminate disease or to create a more perfect human. Their goal was to create the most powerful weapon in human history. A weapon that lives, breathes, and *is* a human itself. They succeeded."

The phone rings, and Azure's eyes snap back to the hotel room. I wonder who could possibly be calling as Azure touches the receiver.

"Hello?"

She doesn't even pick it up, just leaves it sitting in its cradle.

"Don't worry about it. Don't call again."

She pulls her hand away abruptly.

"The hotel manager. Worried the receptionist offended us."

I assume *she* usually does the offending, not the other way around.

I try to choose one of the million questions racing through my mind to ask next, but all I can think about is how good it would feel to lie down on the bed. My eyelids grow heavy.

"You need more sleep," Azure says as though she can read my mind. "I'll stand watch. We should be fine this high up, though. It's hard to trace a pulse from that far down. They usually don't think to look for us in luxury hotels, anyway."

"Azure . . ." I want to ask her more questions, but the need to sleep is hitting me hard and fast. "How long do we live? If we don't get killed, I mean. Do we have a normal life span?"

For the first time today she looks me right in the eye and actually sees me. "None of us has ever lived long enough to find out."

My stomach growls so loud it wakes me from a deep sleep. I sit up in the white hotel bed, hunger tearing through my body like a wildfire in a dry forest. The smell of fried food wafts through the room and stirs a primal beast deep inside me.

Azure is nowhere to be found, but I don't think much of it. I need food. Now.

Room service trays sit on a table pulled right up next to the bed beside me. I lift the metal lids and begin ravenously tearing into the feast. I eat and eat, but nothing satisfies me. As I stuff my second or third burger into my mouth, I take a moment to observe the view. The sun is starting to set and the sky is a burning orange. Light glitters off of the other buildings downtown. I lean off the bed and look down below at verdant green trees, swaying in the wind, that surround the manicured lawn of what looks like some sort of bus depot. People walk in and out of buildings. Restaurant signs begin to glow in the fading light. The water in a half-empty river sparkles in the light just past the buildings, past the roof of the tornado arena.

I come to the end of what I thought would be an endless hunger with stacks of empty, ravaged room service trays sitting on the bed.

A pang of concern shoots through me, and I check my back pocket. There it is.

My journal.

I'm ready to start another life—I don't have any other choice at this point—but I don't want to completely forget my old one. I don't want to lose *everything*. My journal is just about the only thing I ever really did have. My fingers trace the grains of the leather cover and I think about Patricia and Carl. I wonder if they suffered much when they died. Guilt bubbles up in my gut for not feeling more—more sadness, loss, remorse, anger, anything. I think of Jonathan—

Jonathan.

My best friend. The only person in my life I've ever actually loved. I can't believe it's taken me this long to think of him. What must he think has happened to me? Surely everyone in town knows about Patricia and Carl by now. Then there's me—missing, without a trace. Jonathan is the closest thing I've ever had to family, and I've left him. I left him on the night of his mother's death and, by the sound of things, will most likely never see him again.

There they are: sadness, loss, remorse, anger, all of them. They all shoot through me like bullets, each snagging the flesh and pushing through my body from one end to the other.

I wonder how much of my humanity I'm allowed to retain now that I'm a Robot.

I am a Robot.

The words feel too fresh, tender, alien, to say aloud. They sound utterly insane, even in my head.

A Robot.

I grip the journal tight, hoping that I'll be able to hold on to all of the memories, all of the good ones at least, the same way. I know they'll help me retain my humanity, even if I am technically a Robot.

They have to.

I don't want to be a monster.

A searing flash of white burns in my closed eyes, and a piercing, droning sound rings deep inside my head. I shoot up out of the bed. The room is pitch-black. I glance at the clock.

Midnight.

"Get up now. We need to move."

Azure throws her jacket on. She must've returned while I was sleeping.

"What was that?"

She seems to have seen—felt—the same thing that I did.

"A Flare."

She opens the curtains a few inches and peers outside, remaining hidden behind the fabric.

"What's a Flare?" I sit on the edge of the bed and put my sneakers on quickly.

"It's a signal, activated using a sophisticated sequence of codes that sends a ripple through cell towers, radio waves, everything. A distress beacon for Robots. We used them to find new Unreclaimed until the SHRF cracked the code and began using them as traps. We lost many before we figured it out. Too many." Her eyes scour the ground below. "We haven't used them in several years."

She grabs the belt lying on the table by the window and slides it on.

"Either there are some Sheriffs downstairs, looking for us, or there is someone on our side who might be of use."

"Well, what are we going to do?" I ask, pulling my arms through my hoodie as I follow her to the door.

"We're going to find out which of the two they are. Then either kill them before they can kill us, or kill them for being fucking idiots."

The door clicks shut behind us.

The elevator doors open to the cavernous marble lobby with an echoing chime. A couple in formal evening wear sits on one of the large, velvet lounges off to our right, sipping champagne and tipsily cooing into each other's ear. I watch them with caution as we make our way out of the hotel.

The humid night air still sizzles with the heat of the day. Azure swiftly leads me down the sidewalk, but she doesn't need to. I already know—feel—exactly where the Flare went off.

We turn left out of the hotel and silently make our way, walking as fast as we can without running. There isn't a single person on the street besides us. Every step we take echoes off the buildings. If someone is waiting to kill us in the shadows, they will definitely hear us coming.

My heart is pounding. I worry my heartbeat is echoing louder than our steps.

Azure turns left in between two tall brick buildings. The alley is narrow and pitch-black.

We're getting close.

We approach the end of the alley where it opens onto another street, and stop. We toe the line where the light from a streetlamp cuts the shadows, and watch.

Directly across the street from us is a Greyhound station, awash with buzzing halogen light. The building is surrounded by a dark, open parking lot on all sides.

If it is a trap, it's in the best possible location in the entire city. A bright, isolated island in the middle of a dark lake.

I wonder how they will kill us. What will happen to our bodies.

Azure watches the building.

My heart feels like it will explode. Whoever was trying to call for us is right there. Right across the street.

Azure steps out of the shadow and heads straight for the station.

I take one last look back over my shoulder, across the dim, orange glow of the empty street, and follow Azure into the harsh fluorescent light of the station. A few plastic benches are occupied by sallow-faced zombies. Meth has a way of turning her prey into walking dead, and bus stops in the Midwest are usually filled with such corpses. When you grow up in a small town in the middle of nowhere, you recognize them instantly.

A man with bloodshot eyes and fake gold chains hanging from his neck sits between two women. He holds one of each of their legs firmly in his hand and gives me a look as I walk in. One of the women grinds her jaw as her leg shakes uncontrollably, while the other nods in and out of consciousness. He watches my face and slides his hand up the semi-unconscious woman's leg invitingly.

I quickly avert my eyes and see them: A young woman with long, thick black hair and chestnut skin stands in the corner. Her bright brown eyes lock on to me with the intensity of a hawk. A guy sits next to her on one of the benches, the glow of a laptop screen reflecting off his face. With broad shoulders and a square jaw, he looks tall and physically imposing even while sitting. His eyes—almost painfully blue—flick up to mine from the screen, and I look away. Azure seems to take no notice as she approaches the ticket window and presents a credit card from her back pocket.

"Two for Little Rock, please."

The girl's eyes bore into me from across the room. She places a hand on the guy's muscled shoulder as she notices Azure.

"Declined."

The woman behind the glass slides Azure's card back toward her apathetically.

"No, it should work. Try it again."

The girl from the corner approaches as Azure slides her fingers through the opening of the glass at the bottom toward the credit card machine.

"Do you need a ride?" The girl's eyes now lock on to Azure, who fixes her gaze in return.

The woman behind the glass rolls her eyes and goes back to the screen of her phone.

"It depends where you're going," Azure says, studying the girl's face.

"West." The girl's eyes shift to me. "We're heading west."

The guy in the corner snaps his laptop shut and shoves it into his bag.

Azure is locked in a staring contest with the girl—both of them stand firmly, bodies tense. I suddenly get the feeling they've met before.

The guy stands and slings his bag over his shoulder as he approaches. He's a lot taller than I thought.

"We need to go," he says to the girl. "Now."

"We have some company," she replies sternly.

His eyes quickly drift over Azure and land on me. "Nice."

"Let's go," Azure says as she heads toward the glass door in the back of the lobby.

We follow her out the door and down the steps.

The guy and girl lead the way to a lone black Jeep parked about fifty feet from the building. Three black SUVs appear down the street, heading right for the Greyhound station.

"Fuck."

The guy clenches his jaw and hops into the driver's seat as the girl dashes into the front passenger side.

"Get in." Her voice comes out as a hiss. "Hurry."

We slam the doors shut just as the Jeep lurches forward and pulls out of the parking lot. The girl and I turn to look out the rear window.

My pulse races. These are the people. The people with the

guns. There are more of them this time. I stare, waiting to see if the headlights turn to follow us away from the Greyhound parking lot.

We all watch.

The headlights of the SUVs turn in the opposite direction. The street behind us is dark once again.

We all let out a collective breath. I feel the pump of my blood begin to normalize once again. I realize I'd been clinging to the seat so hard my knuckles have turned white. I take a deep breath and let it out slowly.

We're all right.

As we cross an intersection, bright headlights blare into the windows on both sides of the Jeep.

"Drive!" the girl shouts as the guy slams on the gas.

I turn to look out the rear window again and see a line of SUVs following right behind us, engines roaring.

Our speed continues to rise as we tear through a red light.

"Get down," Azure says calmly.

The first bullet hits the back of the Jeep, near the rear window.

I comply.

Another gunshot. This time the rear window shatters.

I feel the wheels leave the pavement momentarily before landing with a jarring bounce at the bottom of a small hill. The Jeep swerves left.

I peek. The SUVs swerve too.

Gunshots continue to fire behind us as we speed onto a long parkway running parallel to the river.

Seventy-five miles per hour . . .

Eighty miles per hour . . .

Eighty-five miles per hour . . .

The girl in the front rolls down her window as she slides two large silver handguns from her pockets. The echo of the tunnel we've just entered fills the car as she turns around and in a single, fluid movement thrusts half her body out the window. She keeps her legs inside, wrapped around the headrest of her seat as her anchor.

She raises the guns and fires.

Each loud clap resounds painfully against my eardrums, still sensitive from the night before. I want to see what's happening, but I can't fully raise my head. I'm terrified that another bullet will come tearing through the window. Through my skull.

I hear a loud crash behind us and look up to see the guy reach over and pull the girl in, hanging on to her tightly as he swerves a hard left again.

"That should give us a second," the girl says as she reloads each gun. "We need to get to the interstate. Now."

"Working on it." The guy's eyes remain locked on the road.

I notice Azure taking all of this in with an unfazed air of indifference. We are being chased down the road in a firestorm of bullets, and she barely even seems effected.

I feel the Jeep lurch harshly to the left, and this time the speed picks up quickly.

We're on the interstate.

I finally raise my head fully and turn back around to look.

The headlights are still right behind and gaining the difference between us.

Another gunshot.

I throw my head back down between my legs and silently beg for this all to be over. I'm terrified and can't fathom how the ones in the car with me have spent so much time running from these people. I've never known fear, real fear, until this moment.

Another gunshot.

I peek up enough to see that we're on a bridge, crossing the river. The SUVs are almost upon us.

I look and see the odometer about to hit ninety-five miles per hour as bile rises in my throat.

"See you on the other side," Azure says, leaning up from her seat.

I look up in horror as she jumps out the back window.

My ears hear only air, gunshots, and roaring engines as I scream her name. This is the woman who saved me, who was going to help me. She isn't supposed to go like this. I turn and watch her body tumble out into the dark.

The glaring headlights blind me as I watch Azure's silhouette effortlessly plant her feet and lock into her landing like a magnet snapping tightly into place. She raises a hand and engulfs the two westbound lanes of the bridge in a crackling, electric-blue wall.

The SUVs crash into the veil and explode upon impact.

Flames rise high in the warm night air. I watch in horror and awe as it all registers.

"See you on the other side."

I feel foolish for thinking she'd meant anything besides the other side of the bridge.

The guy pulls the Jeep over, and within a few seconds Azure pops back in.

"Nice work." The girl in the front nods in approval.

"Go." Azure ignores the girl's compliment. "We need to get as far away from here as quickly as possible."

The guy steps on the gas in compliance.

"More of them will come for us," Azure says, gazing out the window. "They're probably closer than we think."

The wind whips through the hole where the rear window once was, and I can see the soft, pulsating glow of the blue patch of skin underneath her fluttering bangs. I see the sadness creep back into her eyes and wonder if she is thinking about all those who just died, all the lives she just claimed in a single, brief, electric flash, or if something else haunts her.

Lightning flickers in the distance and splinters across the sky.

I slowly catch my breath and try to shake my nausea.

I hope she's wrong about the Sheriffs being close behind, at least for tonight. But I know she isn't.

The hunt is just beginning.

IT

I don't want to do this.

She sat in the plane, fidgeting in her straps. She always hated how tight they were, how they chafed her neck. Most of all, she hated how there were no windows. Hated that she was never able to see the land they flew her over. She knew the plane flew up into the clouds, but she was never able to see them. Surely it would be an amazing sight to behold, surrounded by clouds and sky, all the world below her.

She'd lost track of how many times she'd done this now. Since she'd come of age, it felt like every other week she was reading a memo at lights-out, instructing her to be ready and waiting for transport at 0400 or 0500 or whatever other insufferable hour. She never knew where they were going, or why. She just did as she was told.

The moments before takeoff were always the most maddening. Questions that burned in her mind at night before she fell asleep always fizzled to dying embers during the waking hours, but at times like these, fastened in the big, windowless aircraft, with the straps so tight they cut into her neck, it took every fiber of her being to not scream *"Why?"*

Her entire life was a never-ending series of unanswered questions. She'd learned long ago how to pacify her mind, how to calm herself down until she forgot to ask the questions in the first place. The earliest bits of her memories, stitched together like a shoddy quilt, never seemed to hold any answers at all.

Most of her memories were white—white walls, white surfaces, tables, doors, linens. It was as though she'd been born into a void. There was never a mother in these memories, or a father, for that matter, but she did remember the caretakers. Some of them at least. She remembered the one with the white hair and the white mustache who gave her blocks of all sorts of shapes and sizes—all white—and asked her to fit them into assorted holes. She always accomplished this so easily. His face remained ever expressionless as they whittled the days away— him presenting her with new tasks disguised as toys, which she always navigated successfully on the first try. He'd watch her and then write his notes in his white notebook. She couldn't remember what color the ink was. It was probably white.

He'd take her to the commissary, where they would eat from white trays, alone. She was always alone with the caretaker, wherever she went.

The programs began soon after that. After the days of the toys, the games, and the tests. Long days spent in front of a screen, learning about science, math, and language. The caretaker would come in after a time and ask her questions about what she'd seen. She always knew the answers. He'd write his notes and leave.

During recreation they began showing her other programs—violent, bloody ones about history and war. She learned why America was so important, how good she was, and that anyone who served her should be proud. They always called America—a country, incapable of feeling, breathing, or even living at all—"her."

But for as long as she could remember, the caretaker had called her "it," as though she were a thing, incapable of feeling, breathing, or even living at all. She was a little girl though.

Why would America be "her" and she only ever be "it"?

She never understood.

Every day, recreation was devoted to the programs. Looking back, it wasn't recreation at all. Not really.

One time, just one time, she was allowed to watch something different. Something other than the endless programs depicting an entire history of war and the myriad ways mankind enjoyed destroying itself. She had a new caretaker. A woman this time. She'd been there for about two weeks and one day, during recreation, the woman came into her room, put her finger to her lips, and pulled out a colorful box that held one of the shiny discs that played the programs. This disc didn't play one of the regular programs though. This one was bright and loud and exuberant and colorful and completely, utterly mesmerizing.

It was like nothing else she'd ever seen.

In it, a group of talking animals, who weren't *real* animals, plotted to escape their prison. They were "animated," her caretaker told her, and they weren't in a prison, but a "zoo." The animals laughed and played and eventually made their way to a faraway island where they ate strange fruits and never cared or worried about anything ever again.

This program—this strange, vibrant one—changed her life that day.

She never saw it again after that, and never saw the woman who showed it to her either. It didn't matter though. One viewing was all she needed to let it replay in her mind over and over again.

Animated.

The word haunted her like a demon for years after the woman disappeared.

They weren't real. They were animated.

She'd lie in her bed at night and wonder if she was animated herself. She'd been told she wasn't real. She knew it from the day she was able to know anything at all. If she were animated, like the loud animals, then maybe one day she could escape and find an island of her very own. She'd even eat the strange fruit, as long as she could get there someday. She would be so . . . what was the word?

Happy.

A few years later she was finally introduced to the others. There were several, but she was only supposed to interact with three of them. They had more caretakers now—sometimes several at once—all throughout the day. She loved the company, loved being around new people.

The new children didn't take to her in the same way though. She could feel herself smile and hold out her hand in the method of greeting she'd been trained in, and while the others always held their hands out, their faces seemed to shrink back. Anytime she said hello, the eyes she was trying to make contact with would flit around, search out anything to look at besides, well . . . *her.*

The other three, the three she was to be the closest with, were the very worst.

When she first met them, the two boys hid behind their caretakers and the girl, the first girl she'd ever met that was close to her own age, screamed. The little girl clung to her care-taker as big, wet tears streamed down her face. All she could do was scream. Finally one of the boys, with bright red hair and matching spots all over his face—*freckles*—came forward and held out his hand.

She didn't know what to think back then, but she remembered to this day just how much it meant to her that he was able to see past the other little girl's horror and shake her hand.

It was the first time she'd ever felt like a "her" and not an "it."

Their learning time was spent together from that moment on. The four of them, two boys and two girls. Eventually, the other girl stopped being afraid of her, which made her happy at first. In time, however, she realized that the other little girl had merely replaced her fear with loathing and would never truly be her friend.

One night, after lights-out, she heard a noise in the hall. She got up from the hard, white bed and went to the door. She pressed a sequence of buttons on the little screen that controlled everything in the room—she'd figured out how to manually override the systems long ago—and slid the doors open a bit.

The dim hallway lights revealed a man sliding open one of the doors across the hall from her room. The girl with the yellow hair lived in that room. She'd only ever seen her a few times at the commissary and had never spoken to her, but she knew that's where she lived. Her long golden hair made her recognizable.

Why would that man go in there so late at night?

She waited for him to come back out, but minutes went by and he still hadn't returned.

Her heart pounded in her chest as she crept across the hallway. She'd never ever, not even once, snuck out of her room after lights-out before, even though she knew how to. She didn't know what they'd do to her if she got caught. That man was out walking around past lights-out though, so why couldn't she?

Her hands shook a little bit as she leaned in and pressed her ear against the cold, white door.

She heard whimpering—no—crying, and a man's voice saying something.

The crying got a bit louder, but the man stopped talking. She heard a deep, guttural grunt and the sound of something shaking, or creaking.

The grunts got louder and louder and the shaking turned into a steady pound. Finally, she heard a cry, the loudest one yet, that was immediately stifled, like something was put over the mouth, just as the deeper voice cried out as well. The deeper voice was not stifled.

She heard a rustling and a soft whimper that was followed by footsteps.

She bolted back across the hallway and slid her door nearly shut just as the one across the hall opened. She peered out the tiny crack she'd left and watched the man walk back down the hallway and into the dark. The hallway lights went completely black, so she closed her door all the way and went back to bed.

She tossed and turned and simply could not fall asleep that night. Her mind burned and raced with a million different questions.

Eventually she would learn to pacify her mind, calm herself down, until she forgot to ask the questions in the first place.

Sometime after that she began to notice the way the male caretakers and assistants would look at the other girl in her group. The way they'd stare at the yellow-haired girl from across the hall when they'd all eat together in the commissary. She wondered why they never looked at her like that.

The feeling it stirred within her was something she wasn't able to describe. It burned, made her blush, made her angry and hateful and sad and something else so foreign that she didn't even know what it was called, all at once. For the first time in a very long time, she began to feel like an "it" again.

She heard noises again that night. They'd happened so frequently since that first night so long ago that she stopped thinking much of it. This time, however, when she got up and slid the door back to look, she saw several men going into the room. There had to have been at least five or six.

The crying had stopped ages ago, but that night she heard screams.

The burning feeling came back, and although she knew that whatever was happening across the hall wasn't good, she lay down in her bed and cried herself to sleep, wondering why no one ever looked at her, feeling guilty that she'd ever let this horrible thing that happened to the girl across the hall make her feel like this, make her burn. Crying because she didn't know how to help.

She thought of her first caretaker, the man who wouldn't look at her, who called America "her" and called her "it."

The next day at lunch in the commissary, she looked over at the girl with the yellow hair as she sat down with her white tray. She wanted to make eye contact, to say something, anything, to the girl, but she never looked up. She just stared at her tray and didn't eat.

Two of the caretakers' assistants stood in the hallway with two of the men with the decorated suits. They wore strange hats and often had layers of shiny, colorful badges adorning the breasts of their jackets. They'd started coming in and chatting with the others during lunch and often stayed throughout recreation to play games, or talk, or sometimes just watch.

These four men were all watching the girl with the yellow hair now, and smiling. One said something that made the others laugh. The girl with the yellow hair got up, threw away her untouched meal, and left the commissary.

The burning came back to her cheeks, and before she even knew what she was doing, she'd knocked her tray off the table, spilling the contents of her half-eaten lunch all over the white tiled floor. She watched as everyone's eyes shot toward her, including the four men lingering by the doorway, before immediately drifting elsewhere.

She got up from her seat and began to clean up the mess she'd made, with not a single person watching.

She left the commissary and headed to the new recreational common room, where they were now allowed to spend a portion of their days mingling with one another. She often found herself heading to her own room during this time. She'd rather sit by herself in an empty room and be alone than be forced to sit by herself in a room full of people and *feel* alone.

Today, however, she charged through the double doors and went straight for her caretaker. "I want to see a . . ." She searched for the right word. "One of the . . . a . . ."

Her caretaker and his assistant looked concerned. They'd never seen her like this.

She scrambled for the word. "I'd like to see a . . . mirror." That was it. A mirror. "I'd like to look into a mirror, please."

The caretaker and his assistant shared a glance over their cups of coffee.

"Unfortunately there aren't any mirrors on this floor."

"I've heard the others talking about them. They have them in their rooms. I don't."

The caretaker looked stumped.

"I'd like to see one, please."

He set down his cup of coffee with a look of defeat and led her into the hallway.

For the first time in her entire life, she was going to see what she looked like.

The caretaker walked her into a room that wasn't her own. She'd never seen anyone else's living quarters before. She was shocked to see color—color everywhere. The couch was olive green, a blue lamp sat on a brown desk in the corner, and on the opposite wall at the far end of the room was a mirror. She approached slowly and tried to calm the thumping of her heart. She didn't know why she was so afraid.

She walked up to the glass and beheld a startling being— skin as white as the walls that held her her entire life. Her hair was white and thin. Her white scalp showed in patches. The worst part was her eyes. Like everything else on her body, everything else in her entire life—they were white. Where they should've been brown, or blue, or green, or hazel, or any other color in the entire world, there was no color at all. They gave her away, too, these horrible white eyes. Had they not been moving, not flitting around with the exact same motions as the ones she was seeing out from, she would've never believed the creature before her was . . . *her*.

No, not her, she thought as she crumpled to the floor and began to sob.

It.

More time passed, and they were gradually sent back into isolation. Time allowed in the common room became less and less frequent. Eventually, all of their meals were spent with only their respective caretakers and caretakers' assistants. It hadn't been like this in so long. It felt unnatural.

She didn't mind, though. She never enjoyed socializing, and she had a new CA that she enjoyed looking at. His features were so . . . appealing. The sight of him made her blush and feel a different kind of burning—more like a warmth.

She didn't know how to describe it.

Best of all, though, was that every so often, he looked at her and made her feel like he saw a *her*. She loved it when she caught those glances. His blue eyes, darting quickly away after she caught him looking. She thought of them at night when she lay in bed—of his smile, and how he was the first person to ever talk to her and try to make her laugh—and it all made her so warm she couldn't sleep.

Not long after she started feeling this way for the new CA,

she was taken through a pair of doors she'd never entered before, down a hallway she'd never seen, and into a room she'd never known existed. The room was lined with white padding and completely encircled in a continuous line of mirrored glass placed about halfway from the floor to the ceiling. The caretaker took her inside, told her that he would see her soon, and sealed the door behind him.

The door sealed so seamlessly into the wall that after a few moments she forgot which wall even held the door to begin with. Everything around her was white, but nothing was more white than the creature in the mirrors along all four walls.

She hated looking at it.

She finally sat down so she wouldn't have to see the reflection anymore and leaned against the thick, padded wall behind her.

She felt a buzz in the back of her head, like the beginning of a headache.

One that had been building for days.

Several days later, after an excruciating twenty-four hours in the mirrored chamber and a following day of hunger and sleep, she began a completely new itinerary. Days that were once filled with learning and testing and socializing were now spent in combat training and deeper, more rigorous testing.

She didn't know what they were trying to accomplish, or what they were trying to find within her. Her body felt so different now. The world around her felt different. She didn't know how to describe any of it.

They were all slowly reintroduced back to one another. Apparently they'd all gone through the same thing, felt the same way. She spent most of her new training time with the other three, holding hands, feeling the surges of energy that connected them now when they touched.

They ran test after test. After a while she sensed frustration from the caretakers. Whatever was supposed to be happening, wasn't. For the first time in her life she wasn't passing any of their tests.

What do they want?

She simply could not figure it out.

One night, after yet another long day of testing, she lay in bed and let the questions flow through her. Not the churning rapids of her younger days, but a peaceful, flowing river. She had so many questions.

She was almost asleep when she heard a knock at her door.

Startled, she crept up to the glass panel where she used to type in the passcode to unlock the door and let a little energy flow into it through her fingertips. The little light turned green and she slid the door back.

There he was: the CA.

Without speaking, she let him into the room and sealed the door. He stared at her in the dim glow of her nighttime lighting, and she felt the warmth bubble up in her stomach. His crystal-blue eyes bore into her, and as his hands wrapped around her waist, she felt the warmth come to a boil.

She held his face in her hands as he pushed her against the wall and kissed her.

The warmth boiled over.

She felt, in that moment, a feeling so intense, so deep and primal, that it threatened to take her over completely. She pushed him back toward her bed and threw him down, amazed and surprised by her newfound strength. He laughed as he pulled her in gently and kissed her again—this time letting his lips linger against hers, his tongue parting them.

His hands slid around her back, up her smooth, white skin, as he lifted up her plain cotton nightclothes. She pulled back and lifted the rest over her head, exposing her naked body before him. His eyes rapturously took her in, elated, aroused.

She'd never felt so free in her entire life.

The primal feeling surged as she ripped off his shirt and kissed his smooth, marble chest. She'd never seen this much of a naked man before, and she wanted more. She took off his pants and felt his foreign anatomy standing at attention beneath his underwear, between her legs. He kicked off the last pant leg and pressed his hips against hers. The sensation was overwhelming. She felt it pulse through her thighs, her waist, up into her spine, and to the very ends of her fingertips.

She kissed him deeply as he rolled on top of her. She pressed her hands down his back, her fingers gently slipping beneath the elastic waistband of his soft underwear, and slid them down. She grasped the firm muscles and felt his body enter hers.

She pulsed and vibrated with an electricity she'd never experienced before. There was discomfort at first, but she didn't care. It was the best thing she'd ever felt. His eyes locked with hers as his hips moved. She saw how much they looked like the oceans in the programs she'd watched as a child. She wished she could swim in them forever. That she could drown in them.

He started thrusting faster and faster, and the electricity built within her. He made guttural, panting noises now, sweat beading across his brow, and she knew that his ecstasy was about to crest in tandem with her own.

His jaw locked, open, as he thrust into her, and her toes curled as she felt him pulsate. At the same time, the electric dam within her burst—

She felt her body convulse and spasm in ecstasy as tall, splintering fingers of real, violet electricity sprouted from her skin. The CA's eyes rolled into the back of his head as his own body began to convulse violently. The hair on his head began to smoke and smolder, and patches of red began to sprout up along his body where his skin burned away.

She screamed in horror at the man frying on top of her, inside of her, but she couldn't get him off. The electricity held him, ensnared him, and jolted through him like a terrible storm.

By the time she was able to push him away, what had once been the beautiful CA's body was a horrific, smoldering, lifeless abomination.

She continued to scream into the dark. When the men came, they didn't take her away and punish her like she thought they would, like she thought she deserved. Instead, they hurriedly said something about reviewing the footage, and seemed, for the first time in weeks, pleased with her somehow.

They carted the body away, cleaned the room, and soon she was alone in the dark once again. She held herself and tried to stop from shaking, but she couldn't. All she could think about was how he'd made her feel, how no one would probably ever look at her like that again.

No. Not her.

It.

His eyes were burned into her mind. Eyes that saw her when no one else's would. Eyes that looked like the ocean. She wished she could swim in them forever, that she could drown in them.

She pressed her face into her pillow and cried herself to sleep.

Now she sat on the plane again, about to land in another city, where more people would inevitably die. Every time they sent the four of them on a mission, she knew that people died, and she hated it. She hated herself more than anything. All she knew was death, and she was far too good at dealing it. It disgusted her in a way that her reflection never could.

New Orleans had been the worst. So many people died. They didn't tell her, but she found out. She had her ways. Mothers, fathers, families, babies, they all died.

They expected her to kill. It's what they'd trained her for. Her team was the deadliest—capable of wiping out entire cities, just the four of them.

The boy with the red hair mentioned something about how it was all a ploy. That if enough people died, the ones who trained them, the ones in charge, could profit in the end. He tried to convince her that the deaths somehow made them rich and powerful. She didn't understand it.

Yet another question to add to the endless list.

This time they were only going after four people. They'd never gone on a mission for so few, in such a limited range, with such short notice. She'd had to ready herself for transport only ten minutes after receiving the memo in the glass panel on her wall.

During the brief, they said that the targets had just killed several members of their team and were currently traveling along a busy interstate. There was a detour set up to get them off of the highway and corner them in an isolated area in an effort to reduce civilian casualties. This was odd too. The goal had always been to maximize casualties, not minimize them.

Something was strange about this mission.

All she could think of was how much she didn't want to do this, how badly she didn't want to do any of it anymore.

She thought about the animals, the animated ones in the program she'd watched once so many years prior, and how they escaped during a plane crash. She thought of their own plane crashing, right now, and how maybe the clouds would open up, gently envelop her, and lay her down on an island of her very own. She'd even eat the strange fruit, anything, as long as she could get there someday. She would be so . . . what was the word?

Happy.

She desperately did not want to kill these people, but she knew she had to. She knew that there was no way out for them.

They were going to die.

She always did what she was told, no matter how much it pained her.

No, not her.

It.

CHAPTER 3

ISAAK

Flashes of brilliant purple and white light up everything outside at regular intervals now. There's no rain yet, but a storm is definitely approaching. I wonder if it will hit us.

It's been about an hour since we made it out of Tulsa. A thick silence still weighs heavy on all of us. My heart has finally stopped racing. It seems like we've escaped, at least for now. I look over to my left and watch Azure as she stoically surveys the landscape, lit up every now and then by the lightning in the distance. The little patch of blue skin isn't glowing as brightly as it did before—just a little flicker here and there, reflected onto the black window next to her face.

"We need to get off the highway before Oklahoma City," Azure says, finally breaking the silence.

The girl in the front nods reluctantly. "They'll be expecting us if we arrive tonight," she says, as if she mentioned the idea in the first place. "If we wait out the night in the middle of nowhere—"

"Then we might be able to throw them off our trail and evade them in the city," Azure finishes.

Something tells me they are both used to running the ship.

I keep my mouth shut.

"Well, ladies, it doesn't look like we have much of a choice," the guy says as we enter what appears to be a construction zone. Orange cones narrow the highway down to a single, slow-moving lane.

INTERSTATE CLOSURE AHEAD—DETOUR

The yellow-orange lights of the flickering construction sign cut through the darkness.

"We can just stop in Stroud. We're about to come up to the exit anyway," the guy says as he tries to see beyond the cones.

I watch the girl slide her palms over her pockets. Knowing that she has guns in them makes me watch her hands closely.

"I don't like this," she says, pursing her lips, staring out ahead. A flash of lightning illuminates her face. I look out the back window—shattered and open to the elements—as thunder rumbles in the distance.

"There used to be a huge outlet mall right over there," the guy says. I turn back around and catch him looking at me through the rearview mirror.

"Years ago, a massive F5 hit and completely obliterated it. The entire town's economy was built around it, and within seconds, it was gone."

I look out the window to my right and can barely make out a vast expanse of concrete in the darkness.

"The only thing left was the parking lot. They never bothered getting rid of it, so when you drive by you just see this big patch of flat cement out in the middle of nowhere."

Another purple flash lights up the entire length of the ruin and a chill runs down my spine.

"It's like looking at a shipwreck," I say.

"Exactly."

I look again to the rearview mirror and I notice his blue eyes already on me.

We slow down even more as we take the exit. The vehicle leans as we bend in a slow, tight circle off the interstate. We turn right at the light. I think we're going south.

"Don't stop here. This town is too close to the interstate." Azure holds her gaze out the window as she speaks.

"I don't think there even *is* anything past Stroud."

The guy looks to the girl for command.

She gives a subtle, reluctant nod forward.

Another flash of lightning cracks, closer this time. The thunder follows only a few seconds behind.

We're heading right into the storm.

Hardly anything has appeared on the road around us since we left Stroud twenty minutes ago. Not even a streetlight. Lightning streaks across the sky ahead every few seconds now to reveal a dark sea of flat nothingness. A sign announcing the town lights up in the headlights.

WELCOME TO PRAGUE

Droplets begin to pelt the windshield.

Just in time. I really wasn't looking forward to getting caught in this storm.

We make our way into the tiny town. Our eyes search for a place to stay as the rain begins to pick up. The drops echo loudly through the car, and I can feel the tension mounting. I don't think any of us want to get stuck out in this. A glowing yellow sign for a motel pops up in the distance just as the rain begins to pour.

By the time we pull up to the office at the front of the motel, we can't see more than a foot from the windows of the car through the rain. The guy hops out and runs in, returning a few minutes later, completely soaked, a room key in hand.

"We're down at the end."

He puts the car into drive and starts toward the parking area in front of the rooms.

"Park at the gas station." Azure doesn't look from the window as she issues her command.

"That's all the way down the road," he says. "No one is going to be able to spot the car in this weather. We'll be fine in the lot."

"Do it," says the girl up front. "We can't take the chance."

The guy lets out a sigh and turns out of the lot and heads back up the road to the gas station we passed on our way in, about a quarter mile away from the motel.

I guess we're getting wet after all.

The motel room door clicks shut behind me just as hail begins to come down in heavy, thundering pelts. We all look like we just went swimming in our clothes.

I throw the heavy black trunk I helped carry from the car onto the floor and take a look around the room. Thin, brown carpet with a few pale green stains here and there rests underneath two full-size beds that look like they haven't seen new sheets since the 1970s. The walls, with their faded, dull, creamy color, and the dark brown table holding the bright orange phone confirm the era.

Right now, though, it's dry, and might as well be heaven.

I look at the orange phone and wonder if they would let me call Jonathan, just to tell him that I'm alive.

The guy interrupts my thoughts. "I have some sweats you can borrow."

"Oh, thanks." The sound of the rain intensifies. "I appreciate it."

The guy smiles. "It's all good. Glad to help out."

I see the dark-haired girl watch him for a moment as she leans over to open one of her bags.

"Hey, will you help me with this in the bathroom?"

She's holding a clear plastic bag in which I can plainly see a toothbrush, toothpaste, and a razor. He responds with a puzzled look.

"Now."

She goes into the bathroom. He follows her inside and shuts the door behind them.

Azure touches the remote by one of the beds, and an extraordinarily large, boxy TV near the wall slowly comes to life. A hazy infomercial begins to buzz through. In the right-hand corner of the screen is a superimposed outline of the surrounding counties under the words TORNADO WARNING. A red, swirling mass moves across the map.

"Lovely." Azure scowls as she watches it.

"Where are we?" I ask, trying to figure it out in my head before she can answer.

"Right here." She points to the middle of the map, directly in the path of the red slash. She sits in a chair next to a small desk in the corner, still dripping wet, and closes her eyes.

The girl emerges from the bathroom, towel in hand, followed shortly by the guy, no longer smiling.

"You guys can go ahead and get showered up," he says.

Azure gets up and steps into the bathroom.

"I'm pretty sure we're the only guests checked in right now, so there should be plenty of hot water to go around."

Azure closes the door and locks it before he finishes speaking.

"She's sweet," he says.

I look back at the TV so he can't see me stifle a smirk.

"We're under a tornado warning." The girl sits on the edge of the other bed. She stops toweling her hair and studies the fuzzy screen.

"Watch or warning?"

"Warning."

"What's the difference?" I immediately feel stupid for asking.

"One means it *could* happen," the guy says.

"The other means 'get to shelter and wait for the sirens.'"

This girl is almost as sweet as Azure.

I watch the screen as the red line inches its way closer to where we are, and my stomach drops a little bit. "But that doesn't mean a tornado has actually touched down, does it?"

"No, not necessarily," the guy says. "You can never predict where or when they're going to hit, only monitor the conditions and the likelihood of one happening."

The girl points to the screen. "That just means it's pretty damn likely."

"So what do we do?"

The bathroom door opens and Azure walks out, clad in a stiff white robe. "You take a fast shower, that's what." She throws me a towel.

I head to the bathroom and try to wrap my head around the logistics of the shower she just took.

"You didn't even have time to lather," I hear the guy say to himself as I close the bathroom door and try to stifle another laugh. I'm glad I'm not the only one totally bewildered by her weirdness.

I strip down, turn the slightly rusted nozzle, and wait for the room to steam up. I will not be taking as short of a shower as Azure, tornado warning be damned. My toes test the water before I step in and let it stream down my body, almost scalding. I can't believe it's been only a few hours since I woke up to the piercing sensation of the Flare in the hotel room back in Tulsa. Every hour has felt like an entire lifetime the past couple of days.

The steam opens up my pores and works its way deep into my skin, and I remember how good the hotel bed felt. Hell, after the past few nights, the shabby old bed in the room next to me looks heavenly. As long as I actually get to sleep.

Thunder shakes the entire building.

I stretch my neck and let the heat work out some of the kinks from my night on the train. That was only last night. I really can't believe it.

How the hell did I wind up here?

One of those inexplicable late-night anxiety attacks sneaks up on me and clamps down on my neck with vicious ferocity. I press my forehead against the cold, white tile as I try to stop myself from hyperventilating.

A droning, wailing sound like the cry of a thousand mournful ghosts begins to crescendo from the outside and fills my head over the din of the shower and the thunder.

That must be what a tornado siren sounds like.

Everything goes black.

The building begins to shake around me, and I hear what sounds like a giant train approaching in the pitch-black darkness, just like the other night.

That must be what a tornado sounds like.

Someone pounds on the door and screams in the dark. A bigger sound swells around me, and the shouting is drowned out. I push aside the shower curtain and fumble in the dark for a towel as the locked door bursts from its hinges and flies toward my face. A flash of white blazes in my eyes as a corner of the flying door jettisons into my cheek. I feel the skin tear away and the bone underneath crack with the force, and I fall back into the shower curtain as the cataclysmic train sound arrives.

Lightning flashes, and I see the windows of the motel room shatter inward. Bits of everything shoot out toward me. A hand grasps my arm and pulls my naked body up and out of the tub and into the doorway, clutching me so tight it feels like my arm will break. A roar unlike anything I've ever heard bears down on the room as a brilliant blue dome of electric light surrounds me and everything goes silent. I look up from under the pulsating canopy and watch as the beast outside tears away the roof, the walls, the beds, *everything*, in a swirling, violent mass of debris.

Everything around me flies up into the sky. I'm in a vacuum, anchored safely to the ground under the protection of the dome. A car smashes into the side of the blue wall, right in front of my face, and crumples into nothing. I instinctively clamp my hands over my ears, waiting for a booming crash that never comes. The sound is muffled.

Before my brain can fully register what's happening, it stops. Everything settles into place around us, the noise dies away and, just like that, it's over. Discarded remnants of the motel and the entire surrounding area flutter to the ground. I can't catch my breath. The blue dome flickers out of existence, and I finally look around to see that Azure, the guy, and the girl were all in the tiny blue dome of light along with me. I force myself to inhale and remember that I'm naked.

Perfect.

"Are you okay?"

Azure's stern voice cuts the buzzing silence. The mark on her forehead is glowing again.

"Yeah, I'm fine," I say as I try to stand. "What was that?" My eyes search the piles of debris around me for something to cover up with. My face hurts.

"An F4 at least, if the state of this motel is anything to go by," the girl says as she grabs a crumpled bedsheet from the corner of the decimated room, shakes it out, and hands it to me. "It's full of glass."

I nod in appreciation and wrap it around my body, still dripping wet.

Her eyes linger on Azure in anger or disgust or something I can't fully catch. She starts gathering what's left of our things.

I take a quick look around. The motel has been destroyed. The roof is completely gone. The wall behind the old TV is the only part of the structure left standing in the entire building. The girl's big black duffel and the guy's backpack made it into the protection of Azure's dome and sit right by our feet, undisturbed. Everything else has been razed to the foundation, left in a pile of messy debris. I take in the horrific sight and realize that the silence is what is most disturbing. How many people just died around us?

"We need to go." Azure punctures the silence dismissively.

"There might be people trapped out here. Shouldn't we stay and help?" I ask, looking around at the endless field of destruction. Surely she will consider helping. Anyone who might be buried alive under this wouldn't have much time.

"No." She turns and walks away.

"She's right," the girl says, still regarding Azure with the strange look as she leaves. "The fire department, and whoever else they can get, will be arriving any minute. Followed by news crews." Her brown eyes lock with mine, and I can't tell if it is pity or sadness I see for a brief second. "We have to go now."

She dons the stoic, resolute look of a hardened leader—a look I'm starting to suspect might be a mask. She grabs her duffel, turns, and heads out through what used to be the bathroom. She strides past the toilet that still stands, steps off the foundation of the building, and into the grass after Azure. Her footsteps crunch in the shards of glass and splintered wood that litter the ground.

The guy follows as I realize I am barefoot. *Great.* I remember the sight of my forehead stitching back together just a few days ago . . . or was it yesterday? Everything is such a blur. Pacific feels like a lifetime ago. At any rate, I think I can make it over some glass and other assorted bits of obliterated motel.

Crunch.

I feel shards of glass drive into my skin and take another step.

The wet grass changes into pavement, and I wince slightly as chunks of glass push deeper into my feet. The car is right where we left it, the gas station behind it completely untouched by the tornado that decimated the motel just a few hundred yards away. The others are climbing into the car, but the guy stops and digs something out from his backpack.

"Here."

He extends his arm, clutching a folded pair of sweatpants and a plain white T-shirt. I notice the muscles in his forearm and feel a sudden flush in my face as I remember just how naked I am under the bedsheet. He looks right at me with his bright blue eyes and lets a half smile spread across his face.

I fumble in my head for the right word. "Thanks."

I awkwardly look to my left and right for a place to change, away from the gaze of the blue eyes that have thrown me so off guard.

"Sorry," he says as hops into the car and spares me any further embarrassment.

I slip my legs into the sweats, letting the sheet fall as I pull them up, and pull the T-shirt over my head. The guy is almost a foot taller than me, and his clothes show it. My wet skin clings to all of the excess fabric, but I'm more comfortable than I was, and I'm grateful.

I jump into the back beside Azure as the girl in the front pulls her long black hair into a ponytail. The guy starts the engine. A blast of ice-cold air shoots back from the AC. I hadn't realized how hot it still was outside, even after the storm. The guy puts the vehicle into reverse, and a gust of the muggy, hot air comes in from the open, shattered back window. He puts it in drive and takes a right, back out onto the road. We head south.

In the silence, a thought occurs to me, and I suddenly feel ridiculous. "I'm Isaak, by the way."

The girl turns around to face me and gives a reluctant smile that I'm sure is rarely seen. "Kamea."

I repeat it back to her, making sure I've got it right. It's a name as beautiful as she is. It suits her.

The smile dissipates as she looks to Azure. "Hello, Azure," she says.

I knew it.

Azure nods to the girl without expression, then looks to the guy in the mirror and gives him one as well. He returns it, and I realize that they all have met before.

"JB."

He looks to me as he speaks and I get caught by his gaze again. The subtle half smile creeps over his face once more, and I have the sudden urge to avert my eyes and pick shards of glass from my feet.

I watch the cuts and loose bits of skin stitch back together and smooth over, as if they were never there, and hope that no one in the dark car can see me blush.

I wake up with my forehead pressed against the window. The first light of day casts a pale pink glow over the flat stretch of plains outside. Buildings appear more frequently, and a few car dealerships flank the highway. I look to my left and Azure is sitting tall, alert, gazing out the window. She hasn't slept.

The vehicle slows as we take an exit off of the highway.

"Where are you going?" Azure asks, clearly irked by our sudden detour.

"Well, unless you want me to drive off into a ditch somewhere, I need caffeine," JB says. "And I need to pee, bad."

Kamea cracks her neck in the front seat, followed by each and every joint in her fingers. The noises punctuate the tension in the car like firecrackers.

Azure leans back silently as JB spots a big chain coffee shop and turns into the parking lot. He parks in the far edge of the lot, away from other cars, and kills the engine.

"Five minutes," Azure says as she gets out. She closes the door behind her with more force than necessary.

"Someone isn't a morning person," JB says to no one in particular. I notice his eyes dart up to meet mine, and I suddenly feel the need to search for the door handle.

"Please don't get in a fight with our new friend," Kamea says as she unbuckles her seat belt. I look up and catch the end of an eye roll from JB.

"What? Who, him?" He points back to me with his thumb, the smile returning. "I don't think I'm gonna fight him. He seems nice enough."

Kamea gets out of the car and looks at me.

"I'm not worried about you *fighting* him."

She turns to head into the coffee shop as the blood rushes to my cheeks once again.

I let the door of the coffee shop close behind me and head for the bathroom. I didn't realize how badly I had to go until we stopped. Azure is in line at the counter with her back facing the door. A man in a shirt and tie stands in line behind her and eyes her up and down, but her gaze remains fixed directly ahead. Somehow, I know she still has full awareness of everything going on around her. I feel her eyes on me through the back of her platinum-blond head.

I make it to the bathroom door and try the handle. Locked.

A moment later JB walks up to wait in the hall beside me.

Perfect.

He looks to the wall in front of us, but I can practically feel the smirk on him. I do my best to keep the blushing at bay.

"Thank you, for what you did last night . . . today, I guess." I'm so bad at this. "I know you pulled me out of the shower. You didn't have to risk yourself like that. I really appreciate it."

I feel like a stammering dwarf next to him. He's one of those people who are so nauseatingly tall and pretty it makes them difficult to look at. He looks at me again, still grinning. Even his teeth are perfect. *Ugh.*

"I'm pretty sure you'd have done the same for me."

There's a hint of something behind his bright eyes that I can't quite put my finger on.

"Of course."

The door unlocks behind me and an older man steps out of the bathroom. He nods at both of us as he passes and walks down the hall. I step inside.

I'm about to close the door when JB pushes his way in as well. He closes the door behind him and quickly locks it.

I'm panicked, kind of aroused, and totally confused, all at once.

"Okay, I don't know what your relationship with Azure is, but you need to know that you shouldn't trust her."

My mouth goes dry. "What are you talking about? She saved me."

"Did she? Because a few hours ago she was about to let you die."

"I don't know what you're talking about."

"You were in the shower. She wasn't going to save you. She tried to stop *me* from saving you."

"That doesn't make any sense."

"I didn't think so either. That's why I wanted you to know."

His words hit me like a punch to the gut.

"But I thought we were all on the same side?"

"There are lots of sides out here, Isaak. And from what I've heard, I don't think you'll find yourself on hers."

His eyes look deep into mine before he unlocks the door behind him.

"I'm glad we found you," he says as he pushes the door open and steps back into the hall.

When I leave the bathroom, I hold the door open for JB at just the right angle as to avoid eye contact. He brushes past me without saying a word.

Azure is waiting for me at the end of the short hallway with two bottles of a neon-colored sports drink. She eyes the spot where JB was standing and hands one to me.

"Oh. No, thank you. I don't really like that stuff," I say.

"You do now." She puts it in my hand. "We get more out of it than the average person." She scans the room and then looks back at me. "Electrolytes."

Kamea approaches from the counter with a small bag and two cups of coffee as JB comes back from the bathroom. We move toward the door.

As we walk past the man in the shirt and tie, sitting at a booth with his laptop, Azure slides her fingers along the top edge of the screen. The man stares at her openly, and she returns his gaze with a raised eyebrow and pursed lips, almost challenging him to say something.

He doesn't.

She pulls her hand away and wipes it on her shirt as if she's touched something contaminated, before walking out the door like nothing at all awkward has just happened.

Kamea stops as though she means to say something, gives me an unreadable look, then follows her out.

"I think they're going to be really good friends someday," JB says as he watches Kamea follow in Azure's wake.

Confused, I pop the lid of my drink and take a sip as I step back out into the morning air.

It tastes like salt.

●─●─●

The sun is fully out from under the horizon by the time we get back to the car, which is when the drink hits my bloodstream. It's like manifesting all over again. Everything rushes into me— morning radio shows, cell phone calls, credit card machines taking payments, e-mails, texts . . . everything. It doesn't hurt like it did the other night, but I'm fully aware of it once again. It's like I'm standing knee-deep in a river teeming with bright, silvery fish gleaming in the sunlight, and all I have to do is reach into the water and grab one. I reach for one, and miss.

"Don't get lost in it right now," Azure interrupts. "This stuff heightens our awareness. I need to be fully alert today, but you don't know how to navigate it yet, so try to just accept its presence and move on."

"Then why did you give it to me?" I hold out the bottle.

"Because you need to learn how to ignore it just as much as you need to learn how to use it." She opens the back hatch of the car and grabs the bags. "Leave the keys," she says as she turns and heads out of the parking lot and into the grass alongside the road.

"I guess we're not taking the Jeep," JB says to no one in particular.

"Guess not." Kamea watches Azure carefully.

We follow.

I feel the heat of the day rise along with the sun as we trudge through a grassy ditch along the road. I'm damp with sweat as we reach the shade of an overpass, but it's hot under here too.

"So are you going to tell us where we're going?" JB's voice echoes in the cavernous space under the sound of rush-hour traffic. Azure remains silent as we step back out into the sun and see one of the car dealerships alongside the highway.

I think I know where this is headed.

We come to the edge of a sprawling lot full of cars and step onto the blacktop. Without missing a beat, Azure approaches a car near the road in the corner of the lot. It unlocks itself before she even touches the handle for the back hatch. She opens it, tosses the duffel and the backpack inside, and hops into the backseat. We all follow suit.

JB takes the driver's seat once again.

"Do you want me to drive?" I ask, feeling bad that he's done all the work thus far. Then again, I don't know how well I'd handle a car chase with a horde of government killers should the situation arise, so maybe I've spoken too soon.

"Nah, I'm fine. Sheriffs, tornadoes, endless driving without sleep . . . I'll be good." His sense of humor is in stark contrast with the JB who pushed into the bathroom with me.

"He likes driving," Kamea says as she passes back an open brown paper bag from the coffee shop, filled with sandwiches and small pastries. I take a turkey sandwich and say thanks.

Azure waves it away.

"I prefer driving something with a little more power, personally," JB says as he looks up at Azure through the rearview mirror.

The car starts and goes into reverse without him touching

anything. He jumps and grabs the wheel, taking control of the possessed vehicle.

"I love hybrids," Azure says slyly as she watches the office from the edge of the lot and takes a sip from her bottle.

We pull out of the lot and head back onto the highway. The morning sun shines bright and golden in our eyes.

I really can't explain the new sensations flowing through me. The entire world is alive in ways I've never known or even suspected. We're out in the middle of nowhere now, out past Amarillo in a desert wasteland, and even here I can feel it. Invisible lines of every kind of energy enveloping me, emanating from everything and everywhere, and I can feel them all. It's almost enough to make me forget about what JB said earlier. Almost enough to get me to stop worrying about who I can trust.

Almost.

"We're going to LA, aren't we?" I ask.

The car is silent.

JB glances over to Kamea, but they don't speak.

"And you guys are all working together somehow?"

The fact that I know so little about any of what's going on is really starting to get to me. The adrenaline from all of the chasing and Sheriffs and tornadoes has subsided, and I'm left with questions that need to be answered.

"I think I have a right to know what's going on here."

Finally Azure looks at me.

"The three of us are part of a movement known as the Underground. We work in secret, all over the country, to find Unreclaimed before the government does, and shepherd them to safety."

"And you've met before?" I ask Azure, then look to Kamea.

"A few times," Kamea says, looking ahead. Azure says nothing.

I guess that's all I'm getting about that particular story for the moment.

"And the safe place you're talking about . . . it's in LA, isn't it?"

"Yes." Azure looks out the window to the flat landscape zooming by.

"How did you know?" Kamea turns back and really looks at me for the first time. She has high cheekbones and her chestnut skin is the texture of silk. She really is beautiful.

"Just a hunch. LA seems like a good place for a bunch of freaks to hide."

JB looks at me through the mirror.

"I've always wanted to go there," I continue as I look out at the desert around us, vast and lifeless.

"Unfortunately you're not going to see much of it." Azure doesn't break her gaze out the window as she speaks. "The bigger cities make it easier to hide, but they're also easier to get caught in. You probably won't even see daylight while you're there."

"Now, don't get him *too* excited about it," JB says.

"He shouldn't be excited. He should be cautious and alert. *You* should be driving."

"Do you enjoy being a black hole of negativity, or do you just have something against organics?" JB sounds like he's losing patience with her.

"Organics?" I ask. I have no idea what he's talking about.

Kamea looks back to me. "It's what we call ourselves instead of 'human,'" she says. "We believe it's dehumanizing to Robots for us to identify as 'human' as a means of differentiating ourselves. As if to say that Robots are not human."

"But we're not *human*," Azure says. She glares at Kamea.

"Some Robots choose not to identify as human. Personally, I'm not comfortable talking to a person as though they're not a *person*, and like to make sure the words I use reflect that level of respect," Kamea says.

"And some humans choose to patronize us by assuming they are our equals and by giving themselves asinine names that insinuate such."

"Synthetic, organic, whatever. I only have a problem with assholes," JB says, staring at the road ahead.

Kamea turns away from us and the car goes silent once more.

Somewhere after the New Mexico border, JB reaches into his pocket. "Kam, will you see how far the nearest gas station is?"

He pulls out a phone and hands it her.

"Are you insane?" Azure shouts, and practically jumps out

of her seat. "What the hell do you think you're doing? Are you trying to get us all killed?"

She pushes my chest back against the seat and holds me with one hand, as if she's trying to protect me from it.

"It's fine. I swear," Kamea says as she turns back and looks to Azure, holding her hands up in a peaceful gesture.

"I'm so confused," I say, my chest pressed against the seat. Azure's fingers are rigid and strong.

"Have you told him anything about what he is? I mean, anything at all?" JB asks as he glares back at Azure through the rearview mirror.

She doesn't look at him.

He sighs.

"Robots connect to anything with an electrical current," he says. "When you connect to something connected to the Internet, connected to the grid in any way, you then connect to it yourself. But it's incredibly dangerous because the second you do, *they* can see it. It's like a beacon to them. It takes a lot of training for a Robot to learn how to connect just long enough to do what he needs and sever the connection before getting caught."

"And even then it's incredibly dangerous," Azure says through a clenched jaw.

"With phones, sometimes a Robot doesn't even need to touch one in order to connect." Kamea continues JB's explanation. "Sometimes, depending upon the Robot, he, or she, can unknowingly connect just by being near one."

"Which is why I'm wondering why you've chosen to keep one

in the car with two Robots now?" Azure is a lion ready to pounce.

Kamea tries to look into her eyes and diffuse her. "Custom parts, custom software. The operating system was designed and built from the ground up," she says.

"By yours truly." JB grins.

"It's completely off grid and totally Robot-proof," Kamea says. I can see her eyes waiting to gauge Azure's expressions.

Azure finally releases her hand from my chest and eases back into her seat.

Relieved that the moment of tension has passed, I lean up and grab for the phone.

"Let me see. I love gadgets," I say as my fingers barely graze the edge.

Kamea pulls it away as Azure grabs my wrist. "I still wouldn't mess with it until you know what you're doing," she says as she looks to Azure and waits for another outburst.

Azure grits her teeth, shakes her head silently, and looks back out the window.

"We need to stop and get camping supplies," Azure says, cutting the silence as we make our way closer to Albuquerque. The afternoon sun is still high and bright. "No more motels."

JB glances at her. "We have only one more night until we get there."

"Are you sure about that?" She looks right back at him.

"She's right," Kamea says, staring ahead as she speaks. "We've been on the interstate too long."

Azure looks Kamea up and down, then faces the window once again.

The highway winds around a mountain and descends down into the city. We take the first exit.

"Turn left up here." Azure seems to know where she's going.

After about a mile, she has JB park in front of a bank.

"Wait here." She gets out of the car and walks over to the ATM.

"Your friend is going to get us in a lot of trouble," JB says, shaking his head as we all watch Azure place her hand on the machine.

Is she my friend?

I bite my lip as anxious nausea starts to bubble in my stomach.

Outside, Azure pockets a thick stack of bills and returns to the car. She hops back in.

"There's a store just up ahead. Let's be quick." She closes the door behind her. "We need to get out of the city and off the road."

"The car is loaded up. Grab whatever else you'd like and let's get out of here." Azure walks back over to the registers at the front of the giant superstore and gathers some more sports drinks from one of the little refrigerators nearby. She just bought us enough camping gear to last a week stranded in any terrain or climate imaginable. I, however, am still deciding on what kind of footlong I'd like.

"I don't know how you guys eat this trash," Kamea says as she munches on a handful of almonds.

"This is food of the gods. How dare you," JB says as he grabs a bag of chips. "Yeah, I'll do the combo. Thank you." He grins to the young girl at the register, who blushes as she takes his cash.

He's obviously aware of the power his looks have over people. I make sure to take note.

After my order is finished, I pay, take the bag with my sandwich, and turn to find JB and Kamea whispering a few feet away by the soda fountain. They go silent when I face them.

I walk up and hold out the bag. "I need to go change."

JB takes it, and I make a beeline for the bathroom on the other side of the store with the bag of clothes I just bought.

I step into the bathroom and stop in front of the mirror to examine my face for the first time today. I don't even know who I am anymore.

My hands fumble for the faucet, and I splash cold water onto my face. I let it soak in.

I cup another handful of water and notice a tiny, triangle-shaped mark that has appeared on my inner right-hand wrist, like a tattoo or a birthmark. I scrub at it, but it doesn't budge. It's *inside* my skin.

I wonder if Azure knows anything about this.

I change into the new clothes as quickly as possible and stuff JB's damp sweats into the empty bag.

I step over to the urinal and unzip.

As I go, I start to think about what JB said to me earlier this morning. *Can I trust Azure? Why would she try to stop anyone from saving me? Was JB lying?*

It wouldn't shock me if he was. He changes face so quickly, so expertly, I don't know what to believe is real. If I looked like that I'm sure I'd be a master manipulator too.

But why would he lie about something like that?

It doesn't make any sense. Any of it.

I just wish I knew whether or not I could trust Azure.

But she saved my life. She's helping me. There is good and bad, and she's obviously good.

But what if there's a gray area in between?

Or what if they're just rounding me up for another interested party?

The thought hits me like a slap to the face. What if these people are part of a Robot-trafficking ring, catching kids after they manifest and selling off their synthetic organs piece by bloody piece to the highest bidder?

I laugh at my paranoia and finish. As the toilet flushes, I pull the elastic waistband of my underwear back up and start to zip my pants.

The lights go out.

I can feel the size of the building as everything shuts down—air-conditioning units, lights, the registers outside the bathroom door.

Everything goes completely silent as I stand in total darkness.

Shit.

THE SHERIFF

You're doing this for her.

He had to stop and remind himself every now and then to remember why he did all of this in the first place. It hadn't always been like this. He'd been great once. People loved him. Respected him. Admired him, even. There was a time when he lit up every room he entered with only his smile. When he could've talked to any girl and felt good about his chances that she wanted to talk to him as well. When his parents looked at him as though they couldn't be more proud of anything on Earth.

He hadn't seen them in years.

He didn't even know if they were still alive.

Would they even recognize me now?

He thumbed the ridge of the thick scar running down his cheek.

He didn't recognize himself anymore.

The final drag of his cigarette burned his fingertips. He flicked the butt onto the ground and stomped it into the lifeless gray dirt with his boot.

They'd be coming soon, and most of the guys here would

die. This one was special. Had to be. There had never been an operation like this that he could remember, and he'd been on almost since the beginning. How many had it been now? How many innocent faces haunted him? Crying, begging, running— he killed them all. He had to. He had no choice.

At least that's what he told himself.

It kept him from ending it all.

You're doing this for her.

He closed his eyes and let the afternoon desert sun burn into his skin.

He remembered feeling the sun like that on his face after football games back when he was young. Back before everything had gone wrong.

It was senior year. He peeled off the helmet and let the rays bake into his sweat-soaked skin for a moment as the crowd cheered. He opened his eyes and saw his parents up in the bleachers, beaming. They'd won the game. The state championship.

"Hey!"

A shout from across the field brought him back to earth, and a smile crept across his face. There she was.

Alice.

His best friend. His love. His everything.

She tucked a stray lock of her wavy brown hair behind her ear and waved as he ran over.

"Great game, mister."

Her eyes sparkled in the summer sun.

"What happened to the debate? I thought you couldn't make it?" He wiped sweat from his forehead as he approached.

"I let Alex take the reins for the day. I couldn't miss this."

He took her in his arms and kissed her. She was the cocaptain of the debate team to which she had devoted most of her high school career.

"You're so sweaty." She laughed playfully as she pulled away.

"I can't believe you're here. Thank you." He couldn't help but beam.

She tucked her hair behind her ear once again. "I knew how much it meant to you. Wouldn't have missed it for the world."

He grinned as he took her hand and went to find his parents.

"I just don't understand how none of them are offering any scholarship money," his mom said again as she read the letter.

"It's really competitive now, Mom. I don't have enough extracurriculars, and my GPA isn't that great."

"You have a 3.8. This is ridiculous." She leaned against the counter and grasped her temples with her free hand.

"Mom, it's going to be okay. It's not the end of the world. I'll figure out how to pay for it."

"Between football and all the time you spend with those kids, you think that would count for something."

"Mom, you know I don't do it for that."

"I know, sweetheart. That's what makes you amazing," she said as she put her hand on his shoulder. "I just wish they could see what I see."

He felt the light shining on his face as he stood on the stage and looked out into the audience. Alice held his hand. It was trembling. He gave it a squeeze and drew her attention to his eyes. He smiled and, for the moment, cracked her nerves and got her to smile back at him. He walked up to the microphone as they placed the crown on his head.

Alice tucked her hair behind her ear and blushed.

"This is such an incredible honor, guys," he said to the crowd of faceless silhouettes hidden behind the white beams. "I think I can speak for both Alice and myself when I say that we are proud to call you guys not only our peers, but also our friends."

The crowd was silent. They were always silent when he spoke.

"It's been such an incredible experience growing up with you guys, going on this journey together, and now that we're on the verge of entering a new chapter of our lives, I think it's really important that we all stop and take a moment to appreciate every single person in this room."

He scanned the crowd in vain for two faces.

"In particular, I wanted to take a second to appreciate two of the kindest, most incredible people I've ever met. I've learned so much from them over the past four years, and I will never be able to thank them enough for the lessons they've taught me."

There they were.

"Edwin and Kimberly, could you guys come up here?"

Two figures stirred from the side of the streamer- and balloon-littered conference hall and made their way up to the front.

The light caught both of them at the same moment—Edwin, with red hair and freckles in a suit two sizes too big for him, and Kimberly, in a lavender dress with matching eye shadow and a purple corsage on her wrist.

"You guys have changed not only my life, but the lives of every person you've come into contact with here. I think I speak for all of us when I say you deserve this moment to shine."

With that he took his crown from his head and placed it on Edwin's as Alice placed hers on Kimberly's.

"Everyone give it up for your prom king and queen!"

The crowd erupted into cheers.

I love you, Alice mouthed to him over the roar.

Love you, too.

The entire town buzzed for weeks about how the quarterback and his girlfriend had given up their titles as prom king and queen to the two students with Down syndrome they'd tutored. The local news wanted to run a story on him, but he'd turned them down. That wasn't why he'd done it.

He wanted two people he cared for to feel the light shining on their faces. To make sure they knew how special they were.

He'd had enough time in the light.

His parents beamed at him the same way as always when he graduated from basic training. He had to pay for college somehow, so he'd enlisted after graduation. Now here he was, head buzzed, standing in rank, everyone he cared about smiling at him from the audience. Pride radiated from every angle.

Alice. There she was. Today was going to be the day.

The night of the wedding, as he held her in his arms and swayed to a love song he would've found cheesy on any other night, she looked up at him, right into his eyes. "I need you to be okay." Her voice was barely a whisper.

"I'm going to be great. *We* are going to be great."

He let her head rest upon his shoulder.

"I hope so."

When he came back, everything was different.

Everyone had warned him before he left.

War changes people.

They all said the same thing, but he didn't understand it then.

He did now.

Nothing felt right. Everyone took everything for granted. No one understood the brevity of our freedom, of our existence. Everything was given, nothing was earned. Everyone around him was so entitled it made him sick to his stomach, and nothing he'd seen could be unseen.

He didn't know where he fit in anymore.

Worst of all was the divide with Alice.

He didn't want it to be there. He tried to ignore it for months. But there it was: a gaping canyon of understanding separating him from the only person he'd ever truly loved in his entire life. He didn't know how to cross it and, even more painfully, neither did she.

He tried school for a semester and dropped out. Nothing made sense. It was a waste of time. The people around him were spoiled children and he couldn't stand being around them.

When he closed his eyes, gunfire. When he lay down to sleep at night, the feeling of explosions shook the ground beneath him. He couldn't sleep, couldn't cope.

So he drank.

He drank, and signed up for the police academy.

The distance between him and Alice grew wider every day. She didn't understand him anymore. He wondered if there was anything left of him to understand. They tried to get pregnant, but it wasn't working.

Secretly, he was glad. He couldn't bear the thought of bringing a child into this broken, senseless world, but he'd never tell Alice. It would've destroyed her.

Alice gave birth the day of the shooting.

He'd chased two men who'd held up a gas station clerk at gunpoint down an alley. He shot one, and the other got away. The one who escaped looked back at him before he jumped the fence. Their eyes locked. He could feel the man studying his face before he dropped to the other side and vanished. The other gunman lay in a lifeless heap on the concrete. Blood pooled out from his back and formed a twisted, scarlet imitation of a snow angel.

He'd never shot a man here at home before. It brought everything back—the war, the death, and endless, mind-numbing pain.

They waited until he'd finished giving his testimony, recording every detail of his account, to tell him that his wife had gone to the hospital around the time of the shooting and had given birth.

It was dark when he got to the hospital. The scent of saline filled his nostrils as he caught his breath and signed in at the front desk.

He would never forget the look on his mother's face when he got off the elevator and walked into the waiting room upstairs. She'd been crying. They all were.

The blood drained from his face as he walked into Alice's room. Her eyes were wet and red, her skin drained of life. She looked up to him and managed a smile. "Come meet your baby girl."

He walked over and grasped Alice's outstretched hand. There, in a bundle in the crook of her left arm, was their newborn baby.

She was born with Down syndrome.

He was on paid leave when it happened. For months everyone said he'd grown paranoid and that he was drinking too much. The drinking had gotten a bit out of hand, he knew that, but he wasn't paranoid. The phone calls in the middle of the night, the car that followed him to and from work, a silhouette of a man always lingering in the corner of his eye—he wasn't paranoid; he was being followed. He'd tried explaining to the chief that the man who'd fled the scene last year was stalking him, and he was put on leave. No one believed him, not even Alice.

Alice had her hands full then. Daisy was a happy, bubbly baby, and Alice eagerly devoted every waking second to her. It helped her avoid acknowledging just how much of a hollowed-out shell he'd become and how little of the man she loved was even left.

He dreaded coming home those days. His mom had moved in after his dad had the stroke. His social security checks paid for the home they sent him to, but she couldn't afford to keep their house. He hated seeing her lose the house he grew up in, but Alice needed the help with Daisy anyway, so it all worked out. Still, he couldn't help feeling like a failure when he came home those days. A wife who didn't recognize him, a mother whose only son was a failure, and a daughter he didn't know how to love.

It was easier to just have another drink.

It was raining the day it happened. He'd driven home from the bar drunk, watching the rain splatter on the windshield. It reminded him of the body splayed out upon the concrete before him. A life ending right before his eyes. It had been one year to the day. Each drop on the windshield played it again in his head. So much had happened since that day. So much had gone wrong.

He couldn't help but notice the headlights that followed his every turn, and gripped the wheel tighter.

He parked the car crookedly on the street and wondered why so many other cars were there. When he stumbled into the house, it hit him that something else had happened a year ago today.

Alice turned from her conversation with the neighbors and looked at him with disgust. They all did. They were already eating cake. The presents had been opened. His mother couldn't even look him in the eye.

Daisy sat in her high chair, icing on her hands and face, happily playing in the mess of cake on the tray before her.

Everyone went silent.

"Well, here he is. The drunk." His words sloshed out of his mouth a bit clumsier than he wanted them to.

Alice came to him and placed a hand on his arm. He brushed it aside.

"Did she tell you I lost my job? Did she?"

She pleaded with him under her breath, tried to guide him to the bedroom down the hall.

"Of course she didn't. She probably doesn't even mention my name." He stumbled forward. "Why would she? What's there to be proud of?"

He looked at his mom. She stared at the floor.

"Do you, Mom? Do you ever mention me?" He leaned down and got in her face. "Are you proud of me?"

The words slurred. They tasted foreign in his mouth.

"Your ex-cop son. The failure." He raised a shaky finger and pointed at Daisy. "I couldn't even make a fucking kid right."

Alice's slap sent stars across his vision.

He didn't remember much after that. Just people shuffling out awkwardly, hushed good-byes and apologies. His mom crying as Alice packed her things into suitcases. He watched from the window as they embraced in the driveway. Alice buckled Daisy into the car seat in the back, gave his mom one last hug, and drove away. He stumbled back to the couch and passed out.

Visions swirled in his head for the rest of the night. The face of the man who'd escaped last year staring into his soul, seeing every fiber of his being, every failure, every flaw. He laughed and sneered and plotted his revenge. He chased him down the alley now, roles reversed. His teeth grew long and jagged in the moonlight, and he snarled like a wild beast, hungry for his prey.

The jiggling of the front door handle startled him awake. He didn't know how long he'd been asleep, but it was pitch-black out, and the house had gone quiet. The door handle jiggled again.

Someone was trying to break in.

Calmly, silently, he got up and crept to the desk against the wall. He slowly slid open the drawer and grabbed the pistol inside. He clicked the safety off and cocked it.

The door finally gave, and in crept the man. The man from the scene. He'd finally come.

Two shots rang into the night. The flash lit the room like bursts of lightning.

Only it wasn't the man from the scene.

It was Alice.

Her body lay in a lifeless heap on the entryway tile. Blood pooled out from her chest and formed a twisted, scarlet imitation of a snow angel.

He'd been in three years when they approached him with the deal. It was all top secret. They couldn't even tell him which branch of the military they were operating under, but they wanted to recruit him. They needed soldiers. Soldiers who could slip away and never be missed. It was a tough criterion to meet, but he fit the bill perfectly. In exchange, his mother and Daisy would be taken care of. His father too, if he was still alive. There was a lifetime pension. A good one.

All he had to do was shed his identity in exchange for a

number and pledge his service. It was an easy exchange to make. Anything beat prison. The memory of Alice's dead body on their entryway floor was all the punishment he'd ever need.

He thumbed the thick scar on his cheek as he contemplated their offer. He'd earned it in a brawl his first year in. A gaping slice that ran from right under his left eye to his chin.

He shook the man's hand and took the job.

He trained for almost a year before they sent him on his first mission. He was one of the very first members of the SHRF and one of the first to face the greatest threat ever known to mankind.

They'd learned of the synthetic humans that now populated the country, possibly the entire world. They were meant to be soldiers, designed to spare human casualties in future wars, made so that kids like him would never have to trade in their futures ever again. The scientist who had led the team working on the project sabotaged their efforts, introduced the synthetic cells into sperm banks, fertility clinics, blood banks all across the country. American citizens had been unknowingly giving birth to powerful weapons for two decades now, and they had to be reclaimed before they could cause real damage. The future of not only the entire country, but the entire world, now rested upon the SHRF's shoulders. If they didn't reclaim each and every one of these synthetic weapons, all of humanity could be compromised. He was going to save the world.

The first time he drove one of the metal spikes into a crying girl's head, he thought of the videos they'd watched. All of the children smiling, the president saluting them, the flag waving proudly behind him. The girl's skin lit up and fizzled away in his hands, just like they'd said it would, but it didn't change anything. It felt like murder. She'd looked him in the eyes and begged. She said she didn't know what was happening, begged him to help her. He drove a thin metal rod into her temple instead. The heat from where her body burned away charred the fingertips from his gloves.

He was sure to not touch the skin when he reclaimed the next one.

He finished stomping his cigarette into the dirt and thought of Daisy. He wondered where she was. If his mom was still alive, still doing the job that he wasn't man enough to do.

He'd killed too many at this point. They all haunted him. Every face. Every scream. He couldn't do it anymore.

He was going to submit his resignation after today. Once this mission was over, he was out. No matter the cost. He'd go back to prison, serve whatever time he had left on his sentence, forgo the pension, whatever it took. He wanted his daughter back. It was time to be a father, time to be the man he always knew he was meant to be.

They weren't supposed to kill anything today. In fact, they'd been strictly forbidden from it. These ones were to be kept alive. He couldn't understand. They'd never received an order like this during his time with the SHRF, never taken a single human hostage before, but he didn't question it. It wasn't his place. He was just glad he wouldn't have to add yet another face to his already-filled nightmares.

He took one last breath in the hot sun before the voice sounded over the com unit in his ear.

"They're here. Everyone in position."

He thumbed the scar on his face one last time and stepped inside.

You're doing this for her.

CHAPTER 4

ISAAK

My pulse is pounding.

Hushed voices of confused employees and customers waft through from the other side of the bathroom door. I pull the handle and slip out into the store.

The only light left in the entire arena-size store is coming in from the glass doors at the front. It reminds me of the caves back in Pacific.

A child starts crying, and the sound echoes down the aisles.

I have to find the others. Immediately.

I run past the registers, beyond the point where the light can reach, and into the blackness. "Azure!" I call out.

I hear footsteps filing in behind my back.

That might not have been the wisest decision in the world.

Click.

I turn to face the noise and a row of men—or women, I can't tell—stand silhouetted in front of me. There must be thirty of them, all with their rifles pointed toward me.

Their triggers *click* in unison, and the sound of the strange buzzing bullets fills my ears. Before I can react, an electric-blue veil springs to life between me and the Sheriffs, cutting me off from the barrage. Each of the odd bullets sparks against the shield, then falls to the floor, spent.

"Come on!" Azure says as she grabs my wrist and pulls me down the aisle.

I feel so much faster than I did the other night, but it still isn't fast enough to outrun a bullet. I can hear their feet on the tile behind us and the click of the triggers as they prepare to shoot. Each of my senses is heightened. I can *feel* everything happening around me.

Azure flares the blue veil behind us at regular intervals.

Why doesn't she just leave it up?

When we reach the back of the store, Azure turns and pulses one of her shields up the side of the aisle we just came down, sending it crashing to the floor. Ten feet of metal and assorted home goods slam down onto the Sheriffs. She grabs my wrist once more and guides me through a pair of swinging doors.

We tear through the cavernous back area of the store until we come careening out of an emergency exit. The midday sun hits me like a smack in the face.

Squinting, I watch as a small fleet of the Sheriffs' black SUVs tear out of the parking lot and into the street.

Azure stands by ready to pounce, one of her glass grenades in hand.

A gun fires in the parking lot at the front of the building. I jump and press my body to the wall as Azure grits her teeth and remains where she stands.

"No!"

A voice screams from the lot.

Another gunshot.

"No! Get back here!"

It's Kamea's voice.

Two more gunshots.

Azure abandons her post at the emergency exit and runs toward her in the parking lot.

I take a deep breath and follow.

"We can't just let them have him. We can't let them get away!" Kamea screams in Azure's face. I've not seen her even temper falter until now.

"We can't go after him. You have two Robots with you now. Those lives are worth more than that of a human hostage."

The sound of the smack across Azure's face makes my jaw hurt.

"How dare you," Kamea says, shaking.

Azure doesn't even flinch from the hit.

"Do you have any idea how many of you he's saved?" Kamea continues. Her eyes boil with rage and tears and the deep, terrifying dread of loss. "Do you have any idea how much of his life he's given up to help you and your kind, just because he believes in your right to *exist*?"

She begins to tremble as she fights back her tears and braces herself against our stolen car. She lets out a single, heaving sob and then regains her composure. The smooth indifference of a leader comes back to her face, in stark contrast with the tears glistening on her cheeks, as she raises her chin to address Azure once more.

"You're right." She nearly chokes on the words and takes a moment to get ahold of herself. "We need to move on."

She opens the passenger side door and sits down. Azure moves to the driver's side.

None of this makes sense to me.

I get into the backseat behind Kamea as it finally hits me that I'm never going to see JB again. I barely even got to know him, and yet I feel like he might've been the only person who genuinely wanted to help me.

I *felt* something with him.

"I can't believe we're not going after him."

I say it to no one in particular.

Bile rises up from my stomach as I look out across the parking lot. Stunned customers flock around the glass doors at the entrance as police sirens approach. Mothers clutch their crying children, and dumbfounded employees gesture wildly with their hands as they cry into their phones.

We turn out of the lot and head back toward the freeway.

About an hour later, with my forehead pressed against the glass and the sun roasting my face, I feel a tingle in the back of my head, a *ping* in my consciousness. I haven't stopped thinking about JB since we left—his eyes flashing up to meet mine in the rearview mirror, his smile, how little of him I actually knew—and it's as though my thoughts of him are coalescing into a single point in my head.

I grab one of the sports drinks from a plastic bag on the floor and take a sip. A deluge of sensations washes into me. I sift through them as they pour and home in on the one I'm looking for. I can feel it. I *know* it.

Then it hits me. "I know where he is."

Azure doesn't visibly react, but Kamea turns to face me.

"What do you mean?" Her eyes scan my face for any sign of a bluff.

"I don't know how, but I know where he is. I can feel it."

Kamea looks to Azure. She doesn't take her eyes off the road.

"Azure, we have to go back. We can't leave him with them," I say, trying to make eye contact with her in the mirror.

She doesn't react.

"Azure, please." Kamea's voice is barely a whisper.

Azure slows the car and moves out of the left lane into the rocky median to our left. She makes a U-turn into the left lane of the east-bound side of the highway.

A trail of brown dust floats in our wake.

About twenty minutes later I tell Azure to take the nearest exit. We are still outside of Albuquerque, out in the middle of the desert somewhere. I don't know exactly where we are going, but I know we are only a few miles away.

We make a left over an overpass and head north.

Very quickly, red rock terrain shoots up all around the

road. No one else seems to be out here. The rock formations turn into cliffs on either side of us.

Azure huffs in the front seat.

I know what she's thinking: This road would be the perfect place to set a trap.

I grip the handle above the door and my breath quickens as I wait for something to happen.

But nothing does.

The rocks give way on our right and a wide, flat expanse opens up before us. Mounds of the red rocks dot the entire field, and at the far end lies a remote industrial park and a large gray warehouse.

"There!"

How do I know this?

Azure doesn't slow down.

"What are you doing? I said he's in there!"

"So should we just pull up front and wait while you ring the doorbell and ask for him to come out?" Azure says, glaring back at me in the rearview mirror.

I bite my bottom lip and watch as the valley disappears from view behind another giant mound of rocks.

About a half mile farther down the road, Azure slows the car. She takes a right into an open patch of gray dirt. The car bucks and tumbles until we pull behind another one of the rock mounds and park.

The car shuts down and the silence is deafening.

I take a deep breath and open the door.

The dry, desert air drapes over me like a blanket. The sun is bright and warm, and what little breeze there is only seems to deaden the sound around us.

Azure scans our surroundings and points behind us, toward a ridge of rocks.

"The warehouse you saw should be a little less than a mile that way. We walk, single file, and keep as close to these rock formations as we can. Once we are in range, we'll assess the building and develop an entry plan from there."

Azure looks to Kamea like she's waiting to be challenged. Kamea nods and opens the back of the car. She unzips her big black duffel and turns back to us.

"Grab some gear," she says, and steps aside.

Azure looks at her suspiciously, then peers into the bag.

"You've had all of this the entire time and haven't mentioned it until now?" Azure asks, anger rising in her voice. "You realize your friend might not even be in this predicament had you thought to include me in this little secret sooner?"

"I wasn't sure that I could trust you. I'm still not. But I really don't have a choice now, do I?"

They stand practically nose to nose, glaring into each other's eyes with hard fury. Azure's cold steel to Kamea's smooth obsidian.

"Guys," I say, voice slightly cracking.

They both turn to me and back down.

"Come, Isaak," Azure says as she beckons me over to the

bag. I lean in and take a look at the glistening array of metallic tools unlike any I've ever seen before.

"Laser gun," she says as she removes a pair of mundane-looking silver rings from a pouch at the side. She slips one onto her forefinger and the other onto the thumb of the same hand.

I don't even bother asking.

She finds a case of several more of the glass orb grenades. Seeing them sparkle in the sun turns my stomach, remembering what they did to the Sheriffs that night. She empties the entire case and keeps looking.

"Here we are," she says as she pulls a gleaming chrome rod from the bottom of the bag. The entire surface is smooth except for a crown of metal prongs at one end. The opposite end has a rubberized handle. She hands it to me, and I take it by the grip. A subtle vibration rings to life inside of it the moment my hand clasps around it, like gripping the metal of a gong after it's been rung.

"This is a Kinetic Disruption Pulse Rod."

"What does it do?" I examine the metal prongs near the top, and Azure bats it away from my face.

"Be careful," she says as she regains her composure. "That," she continues, "is capable of creating a pulse of kinetic energy that catalyzes a domino effect of energy and releases upon impact."

"Think of it like a gust of wind that makes lots of smaller gusts in every direction once it hits something," Kamea says.

"A very powerful gust of wind," Azure adds.

I can't help but keep the look of disappointment off my face. There's an open trunk of superweapons in front of me and I get stuck with a wind stick.

"It's really powerful, and really dangerous," Kamea says, as though she can read my mind.

I look at it again. It is a beautiful piece of equipment, I must admit—simple, clean, and perfectly weighted in my hand. I wonder what it's like to use it.

"They're incredibly useful in small spaces when you need to create some chaos," Azure says as she pockets a few more items. She closes the hatch and dusts off her hands.

"When it comes time to use it, squeeze the handle to start the charge. You'll feel the vibration inside intensify rapidly until it almost makes your hand go numb. It's very quick. Then, aim it at your target and release your grip. It won't make impact as fast as a bullet, but when it does, you will know."

I lift it up and take aim at a boulder across from the car. A subtle yet powerful vibration sends chills up my arm.

"Don't fire that out here," Kamea says. "If they're not aware of our presence yet, then they definitely will be once you set that off."

I lower the rod, and the vibration fades.

The sun bears down on the back of my neck as I crouch down behind a rock formation a few hundred yards away from the building. It took us almost an hour to make it to our current hiding spot, and Azure has been gone almost another hour, scouting the perimeter of the building. Thus far there hasn't been any sign of occupation. There hasn't been any sign of life at all. I fixate on the point in my head that I felt before.

JB is inside. I don't know how I know it, but I do.

Kamea sits in the dirt with her back to the rock, eyes closed. I wonder what her life must've been like up until this point—how she became a part of the Underground, when she met JB, if she still has any family. I doubt it. These people don't seem as though they have any ties left to the outside world.

Outside world.

I can't believe I no longer feel like a part of the world I grew up in—the only world that I knew existed up until a few days ago. How long have these people been fighting? How long has someone like Kamea been running? I think about Jonathan and wish I could talk to him, if only for a moment. I hope he's okay.

A crunch in the sand gives Azure away only a few short feet from us. If she were an enemy, we'd be dead.

Kamea opens her eyes and waits for her assessment as she crouches down in front of us.

"That's your only way in," Azure says, barely above a whisper. She nods to a large cluster of air-conditioning units sitting against the gray wall of the warehouse. A pair of narrow ventilation ducts connect them to the building near the roof. "Can you make it up?" she asks Kamea.

Kamea gives a nod.

"You'll go in and locate him. If you make it into the ventilation system, it shouldn't take very long. I'll give you exactly half an hour, at which point Isaak and I will come in the front doors and create a diversion. We should be more than enough to draw them off while you get him out. The timing will be tricky, but I don't see any other option."

"There might be another way," Kamea says. Her hushed voice sounds as dusty as the hot air around us. She reaches into her pocket and pulls out a phone. I can see Azure shrink back.

"If this isn't timed perfectly, it will be for nothing," Kamea says. "Who knows when I will find him in there. It might be in an hour, maybe in five minutes. A diversion has no chance of working if the timing is off."

Azure clenches her jaw and studies Kamea's face.

She reaches out and swipes a single finger over the phone. The screen lights up. I lean over to see what it says, and Kamea tilts it toward me. A new message has arrived from a long sequence of seemingly random letters and numbers.

FINE.

Kamea types out a reply and sends it.

Azure nods in response. She received the message in her head.

Kamea stands and cracks her neck. She puts a hand on my shoulder and locks eyes with mine. They are deep and dark and full of emotions I can't even begin to sift through. She gives me a wink and takes off. I carefully peer around the edge of the rock to watch her.

She bolts across the dirt as fast as she can. In a span of seconds that feel like years, she makes it behind the AC units.

I crouch back behind the rocks and release the breath I'd been holding.

Azure stares ahead.

Now we wait.

It's been two hours. Or maybe it's been twenty minutes. I don't know. All I know is that it's been too long. The sun is on the far side of the horizon now, and the bright, golden heat is melting into a rusted orange. She's been caught by now. I know it. They're probably torturing her alongside JB, prying out whatever information they can about the Underground from their bloody, screaming bodies. I put my middle finger in my mouth and start to chew the nail.

Azure stands up and looks at me. "Remember: Squeeze the handle, aim, release."

My pulse quickens.

"Let's go." She offers a hand and lifts me up from the ground. This is it.

I follow her around the rocks and into the open space. She saunters at a cool, even pace toward the front of the building, and I follow. I feel exposed and terrified. It's too quiet out here. If the Sheriffs are in there with JB, then why isn't anyone out here guarding the place? It doesn't make any sense.

Azure stops in front of the building. "Remember, Isaak, they will kill you if they can. Don't let them live long enough to try. Stay behind me." With that, she walks toward the doors.

My head is spinning as we approach. Azure looks calm and

collected, taking deliberate, assured strides across the desert floor to our potential doom. She looks cool and powerful, and I feel like I'm going to vomit. My legs won't stop shaking.

"Kill the ones with Taserifles first," she adds.

Without missing a beat, she reaches the door and kicks it in. The sound of crashing metal smashes the silence into a million pieces as the door goes flying down the hallway behind it, hinges and all.

She charges into the debris and sends up one of her shields just as the sound of gunfire fills the air. A deluge of bullets is unleashed upon us in a narrow hallway, but none make it past her electric veil. She pulses it out before us with every wave of bullets, predicting exactly when they will fire. Her stride is uninterrupted as we march down the hallway. Near the end, I notice her hand dart into her pocket. She lets her shield flicker away for barely a moment, just long enough to toss the glass orb into the room beyond.

She sends the concave wall of blue light up as the entire building shakes in the blast of the grenade. She lets the shield down again once the explosion subsides, and we walk into the smoke.

The narrow hallway opens up into a wide lobby. Two metal staircases stand on opposite sides of the room. Everything else that was in the room two minutes ago is obliterated, and fragments of charred bodies line the walls.

My stomach lurches at the sight of so much carnage.

Footsteps rumble from the stairs at both ends of the lobby.

"Cover my back." Azure's eyes dart back and forth across the room. They are radiating blue light—sapphire beacons through the smoke and dust.

The Sheriffs pour in from every door. A few of the guns fire, but her shield appears just in time with every shot, deflecting every bullet. They charge us.

The first few run toward us wielding staffs that flicker with violet light at the tips. Azure bends backward impossibly as the first swipes out toward her with the electric spear. Her body arches under the flickering tip as she grabs it from the middle, pulling it from the Sheriff's grasp. She spins it around to face him as her body lurches forward once again, using her momentum to thrust it through his throat. She kicks his chest to pull it free and jabs it into the noses of the next two. The sound of the bones in their faces cracking sends chills down my spine.

Everything happens so quickly, I don't know what to make of any of it. Azure spins and slashes and kills every single one of them as quickly as they can approach, but there are more pouring in every second, coming at us from every angle now. I watch in horror as they pile in around us. She moves faster than any of them are physically capable, but they're crowding in. She won't be able to handle them all.

A row of them form at the landing above us and take aim with Taserifles.

"Isaak!" Azure shouts above the clamor, and spares a millisecond to give me a reprimanding look for my ineptitude. In that single, brief moment, a Sheriff grasps her neck with a thick black glove. It isn't an ordinary glove. The light beaming from Azure's eyes goes out, and her body goes limp.

I feel their eyes lock on to me now as the woman with the glove draws a thin, metal rod from her belt.

My stomach lurches and my head spins. Just as I'm on the verge of hyperventilating, I feel the weight of the metallic rod in my hand, and I squeeze the handle as hard as I can. The gong sensation throbs to life and fills my bones with vibrating energy. The power connects to the fibers of my body, the tissues, the nerves, my mind. I point it at the woman holding Azure by the neck. In a split second, my hand is numb, the vibration is so powerful.

I release.

The air between us ripples, like waves of heat rising on the horizon. She thrusts the silver stake in her hand down toward Azure's temple, but before it can reach Azure's skin, the ripples reach the Sheriff's chest.

I feel the tremendous energy leave my arm through the rod and make contact as her body launches back toward the wall like a cannonball. The sound of her skull cracking against the cement reverberates above the din and makes me wince. I look to Azure as her eyes flare back to life, and she regains her balance. If anything, she looks even more fearsome than before. Now they've pissed her off.

Before anyone in the room can move, the stairs above the Sheriff's splattered body blast up toward the ceiling. Other

Sheriffs start to rocket off toward the walls like dolls being thrown haphazardly around a playroom. Azure grabs my wrist and shields us once again.

As each body makes impact, it creates another wave of ripples in the air, which sprays out in every direction. The Sheriffs are helpless as they go flying about the room. My breath heaves loudly in the silence of Azure's shield. Bodies bend at horrifying angles and break against the walls around us.

"Let go of your fear, Isaak."

She watches the room as the ripples begin to die down.

"Fear is a useless emotion. It makes you weak and clouds your judgment."

A Sheriff slams against the shield, face-first. The snapping of his neck should've sounded like a gunshot, but we can't hear anything inside the dome of light.

"Now let's kill the rest of these fuckers and get out of here."

The last of the bodies slides slowly across the floor, and the ripples fade away.

The shield blinks out and we march toward the door on the far end of the room, stepping over bodies and crooked, contorted limbs along the way.

We step into another hallway lined with doors. Azure pulses out her blue shields from both hands, crunching the doors back into the frames. If anyone is waiting behind any of them, they won't be much of a threat after these impacts.

We take a right at the end of the hall and approach a landing of stairs. More footsteps thud down to meet us.

But it's not another horde of Sheriffs.

"Look who finally showed up."

How JB can muster a grin in a situation like this is beyond me. I'm sweaty and panicked and about to vomit on the floor, but his eyes are sparkling and confident and he's cracking jokes.

"Get going. We'll take the rear," Azure says, giving a slight nod to Kamea as she reaches the last step behind JB. "Go!"

They break into a run and race toward a door at the far end of the hall.

I'm a few feet behind Azure as she bursts out into the sunlight before me. I'm about to make it over the threshold myself when a black glove reaches from an open door near the end of the hallway and takes hold of my neck.

Everything shuts down. My body goes completely slack, but I can hear and see everything around me. Strong fingers wrap around my throat, and I see the man holding me.

He's not wearing a visor like the others, like every Sheriff I've ever seen. His dark eyes scan my face, and I see something almost like sorrow behind them. A long scar runs down his cheek. He holds his thin metal spike near my temple but doesn't thrust it in. I take in the lines of his face and in that moment I no longer feel afraid. A sense of sadness washes over me as I notice the tears welling up in his eyes. He nods and starts to release my neck. The metal rod falls to the floor as he begins to let go.

In a flash Azure's hands wrap around his jaw from behind.

She snaps his neck in one powerful thrust, and his dark, sorrowful eyes go blank.

The nerves in my face reactivate as his glove loses contact with my skin.

"He wasn't going to kill me." My tongue and lips feel foreign as they come back to life.

"Come!"

She yanks me out the door, and I stumble behind, barely able to fumble for the weapon I dropped before she pulls me out. I look back and spare the dead Sheriff a glance as we run into the fading orange light.

Turning forward once more, I see JB and Kamea sprinting across the open desert a few hundred feet ahead. I push my body to keep up with Azure as she begins to close the distance between us.

We're only a few hundred yards away from the building when I hear something loud and turn back to see hangar doors begin to open. The groaning of the metal echoes out in the valley before us like a death knell. I don't know what's coming, and I can't bring myself to watch.

"Run!" Azure screams to the others as she grabs my wrist and pulls me to keep up.

Engines roar to life behind us.

I squeeze the handle and aim the stick blindly behind me. I release it once my hand goes numb and turn to see what happens. In the daylight, I can see an orb of rippled light jettison off from the end of the rod and flow through the air. It slows and dissipates into nothing just as a fleet of black SUVs tear out into the valley.

I'm out of range.

I watch in horror as they race toward us. There's no way we will be able to outrun them.

My foot catches a rock and I crash to the desert ground beneath me.

I catch myself with my shoulder and hands, tiny rocks and dirt ripping into my skin as I make impact. Before I can get back to my feet, a line of bullets fires into the sand near my head.

I lie still, paralyzed in fear as the vehicles close in. The sound of bullets fills my head.

A blinding beam of white light shoots out from above me and hits the vehicle in the lead. It explodes upon contact, sending the rest of the fleet careening to avoid damage. Tires swerve and one of the vehicles flips and rolls, crumpling against an outcropping of red rocks.

Azure yanks me up from the ground by my collar, and I notice her fingers are held like a child playing guns, the silver rings glowing. Her face is unreadable, but I know she must be furious with my incompetence. I just cost us our escape with my carelessness.

She pulls me forward again with her right hand and sends up a shield behind us with her left as bullets begin to fly.

JB and Kamea are far enough ahead that they might make it. If they can reach the ridge, they have a chance of hiding and making it to safety.

Azure and I won't be able to reach it before the Sheriffs catch up, and it's all my fault.

Another round of bullets pelts the ground, and Azure flings her shield up behind us. I'm running so hard I no longer feel the sensation of my feet connecting with the ground.

Another round of bullets.

And another.

Then I hear a different sound emerge from the hangars and I can't help but look.

Drones.

Massive black drones, the size of large helicopters, fly out of the hangar doors and over the valley. They're moving faster than the SUVs, and something tells me their artillery is way more powerful than the Taserifles firing at us now. Six of the gigantic flying war machines speed toward us like monstrous ravens, bringing death on their wings. JB and Kamea won't be able to make it after all.

None of us will.

"Run!" Azure screams again, desperation finally cracking her steely veneer.

Bullets shower down all around us now. Azure flares her shields up in every direction, but they're dimming and flickering with every step.

I realize that she can't make these things forever, and she's about to run out of power.

The vehicles are only fifty feet behind us now. The drones

approach even faster overhead, their propellers buzzing in a horrifying wail as they fly.

Azure throws up her hand and nothing comes. Her energy is spent. Her shields have run out.

A large, whizzing bullet strikes the back of her neck and her body crash-lands into the dirt, her face sliding over rocks and sand. Paralyzed.

I turn and face the approaching envoy. I know I'm going to die.

They're ten feet away, charging at full speed. They're going to run me over.

I brace myself for death and throw my hands up in front of my face. Seconds before the grille of one of the SUVs pummels into me, I feel a charge surge through my fingertips.

Without a thought, the charge ripples out from the tips of my fingers, and my veins fill with fire. A nuclear blast erupts inside of me as a wall of blazing purple light springs to life across the entire valley floor.

Everything careering toward me crashes into the wall at full speed and explodes. The SUVs pile into one another and the drones fall from the sky like firebirds, dying in their own flames. The violet, electric light reaches up into the sky as far as I can see, spanning the entire length of the valley. A blazing wall of fire and destruction lies neatly on the other side.

I can feel light streaming out from within me, an energy unlike anything I've ever felt before. Currents of radiant, magnificent power churn inside me and flow out through my fingers, and my mind opens to the world around me. I can *feel* Azure. I know her pain. I know her sorrow. I know her power.

And I'm using it.

I let the energy flow up through my hands and look around in awe. The purple shield is ten times greater than anything I've seen Azure create, and I don't even know how I'm doing it.

The seconds pass and each feels like a miniature lifetime. The subtle vibrations of every single living thing in the valley flow into me as the power flows out. I'm connected to everything around us. I close my eyes and bask in the sensation.

Quickly the feeling begins to drain me from the inside. I don't want to let this energy go, but I have to.

I release my grip on it, and the purple wall of light unceremoniously blinks out of existence. The valley goes back to the burning orange glow of the sunset and the flames of the destruction in front of me.

I collapse onto my knees in the dirt beside Azure and pull the large, dart-like bullet from her neck. She remains still.

The sound of running footsteps crunches toward us.

"Oh my God. Isaak. What was that?" JB looks as though he doesn't recognize me.

I can barely lift my head to look him in the eyes. "I don't know."

Kamea crouches in the dirt next to Azure and places a black, handheld device against her neck. Azure's body gives a single startling convulsion, and her eyes open.

She pushes herself up on her hands wearily as her eyes flick back and forth from my face to the wreckage in front of us.

Now they're all looking at me.

"Isaak." Kamea's voice sounds distant. "Isaak, are you okay?"

Darkness creeps around the edges of my vision, and their faces begin to swirl together. I can't hold myself up any longer. My body wants to lie down on the ground, so I let it.

My eyelids are too heavy to keep open. My head rolls to the side and my cheek rests in the bits of rock and sand.

The world begins to fade.

The last thing I see is the body of a hawk, lying in the dirt a few feet away from me.

Dead.

THE MUTE

Anytime I open my mouth, somebody dies.

The words rang through his head as he held his mother's lifeless hand. She wasn't actually his mother, not his real one at least, but she was the only mother he'd ever known and probably would ever know.

Her last breath had rattled out of her pale, blood-drained lips minutes before. The only sound left was the monotone wail of the heart monitor, alerting all who could hear that the patient had died. They all heard, but they let him be.

He said good-bye to his mother for the very last time.

The sound droned on, drilled into his head until his brain was nothing but an empty, numb void, just like it had that night years ago. The night with the sirens and the police, when he sat in the backseat of the squad car and watched them pin down his first mother as she spat and cussed and screamed and fought. Watched them press her face to the ground, the whites of her roiling eyes flashing red and blue with each passing of the spinning lights.

In that moment he knew he would never see her again, the first woman he called "Mama." The feeling couldn't have been more different from how he felt right now. This mother, the one who held his hand, who sang him softly to sleep on all of those endless nights filled with terrible nightmares, this one who *loved* him, why was she the one who had to die?

He remembered all the times he'd wished the first one would die, all the times she *should've* died. He thought of all those men, holding her facedown in the mud that night as she fought and screamed like a wild beast.

She deserved this.

He held on tighter to the dead hand in his.

Not you.

The first days of his life that he could remember were in a trailer—a beat-up brown double-wide with rust stains by a squeaky screen door. The sound it made when she would come in at night still haunted his dreams. He'd lie in the little room in the back, on Batman sheets that reeked of urine, and hope he wouldn't hear that noise.

It meant she'd failed, that whatever she went out looking for night after night had eluded her, and she had to come home. Whenever this happened, she was always so angry. Her breath would stink as her mouth fumbled over words she could no longer pronounce. The screen door would squeak open, the sloshy, slurred yelling would start, and then the stumbling footsteps down the tiny hallway to the room would signal it was time for him to squeeze his eyes shut as tight as they could go. Maybe she'd leave him alone if they were closed tight enough.

He never seemed to get it right. She never left him alone. Not on those nights.

"Get up, you little fucker."

Her pungent breath was enough to cut the stench of piss.

He pretended to still be asleep as she wrenched him out of the little stinky bed by his arm. Her bony fingers dug in deep.

"Nobody wants me," she slurred as she dragged him out into the hallway, brightly lit by a flickering yellow bulb. "Nobody fucking wants me."

She leaned in and grabbed his face, hard. "And you wanna know why?"

The answer was the same every night. "'Cause of *you*." Her makeup was smudged and smeared and gave her the appearance of a rabid raccoon. "Nobody wants a woman with a kid, and you ain't even fucking *mine*!"

She was getting angrier now. "Say something, goddammit!"

She hated that he never spoke, and on these nights it only fueled her rage. He didn't know why she was so angry, or what he'd done wrong. It didn't matter. He never said a single word.

He knew *how* to speak. If he wanted to, he could've. But he never wanted to. Ever. The world was loud enough inside the trailer. He didn't want to add to it.

He just wanted to go back to bed.

She started pinching him in his side, hard. "I said talk, you little shit." She dug in harder. "Talk to your mama!"

He let out a tiny whimper and began to cry.

"Oh, you can cry, but you can't talk? Let's give you something to cry about." She let go of him and stumbled to the ashtray by the door to retrieve her neglected cigarette. "Now tell Mama you love her."

She came back with the lit cigarette, holding it like a doctor would hold a syringe. He remained silent. "I said, tell Mama you love her." The glare in her eyes burned like the end of the cigarette she was wielding.

He said nothing.

"Tell me you love me!"

His lips didn't budge.

She grabbed his arm with her free hand and held it so tight he could feel his hand going numb. "Say it now, goddammit!"

Nothing.

She pressed the burning end of the cigarette into his arm, and the glowing tip seared his tender flesh. "Tell me!" Her eyes widened and her lips trembled as she pressed the cigarette in harder.

He shook as silent tears poured down his face. The burning hurt so bad. Still, he said nothing.

"Goddamn you!"

She collapsed back onto the grimy brown carpet. A muddled look of shock and confusion bloomed on her face as she blinked and saw him crying in the hallway, saw the cigarette in her hand.

She shot up and tore past him to the bathroom. She threw the cigarette into the sink and collapsed to her knees before the toilet. She'd barely flipped it open before she began vomiting violently into the water, droplets of brown splattering back onto her face, strands of her lank hair falling into the bowl.

He waited until she finished and passed out on the linoleum before heading back into the room, back to the bed that smelled like pee.

He tried to squeeze his eyes shut as tight as they could go.

Maybe she'd leave him alone if they were closed tight enough.

One day he woke to discover that she'd finally found what she went looking for night after night. His name was Jim.

Jim had long, greasy brown hair, a tattoo of a cross on his arm, and smelled more like cigarettes than she did. In the beginning all they did was laugh and kiss and spend time in her room. He didn't mind. When they were in her room, they left him alone.

He remembered Jim asking once why she even had him in the first place, and she said that her "dumbfuck sister got herself knocked up, refused to get rid of it, took one listen to him crying once he popped out, and died, right there and then." She was her only living family, so she had to take him in.

He took another swig from his bottle. His fourth or fifth of the afternoon. "The least she could've done was left you some money."

She sat down on his lap. "She always was a selfish bitch."

"Well, you ain't selfish, babe." He kissed her neck. "You're pretty much a saint for taking the little fucker in, bending over backward to take care of him."

"I just did what anybody would. It's the Christian thing to do." She leaned in and smiled while he continued nibbling under her ear. "And besides, he's *my* baby now."

He pulled back abruptly. "The fuck he is!"

Before she could respond, his face broke into a wide grin. "*I'm* your baby now."

He dove back into her neck as she laughed and cooed.

It didn't take long before everything got worse. He thought Jim would finally make her happy, that he was what she had been searching for so desperately, but ultimately he wasn't.

It was only the second week when Jim started hitting her, and it was terrifying. He'd hide under the little bed, close his eyes, and wait for the yelling to end. Sometimes the yells turned into screams and he could hear the sound of a fist colliding with her face.

Sometimes, when the screams grew too loud, the neighbors would call the police. The shouts would be interrupted by a knock on the door and officers would ask them questions, staying long enough to make sure no one would get killed if they left. The yelling would stop for a few days after these visits but, like clockwork, it would eventually pick right up where it left off.

On that night—the bad night—they'd both smoked so much from Jim's special glass pipe that their hands shook and they could barely see straight. One thing led to another and, sure enough, the yelling started again. He just wanted to get past them down the hallway. To hide under his little bed, where he could ride out the storm like always. But when he tried to pass Jim, he accidentally knocked the pipe off the coffee table and spilled the contents all over the dingy floor. The pipe cracked in half.

He could feel the fist flying toward his face before it made impact. In a flash of pain, he was suddenly on the other side of the room, seeing stars. He started to cry. The woman wailed and began an all-out physical assault against the man. He picked himself up and dizzily made his way to his safe place as the two of them went at it.

It felt like hours before the police finally showed up that night. He heard the men talking to Jim right outside the door. Though he didn't know why, he knew he had to get to them.

He stepped into the living room as a light shone on his face.

"Hi, young man. Would you mind stepping a little bit closer, please?" asked the voice behind the light.

"Get back to your room, boy," Jim hissed through his crooked yellow teeth.

"No. We'd like to ask you a couple of questions, if that's all right." The voice behind the light sounded powerful, and safe.

As he walked out into the light, someone gasped.

"Jesus Christ, Dave, look at him."

There was another voice behind the light.

"Come here, son. We won't hurt you," said the first voice.

He went forward toward the voice, as the second talked into his walkie-talkie. He could see them now, the two officers. Both wore belts just like Batman did on his sheets, but each of these guys also had a gun. He walked up to one and stood by his side.

"We're gonna need you both to step out of the house." The first voice now issued commands to Jim. He obeyed and stumbled over the threshold. She followed him out and stood next to him, shaking her head slowly in the blinding light.

"All right, son." The man with the first voice leaned in. His eyes were kind. "Can you to tell me who did this to you?"

He looked to the ground and his face burned. He didn't want to do this. He knew it'd get him in trouble.

"I promise you won't get in trouble."

It was like the man could read his thoughts.

"We're going to help you. Just tell me who it was."

"He don't talk none, Officer," Jim said as he scowled into the light. "Kid's retarded or something."

The officer looked back at him, and for a moment they all lingered in silence, the tension palpable and thick.

"Can't you tell me?"

The officer began to realize it was futile. "I promise I'm only trying to help."

A deafening silence hung in the night air.

Finally, he raised his finger, pointed it at Jim, and stared at him through an eye that was almost completely swollen shut. "Him." His lips barely moved when he spoke.

Jim lurched forward and slid something metallic out of his pocket. "You little piece of fucking shi—"

Before Jim could finish pulling out his gun, a loud bang

resounded and a patch of red blossomed on his white wife-beater. He fell back onto the rusted trailer and slid down into the filthy dirt.

The woman screamed. Her man, her happiness, her Jim, was dead.

They'd killed him.

Another cop car pulled up just as she charged toward the first officer. He tried to subdue her but couldn't. She was fueled by rage and whatever she'd been smoking all night.

One of the officers picked him up and put him in the second car just as it started raining.

He sat in the backseat of the squad car and watched them pin her down as she spat and cussed and screamed and fought. He watched them press her face to the ground, the whites of her roiling eyes flashing red and blue with each passing of the spinning lights.

He knew he would never see her again.

Thoughts of that night came to him often—how all he had to do was open his mouth and, in an instant, Jim was dead. It only made him more reluctant to speak. Now he truly was a mute.

Even when he went to live with the new family, he kept his mouth shut.

They were nice, the new ones.

The man was tall with gray hair and dark brown eyes and didn't really say much either. For the most part, the man kept to himself. He went to and from work, took hikes in the woods behind the house, and quietly regarded him as a sort of strange alien. He wasn't mean, though, not like Jim, and that's all that mattered.

The woman was the kindest person he'd ever met. Her brown hair was just beginning to show the faintest touches of gray, and the only lines on her face surrounded her warm green eyes. Lines that only existed from smiling and laughing.

She made him smile for the very first time a few weeks after he'd moved in. A real, true smile. He still remembered how strange it felt.

She drove him to school, laughed and played with him when he got home, and took him on walks into the woods to tell him all about the different kinds of trees. His favorite time of day was bedtime. Every night she would follow him into his room, help him change into his jammies, and make sure he brushed his teeth. Then, after he crawled into bed, she'd choose a book from the colorful shelf by the door, sit down next to him, and read to him aloud. There were only a handful of stories to choose from, but even still, they were always different. The way she changed her voice for every character and how she had the perfect way of building suspense, or wonder, using only her tone—she'd weave a blanket of words to wrap him up and send him off to sleep every night. He finally knew what it felt like to have a mother.

A *real* mother.

Some nights, though, the *other* mother would visit him in his sleep. Terrible dreams in which she found him at this new safe place with his new family and dragged him out into the woods. There, she'd pin him down and press burning cigarettes into his face until he woke up screaming. On these nights, his new mother—his real mother—would come to him, wipe the hair gently from his brow, and sing him back to sleep.

There was nothing in the entire world like her voice. It made him so happy, filled him with a warmth and comfort he'd never even known existed. She never asked him to speak, never tried to force the words from his mouth, but he thought it every night as she held him: He loved her.

The day she was late to pick him up from school still haunted him. He noticed her red, watery eyes the moment he sat down in the car, and the awkward silence on the drive home alarmed him. They pulled into the garage, where he hopped out and made his way in through the door to the kitchen, but he noticed she stayed behind, staring at the empty white wall before her. She started trembling and tears began to pour down her face. He gently closed the door behind him. He felt like he'd seen something he shouldn't have.

He got off the bus and headed down the road toward the green house he now called home. Since she began treatment, his mom wasn't able to drive him to and from school anymore, but he didn't mind the walk. He just wanted her to get better.

He walked in through the open garage, set his bag on the kitchen table, and saw her standing out on the back porch.

The dangling ends of the peach kerchief tied around her bald head fluttered in the wind. Standing there in the light of day, he noticed how frail she'd grown. She didn't really go outside much anymore, so he went to see if she was all right.

He slid open the glass door that led from the kitchen to the deck and closed it behind him. She turned around and grabbed his hand, lighting up at the sight of him. Her light had dimmed to a flicker these days.

She walked with him slowly, hand in hand, down the steps, onto the lawn, and into the trees.

"Do you know what happens to the trees every winter, my darling?"

He said nothing. He always said nothing.

"Well, first all of the color drains from their leaves. One by one, they slowly begin to fall to the ground. Then shortly after that, they die."

The clouds loomed low and gray overhead.

"Do you know what that means, darling? To die?"

Still, he said nothing.

"It's when you fall into a deep sleep and never wake up."

The wind rustled the crisp remnants of leaves on the trees as she adjusted the powder-blue cardigan draped over her shoulders.

"But every spring, as soon as the weather begins to change and the sun begins to shine again, do you know what happens? Little buds begin to grow on the branches of all of the trees and then bloom into beautiful flowers. Pretty soon the trees are covered in brand-new leaves. They're alive again."

A bird chirped in the branches overhead.

"Now, people, humans, we don't wake back up like the trees do after we die, but we do leave memories and stories. And every now and then, after we're gone, the sun finds its way out from behind the clouds and makes them bloom, just like flowers, within our hearts."

She held his hand tight.

"Do you know what makes my mother come to life in my heart? The smell of her apple pie baking in the kitchen. She died when I was a young girl, and for years and years I was so angry at the world for stealing away the one person I loved more than anything. I grew older and eventually began to forget the details of her face, and even the sound of her voice, but one day I found her recipe for apple pie. I picked some apples from the orchard by our old house and followed it exactly. Two hours later the house was filled with a smell that made the clouds part, made the sun shine on my face, and made the flowers bloom. I sat down, and I wept, as every single detail of her face, her voice, and her love for me came back and flowed through me like she was standing there before my very eyes. I thought I'd lost her forever, but in that moment she was brought back to life. Now anytime I feel lost, or afraid, or when I just need to feel my mother's love once again, I go to the orchards, pick her favorite apples, and bake her apple pie."

She squeezed his hand and began humming the tune she sang to him at night when his old mother came back to haunt him.

The nurse walked him down the hallway and into the little room as he tried to catch his breath. School had just ended for the day when he'd felt a pain. A sudden panic so intense that he ran from the lot where the buses parked to the hospital a mile and a half away. He stepped inside, saw his mother lying in the white bed, her skin as white as the walls and sheets surrounding her, and his heart stopped. He sat down, grabbed hold of her hand, and desperately tried to catch his breath.

He had to tell her something.

He wet his lips and swallowed.

"I love you."

She looked at him and her eyes rose in a feeble attempt at a smile that her mouth didn't have the strength to make. A single tear rolled down her cheek as a faint whisper of a breath passed through her colorless lips.

The machine monitoring her heart let out a long, single, droning note.

The only mother he'd ever known, would ever know, was dead.

He closed the locker, clicked the combination lock tight, slung his backpack over his shoulder, and headed down the hall.

"Hey!"

He heard the voice, a girl's, but he kept walking. She wasn't talking to him.

"Hey! Wait up!"

Maybe she *was* talking to him. He felt a hand on his shoulder and turned around. He looked down—in his teenage years he'd grown taller than pretty much anyone else at his school—and stared.

"I know you don't talk much, but I'm pretty sure you can hear."

The words could've been insulting, but her grin and bright, gleaming blue eyes gave them an entirely different meaning.

"So, prom is coming up, and I know this might be weird because we don't really talk, and I know girls aren't usually the ones to do this, but it's the end of the year, the end of all of this, really, so I figured I should just go for it and ask if you . . . wanted to go with me?"

He blinked in open surprise.

"To prom? Like, go together?"

He let the words sink in for a moment, smiled, and nodded his head.

"Awesome! I think it will be really . . . nice."

She grinned again, and he couldn't help but join her.

"I wasn't planning on going super all-out with, like, the dress and everything, so please don't worry about getting fancy. I just think it will be fun to go and dance and hang out, and maybe even talk . . . if I'm lucky."

He chuckled under his breath, and she laughed.

"All right, then, so see you Friday night?"

He nodded. She began to walk away, but he gently tapped

her on the shoulder. She turned back to him and found him with his hand outstretched, holding his phone out for her.

"Oh yeah, you might need my number, sorry."

She laughed again as she typed her number into his phone, her blue eyes flicking from the screen to his face.

"There you go. See you Friday."

He opened his eyes as the morning sun shone through the window. The light flitted on his eyelids and kept him from falling back asleep. It was Friday.

He shot up out of bed and got dressed for school. Everything felt buoyant and effervescent. The day seemed to glow around him. In the bathroom, he splashed water on his face, ran his fingers through his sandy brown hair, and wondered what it'd look like if he grew it out long. He smirked in the mirror at the notion, grabbed his bag, and bounded down the stairs.

When he came into the kitchen, he saw his dad at the table reading the newspaper. His hair and beard had turned white several years earlier. The tall man set the paper down at the sight of him, stood up, and handed him a pale blue envelope. As he pressed it into his hand, his dad placed his other hand upon his shoulder, squeezed, and let out the faintest hint of a smile. The man never said much, but they'd come to understand each other over the years.

He parked the old red pickup, the one that used to be his dad's, in the school parking lot and picked up the envelope from the passenger seat. He stared at it a moment before he slid his finger underneath the edge at the corner and gently ripped it open. He pulled out the card and read the gold script embossed on the front.

To a wonderful boy, now a wonderful man:

Watching you grow into who you are today has been the greatest gift a father could ever hope to receive. I've cherished every moment with you and could not be any more proud to call you my son.

He opened the card to the inside flap.

Happy 18th birthday.

In pen after the printed script, was written, *Love, Dad.*

He closed the card and withdrew one of the comics from his bag. After his mom had died, the comics were what brought them together. His dad collected them, and he loved reading them. They finally had a bit of common ground. It wasn't much, but he'd always felt like their entire relationship was forged in the battles of the heroes they used to read together. It was never anything like how his mom used to read to him, but it was something, and it meant everything once she was gone.

He zipped up his bag, opened the truck door, and winced. He felt a buzz in the back of his head, like the beginning of a headache.

One that had been building for days.

His fingers were clammy with sweat as he pulled into her driveway. He didn't know if he could do this. He wasn't nervous about the dance; something felt wrong. The headache had grown into a tremendous, head-splitting pain, and he couldn't seem to shake it. A buzzing, like millions of bees, kept intensifying in waves. Each wave left him unsettled and slightly nauseous.

He wasn't going to disappoint her, though. He still couldn't believe that she'd asked him in the first place, that he was getting to take her, but here he was, in her driveway, sweating in a rented tux and debating whether or not he should turn around and go home.

There was no way that was going to happen.

He hopped out of the truck, wiped his forehead, and walked up to the door. He could feel his heart pounding as he rang the doorbell.

Her mother let him in and before she could even speak, there she was.

She was the most beautiful thing he'd ever seen. A simple, pale blue dress hugged her athletic frame and made the color of her eyes almost electric. Her honey-colored hair sat in loose curls on her bare shoulders. Everything about her was radiant.

It was almost enough to make him forget about the headache.

Almost.

He winced in pain.

"Are you okay?"

He nodded. Her mother didn't look convinced.

"You guys be careful, okay? No drinking, no drugs, keep your phones on you . . ." She looked at the two of them and then let out a pensive smile. "And if you *do* get drunk, please do not do anything stupid. I'll come pick you up. Just promise me you won't do anything dumb."

She gave them a knowing look as her daughter rolled her eyes and gave her a kiss on the cheek.

"Bye, Mom."

He leaned back in the passenger seat and moaned in agony as she brought the truck's engine to life. He'd only made it through a few songs before he passed out on the dance floor, and when he came to, he insisted on going home instead of to the hospital. She was reluctant but did as he asked.

He faded in and out of consciousness as she drove, the pain was so great.

He couldn't be sure, but whenever he opened his eyes, he thought he saw a pair of headlights behind them, making all of the same turns, following them.

He moaned and yelled and writhed in pain for hours. Fevered visions came to him of a beautiful angel helping his dad keep a cool, damp washcloth on his forehead as he tossed and turned in agony on the couch in the living room. In a moment of clarity, he opened his eyes, saw her sitting above him, and let out a weak smile.

"I like you."

He was barely able to whisper the words, but he'd said it.

He'd spoken to her for the first time.

A warm, joyful smile spread across her face as she gently caressed his forehead and then leaned in to kiss it.

Everything was going to be okay.

He woke up in a cold sweat. She was draped across his chest, wearing some of his sweats. He could see in the bright moonlight that his dad was in the armchair across from him, fast asleep. He gently slid out from under her. He'd woken thirsty and ravenously hungry.

He tiptoed into the kitchen, downed a glass of cold water, and scoped out the fridge. There was some leftover spaghetti from last night.

He ate the entire bowl and walked down the hallway to the bathroom. The moon was so bright streaming in through the glass patio doors in the kitchen behind him that he could see his shadow, long and lean, in the tile below his feet.

Another shadow crossed behind his own.

His blood ran cold and a chill went up his spine.

He ducked into the pitch-black darkness of the office next to him. The room was hardly visited since his mom had died; they used it for storage now. He crouched behind a stack of boxes and stared through the tiny space between them and the wall so that he could see down the hallway.

He listened.

He could hear the blood pumping in his ears, his heart pounding. The sound of the patio door sliding open, slowly, echoed down the hallway from the kitchen.

Hushed footsteps filed into the kitchen, and he heard a rustling in the bushes outside the window next to him. The handle of the front door clicked as someone jiggled it from the outside. The faint sound of glass breaking upstairs was followed by heavy footsteps.

His house was being invaded.

He was paralyzed in fear, worried that the heavy thump of his heartbeat would give him away.

He suddenly remembered that she was asleep on the couch, and his father in the armchair, in the living room. Vulnerable. Exposed.

He began to shake as panic coursed through him. Before he could do anything at all, he heard a shuffle in the living room.

"Hey, are you . . . ? Oh my God! Oh my God!"

A muffled gunshot rang into the darkness.

Then another.

He stared through the tiny crack, shaking in fear, and saw them—people, dressed in black, filing down the hallway. They hurried past the office.

Without thinking, he shot up, bolted out from behind the boxes, and sprinted toward the patio door in the kitchen. It was wide open. As he leaped across the threshold and into the night, he turned and saw what remained of his father's head, splattered in a dark, circular spray against the white wall behind the armchair, illuminated by the moonlight.

A voice called out from behind him as he bounded down the patio steps and sprinted toward the trees. He crossed into the woods just as the first strange, whizzing shot buzzed past his ear.

He raced into the trees as thudding footsteps and rattling guns pursued him. He charged up the hill, hoping he'd be able to lose them among the rocks, but it sounded like they were gaining on him.

He knew that if he could make it beyond the clearing at the top of the hill, he could lose them past the creek. Then he would work his way deeper into the forest, where he'd be hidden, and safe. He'd been hiking and playing in these woods for years now, and there was no way these men knew them better than he did.

The moon lit the clearing like a bright, blue sun. He leaped to the other side, pushing his body until his legs were a blur. He jumped over the fallen log at the other end and felt his ankle snag on a branch hidden in the shadows. He tumbled into the grass, face-first.

He could hear the people in black filing into the clearing, just on the other side of the log. His mind swirled, his heart raced, and every nightmare he'd ever had came flooding back to him. The other mother was chasing him, her monstrous, glazed-over stare and her bony fingers reaching for him through the darkness, desperately screaming for him to love her as she pressed burning cigarettes into his face. The flesh sizzled as the face of his dad exploded onto the white wall behind his favorite armchair. The body of the beautiful girl, the first to ever seem like she might understand him, sprawled out in a growing pool of crimson that spilled off the couch and onto the floor below.

Say it.

He heard the footsteps.

Say it, damn it!

They were coming right for him.

Tell Mama you love her!

He heard the rustling of metal in their hands and knew their guns were raised.

The world was always so loud. He just wanted it to end.

Tell me you love me, goddammit!

He screamed.

The sound from his mouth pierced the open air and shook the fabric of his entire being. He could see the men in the clearing drop their weapons. Some began to fall to the ground themselves. He kept wailing, his voice a vibrating beast, as he rose up from behind the log. He saw the men before him crippled over, vomiting violently, uncontrollably, into the grass. Some screamed in agony, the sound completely muffled by the blast of his roaring voice. Energy coursed through him. He let the power crescendo, felt it jolt his very bones, as the men began to convulse. Blood poured from the cracks between fingers clutched futilely over their ears.

The sound droned on, drilled into his head until his brain was nothing but an empty, numb void, just like it had been so many times before this night. Too long had he allowed the world to silence him with its endless chaos, its endless noise, and all the pain it caused him.

He finally let his voice be heard.

He closed his mouth when none of the men had moved in several moments. He collapsed onto the grass beside the log and surveyed the clearing and roughly a dozen men, bloody, frozen in contorted positions of violent agony, lying in pools of their own vomit.

Dead.

He tried to catch his breath as his eyes welled with tears. All the tears in the world couldn't wash away the horror of what lay before him, of what he'd done, of what he'd become. He thought of the woman who'd given birth to him, his first mama, Jim, his real mother, the girl lying dead on the couch back at his house, the pile of bodies before him.

Anytime I open my mouth, somebody dies.

The silence of the night enveloped him as he softly cried into the darkness and wished his mother, his real mother, would come to him, wipe the hair gently from his brow, and sing him back to sleep.

He looked up toward the branches above him.

They were covered in little white flowers.

CHAPTER 5
ISAAK

The taste of the red liquid chokes me and I jolt awake. It spills out of my mouth and onto my chin as I sit up and gasp for air.

I'm in the car. We're driving again. I can feel the tires vibrating on the highway below.

Azure is next to me in the backseat, holding one of the sports drinks. I wipe my chin off and grab it from her. It tastes incredible. Life blooms in my stomach and spreads out into my veins as I guzzle it down.

"Welcome back, buddy." JB gives me his signature grin. He's even charming when he's patronizing.

I gulp down the last of the red drink and finally breathe once again. "What was that? What happened?" I turn from Azure to Kamea. I don't know what I did back there, and I need answers.

"We were hoping that you'd tell us, actually," JB says.

I look to Azure. She watches me with silent, curious eyes. I look to Kamea in the seat in front of me. She watches back through the vanity mirror in front of her, trying to read my face.

"You guys think I know how I did that? I don't. I don't even know what I did."

I can't tell if they believe me or not.

"We'll discuss this later," Azure says. "Right now we need to disappear, and fast. What happened back there will have every southwest unit of the SHRF on us in a matter of hours. We need to hide."

I look out the window into the desert. The violet twilight is fading into a deep, inky blue. It's that weird time of day when the very last bit of light somehow makes it seem darker than pitch-black.

"Where can we go?" I ask, looking out at the last bits of desolate landscape around us in the dying light.

"Take the next exit," Kamea says to JB.

A green sign reflects brightly in the headlights ahead of us.

RT 66

"I know a place."

It's completely dark by the time we see the first sign.

EL MAPAIS NATIONAL MONUMENT

"Down there," Kamea says to JB.

He takes a left down a dirt access road reserved for park rangers. The car bounces harshly on the rocky terrain. Hybrid sedans aren't made for drives like this.

We bump along for what feels like ages.

"Behind that outcropping over there." Kamea points to a large rock formation visible in the moonlight.

JB takes us off the road. I don't think the car will make it.

The tires lumber over shrubs and rocks and finally come to a halt on the other side of the giant boulders.

"Grab everything," Azure says.

I get out, and a chill creeps up into my sleeves. It's colder than I expected.

We get everything out of the car—Kamea's small armory in the duffel and all of the gear we bought at the store earlier in the day—and start hiking back toward the road.

"Wait." Azure stops and sets down the bags she's holding. She reaches into my side pocket and grabs the stick weapon.

Before I can ask what she's doing, she walks back toward the car and tosses one of her glass orbs at it. It smashes on the windshield, and the gel substance inside gives off a soft purple glow. She flicks her wrist, and a blue dome surrounds the car as it explodes in a fiery blaze.

Crickets chirp in the shrubs around us as the car is silently decimated in Azure's dome.

When the explosion subsides, the dome disappears. A wide, black circle of mangled car and charred dirt lies up against the boulders in the moonlight.

She aims the stick at the debris.

I can't see the rippling orb it releases in the darkness, but within seconds the remnants of the car blast toward the rocks behind, dirt spraying up in every direction. Rocks burst and launch into one another until the entire rock formation has crumbled down on top of what used to be the car.

Nothing is left visible. Nothing that looks like a car, at least.

"Now we can go."

She hands me the stick and picks up her bags.

We follow Kamea into the darkness.

I didn't realize how well my new eyes are able to see in the dark until now. Kamea had to let Azure take the lead about a half mile back, instructing her to find a large pillar formation of rocks that looks like a tower. I can see it plainly ahead of us, but keeping Kamea and JB from stumbling over rocks and running into the tiny cacti has made it very clear that I'm operating on a different level than they are.

Azure stops.

I grab JB's arm as he slips and look up. We've made it to the pillar. At least ninety feet tall, the massive rock monolith sits right at the edge of where the brown dirt and shrubbery changes to a landscape of jagged black rock.

I hope that's not where we're going.

"Where now?" Azure surveys the landscape ahead. I think she has the same concerns about the terrain that I do.

"Southwest," Kamea replies. "About two miles from here. We'll be able to camp safely."

A puff of my own breath drifts out into the frosty desert air as I take another look at the flat, black expanse before us.

Great.

●–●–●

We're still walking about an hour later. Kamea and JB can't keep up with us in the dark over these sharp rocks, and it's understood that flashlights aren't an option.

I've been watching the horizon and have yet to see anything but a vast basin of black rock and junipers. The valley is lined with mountains and cliffs, but from where we are currently, they have to be about eight miles away. There's nothing near where Kamea directed us, and now we're two miles out into a jagged minefield of black nothing with nowhere else to go.

I open my mouth to voice my concerns right as Azure comes to a halt in front of me.

"Watch out."

She takes a cautious step forward and begins to descend, sharply.

"It's steep. Be careful."

I take a step forward and follow her down.

After the tents are set up, I take a seat and join the others around the small, crackling fire and set my journal on my lap. I finally have a moment to examine our surroundings. We're in the middle of a deep, bowl-shaped crater. The sides are lined with jagged black rocks, but the basin is covered in soft brown dirt. A small copse of gnarled piñons sits at the far end, about twenty yards away from the two tents.

"This whole park is a volcanic field," Kamea says.

"How did you know about this place?" I turn to face her

across the fire and slip my journal back into my pocket. I can't clear my head enough to write anyway.

"I've been with the Underground a long time," she says, her eyes gleaming in the reflection of the flames. "The last mission of my first year, we were pursued from Albuquerque on I-40."

Azure prods the fire with a long stick and tiny sparks dance up above us.

"The Sheriffs blocked the interstate just before the exit for Route 66," Kamea continues. "It was the middle of the night, but traffic was at a complete standstill. They were going down the rows of cars on foot. We had no choice but to get out and run, which is exactly what they were hoping we would do." A pack of coyotes howls in the distance. "It was a massacre."

Her eyes are lost in the flames.

"How many?" I ask.

"Twenty."

Chills crawl up my arms.

"I was the only human in the group," she says.

"Did anyone else survive?" I ask.

JB and Azure remain silent and avoid eye contact with us.

"One Robot. He'd manifested the day before."

Azure prods the fire again, harder this time.

"So what happened?" I ask, watching Azure as she becomes visibly restless.

"We ran. We ran until we couldn't run anymore. Then we walked. By the time we found a place to hide, I was carrying him, and both of us were covered in blood and sweat and dirt. It was right here in this crater."

Azure's jaw is clenched. Kamea continues her story.

"We were stuck out here for two weeks. He hid near the trails during the day while I hiked to the visitor center at the other side of the valley to get us water and food. Sometimes I was able to steal, but mostly I had to scrounge scraps from the trash cans. The Sheriffs wouldn't leave the area. The size of our group must've convinced them that there were more Robots around. When I was finally sure we could get back on the interstate safely, we stole a car and left. I've used this place several times since then."

Azure throws her stick into the fire as she stands and stomps off toward the trees.

"What's wrong with her?" I ask, looking to Kamea and then JB.

JB looks at Kamea before responding. "No one had ever traveled with a group of Robots that large before," he says. "Kamea was one of the founding members of the Underground and held the record for the highest number of successful rescue missions."

Kamea still doesn't look up.

"Not a single Robot had died on her watch until then," he says, waiting for her to interject.

She doesn't.

"It was the single biggest kill the Sheriffs had made. After that, the Underground established a policy to never travel with more than three of you at a time."

Kamea looks into my eyes.

"I was young, and I was cocky. Saving you guys started to feel like a game, and I was being reckless. I wanted to be known as the best, wanted to leave everyone in awe when I came back with an entire caravan."

Azure's footsteps crunch back toward us in the dirt.

"I was really fucking stupid," Kamea says. Her eyes linger on me for a moment before she looks back to the fire.

Azure drops a pile of dried branches onto the ground next to the flames and takes a seat again. She seems to have cooled down.

"Kamea is a pretty big deal in the Underground," JB says. I can hear his voice trying to bring the conversation to a more positive tone. "She was, and still is, the closest any of us have ever been to catching Asim."

"Who?"

"Dr. Mayur Asim. He created you," Kamea says.

"He's also a madman, and a terrorist," Azure says, her eyes meeting mine once again. "He created the Robots and then sabotaged the entire operation. He might be a genius, but he's the sole reason we are being rounded up and killed. He deserves to die."

"Well, where is he now?" I ask.

"Nobody knows," JB says.

I look to Kamea, but she stays quiet. Her face is still and solemn in the flickering light.

"Why do you guys want to catch him so bad?"

No one answers.

"Are you not able to tell me or something?"

"He knows how to find the Heart," Azure says with a look of reluctance.

JB and Kamea both glare at her. Kamea shakes her head.

"What are you not telling me?" I'm starting to get angry now.

"You saw what he did today. He's going to find out as soon as we get there. The Assembly is going to keep him very close once he's tested." Azure speaks to the others as if I'm not even there.

"What are you talking about?" The frustration starts to boil up in my chest. They're keeping way too much from me.

Kamea sighs and finally looks back at me. "He didn't stop at creating synthetic life. He also created a device that would deweaponize you. A project code-named 'the Heart.' Only a handful of us in the Underground even know of its existence, and none of us really knows anything more about it other than the name and what it does."

"And what does it do?" I look at her over the fire.

"It's supposed to make you real."

The word hits me like a kick to the chest.

Real.

Silence falls back on all of us like a shroud. I see JB give Kamea a look from my peripheral vision, and she grimaces. I don't think she meant to use that word, but she did, and it stings.

"You all should get some sleep. I'll keep watch," Azure says, her voice as cold as the air around us.

"It's okay," Kamea says sheepishly. "I can take first watch if you want to get some rest. You need to recharge."

"I don't need, or want, your help." Azure's voice drops to barely a whisper.

"Come on, Kam, let's go to bed," JB says as he stands and gently holds on to her arm.

Kamea stands and looks at me again. "Good night, Isaak."

I attempt a smile in return as she gives Azure a terse nod. She walks to one of the tents with JB and they climb inside, zipping it up behind them.

Azure takes a seat next to me by the fire, and we sit in silence as the rustling in the tent dies down. I watch as she smooths her pants out with her hands and notice the same small triangular patch on the inside of her wrist that I saw on mine earlier today.

"What is that?" I point to the mark and hold out my wrist in the firelight. "I have one too. I noticed it this morning."

"We all have them," she says, holding out her wrist next to mine. "We don't know what they are, but only we can see them. It helps us identify one another."

She takes a protein bar from a pocket in her jacket and unwraps it. The sound of the crinkling foil echoes off the rocks behind us. I listen to her chew as the events of the day bubble up in my head. "What happened back there?" I break the silence, ready for answers to questions that have been eating me alive all night.

"I don't know, Isaak."

I'm filled with so many more questions and getting so few answers. The entire world is a mystery to me now. Life didn't make sense when I thought I was a human, but now that I know I'm a Robot, I'm even more confused.

No. I'm still human.

Or am I? Can't I be both? What does that word even mean?

Anxiety, fear, and panic rise up in my throat and threaten to choke me. I close my eyes and try to breathe.

"We are capable of incredible things, Isaak."

I open my eyes to find her staring at me intensely.

"Our bodies interact with electricity and other forms of energy in ways that humans can't. We are strong, fast, our senses sharpened to the point of near precognition, and resistant to physical injury in all but one specific, tiny weak spot." She raises a finger and taps the side of her head, right at her temple. "Certain Robots, however, have abilities beyond that. Our only theory is that, much like mechanical weapons, we were all designed with specific intents and purposes. Even within the Underground we categorize and organize ourselves like a general would sort and train her troops—those with abilities suitable for fighting, for defense, intelligence, and espionage. Right now there are those who can spark and wield fire, one whose body and appearance can change at will, even one whose ability to activate and manipulate the senses in a human brain is so powerful that it verges on mind control."

She takes a moment to stare into the fire before she looks at me again.

"There are several of us who can create shields like I can," she continues, "but I've never seen or heard of any of us being able to do what you did back there. They said it spanned the length of the entire valley and went so high into the sky they couldn't see where it ended. I never thought something like that could be possible, given the amount of energy required to make, not to mention sustain, a shield that size. . . ."

Her voice trails off. My mind still brims with questions.

"You mentioned Robots having certain abilities. . . . Is that my ability, then? Making those force fields, like you?"

Her eyes scan the flames as if she can find her answers there. "It could be, but something tells me that's not the case."

"Well, how do we find out?"

She looks up at me finally. "We get you to the Underground so you can be tested and trained."

"Trained for what?" My mouth starts to go dry. I think I already know the answer.

She holds her gaze on my face, and I see a flicker of blue flash behind her eyes. "War."

I wake up in a cold sweat with a stiff neck, bundled tightly in a thermal sleeping bag. I find the zipper and wriggle free from the cocoon furnace and yawn deeply as I sit up. The ground beneath me is hard and lumpy, and my body aches from sleeping on it. Any other time I'd be tempted to lie back down and sleep a bit longer, but the thought of it makes my back hurt.

I unzip the tent's flap and step out into the frosty dawn. My breath comes out in big white clouds, and the trees at the far end are all covered in a shimmering white glaze.

"Well, good morning, sunshine." JB is by the fire in a puffy black coat with a plain white T-shirt underneath, exposing just enough of the top of his chest to allow me a look at his pecs for one brief second. I'm sure he notices. He has a small skillet set up above the low flame, and the scent of food wafts toward me. I'm ravenous.

"Just in time for breakfast, too," he says slyly as he walks over and hands me a plate of scrambled eggs.

"Where did you get eggs?" I ask as a yawn slips out.

"They're powdered," Kamea says in between bites from her seat near the fire, bundled in one of the same oversize black coats.

"They're not *that* bad," JB says in response to the face I must be making.

"He actually did a nice job with them, given the circumstances." Kamea gives him a small smile.

I take a seat on the log beside her and shovel a forkful into my mouth. It tastes like pureed cardboard.

I groan and everyone laughs. Even Azure stifles a small chuckle at my expense.

"Thank you for the delicious breakfast, JB," I say as I choke down the sludge.

"Anytime, sugar. Now eat up." He laughs as he heaps another helping onto my plate.

"You need to eat as much as you can," Azure says, immediately sobering the tone. "He's not trying to poison you, despite the taste." She cracks a small smile.

"Oh my God," JB feigns dropping the skillet and spoon. "Did she just crack a joke? Is the ice queen melting before our eyes? Kamea, grab the first aid kit. I think we might need medical assistance here."

Azure lowers her fork and glares at him. He shuts up.

"So what do we do now?" I ask, holding back a smile. "What's the plan?"

"Well . . ." Kamea sets her empty plate down. "After we pack up, we'll hike to the northern end of the park and up the sandstone bluffs. There's a visitor center there. We'll steal a car from the lot and be out of here by sunset."

I look to Azure, waiting for her to chime in, but she just finishes chewing her powdered egg paste.

I take another bite and try to hold my breath as I swallow.

The icy, gray dawn has burned away in the heat of the searing, golden sun. It has to be around noon by now. It feels like we've been walking for ages, but I don't think we've made it very far. The lava rock makes it difficult to keep a good pace, and the heavy packs don't help. At least there's daylight now to help JB and Kamea keep up.

We spot another rock cairn in the distance.

Kamea told us earlier that we were going to follow the park's main walking path, the Zuni-Acoma trail, from a distance, using the strange rock-pile formations as markers. We'd follow this half the day, then spend the rest of our hike heading due north toward the sandstone bluffs. Because of the rugged landscape of the park, there actually isn't a trail at all to speak of, just the cairns, scattered far enough apart from each other that you have to keep your eyes on the horizon at all times in order to find the next one.

Following them from a distance is even more difficult.

"So where is everybody from?" I break the silence, hoping to pass the time a little quicker. "JB?" Sweat trickles down my forehead. I shouldn't be drawing his attention to me right now, but I'm sore and my stomach hurts from his nasty cardboard eggs and I don't really care at this point.

He takes a sip from a water bottle before responding. He hasn't even broken a sweat. "I'm from Oklahoma. Near where we met you guys."

I step over a fallen piñon branch. "How did you wind up with Kamea and the Underground?"

"Well." He takes another sip, his usual veneer fading a bit. "As you might be able to tell, I like guys."

I start to blush for no reason. He's not even hitting on me. I hope he doesn't look up from the ground.

"Which, if you can imagine, is not always the most accepted thing in that particular part of our great country."

Kamea's water bottle slips from her hand. He leans over to pick it up and tosses it back to her in stride, not missing a beat.

"My parents found out about my boyfriend, my first boy-friend, from one of their friends at church. She was the mom of a kid I went to high school with—a total asshole quarterback who decided to make my life a living hell after we got drunk one night and he blew me. Super cliché. Anyway, I wasn't really hiding anything by the time I started dating my boy-friend, and word traveled really quickly. She got wind of it and ran to my parents at church as soon as she could. I think she was just afraid of what her son was hiding from her."

A hawk cries overhead.

"My parents confronted me, and when I told them that I wasn't going to change for them, or anyone else, they kicked me out."

I watch as its shadow passes over me and races over the lava rock in jagged leaps.

"My boyfriend's parents were amazing. They were kind and warm and welcomed me with open arms when I had nowhere else to go. They were older and had adopted him when he was a baby. The most amazing people I've ever met. I remember his mom holding me the first night. I couldn't stop crying, and she just held me. She barely even knew me. Sometimes people are just made of love, like they don't know anything else, don't know any other way to be. They were like that. He was like that."

Was.

"I'd only been there a week by the night of his eighteenth birthday."

My stomach clenches.

"The headaches came. I remember holding him in his bed while his dad called the ambulance. It was the middle of the night. The hospital was on a skeleton crew. Every machine they tried to hook up to him went on the fritz, and no one could figure anything out. He was just lying in the bed in the emergency room, screaming in pain. We were waiting for a neurologist to come up from Tulsa. I was sitting with him in the room while his parents were getting coffee in the waiting room. Then she came bursting in."

He nods to Kamea ahead of us.

"She threw his jacket at him and told him that people were coming to kill him. Said that he was in pain because something special was happening, something the government was trying to eradicate. I still don't know how she convinced us she was telling the truth. Maybe it was because I saw what he did to the machines, or maybe it was because I wanted to believe he was special, that we were special. We followed her to her car and made it to a safe house that night."

"What about his parents?"

Kamea's silence tells me the answer before he can.

"They went missing that night. No one ever saw or heard from them again. Vanished without a trace."

"Oh my God." My stomach is turning now. "What happened to you guys?"

"We joined the Underground and made it to Grand Central."

I shoot him a confused look.

"The Underground's base in LA, where we're going."

I nod. Yet another answer that only brings more questions along with it.

"I stayed with him," he continues. "I had nowhere else to go, and once I found out about the Robots, what was happening to them, I couldn't leave. I knew then that I would devote the rest of my life to helping them. Helping you."

"What happened to him?"

He walks in silence for a few long moments before responding. "He was killed. 'Reclaimed,' as the SHRF likes to call it."

"I'm so sorry, JB."

He stares at the ground more closely than necessary.

"It's okay. I never would've met Kamea or known about the Underground if it weren't for him. I'm just grateful I got to know him while I could." He picks a few needles from one of the piñons we pass and rubs them in his palms and on his arms and neck. "You learn to be really grateful for life once you've seen so much death."

A breeze picks up at our backs, carrying the sound of another hawk crying in the distance.

"What about you, Kamea?" I ask after a moment of silence. "What's your story?"

She comes to a halt. "Hide. Now."

A chill shoots up my spine. Azure rushes back to me and scans our surroundings. Kamea points to the horizon directly in front of us.

A tiny black speck flies in the distance, heading toward us at a rapid pace.

"Is that a hawk?" My palms are already sweaty.

"No," Azure says. "It's a drone."

My heart starts pounding. I thought we were done with this for now. We're out in the middle of a lava-rock wasteland with nowhere to hide besides scattered copses of tiny desert pines and brush.

"What do we do?"

Kamea and JB run out in opposite directions, frantically looking for a place for us to hide.

Azure watches the drone for another moment and then turns to me.

"You aren't doing anything, Isaak," she says, drawing a black handheld device with two metal prongs jutting out of one end from a pocket in her cargo pants.

Before I can speak, she grabs my neck and presses the prongs to my skin. Cold, hard determination burns in her cobalt eyes.

A burning sensation surges into my neck, and everything goes black.

THE TWINS

Leave her alone.

Here they were again, his brothers—the boys he was forced to call his brothers—trying to tear her down. Trying, as they always did, to make her feel ashamed. She was strong, though. Stronger than he could be himself. Sometimes he felt like their words hurt him more than they hurt her.

He just didn't understand where their hatred came from. No, that wasn't true. He knew it stemmed from fear. They were afraid. Afraid that if she was herself, her true self, it would somehow reflect something within their true selves that they desperately didn't want anyone to see.

Thomas threw the first punch.

"Fuck you, little faggot," he said, sneering as he popped her in the face. As his sister fell, he lunged to hit Thomas in retaliation.

No, fuck you.

The resounding crack of his knuckles against Thomas's jaw sent shock waves of pain through his hand and into his arm.

It felt fucking fantastic.

Girls were cheering in the hallway and taking videos with their phones. His other two brothers charged at him as Thomas reeled back in pain, his nose gushing blood, but they were stopped by two thick, tree-trunk arms.

"What in the blue fuck is going on here boys?" Mr. Anderson's deep voice boomed over the cacophony of the students gathered in the hallway.

With his brothers safely occupied by Mr. Anderson's giant arms, he turned and bent down to help his sister up. Her books had fallen out of her bag and her eye was quickly swelling shut. Her wig had fallen off and was strewn out on the tile by her backpack. "Are you okay?" he said, lifting her up.

"Yeah, I'm good." She grabbed the wig from the tile and stared at it in her hands.

"Put it back on," he said. "Don't let these assholes get to you."

She stared at her feet. "I don't have a mirror."

He put his hands on her shoulders and made her look him in the eye.

"I'm your mirror."

She cracked a smile and winced from the swelling as Mr. Anderson shuffled their three brothers down the hall. He looked back toward them.

"You two. Office. Now."

Just leave her alone. Please.

He remembered the first time he thought of her that way, as *her*.

She was born *he*—his twin, Aaron. His partner both in the womb and the world outside. But as long as he'd known Aaron—as long as they'd both been alive, really—he knew she was *she*.

Even in his earliest memories—riding in Aunt Janet's car, singing along to the radio—he always sang the boy's parts and Aaron always sang the girl's. When they arrived at the store and begged Aunt Janet to roam the toy aisle, he knew Aaron would wind up in the pink aisle. Aaron would beg and plead for toys that he had no interest in, and the toys he wanted Aaron never seemed to care about. Aunt Janet never made it seem like an issue, so it wasn't one.

Aaron's sheets were pink and his were blue, and when Aunt Janet tucked them in at night, she kissed them each on the cheek and told them both how much God loved them and that they should always say their prayers, even if she wasn't around to say them too. She would sit on the edge of one of their beds and together they would sing.

Jesus loves me, this I know
For the Bible tells me so
Little ones to him belong
They are weak, but he is strong
Yes, Jesus loves me
Yes, Jesus loves me
Yes, Jesus loves me
The Bible tells me so.

Then she would turn out the light and tell them she loved them. That's just how it was.

The day of their seventh birthday was the day everything started to change. Aunt Janet got dressed up, went to the hairdresser that morning, and had her best friend Shonda over to do her makeup. The theme was Pirates and Mermaids. All of his friends from school—the boys—came dressed as pirates, and Aaron's girlfriends all came as mermaids. There were two cakes, a ship and an underwater castle. Even the party favors were themed. The boys all got toy swords and eye patches, while the girls got sparkly hairbrushes and seashell-shaped lip glosses. Aunt Janet even let Aaron put on some of Shonda's eye glitter from her makeup kit.

Then Pastor Martin arrived.

The party was halfway over, and all the kids were laughing and eating cake when the doorbell rang. Shonda stopped Aunt Janet before she could answer the door to make sure her makeup and hair were right, and then the loud voice came from the entryway.

"Why, Janet, you look ravishing."

Aunt Janet came into the room with the new arrivals just as Aaron belted out the final high note from his favorite song from the mermaid movie he watched on repeat back then.

"Boys, this is my friend Pastor Martin and his sons, Thomas, Elijah, and Michael."

Aaron stopped singing and brushed strands of the neon-orange wig from his glittered eyes as Pastor Martin looked down at him. The pastor tried to hide the look of disgust spreading across his face, but his efforts were in vain.

"Well, you must be the birthday . . . boy." Pastor Martin's lips curled back into a sneering smile.

"And me." He stepped forward and stood next to Aaron.

Pastor Martin tried to smile even wider, but it only made him look more insincere. "It must be so much fun, having a twin. Double the presents, double the cake." He nodded at the two distinctly different desserts sitting on the table. "Now, boys," he said to his three sons, "go play with the other boys."

His eyes rested on Aaron at the last part. He patted his eldest son, Thomas, on the back and pushed him gently toward the side of the room where the pirates were playing.

"Well," Pastor Martin said, "I think they're going to get along splendidly."

"I think so too." Aunt Janet had a way of smiling through her eyes when she was happy. This was one of those moments. "Would you like some punch?"

"I thought you'd never ask."

She grinned as he offered her his arm and walked her to the kitchen.

The day of the wedding was the first time he saw the other side of Pastor Martin. He and Aaron were playing with the other kids in the community room of the church while they waited for the ceremony to start. The girls had gone outside to pick wildflowers and were making small wreaths of little white daisies to wear during the service. Deacon Jacob, Pastor Martin's best man, called them all inside as the groom's party began to file in. Aaron marched in last, giggling with cousin

Lydia and proudly wearing a crown of flowers like all of the other little girls.

He would never forget the look on Pastor Martin's face as he turned the corner and saw Aaron standing there. His eyes boiled as he strode over to Aaron and ripped the crown to shreds.

"Listen, boy." His hushed voice was like sandpaper. "Today is *my* day, your Aunt Janet's day. You will not embarrass us, running around like some little faggot. Not in front of my entire congregation. Do you hear me?"

He was afraid Pastor Martin was about to hit Aaron, the way his hands clenched around the collar of the little rented tux.

"I said do you hear me, boy?" Flecks of spit shot from his mouth onto Aaron's face.

Tears streamed down Aaron's cheeks and dripped onto the dusting of fallen petals on the floor.

The community room was silent. Everyone watched.

The pastor noticed the silence around him and rose back to his full height, brushing a petal from his shoulder.

"Now," he said to the entire room, "let us have a blessed celebration and a joyous day. I'm getting married!"

The entire room cheered and applauded.

He went to Aaron's side and held his twin's hand as the sniffles and tears subsided. He looked up and saw Thomas, Elijah, and Michael glaring at them from the doorway.

After they moved into Pastor Martin's house, everything changed for the worse. Aunt Janet somehow convinced him to allow Aaron to bring the big box of dolls with them in the move, but that didn't last long. It was only a month until the evening they were all playing baseball in the front yard. He could pitch and bat and keep up with Pastor Martin and his boys—their new brothers—but no matter how hard Aaron tried, there was no way to please him.

"Use your legs, boy. You have to brace yourself. Use your muscles!"

The pastor started to get frustrated, and Aaron began to lose confidence.

Thomas, Elijah, and Michael snickered together near second base.

"He's trying, Martin. Just let the child have fun." Aunt Janet spoke softly from the porch.

"Well, if he wants to be a boy, then he needs to play like one." He repositioned Aaron's arms and elbows gruffly. "You want to be one of the boys, don't you?"

Aaron nodded solemnly.

"Good. Then do it like I showed you."

He held the bat and watched the fear creep into Aaron's eyes. Pastor Martin hovered over and watched like a hawk. Eager for another failure. The other boys went silent behind them.

He tried to lock eyes with Aaron.

You can do it.

He gave a slight nod.

I believe in you.

Aaron pulled back and launched the ball. It spun wildly and flew into a high arch above them all, landing only a few feet away from their makeshift pitcher's mound.

He watched Aaron's face collapse in defeat.

Pastor Martin's boys threw their gloves and howled in laughter.

Aaron burst into tears.

He couldn't take it anymore.

He marched past Pastor Martin, past Aaron, right toward Thomas and the other boys.

"Leave him alone!" He could feel fire boiling in his stomach as he approached.

"Or what?" Thomas took a breath to answer him. "You and your little fag brother gonna do something about it?"

He swung the bat and cracked it into the side of Thomas's face before he even knew what he was doing.

Thomas howled and screamed and began to cry as he collapsed into the grass.

He dropped the bat, stunned by what he'd done, as Pastor Martin rushed over toward them. Aunt Janet shouted from the porch as she ran down into the yard.

"Oh my God, oh my God," she shouted. "Martin! Martin, don't hurt him!"

Pastor Martin grabbed his left ear and clamped down like a vise. Pain shot through his head as he winced.

"Get to your room. Now!" Pastor Martin's eyes boiled with a rage so intense he thought he was going to kill him, right then and there. Livid, the pastor released his grip and threw him back toward the porch as he knelt down to tend to his wailing son.

Aunt Janet ran right past him and Aaron, and went to the grass where Thomas lay howling in pain.

He walked back toward Aaron and reached out to hold hands. Together they walked upstairs to their room.

They waited.

Ten agonizingly long minutes later, they heard Pastor Martin storm up the wooden stairs. Their bedroom door burst open and he charged in.

"Now let me set a few ground rules in my house."

His emphasis on "my" was apparent.

"All of this girly shit"—he grabbed at Aaron's toys haphazardly, flinging dolls from shelves and a stuffed animal from the end of his bed—"is gone."

Aaron sobbed.

"When you are under my roof, you will behave like a little boy ought to behave." He grasped Aaron's favorite stuffed animal dog from the floor by his bed and began pulling at its head.

"No!" Aaron screamed between sobs.

"You will do as I say! I do not condone sin. I will not abide some little fairy living in my house and allow him to drag my household down to hell with him." He spat as he screamed. The dog's head began to split from its body at the seam.

"And you." He turned to him now. Quieting into a softer, more threatening rage. "If you ever so much as touch one of my boys again, I will send you out of this house and into foster care so quick your little orphan head will spin, and I will make damn sure you never see your sissy brother again."

He was right in his face. "Is that clear?"

He nodded.

Pastor Martin let the decapitated stuffed dog fall to the floor and walked out.

He got up from his bed and sat next to Aaron on the bed across the room. Aaron couldn't stop crying. Deep, guttural cries shook the entire bed as they both sat there.

"I'm never going to leave you," he said as he took Aaron's hand.

Aaron's head drooped even lower in defeat and the sobs came harder. He put his arms around his twin, and they held each other.

"Ever."

He remembered the day like it was yesterday. It never left him. He'd had nightmares about it every single night since.

He and Aaron were riding with Aunt Janet to the church for a banquet in Pastor Martin's honor. He had served the church for twenty-five years, and his entire family had come into town to celebrate. Aaron had battled with Aunt Janet for a half hour about the suit. "All of the other boys are wearing them, Aaron," she said. "Please. I don't want any fighting tonight. Would you do it for me?" Aaron gave in, but now they were running very late. He sat in the backseat watching Aaron pout and fidget in the vest and tie, while Aunt Janet went a little faster than usual in order to make it on time.

Red and blue lights flashed behind them and the loud chirp of a police siren announced that she was getting pulled over. Aunt Janet pulled off to the side of the road and grasped her temples. He was convinced she was more afraid of upsetting Pastor Martin than anything else.

The officer approached the car as Aunt Janet rolled down her window.

"I'm so sorry, sir. I'm just running late to my husband's—"

"License and registration."

She fumbled through her purse. "Yes, I just . . . I am so late, Officer. My husband has a—"

"I didn't ask for a story, I asked for your license and your registration. Now."

His curtness struck a nerve. She looked him in the eye and sighed.

He reached for the door handle and flung it open. "Ma'am, I need you to step out of the vehicle."

"What? Officer, I'm sorry. I have it right—"

"I said out of the car, now!"

Aunt Janet was shaking as she fumbled with her seat belt and stepped out of the car.

"Officer, I apologize if I was speeding. I just—"

He grabbed her by the back of the neck and slammed her chest to the hood of the car.

Her gasp for breath sounded like a scream.

"You have the right to remain silent—"

She bucked harshly underneath the elbow he pressed into her back. The officer's partner drew a Taser from his belt and pressed it to her neck as she caught her breath and screamed.

Her cry was cut short. She went into silent convulsions as he sent the first charge into her body.

He released it, and she screamed and gasped for air all at once.

"What did I do?" She was crying, her makeup streaming down her face. "What did I—"

He pressed it to her neck again. It lasted longer this time.

When he finished, a dry, heaving sob came from the back of her throat.

"What . . . did . . . I—"

He pressed it to her neck again and let it go even longer than the last time.

Her body convulsed and shook and went into deep, gut-wrenching tremors. The officer finally pulled away the Taser, but when he did, the air didn't come back into her lungs. Her eyes were rolling into the back of her head and her body still convulsed.

The first officer released his elbow from her back and flipped her over. "Ma'am. Ma'am!" Panic set into the man's voice.

He and Aaron got out of the backseat and stepped out into the steamy Southern air.

"Get back in the car, boys!"

They didn't.

Aunt Janet's body was shaking violently against the car, and she still wasn't breathing.

"What's happening to her?" Aaron screamed, terror rising in them both.

"Get back in the car!"

Aaron ran to her. "Aunt Janet!"

The second officer grabbed Aaron around the waist as the first stepped away and spoke into a small com device, requesting an ambulance.

He walked up slowly. The first officer stood to the side and the second held Aaron, kicking, screaming, and crying. He stood next to Aunt Janet and watched as her body slowly stopped convulsing. She tried to reach a hand toward him but couldn't lift it. Her eyes were filled with fear and her lips were still working in a futile effort to gulp a breath of air. He watched as stillness crept through her body and into her face. Her eyes locked on to his, and then the stillness found them as well.

The sound of cicadas drowned out the entire world around him and his vision began to blur.

Aunt Janet was dead.

Life after Aunt Janet's death was more like a prison sentence than an adolescence. They became the famous orphaned twins of the unarmed woman whose heart stopped from a police Taser. They had nowhere else to go, no other family with whom they could live. With all of the media attention and news cameras around,

Pastor Martin didn't have a choice, really. He had to keep them. Looking back, he wished Pastor Martin had just sent them away. Everything would've turned out differently.

By the time high school came around, things had changed even more. Everyone had forgotten about Aunt Janet and who they were, and stopped talking to them as if they were famous. He did well in school, excelled in both baseball and basketball, and even Pastor Martin had begun to take a sort of quiet pride in him.

That wasn't the case with Aaron.

For all of Aaron's fragility as a child, Aaron the teenager had hardened and developed an impenetrable suit of emotional armor by the time high school came around. Insults and slurs rolled off like raindrops on steel, and a sharp tongue and an air of casual apathy were wielded like deadly weapons. Aaron made terrible grades, smoked weed, and took pills behind the gym in between classes, and began to sneak out of the house at night in women's clothing.

A distance grew between him and Aaron that he'd never felt before. Night after night, Aaron snuck out. He didn't know where or why. It was as if he didn't know his own twin anymore, and even worse, it felt like Aaron didn't want him to.

One night he pretended to be asleep as Aaron slipped into one of the skirts from the box underneath the floorboard. He saw, through barely opened eyes, as Aaron grabbed a small gold clutch and climbed out the window. Once it closed, he shot out of bed and watched. Aaron slipped down the white, ivy-covered trellis at the front of the house and strutted over the lawn in heels. A black sports car was waiting under the orange glow of the streetlight, and Aaron got in.

Whoever it was sped off into the night with Aaron.

His stomach tied in knots, he crawled back into bed and went to sleep.

He woke to the sound of his phone vibrating on the dresser. He got up and slid his finger across a glowing picture of Aaron's face.

"Hey," he said blearily. "What's up?"

Silence.

"Aaron, are you there?"

"I need you to come pick me up." Aaron's voice was hushed and raspy.

"Are you okay?"

"Yeah, I'm fine. I just need you to come get me."

"Send me the location."

Aaron hung up.

Seconds later the screen lit up with a message.

He parked on one of the smaller side streets, away from the lights and music blaring from the next street over. He was in the part of town that was always filled with tourists getting drunk while listening to blues bands and gorging themselves on barbecue.

Aaron noticed his car from across the road, flicked a half-smoked cigarette onto the pavement, and approached. Aaron wasn't wearing any shoes.

He leaned over and opened the door. Once inside, Aaron stared straight ahead, revealing a large purple bruise blossoming in the glow of the streetlight outside.

"What happened, Aaron?"

Silence.

"Aaron, you have to talk to me."

Still nothing.

"Aaron, I'm your brother, and I love you. Please talk to me."

Aaron held up a hand and laughed. "You don't love me. You don't know me. No one does."

"That isn't true. I love you more than anything."

Aaron snorted again and looked off to the sidewalk with watery eyes. "Not if you knew what I really was."

"Try me."

Aaron's legs began to shake.

Minutes of silence went by, but he stared at Aaron's face, waiting for an answer. Finally, Aaron's eyes closed and the sound of a deep breath filled the car.

"I'm a woman." She opened her eyes and looked at him. "I don't know how to explain it, but I've always been this way. Inside. I've always known it." She bit her bottom lip and her eyes glistened.

"I tried to change. I used to be so afraid, I would cry myself to sleep. For years I'd pray and hope that I'd wake up and I'd be fixed. That I'd be normal." Her hands began to tremble. "But it didn't work, and I know what I am now. I've come to terms with it and accepted it. I just don't have any fucking idea how anyone else is going to." A single, silent tear slid down her cheek.

He reached over and took her trembling hand in his. "I've always known."

She looked at him with terrified eyes, relief flooding into them.

"And I don't care what the rest of the world thinks, or what anyone else's dumb fucking opinion is. You are my sister, you always have been, and I will *always* love you."

She squeezed his hand so hard that blood stopped pumping into it as tears fell down her face.

He pulled her into a hug and held her as they both cried tears of joy—joy for the return of a sibling they hadn't even realized they'd lost.

With her brother's help, Aaron found the courage to begin wearing the clothes she felt the most comfortable in by their senior year. Thomas was a senior as well, and now both Elijah and Michael—a junior and sophomore—were all at the same campus with them.

Word of Aaron's new style choices spread very quickly throughout the school. Most of the other students and faculty ignored it, and some of the girls even thought it was cool, but some of the boys, and a few of the teachers, made it very clear that Aaron was not wanted. The ones who harassed her the most were her stepbrothers. At times it felt like they were the only ones left at the school who even cared.

She was tripped, pushed, and catcalled. Threatening notes were left in her locker, and once a bag of used tampons was dumped all over the floor in front of it.

Thomas was behind it all. For whatever reason, he hated her.

He could see it in Thomas's eyes when Thomas saw her approach in the hallway. He was even pretty sure that if it weren't for Thomas, the other two wouldn't have cared. But there they were, every day. At home, at school, outside of school, and back at home again. Always plotting something. Always looking for a way to put her down.

The day she finally had the courage to wear the wig was the very worst. They were walking back from lunch when Thomas, flanked by his brothers, stopped them in the middle of the hall.

"Are you fucking kidding me with this shit?" He glared and blocked her path.

"Move, Thomas," Aaron said apathetically. She was used to this by now.

"No." Thomas's voice rose. "I'm not going to move. You're going to take off that wig and stop being a fucking embarrassment."

"The only thing embarrassing here is your behavior, Thomas," she said, rolling her eyes.

Other students had gathered around. A few of the girls let out audible reactions at Aaron's insult.

"You think you're so clever, wearing fucking dresses and wigs and shit. Do you know what everyone says about you?

You're a disgusting joke and you make everyone fucking sick."

Aaron walked right up to him. "Honey, I think someone's just afraid that he might secretly want to wear a dress too."

Thomas threw the first punch.

After they left Mr. Anderson's office, he drove around town with Aaron in his car, listening to music, talking, and avoiding home. Pastor Martin had come to school to pick up his boys after they'd all talked to the principal, and neither of them felt like facing him right now. In fact, they were dreading it.

When the sun set and they had nowhere else to drive, it was time to head back.

He pulled up to the house and parked on the street. A large white van was parked in the driveway, blocking his usual spot.

When they stepped inside, the lights were dim. They thought they'd be able to make it upstairs and avoid confrontation altogether.

They were wrong.

The entryway lights flicked on when Aaron closed the door.

"In here, boys."

Pastor Martin's voice rumbled like a thunderhead on the horizon.

They slowly stepped into the living room.

Pastor Martin sat on the couch with his three boys. Thomas's face was bruised and swollen—much worse than Aaron's. Of all the times they'd seen Pastor Martin upset, he'd never been as frightening as he was in that moment.

"Have a seat, Aaron." The pastor gestured to the armchair across from him. "We need to talk."

Aaron hesitantly sat on the edge of the recliner.

"I have warned you ever since you were a little boy that I would not condone"—he looked Aaron up and down—"this."

He stepped up beside his sister as Pastor Martin spoke and placed a hand on her shoulder. It was trembling.

"You have chosen a life of damnation and have tried to drag my boys down with you."

Thomas sat next to his father and scowled at both of them.

"I will not let that happen, and I will use whatever means necessary to ensure that it never does."

Pastor Martin stood up from the couch, and Thomas's face broke out into a wide Cheshire grin.

Two large men in white polo shirts and khakis emerged from the dark kitchen and swiftly made their way toward Aaron.

He tried to block them as Aaron shot up off the armchair.

"Get away from her!" he shouted as he ran toward the men, trying to protect his sister.

Pastor Martin made a look of disgust and nodded to his boys. The three charged him and took hold of his arms, binding them behind his back.

"'Her'?" Pastor Martin sneered as the hulking men apprehended Aaron. "Listen to me right now, boy. This shit ends here. *Tonight.*" He got right in his face, his breath hot and putrid. "You and your queer brother have made a laughingstock of me and my family, and I am putting an end to it."

His eyes gleamed with hatred. "If you ever want to see him again, I suggest you toe the line very carefully with me from here on out." He turned and nodded to the men.

They dragged a flailing Aaron to the door and out into the driveway.

Silent tears streamed down his face as Thomas sharply bent his elbow behind him. A searing spark of pain shot up through his arm up into his shoulder, and he gasped.

Thomas leaned in to his ear. "Fuck you and that faggot."

He let his body go limp and stopped fighting.

Aaron's screams were shut behind the sliding metal of the van's side door. The engine started, and as it drove away, the night went silent once more.

Thomas threw him to the ground at Pastor Martin's feet.

"This is for his own good," Pastor Martin said. "The boy needs salvation. You'll thank me one day."

Pastor Martin started up the stairs and gestured for his boys to follow. "Come on, boys. Leave him alone."

He lay with his face on the floor for what felt like hours.

His twin, his sister, his everything, was gone.

And he had no idea how to get her back.

The next month was a daze. Graduation was swiftly approaching, but nothing else mattered while she was still missing. A few of the girls at school asked about her, but besides that, her name was barely mentioned. At home Pastor Martin and his sons acted like she'd never existed. He kept his head down and played along. It was the only way he was going to find her.

The Saturday before their birthday, with humid, early-summer heat looming heavy under the afternoon sun, he pretended to nap up in his room as Pastor Martin and the boys left for Elijah's basketball game. The front door closed and his eyes shot open. His ears strained to hear the sound of Pastor Martin's car driving away.

He leaped off of the bed, heart racing, and ran downstairs. In front of the locked door at the end of the hall, he withdrew a bobby pin and a long, thin nail from his pocket. He'd been learning how to pick a lock for weeks now, waiting for a moment exactly like this.

You can do this. Do it for her.

The lock clicked and he opened the door to Pastor Martin's office.

Inside he rifled through drawers and files and anything he could get into. He stopped when he got to his desk.

There it was. Exactly what he'd been looking for.

He picked up the glossy white pamphlet and traced his fingers over the embossed logo of two blue doves, flying side by side.

NEW BEGINNINGS: A FAITH-BASED REHABILITATION AND SPIRITUAL RESTORATION CAMP—SERVING WAYWARD TEENS. SERVING CHRIST.

He took a picture of the address with his phone, raced back up to his room, threw clothes and toiletries for both Aaron and himself into his gym bag, then ran back down to grab his car keys off the hook in the kitchen. He stopped before the open front door and debated grabbing some medicine before he left. There was a buzz in the back of his head, like the beginning of a headache.

One that had been building for days.

It was almost ten when he pulled up to the gate. The camp was on the other side of the state, right on the edge of the national forest. He'd been driving for six hours and his head felt like it was going to implode.

He shook it off and pulled farther down the road. He would need to be clearheaded and strong for this.

If the camp was laid out as the map detailed, he would have to trek about a half mile through the woods before coming to a lake. The dorms sat in a row along the opposite shore. Hopefully there would be an easy way to walk around; otherwise he was going to have to get wet.

His shoes were soaked and heavy with mud by the time he reached the shore. He could make out the row of small, dark trailers on the other side. A small trail stood out in the moonlight to his right, running alongside the lake's edge. He stayed close to the trees and followed it.

Once he got closer, he realized they weren't trailers at all. They were shipping containers. Each had a door cut into the side. They were dark because there weren't any windows. Not a single one.

He bent over as a wave of pain pounded through his head. He had to find her, fast. Otherwise, whoever ran this place would find him crippled with agony in the grass come morning.

He caught his breath and stood once the wave of pain subsided. He took a deep breath and listened.

A voice was coming from one of the containers.

He crept through the wet grass toward the sound until he stood right next to the source.

It was Aaron's voice. Screaming. Crying. Yet distant somehow.

His heart raced, and he ran to the front of the container, facing the lake. He stepped into the light of the fog lamps, but he didn't care. He was getting her out.

The door was locked from the outside with a padlock. His stomach twisted as he worked on picking it.

The lock clicked and he dropped it to the ground.

When he pulled the door open he was smacked in the face with a blast of hot air and a stench unlike anything he'd ever smelled before. He stepped inside and his stomach dropped.

The tiny container had to be well over one hundred degrees inside. The floor was dirt, and the walls were bare metal. A bucket of filth sat in one corner, and in the other, illuminated by the blue glow of a wall-mounted screen, lay Aaron.

Her body was curled into a ball, naked except for a pair of soiled girls' panties. She glistened with sweat and was covered head to toe in filth. He stepped inside, horrified, and went to her, crouching in the dirt beside her.

He held his breath as he shook her lifeless body.

Please. Please, God. Please

Her body began to stir, and tears of joy welled in his eyes.

"Come on," he whispered. "I'm getting you out of here."

She could barely moan in response.

The screaming he'd heard from the outside happened again, and he turned to the screen on the wall.

A video was playing. Aaron, dressed in a wig and women's underwear, was tied to a chair. A man holding a belt whipped her repeatedly, shouting about repentance and sin, as she howled and begged them to stop. Other boys stood around the room and watched, naked and expressionless. The video went for about a minute and then started over again, on a loop.

His blood boiled inside as he lifted Aaron up off of the ground.

When her eyes opened and she saw him, she jolted to life in response. She held him so tight he thought she would never let go.

"We have to go. Right now." He was starting to panic. They'd lingered too long already.

She nodded and struggled to her feet. He held her hand, and together they walked out into the night. Even the muggy summer air was a cool relief.

They both took a deep breath.

An air horn sounded three times as another light came on behind them in the distance.

"Are you able to swim?" The racing of his heart over-powered the pain in his head.

She gave a single nod.

He grabbed her hand and ran toward the water as the sound of men shouting began to fill the air.

They splashed into the black water and then dove in.

He had to let go of her hand to stay afloat, pushing the water with his legs and arms, choking for air between thrusts. He turned to look back every few seconds to make sure Aaron was still with him, but she never fell behind. As they approached the far shore, a group of men came into view in the fog lights, hunched over, gasping for breath after their run.

"Get back here!" one managed to yell across the black water.

He stood in the mud on the opposite shore and pulled her out of the lake. They ran together into the trees and never looked back.

They stopped at a small roadside motel. He'd planned on making it all the way back home tonight, but he was in too much pain to continue driving. She was too. They could both feel the exact same pain shooting through their skulls, threatening to explode like a bomb.

In the room, they both collapsed onto the grimy bed. He wrapped his arm around her and held her as she began to sob.

The pain grew worse, coming in wave after wave. He did his best to stifle his own moans of agony and comfort her. The room swirled and his vision faded in the pain. He was afraid they were both going to die, but he didn't care. He had his sister back.

That was all that mattered.

The next morning he woke to a pounding on the door.

"Check out was at eleven!" the hoarse, smoky voice of the manager yelled. "If you want to stay another day, you need to pay. Otherwise, out!"

He picked up his phone and checked the time. It was noon.

He felt a tingling sensation as the screen flickered in his hand.

Aaron looked at him. "I can't go back. Not yet," she said.

He nodded and went to the door. "I'll pay for another day," he called. The manager grumbled and walked through the gravel back toward her lair.

He looked back at Aaron. She was staring at her hands. "I feel so strange."

He looked at his phone where he'd left it on the bed. "Me too."

"You need to come see this," Aaron said.

He'd just returned from his third trip to the greasy burger stand a few miles down the road. Neither of them seemed to be able to satisfy their appetites.

"Promise me, though, you won't freak out." She was in the bathroom, talking through the door.

"What are you talking about?" He stepped closer, confused.

"I said promise me. Seriously."

"Okay, okay. I promise." He took another step and waited for her to come out.

A silent moment passed. Then the door handle turned,

and out stepped Aaron, wearing a T-shirt and gym shorts.

"This might scare you. To be honest, it's scaring me."

"What are you—"

"Just watch."

Aaron lifted her hands slightly and closed her eyes.

After a few seconds, he realized her hair was growing longer by the second, her nose changing shape completely. The process stopped, and he looked at her, dumbfounded.

"What was that?" he asked. His mouth hung open.

"I don't know." Her eyes welled with tears as she spoke. "My whole life I've seen something different from my reflection whenever I look in a mirror, and while you were gone just now—" Her voice faltered, and she took a breath. "My body just started changing with my thoughts. I don't know how to explain it. Watch."

She ran her fingers down her new long hair and it instantly shifted from black to red and then to an iridescent shade of pink. With a quick shake, it went back to black.

He didn't know what to say. There were no words.

"I need you here while I try this." She took a deep breath and closed her eyes. After a few moments her entire body began to change in front of him. Her shoulders slimmed, her nose grew narrower, and breasts began to lift beneath the fabric of her T-shirt. More and more parts of her body began to shift and remold themselves right in front of him. Everything about her was a shifting mirage, glistening and changing. She opened her eyes and a soft, pink glow began to fade from them as her body stopped shifting.

She stared at him in terror, waiting for him to react.

His eyes welled with tears. "It's you," he said.

Tears filled her eyes as well. "It's me."

They drove around a few more days, slowly making their way back toward home. He didn't know what had happened to them, but he knew they needed to get back to Pastor Martin's house, get the money from the fund started after Aunt Janet's murder, and start a new life.

Surely Pastor Martin would be glad to be rid of them forever.

He pulled into the driveway and killed the engine.

"Are you sure you want to go in like this?" He looked at Aaron in her new body. She could change everything about her physical appearance at will now, but the current iteration was the *real* her.

"I'm never going any other way again."

He gave her a small smile, and they got out of the car.

They stepped into the kitchen just as Pastor Martin finished praying over their meal. Thomas, Michael, and Elijah sat around the table with their heads bowed. Pastor Martin saw him first.

"Boy, where have you be—"

Then he saw her.

Their chairs all slid back from the table as they stood and got a full look at her new appearance. She was completely different, but they knew damn well who they were looking at.

Pastor Martin's mouth was open. A look of shock, terror, and disgust swept over his face.

"The devil is in my house."

"Pastor Martin, we just want to pack our things and leave," he said.

"And our money. The money that was raised for us after Aunt Janet died," Aaron said in her new voice.

This pushed Pastor Martin over the edge.

"Your money?" His eyes went wild in rage. "*Your* money? Who do you think paid for your groceries, and your clothes, and everything else it took to raise you little demons after she died?"

His hands clenched into fists at his sides.

"Do you honestly think I paid for *anything*? That I took money that I needed to raise *my* boys to care for you degenerate orphans?" He shook as he screamed. "You killed your mother when you crawled out of her and sucked away her sister's ability to love anything else in this world. You honestly think that I would let you little parasites drain me and my boys as well?"

He turned abruptly and bolted from the room.

"You and the faggot need to leave now," Thomas said from the other side of the table.

"What did you call me?" Aaron's eyes glowered.

"You heard me."

In one quick step Aaron reached over the table, grabbed him by the neck, and dragged him across it. Plates shattered and food spilled onto the floor as his feet scraped over the surface. Aaron effortlessly held him up by his throat like a doll.

The sound of a gun cocking interrupted them.

"Put him down and get out. Now." Pastor Martin held a small pistol, aimed at Aaron.

Slowly, she set Thomas back on the floor as he sputtered and gasped for breath.

Thomas clasped his throat and gulped. "Faggot," he whispered.

Her fist collided with his face so hard it sent him flying back over the table and into the wall. His head sank into the plaster and the crack of his arm breaking against the countertop was like a gunshot.

Then Pastor Martin fired. A real gunshot tore through the room, and Aaron stumbled back, blood spraying from the top of her chest as the bullet ripped into her.

He watched in horror as his sister fell to the ground and blood pooled around her. The strange electricity that he'd been feeling for days welled up inside of him. His fingertips tingled. He turned and lunged for Pastor Martin, seizing him by the throat.

At his touch Pastor Martin's body went limp. Every fiber of his being felt malleable. His movement, his breathing—every single function inside Pastor Martin's body felt connected to his fingertips.

Even his heartbeat.

Anger and sorrow and a lifetime of pain coursed through him as he took control of Pastor Martin's heart—a heart filled with hatred, spite, malice, and jealousy. He stared into Pastor Martin's eyes. This was the man who had kept him and his twin sister in fear because she'd dared to be born different, the man who had sent her away to a torture camp because he'd refused to understand her, the man who'd abused Aunt Janet and drained the light from her smile, the man who had squandered away their inheritance.

Elijah and Michael screamed for their brother and father, but he didn't care. Aaron, his whole world, was lying on the ground, her life bleeding out onto the kitchen floor. He wasn't going to let Pastor Martin get away with what he'd done.

He felt every pump, every beat, every pulse of warm blood flowing in and out of the chambers in Pastor Martin's heart— and he stopped it.

Leave her alone.

Just like that, he was dead.

He removed his hand from Pastor Martin's neck and watched the corpse collapse on the tile.

Elijah and Michael howled and ran to their father's side as he went to Aaron's body and fell to his knees. Hot, angry tears poured from deep inside of him. He grasped her still hand in his and clutched it to his chest.

It twitched.

He opened his eyes and wiped away the tears as Aaron

began to stir. Panic and hope raced through his mind all at once, and before he could release his grip on her hand, her eyes opened.

She gave a faint smile and lifted herself up off the ground, helping him to his feet as well.

Elijah knelt by his father's lifeless body, weeping, and Michael's voice echoed from the living room. He was calling an ambulance. Thomas's body still lay in a crumpled heap by the wall.

Aaron led the way out of the kitchen and back out the front door. They sat down in the car, and Aaron flicked on the overhead light. She flipped the vanity mirror down and pulled the collar of her blood-soaked T-shirt. They both watched as the last remaining portion of the bullet wound healed. The open patch of skin sealed up before their eyes.

She began to laugh and cry at the same time.

He gave her hand a squeeze and pulled out of the driveway.

As they crossed the bridge over the river, past the pyramid and all the buildings downtown, he looked over and saw Aaron staring out the window, watching everything pass by.

> *"Jesus loves me, this I know*
> *For the Bible tells me so*
> *Little ones to him belong*
> *They are weak, but he is strong*

Yes, Jesus loves me

Yes, Jesus loves me

Yes, Jesus loves me

The Bible tells me so."

Her voice faltered at the end.

CHAPTER 6

ISAAK

Light and air surge back into me. I'm lying on the ground, in the dirt, with my head in Azure's hands.

Azure.

I try to scramble away from her in fear. The last thing I can remember is her attacking me with her Taser.

"Shh. Calm down." She holds me firmly in place as I try to get away, small rocks biting into the meat of my hands. "Everything is okay, Isaak. Calm down."

I look around and see Kamea and JB hovering over her shoulder, watching me wake up. A bit of relief bubbles up in my stomach.

"What happened? Why did you attack me?"

My voice feels caked in dirt.

"She didn't attack you, Isaak," Kamea says. "She knocked you out so the drone wouldn't pick up your electrical signature."

"As soon as she put you down she had Kamea knock her out along with you, if you can believe it," JB says.

I start to sit up. The rocks hurt underneath my tailbone.

"What was it?"

"It was an SHRF drone," Azure says, grabbing my hand to help lift me up to my feet. "They're scanning the area for abnormal electrical activity. That's why we had to be knocked out: Our bioelectrical output is nearly that of a human's while we're asleep."

"Once you guys were out, we hid you in that lava tube," Kamea says, pointing to the opening of a small cave a few yards away from us. "We kept walking like we were hikers and waited for the drone to leave the area."

"How long were we out?"

"About four hours," Kamea says.

I groan. "We're going to have to camp again, aren't we?"

"Not if we can get to the visitor center before sunset," Kamea says. "That drone stayed here way too long. This place isn't the safe haven it used to be. At least if we get on the road, we should be able to make our way to a safe house and hide for a bit. I know of one only an hour from here."

"Then what are we waiting for?" I spot the nearest cairn in the distance and start walking.

"Isaak," JB calls over to me as I trudge away. "This way."

I look at him as he nods over his shoulder in the opposite direction. I turn and follow the others as they start our long march in the correct direction. JB gives me a small grin and follows behind me. I look around for the lava tube so I can go crawl inside and die.

●–●–●

The sandstone bluffs rise up before us in the distance. The sun is sitting low and orange in the sky, and I can't tell if we're going to make it.

We don't.

By the time we get to the rocky base of the cliffs, the sun has started to set. Kamea says that most day hikers would already be back at their cars by now and that we missed our window for stealing one. We're going to have to camp again.

My back aches in protest.

We climb up into the rocks until we come to a wide, flat landing hidden between a pair of massive sandstone boulders, and decide to set up camp. The ground is soft and sandy, much better than the ground we slept on last night. Azure goes back down to collect firewood as Kamea takes a moment to stretch by her tent. I spot a trail in the rocks behind one of the boulders and decide to explore a bit.

The gap between the boulder and the cliffside is narrow, but I squeeze myself through, round the corner of the cliff, and come upon a breathtaking view. A ledge juts out in front of me, perched above the entire valley. The sun is setting in the distance and everything is awash in soft, golden light. I cautiously approach the edge and try to not look down. My knees are shaky from the height, but I manage to sit.

I settle in, my feet dangling off the edge, and look out at the view. The sky is a stunning swirl of orange and rose and violet, and I feel like I can see miles out ahead of us. An endless, flat expanse of brown dirt, black lava rocks, crooked desert pines all trail out into the horizon.

I lean over and reach into my back pocket to pull out my journal. I slide the pen from its nook in the spine and start writing.

Clinging on to daylight
Basking in the sun
Holding on to grains of sand
That, through my fingers, run
Melting in the sunset
The day it fades to night
The petals of a flower
Curl in without the light
But frost that settles on the land
In white and black and blue
Will wither under softer rays
And melt to morning dew
For with the dawn the sun will rise
The cycle starts anew
And like the ever-changing Earth
I shall be changed too

"Isn't this amazing?"

JB rounds the cliff face behind me, his feet crunching in the gravelly sand. He doesn't even flinch as he approaches the ledge and sits down next to me.

"It's incredible."

His leg casually bumps into mine as he settles in. "What're you writing?"

"Oh, nothing important. I just write poems sometimes." I fidget with the journal and wish I weren't holding it. "It's stupid."

"That's not stupid at all," he says, looking at me. "I think that makes you really intriguing."

I don't know how to reply. He looks back out to the view. Everything is silent around us except for the wind.

"Thank you, by the way," he says. "Kamea told me what happened. If it weren't for you, I would still be tied up in that warehouse. I might even be dead. You saved me."

"I don't think I can take the credit for that."

"Of course you can."

I fixate on a pair of rabbits running through the brush below, hoping to avoid direct eye contact.

"Isaak, they never would've found me if it weren't for you. I owe you. More than you realize."

The warm wind starts to cool as the sun sets even lower. I stare out at the mountains in the distance, purple in the fading light.

"I used to have a view like this back home," I say, trying to combat the awkward silence. "I mean, not anything like *this*, but it made me feel the same way."

"How does it make you feel?"

I can feel his eyes on me.

"Like the world is more than me, more than us. Like there's this whole magical, vast expanse of wonder out there that we never take the time to appreciate. Like if we all stopped to have moments like these, to look at views like this, the world would be a better place. Sometimes it's good to step back and realize how small and insignificant you are in the grand scheme of things. It forces you to not take anything for granted. It's what I imagine standing at the edge of the ocean is like."

"You think you're insignificant?"

"I don't mean it as a negative thing. I just think it's important to maintain a sense of wonder, if that makes any sense."

"It does."

His leg inches in closer to mine. They're fully touching now. I look over at him. His eyes are like sapphires in the copper light.

"You have a really beautiful soul, Isaak," he says. His voice is hushed and his shoulders lean in to me ever so slightly.

"Do I even have a soul?" A nervous laugh slips out. I can feel a blush rising up to my cheeks.

"I don't think anyone without a soul could be as special as you are."

He leans in closer to me. His lips are full and I can feel heat radiating from him. None of us have showered since the day before yesterday, but he smells amazing. Like pine and sweat and man. The blood drains from my cheeks.

"You think I'm special?"

My palms are sweaty. He gives the smallest of his painfully perfect grins as he puts his hand on my leg and leans in further. "I think you're very, very special."

His hand slips up my thigh to the side of my back. His muscled arm effortlessly pulls me in to his chest, and he angles his face. I feel his breath on my lips and brace myself for my first real kiss.

"JB," Kamea announces her presence behind us.

I jump and slide out of JB's arms. I can feel my face going white. I place my journal over my lap so she can't see what's obviously happening in my pants.

"Yes?" JB says flatly.

"You have the lighter. We need it to start the fire."

Kamea doesn't sound too happy, either.

"I'll just go do it," he says, pushing himself up to his feet. "Don't stay out here too long, kid."

I turn and watch him round the corner and go back down to camp with Kamea. Neither of them speaks to the other.

Kid.

He's not even that much older than me.

The next morning I sit in front of the rekindled fire, warming my hands over the flames. Everything is gray and blue in the dim light before sunrise. The night's frost has me chilled to the bone.

JB is boiling water to make oatmeal, while Kamea breaks down their tent.

"All right, who is ready for flavorless slop?" he says, his voice still raspy from sleep.

"Sounds delicious," I say, expressionless. My eyes feel puffy from two nights of unfulfilling sleep. "But I think I might miss those eggs from yester—"

"Be quiet." Azure's voice is hushed and firm. Something is wrong.

We all go still.

She's standing at the far edge of our camp, next to one of the large boulders, peering down the trail behind us.

I strain to hear anything.

"What is it?" I whisper.

"Shh!"

Then I hear it.

A faint thudding and a soft, metallic chime echoes in the rocks around us, like a delicate set of gears shifting.

I stand up as the noise gets closer.

JB and Kamea look at each other, puzzled. They must not be able to hear it yet.

JB stands and begins walking toward Kamea, but Azure holds up her hand in signal for him to halt.

Then they can hear it as well. It's coming up the bluff, right behind us. My heart starts to race.

Kamea's eyes shift to the duffel bag of weapons sitting in front of her. The KDPR I've kept in my pocket the past two days is sitting on top of it, its smooth metal surface glistening blue in the morning light.

The noise gets closer.

And then goes silent.

We all stand perfectly still.

Then the gear noise sounds again, louder than ever, and a creature appears on top of the boulder behind Azure.

At least I think it's a creature.

It has four, multi-jointed legs and a narrow, triangular head housing a single, large eye. The creature freezes, perched on the rock above us. A smooth, matte black metal finish covers its entire body. The oddly jointed legs splay out to the sides a bit, perfectly gripping the rock. It looks like it's incapable of losing balance.

The large, round eye in the middle of its head begins to shine a brilliant green light over us. Its body is frozen in place. Its head tilts up and down, then side to side, scanning each of us in turn.

And then the light turns red.

In a flash it leaps over our camp and begins climbing the rocks to the top of the bluffs behind us.

Azure dashes to the duffel, grabs the KDPR, and races behind it.

"It's a drone!" she shouts as she bounds around the cliff.

Kamea and JB follow, so I take off as well.

Azure keeps a close distance behind the machine, leaping fearlessly from rock to rock in pursuit. The machine's limbs are nimble and precise, locking on to surfaces and into crevices with accuracy only a computer could achieve. It looks like a massive black wolf, bounding up the bluffs, bouncing from boulders to sheer cliff face and back again. Azure remains firmly on its trail.

I'm able to keep up once I begin to let go of my fear of falling.

My body is more sure of itself than I give it credit. I spot spaces for my feet to land and propel myself from them before I'm even conscious of it. I'm still not used to my newfound strength. It's exhilarating.

I keep my eyes on Azure and race behind her.

Kamea and JB do their best to keep up with us. JB fares a bit better than Kamea simply because of how long his legs are. We leap through the trails and rocks and strain to keep up.

Several yards ahead I see Azure lift the KDPR, and a pulse of rippling air flies toward an outcropping of rocks above the dog machine. A massive boulder explodes ahead of us, the fragments of which begin to explode in chaotic, random bursts around us.

The machine leaps from the flying debris, unscathed, and crests the top of the cliff.

Azure follows right behind it and, without thinking, I make a leap for an outcropping near the top. My feet leave the rock underneath me as I launch toward the cliff. My hands barely grasp the edge of the rough sandstone, but it's enough for me to pull myself up. With a grunt, I lift myself over the edge and scramble to the flat ground in front of me.

Azure is ahead, running after the machine at full speed.

I chase after them.

I can't believe how fast the machine is, bounding over the flat terrain now at what has to be close to fifty miles per hour. Azure is just behind it. Flashes of blue start to light up in front of the machine as it runs, but it dodges them expertly. Azure's arms fly through the air in front of her as she sends up shield after shield, trying to impede the machine.

Suddenly, Azure stops, allowing me to catch up with her.

Before I can ask what she's doing, she opens her eyes. Radiant blue light shines from them, brighter than I've ever seen before. She lifts both hands and flicks her wrists in unison.

A shield, twenty feet wide, sprouts up before the machine. It crashes into the veil and stumbles.

With another flick of her wrist, Azure wraps the shield into a dome around it, trapping the mechanical beast inside.

She holds the blue light in her eyes and walks over to the dome, shrinking it with every step.

By the time she's close, the dome is little more than an airtight cage, holding the machine perfectly in place.

In less than a second the shield blinks away and Azure's hand darts down. Sparks fly from the machine as it stumbles to the ground, lifeless.

Azure walks back to me and drops the machine's triangular head down into the dirt. It's ripped cleanly from its fallen body.

"What was that?" My breath is short and my legs start to tremble as the adrenaline leaves my system.

"Another drone."

She walks past me and starts her descent back down the cliff toward camp.

"That was a drone?" I lower myself down to some rocks that form a small trail at the edge.

"Yes. A new model, apparently."

We make our way farther down, and it hits me: Kamea and JB aren't with us.

I race past Azure, adrenaline back in full.

I jump down from rock to rock and round the last corner where I remember seeing them.

And there they are.

Kamea is kneeling over JB. He's lying in a pool of blood.

His blood.

And he isn't moving.

"Oh my God." My breath is short and panicked as I approach and see the damage.

His left leg is broken nearly in two. Bone is jutting out from the side at a horrifying angle, and blood is pouring out all around him. His head is cocked lifelessly to the side. My heart stops for a moment until I see his lungs rise.

He isn't dead. Yet.

Kamea's hands are covered in scarlet red as she tries in vain to hold pressure on his thigh and curb the blood loss.

"What happened?" Azure says as she runs to his body.

"You used a stick on a cliff full of boulders and rock," Kamea says, her voice full of acid. She takes a breath to collect herself, redoubles her efforts on his thigh, and looks to Azure, pleadingly. "You have to do it."

Azure clenches her jaw and looks away from his dying body. "No," she says, and stands.

Kamea clenches her jaw tightly as tears fill her eyes. Then she looks to me. "Isaak, I need you to help me."

"He will not!" Azure stands between me and Kamea protectively. Shielding me as if Kamea means to attack.

"He's going to die if you don't!" Kamea screams through her tears.

Blood continues to pour from JB's dangling leg, and the whites of his eyes roll out from under his eyelids as a nauseating gurgling noise comes from his throat.

All of my anger and confusion flare up inside. I am so fucking sick of being surrounded by endless mysteries and questions and not getting answers to any of it.

"Azure. Move." The brevity of my voice scares even me.

Stunned, Azure steps aside.

I look at Kamea's dirty, tear-strewn face and into her eyes. "Tell me what's going on." I try to gentle my voice, but I'm angry and scared.

Kamea opens her mouth to speak but is interrupted by another painful gurgling noise from JB's throat. His breathing is heavy and slowing down. She looks at Azure instead.

"Please." Her voice is barely a whisper.

I turn to face Azure, looking for answers.

She heaves a deep sigh and kneels next to JB as she draws a knife from one of her pockets.

"Robot blood," she says as she presses the edge of the knife into her palm, "functions almost exactly as human blood." She drags the knife through her skin, slicing it open the entire length of her hand.

"Except that our blood cells are a nanorobotic technology

capable of healing virtually any human ailment, illness, or injury."

A crimson stream pours from her hand. She drizzles it over JB's open wounds.

"The downside, however," she says as she grasps the exposed bone and forcibly shoves it back in place, "is the human immune system's potential reaction to the new cells." JB's body begins to convulse as she clamps down. "Human bodies that receive Robot blood each react to it differently. Some accept the cells without issue. Most seem to suffer in varying degrees—a rash, or achy joints, or even heart disease and kidney failure. The human body does not know how to interact with the cells and inevitably fights itself to death trying to rid itself of them."

JB's body stops convulsing and his breathing begins to even out.

"Once Robot blood is introduced to a human system, the human's germ cell reproduction is controlled by the synthetic cells. The question becomes: Do you die now, as your human body intended? Or do you cheat it and run the risk of decaying in your own skin for the rest of your cursed existence?"

I look over to Kamea and wonder if she knows the gamble she just took with JB's life.

Azure lifts her bloody hand away from his leg. Her sliced palm begins to seal immediately. I watch in wonder as JB's leg begins to as well.

"He should be fine in a half hour or so," she says as she wipes her hands on the front of her pants.

"So wait. Germ cells . . . That means a person—a human—who uses Robot blood will only produce Robot children from that point on?"

I look at all of their faces, in wonder of how little I know about myself and what I am.

"For men, yes," Azure says, trying to wipe more of the blood from her hands.

"For men?" I look to her face, awaiting more answers.

"Women," Kamea says, her bleary eyes fixed on JB. "We go sterile."

Wind whips up through the rocks around us, and everything is silent except for JB's labored breathing.

"Isaak, come with me," Azure says. "We grab the weapons and nothing else." She looks up along the ridge above us. "We won't be camping anymore. If we don't make it to a safe house today, we won't be making it, period."

She turns and starts back down the cliffside toward our campsite.

I look to Kamea and try to think of something to say, but her eyes stay firmly on JB. His head is leaned back on a rock, eyes closed. His breath is finally starting to normalize.

I turn and follow Azure down the rocks.

Everyone sits in tense silence as we make our way toward Flagstaff. The safe house Kamea spoke of didn't exist anymore—the only thing left was the charred frame of a two-story house in a neighborhood that made Pacific look like a utopian luxury colony. We didn't even bother stopping. We simply drove past and began the long drive back toward the interstate.

It was only a five-mile detour, but it felt endless.

Now we're back on the highway, and every minute feels like an eternity—exposed, vulnerable, waiting for yet another attack. I keep an eye on the black duffel bag on the floor next to me. The KDPR is in my pocket.

At least I can stretch out a bit in this minivan.

"I really hate this, by the way. Stealing cars from people." I speak to no one in particular. Inside, I think I blame Azure more than anyone. For whatever reason I feel like she takes pleasure in it.

"Well, what would you prefer us to do, Isaak?" Azure says from the driver's seat, eyes fixed on the road ahead.

"I don't know. It just feels *wrong*." I look out the window and my stomach turns at the sight of the endless expanse of brown flying by around us. I am so sick of the desert. Tired of feeling like hunted prey.

"We really don't have a choice, Isaak," Kamea says gently from the seat beside me. "It's too risky doing it any other way."

"I get that. I just . . . I don't know. A car is a big deal. It's not like stealing food or something. It feels like bad karma."

Azure snorts in the front seat.

"Isaak, you are currently a member of what is essentially the most endangered species on the planet. A species that is being hunted viciously by the most powerful military force on Earth. You belong to a group of beings who eat and breathe and think exactly like those who are hunting them, yet have been—in fear of their superiority—deemed unworthy of the right to live. You are currently facing *genocide*." Her voice rises, and I see her knuckles tense around the steering wheel. "Fuck karma."

The sound of the tires on the road below us is the only noise in the van.

"She has a point there, kid," JB says, craning his head around to me from the front passenger seat. He tries to give me one of his grins, the first since he regained consciousness, but it only makes me want to lean back and kick his face.

"I'm not a kid."

He turns back to the front and I gaze out the window.

I might've been a little too harsh.

We stop for gas outside of Flagstaff. Azure parks by one of the pumps at a station near the highway and kills the engine. I can still feel the road vibrating underneath me.

"I need a snack," I say to Azure as I hold out my hand.

She undoes her seat belt.

"Maybe one of the kind humans here will lend you some money. Wouldn't want to taint your karma with what I stole from the ATM."

I leave my hand up.

She slaps a twenty in my palm, and I pull the loud, sliding side door open beside me.

"Anyone want anything?" I look to the other two.

Kamea shakes her head.

"All good," JB says, staring ahead.

I slide the door shut again and walk away.

Guess I pissed him off.

The gas station's mini-mart smells of mopping fluid and cheap air fresheners as I make my way to the snack food. I can't bear the thought of getting back in the van, back on the interstate. I'm ready to drown myself in junk food. I'm browsing the selection of chips when I notice a girl staring at me from the across the aisle. She has caramel-colored skin, strong cheekbones, and a shaved head. She looks hard—severe—and I quickly avert my eyes.

I browse through the doughnuts and the drinks and finally bring my haul up to one of the registers. The girl with the buzz cut sets an armful of brightly colored sports drinks down in front of the register to my left as I hand the clerk the twenty. She glares right at me and slowly slides her left hand away from the drinks.

There, on the inside of her wrist, is a small silvery triangle mark raised in her skin. Exactly like the one I have.

My eyes dart back to the clerk as he hands me my change. I take it and my bag of snacks as my heart starts to pound.

What do I do?

My feet go on autopilot and I start to walk away. I spare a glance behind me as I leave, but the girl doesn't look back.

Did I really just see that?

I walk up just as Azure removes the nozzle from the tank and places it back in its holster.

"There's a girl." My voice falls to a whisper. "In there."

Azure looks at me, puzzled.

"One of us."

Her expression changes instantly, and she turns to watch the glass doors.

"Her."

The girl walks out with her bag full of sports drinks and makes her way to a rusted old car at the pump across from us. She opens the door and tosses the bag onto the passenger seat. Before she takes a seat, she stops, turns to Azure, looks her directly in the eye, and nods.

I look to Azure's face as she returns the nod.

"Get in," she says.

Something tells me we might not be getting back on the interstate after all.

We've been following the girl in the rusted car for a half hour now. We took side streets across what appeared to be the main part of town and now head north and west. Tall pines start to fill the landscape around us. It doesn't feel like desert wasteland anymore. Now we're in the mountains.

The girl slows and takes a left into a nondescript neighborhood nestled in the foothills. Azure takes her time and makes sure to keep her distance, but follows nonetheless. The houses lining the streets are all quite plain. One- and two-story boxes that look like they were once someone's suburban mountain dream but now live quietly on as someone else's consolation prize. Consolation prizes in need of paint jobs.

Halfway up the street, a garage door begins to open on a house to our left. The rusted car slows and stops just ahead of the driveway. Azure slows the van and turns in.

"You're sure about this?" Kamea asks, taking in our surroundings as Azure pulls into the garage.

"No, but what other choice do we have?"

I thumb the handle of the stick in my pocket as the garage door closes behind us. Azure turns the key and the engine goes silent.

"Should we get out?" I ask. My palms are sweaty and my legs are restless.

Before anyone can answer, the door to our right opens and warm yellow light streams out into the garage. A woman stands in the doorway and waves us inside.

"Yes," Azure says as she opens her door and steps out.

I keep my fingers on the handle poking out from my pocket and follow Azure and JB into the house. Kamea comes right behind me.

We walk into a bare kitchen with beige countertops, a brown linoleum floor, a few dated appliances, and nothing else. The woman stands near the sink, arms folded, examining each of us as we walk in. The bulb in the old light fixture hanging above a plain, wooden dining table casts a yellow glow in the room. I can now see that an entire side of her face is covered in burn scars.

"Welcome to my house. You are safe here."

The woman eyes each of us up and down as Kamea closes the door to the garage. "Two of you," she mutters, barely above a whisper.

Before I can open my mouth to respond, the girl with the buzzed hair walks in. She's more intimidating than I first realized, now that she's standing in front of me, face-to-face. She is lean, muscular, and her brown eyes are hard. The muscles in her face tense and flex as she clenches her jaw.

"My name is Griselle," says the woman with the burns.

A younger guy walks in from what appears to be the living room. He's tall—taller than JB—but thin, lanky, and pale. His brown hair is pulled into a small knot on the back of his head, and he's dressed head to toe in black.

"This is Tace."

He gives a slight nod to everyone as he walks to the buzz-haired girl and discreetly grabs her hand. She drops her gaze from the newcomers for a brief moment, looks to him, and squeezes his hand in reply.

The girl looks back over to us, her eyes resting on me. "I'm V."

We sit in the living room and talk. I'm next to Kamea and JB on a long, broken-in burgundy couch, Tace and V sit on a floral-patterned love seat across from us, and Azure sits beside me in a chair she pulled in from the kitchen. Griselle gently sways in a rocking chair on the other side of the small living room. I take a moment to observe the room and notice that it is free of electronics.

"How long have you been working with the Underground?" Kamea looks to Griselle and takes a sip of the tea she poured for each of us.

"A little over a year." Her fingers trace the outline of a white crystal pendant hanging from her neck as she speaks. "These two came for my nephew right after he manifested." She nods to V and Tace across from her. "They saved his life. I offered my service to them, to you all, after that. Once I learned about what's happening out there, right under our noses, I knew I had to devote my life to the cause. In any way I could."

"Where is your nephew now?" Azure asks.

Griselle looks at her but doesn't respond immediately. Tace shifts in his seat.

"He went missing eight months ago," she replies, and takes a sip of her tea.

"I'm so sorry," I say.

"Thank you."

A wooden clock ticking on the wall echoes in the silence.

"Well," Griselle says as she lifts herself from the couch. "I'm going to get dinner started. Does everyone like spaghetti?"

She leaves the room before anyone can answer.

"She's a good person," V says once pots and pans begin clanging. Her eyes rest on Azure.

"I don't doubt it," Azure replies. "I just don't trust humans. Never have. Never will."

JB rolls his eyes and shakes his head.

"You can trust her," V continues. "We've been here for more than a week now. She's proven herself."

"Not to me she hasn't." Azure holds V's gaze. I'm afraid a stare-off is about to begin.

"We're headed to Grand Central," Kamea says, breaking the showdown before it can begin. "Are you guys going that way as well?"

Tace wrinkles his nose and looks at V with concern.

"You can't get to LA from the roads anymore," V says.

Azure, Kamea, and JB all sit up a little higher at this.

"What do you mean?" Kamea asks.

"You haven't heard." V spares Tace a weary glance and turns back to Kamea. "The SHRF have developed something . . . new."

The ticking of the clock is louder than ever.

"Scanning stations. They look like cell towers."

JB closes his eyes and leans back into the couch.

"They've completely sealed off any way in or out of the city."

Everyone is silent.

"Well, what do we do?" I ask as I turn to Azure. "You said I need to get to LA to be analyzed and trained. There has to be another way."

She clenches her jaw as her eyes work, deep in thought.

"Does Flagstaff have an airport?" I ask.

"Robots can't fly, Isaak," Kamea says. "You can't go any-where near an airport."

"What if we flew private?" JB asks.

"We don't have a pilot," Kamea says.

"And it's not exactly easy finding one who will take cash and forgo filing a flight plan," Azure says, her eyes still working out the pieces of an invisible puzzle.

"We won't need one," V says. Tace shoots her an unreadable look, but she gives her head a subtle nod and continues. "We're going to LA as well. We were going to leave tonight, until I came across you guys."

"How?" Kamea asks.

"We're going through Vegas."

JB rubs his temples, and Kamea can't help but look confused. Azure gives a snort and shakes her head.

"What's wrong with Vegas?" I ask.

"It's the only place in the country where Robots will not—cannot—go," JB says, looking at me, exasperated.

I'm confused now as well, and I'm sure I look it.

"During the first years of manifestations," Kamea says, "Vegas became an unofficial Robot gathering place. The electrical output of the Strip proved to be the perfect camouflage."

"That is until the SHRF was mobilized and discovered what was going on," JB says.

I look to Kamea, waiting for more.

"It's where they're based, the SHRF." Azure doesn't look at me as she speaks.

"So why would we even consider going there?" I ask Azure.

She looks at V. "I was about to ask the very same question."

V looks at each of us in turn. "We now have a very powerful ally who has assured us safe passage directly to Grand Central, if we can get to Vegas first."

"And how do we know we can trust you?" Azure asks.

V holds out her wrist for Azure to see. "Do I look human to you?"

Azure lifts her mug from the coffee table and takes a sip.

We sit around Griselle's kitchen table and eat our first real meal in days. It tastes like heaven. After we finish, while Griselle washes the dishes in the sink, I grab a hand towel and begin drying them.

"You don't have to do that," she says, nodding for me to join the others in the living room.

"No, it's okay. It's the least I can do." I locate the cabinet for the glasses and put the first one away. "This was one of my chores growing up, so I'm a pro."

A smile spreads across her face as she rinses a plate.

"You remind me of him, you know." She points to a photo hanging in a small frame. The boy in the picture has brown hair, dark brown eyes, tanned skin, and a big, gleaming white smile.

"He was way better-looking than I am." The words come out of my mouth before I realize I'm saying it.

Griselle laughs as she dunks another plate into the soapy water. "He always spoke his mind. Called everything just like he saw it. Wouldn't have it any other way." Her eyes get lost in the water. "He had a good soul."

I pick up the rinsed plate and wipe the towel around the edge. "How did you know? Earlier, when we walked in, you knew there were two of us before we said anything."

A grin comes back to her face. "You're a very perceptive young man." She dunks the large pot into the water and begins scrubbing. "I don't know how. I just did. I can see it glowing around you guys."

She slides the pot around to scrub another side. "Some people call it an aura, but with you guys, it's different. It's radiance. It's light."

"And you can see it?"

She nods her head as she rinses the pot. "It's beautiful." She unplugs the drain stopper and lets the soapy water out.

"Where do I put this one?" I ask as I start to lift the rinsed pot out of the sink.

"No, no, you go out there with the others," she says as she takes the damp towel from my hands. "I'll finish in here." She gives me a deep smile and nods toward the living room.

I can't help but smile back.

"The entire house is coated in EMF-shielding paint." Griselle flips on the overhead light in the basement as we all head down the stairs. Thin, tan carpeting covers the floor, and a leather couch sits in front of a vintage television set. The walls are paneled in wood, and everything smells pleasantly of dust and incense. "But this"—she approaches a wall-length book-shelf and runs her hand along the wood—"is the safest room for you in the entire state."

She pulls one of the books from the shelf and a loud *click* reverberates throughout the room as the entire bookcase jolts forward slightly. Griselle grabs the wood and pulls it away from the wall, revealing the entrance to a secret room. She flips a light switch just inside the doorframe, steps aside, and I step in.

The room is completely lined in charcoal gray foam pyra-mids, jutting out from the walls and the ceiling toward us like spikes. I go to the center of the room and am struck by the silence.

"It's an anechoic chamber," Griselle says as the others fol-low me in. "Nothing will be able to detect your presence, even from right outside the door."

A large, rectangular Adobe-print rug, colored like the des-ert sunset, covers almost the entire floor, which appears to be polished concrete. Two cots with white pillows and folded blankets lie up against the wall.

"I'll bring two more cots."

Azure steps onto the carpet beside me, examining the walls. She looks to Griselle and gives her a single nod.

Griselle nods back and looks to Kamea and JB. "I have two spare bedrooms upstairs or you can have the couch down here. Wherever you'd like."

"Thank you," Kamea says.

"There are cameras and motion-detection systems set up

around the perimeter of the house and at the entrance to the neighborhood," Griselle says as she kneels down before the rug, "but if anyone manages to catch us off guard somehow, you won't be trapped in here."

She lifts one side of the rug and tosses it back, revealing a steel panel cut into the concrete. A small handle lies flush with the metal near the edge.

"This leads out into the woods behind the house. If anything happens"—she points to a small lightbulb above the door—"this will flash. If it goes off, don't open this door, and don't come back into the house. Just get through the hatch and into the tunnel."

I let my fingers trace the tip of one of the foam pyramids jutting from the wall.

"I'll go get those cots." Griselle turns and leaves the room. I follow to help.

"Oh, Isaak, I can get all of this myself; don't worry about it," she says when she notices me behind her.

"It's no problem. I want to help."

She holds the basement door open for me at the top of the stairs and smiles. "Wait here. One second."

She turns and heads down the dark hallway. A few moments later, she returns with her hand outstretched. "I want you to take this."

She grabs my hand and places a smooth black stone in the center of my palm. It's shaped like a cylinder, with flat, naturally faceted sides and terminations at the top and bottom.

"It's a piece of black tourmaline, said to protect those who wear it and meditate with it. Keep it in your pocket." The smile fades from her face and she averts her eyes.

My fingers close around the stone. "Thank you."

She looks back to me now, eyes welled with tears. She places her hand upon my cheek and gently holds my face for a brief moment. The sadness in her eyes is like a kick to my stomach.

"Let's get those cots," she says. She turns from me and opens the hall closet.

"Good night," JB says from the couch before I step into the safe room.

I look back over my shoulder at him and pause. "Good night, JB. Sorry if I was an asshole earlier. I'm just . . . tired. I shouldn't have taken it out on you."

His lip curls into a small, genuine smile. "It's okay. You're a good guy, Isaak."

I nod as Kamea walks past me and the open bookcase door, coming from the bathroom. "Get some rest, Isaak."

"Thanks, Kamea. Good night."

I step into the room and close the door behind me. It seals with a heavy thud.

A single candle flickers on a small wooden table in the corner and casts wild, roving shadows over the spiked walls. The others have all settled into their cots—V and Tace in adjacent ones on the wall to my right and Azure to my left. I carefully step over the large black weapons duffel and sit on the edge of my cot along the far wall.

I take a moment to examine the black stone in my hand in the wavering candlelight and then slide it into my pocket. I lean over and blow out the candle, and everything goes black. The sound of breathing fills my ears as I lie back and try to relax.

So much running.

So much hiding.

Now I can finally take a moment and really breathe.

Something lingers at the edge of my mind however and stirs restless inside me.

I close my eyes and realize that I didn't take off my shoes.

I decide to leave them on.

Endless punching. A Hydra with nine heads, snarling in front of me. Each of the heads drips putrid, burning acid from its mouth over gnarled, razor teeth. Each head charges into me, punching into my chest and face. I can't breathe.

A legless old woman who is more machine than human sits on top of a pair of wheels, revving an engine, breathing heavily into a mask. She snarls at me through her rasping breaths.

Another punch.

A haggard witch with brown, rotten teeth presses a crooked finger into my cheek and burns away the flesh. I scramble back from her and walk to a shelf along a white wall, where I find an assortment of dolls. I pick up one that looks like a middle-aged woman with brown hair. It crumbles to dust in my hands. I reach for a tall man with gray hair next, but he too crumbles.

I try once again and grab hold of a beautiful young girl with blond hair and a wide, bright smile painted onto her ceramic face. I stare into the eyes and begin to smile myself. She makes me so happy.

Her painted face begins to melt inward. Within seconds all that's left is a pool of blood, trickling from my hands onto the pristine white floor.

A man comes into my room. His teeth are yellow and his eyes glow red. He places a hungry hand upon my thigh and slides his monstrous talons up between my legs.

I scream.

I scream so loud the walls around me begin to crack. Everything begins to crumble. I know I'll be buried under the weight of it all, but I don't care. I need to scream. I need to let out my terror and sadness and every horrible demon that clings to me so tight.

I wake up in a cold sweat.

I'm still lying on the cot, in the muffled silence of the pitch-black safe room. I move my fingers a bit just to prove to myself that I'm awake and that the nightmares weren't real.

I take a deep breath.

You're fine. Relax.

I let it out slowly and stare into the darkness.

You're safe.

I roll onto my side and feel my heartbeat slow back to normal.

The little red bulb above the door begins to flash.

I shoot up from my cot as the tiny room pulses in urgent red light.

Azure rouses from her sleep and throws back her blanket once she sees it, on her feet in seconds. The others stir at the commotion. Tace springs to life once he sees it and begins to shake V awake as Azure moves the duffel bag from the rug and tosses it back, exposing the trapdoor.

My stomach drops. *JB and Kamea.*

Without thinking, I go to the door and start to push it open. It unseals from the wall with a heavy pop, and just as I step out into the black hallway, I hear Azure curse under her breath behind me.

I run in the dark to the couch and shake the first body I touch. I can't even tell who I'm shaking. My fingers grip the skin, and I hear Kamea's voice murmur through a daze.

"What?" She begins to wake up, but it's not fast enough.

"We have to go, now!" I whisper as harshly as I can. I know I'm being a fool, but I can't leave them behind. I can't let them die. Not when we've come this far.

Kamea springs to life almost instantly and JB sits up behind her. They hop off the couch and I run back over to the open bookcase door.

Footsteps move upstairs.

I step into the room of blinking red light. The others have already gone down. The duffel is gone as well.

Kamea darts into the room followed by JB, who strains to

close the door shut behind him. It seals in place with its signature *pop*, and I lower myself down through the trapdoor.

I wait for Kamea and then JB, who slides the cover back in place above him.

The low hallway is pitch-black. I raise Kamea's hands to help her find her way along the wall when a light blinks in the distance.

I hunch myself over and run as fast as I can in the low tunnel, making sure Kamea and JB are right behind me as I approach Azure with the flashlight.

I catch a glimpse of her face in the light. She just shakes her head.

She motions for me to continue on and remains in place as Kamea and JB follow. She takes up the rear as I pursue another blinking light ahead of us. We all run as fast as we can, but the ceiling is only about four feet from the ground. The air around us is damp and cool, and I can't help but think about the night running through caves when Azure first found me. It feels like a lifetime ago. I wonder if this is going to be my life from now on—running in the dark.

I make it to the other light and find Tace standing at the bottom of a metal ladder. V has already climbed up and out of the top. I swiftly climb the rungs and push myself out onto the ground. Pine needles prick my palms as I lift myself up. V stands over the hole and gives me an unreadable look.

One by one they all come out of the hole in the ground. Before Tace can even fully climb out, V is already sliding the steel cover back into place. Once it locks into the grooves in the ground, she kicks dirt and pine needles over the top.

Azure is already scanning the surroundings.

"This way." V waves us on to follow her through the trees.

We run for what feels like an hour. The trees lash out at us with pine whips, and large, white boulders sprout up out of nowhere in the moonlit ground. I have to slow myself periodically to make sure Kamea and JB are able to keep up. The others just keep running.

Suddenly V stops. I know I should be more exhausted than I am, but I'm not. JB leans over and grabs his knees, gasping for air. Kamea's skin glistens with sweat in the frosty night air.

I approach V and see she's standing at the edge of a steep hill, almost steep enough to be called a cliff. Below us, rows of trailers sit among the tall pines, still and quiet in the dark. She slowly begins her descent. I follow, carefully placing each foot before me so I don't tumble face-first into a tree. My body seems to do it automatically though. I don't think I'll ever get used to this.

At the bottom I stand next to V as she assesses the surroundings. She's looking for something specific.

A moment later she dashes out into the open, in between the trailers, to an old, windowless, white van. As she touches the back door, the lock clicks and she opens it. A nod of the head tells us all to get in. I climb into the back. Bare, plastic floor, with no seats, and assorted power tools surround me.

V nods to Azure and then climbs into the back behind me, along with JB and Tace. Up front, Azure climbs into the passenger seat and brushes her finger along the ignition as Kamea sits behind the wheel.

The van rumbles to life.

We peal through the gravel, between the trailers, until we come to a paved road. "Take a right," V says. Kamea swerves accordingly and pushes the engine even harder once we make it to the pavement.

The transmission protests at the abuse, but she doesn't relent.

"Fucking traitor," Azure says, almost under her breath, as she stares out the windshield.

Everyone is silent.

"What are you talking about?" I ask.

"Griselle," Azure continues. She doesn't turn around to face me. "She sold us out. She's one of *them*."

I thumb the outline of black stone in my pocket and see the flashing red light in my head, blinking on and off in the darkness.

I refuse to believe it.

The sun is starting to rise as we turn to take a different highway in Kingman, Arizona. Not much later, Kamea stops to get gas. Azure hops out of the car before she even puts it into park and doesn't bother paying. She touches the pump, and it begins churning out gas at her command. After the tank is full, she scrambles back into the van with an intensity I'm not used to seeing from her.

We are back on the new highway in mere moments, this time heading north, toward Vegas. I lean back against the metal and close my eyes, hoping to get some more sleep.

I feel a nudge and open my eyes again to find JB beside me. He gives a small nod, beckoning me closer to him, and I give in. I'm too tired, too deprived of any sort of human contact.

Human.

His arm wraps around me, and I relax into his chest. It's firm and warm and bringing me a kind of comfort I didn't realize I so desperately needed. The vibrations of the road underneath us rock me into him as he lets this thumb gently caress my forearm.

I close my eyes and try to quiet my mind.

Almost an hour passes before I wake up to the feeling of the van slowing.

"Shit," Kamea says under her breath.

I stir from JB's chest and lean to peer through the windshield. A long line of red taillights stretches out into the road ahead.

"What's going on?"

"The signs say construction," Azure says, watching the road, "but I'm betting it's something else."

We come to a halt as we enter the traffic jam.

Tace and V sit up and peer out the windshield as well.

"This isn't good," V says.

"What do we do?" I ask.

Kamea looks back to me in the rearview mirror. "Just be

alert. Everyone be ready to move in case something happens."

We crawl forward slowly, all of us peering over the seats from the back, trying in vain to spot some sort of warning ahead of us.

HOOVER DAM—VISITORS CENTER

EXIT 3 MILES

As we pass the sign, two highway patrol cars speed by us in the opposite lane, heading south. The traffic begins to move again.

"There must've been a wreck up ahead," I say hopefully.

No one responds.

We speed up as the bottleneck releases in front of us and cars return to their normal paces.

The road slopes upward as traffic picks up. I release my grip from the back of Kamea's headrest and sit back down.

Crisis averted.

"Damn it," Kamea says, alarm in her voice.

I shoot back up and peer out the window again. Near the top of the hill, about a half mile ahead of us, is an access road that merges into our lane. A long row of more than a dozen black SUVs sit right at the crest of the hill—waiting.

Our speed picks up as we keep pace with the other cars around us.

"Just keep going," Azure says. "Don't do anything conspicuous."

Tace, V, and JB all sit up and crouch on their feet in the back, ready to move at a moment's notice.

"What do we do?" I look to Azure, my heartbeat rising.

"Just drive," she says to Kamea. "If we can get by them quickly enough, we won't have anything to worry about. Their scanners aren't sensitive enough to pick up targets moving faster than one of us could run. Not unless one of us is manifesting."

I grip the back of the headrest and watch the SUVs come into view as we approach. Kamea pushes the van faster as we charge up the hill. As we get closer, I realize there must be twenty or thirty of them parked in the access road.

The engine groans as we go faster.

The road begins to curve to the left as we near the top of the hill.

"The bridge is right up here. If we can make it across, we should be good. There aren't any access roads for them to wait on above the canyon," Kamea says, eyes fixed on the road and the Sheriffs we're quickly racing toward.

She begins to turn the wheel left as we come up to the top of the hill and follow the bend. The Sheriffs are on our right. I duck slightly behind the headrest and try to peer into their tinted windows as we pass, but I can't make anything out. I hold my breath.

Azure watches them as we pass from her side-view mirror. "They're not moving. We're good."

I inhale deeply and let my heartbeat catch up with itself.

"No," V says from the back as we round the corner completely. "No, we're not."

She points to the bridge up ahead of us and the rows of what appear to be cell towers lining both sides.

"Those aren't supposed to be there. Those are the scanners."

My pulse lurches back to a frantic pounding as Azure gets up from the passenger seat and climbs into the back.

"What're you doing?" I ask as I make room for her to pass by.

She reaches into one of her pockets. "I'm blowing the bridge."

She retrieves a handful of her glass orbs and reaches for the back door.

"You keep plasma grenades in your pocket? Are you crazy?" V is horrified as she backs away from Azure's palm full of death.

My horror is because of something else entirely.

"Azure, you can't do this. There are too many people." I get up onto my feet. I will fight her if necessary.

"Isaak, you know nothing. Every one of these people would sacrifice your life in a second if it meant saving theirs. We have no other choice."

She throws the back doors open. There they are. The entire fleet of SUVs racing toward us from the access road.

"Aren't you guys going to do anything?" I scream to the others in the van.

We can't let this happen. *I* can't let this happen. This isn't life preservation; this is terrorism.

I spare a split second to see that everyone is silent, all in tacit compliance with Azure's monstrous plan.

Her hand reaches out over the road behind us.

I grab her other arm and force her to look at me. "Please

don't do this, Azure." I stare into her eyes, pleading, begging for another alternative. Anything but this.

She turns, her hand dangling over the road and lets the glass orbs fall to the pavement below. I watch them shatter on the road and quickly fade into the distance.

My legs react involuntarily.

I launch myself out of the van, out into the air behind us. I hear the screams and shouts from the others fade almost immediately as the van leaves me in its wake. My eyes lock on to the cracked glass and the violet gel inside, glowing softly on the concrete. My feet land with surety before the shards and the gel, and I lean over.

I let the sensation of the light flow through me once again, envisioning a barrier around me and around the grenades. A dome of purple light ignites as the world erupts into fire. A cataclysm of light and fire burns the vision from my eyes and swirls into a maelstrom of pain. I wait for the world to go black, for death, but the fire only seems to fuel the light inside of me. I feel it pound into me in waves, blast after blast that churns more and more energy into me.

The fire goes out, but the light blazes inside every fiber of every muscle and nerve in my body. I release the dome, and everything about me burns with a radiant golden light. The entire world has slowed to a halt, and a power unlike anything I've ever imagined courses through my fingertips.

There is no friction, no inertia, no gravity—the laws of physics are mere illusions. I watch as the SUVs appear, crawling to me as ants before a god. I reach for the first as it approaches and lift it as a child would a toy. I toss it over the edge of the bridge into the gleaming blue lake below. More of the toys approach now. I reach for one of the scanning towers looming over this place as sentinels of death. The mere sight of them fills me with rage.

I pluck it from the bridge like a daisy and use it to brush away the ants creeping toward me. Off they go, into the lake.

I'm no longer afraid of death. I *am* death.

The rage fuels the burning light inside as I dispose of them all.

I throw the last into the air above the water and look at the towers lining the rest of the bridge.

A final surge of rage rips open the last of my barriers. The burning light pours out of my skin as I raise my hands toward the towers. It blasts out from my hands, burning the towers to ash when it touches them.

I smite them from the Earth. All of them.

As the last tower disintegrates, I feel the light sap out of my bones. Depletion pulls at my core like a black hole, and I am now powerless in its grasp.

The last ray leaves me and I slide into the abyss.

The life inside of me is gone.

A soft glow flits on the other side of my eyelids. I want to move, but I can't. My body feels weighted to the ground beneath me. My limbs are heavy, immovable lead.

Only I'm not on the ground. This is soft, cushioned. My eyes try to open, but they refuse.

The sound of air-conditioning surrounds me. A zipper opens and the noise of hands shuffling through cloth stirs me even further.

Open your eyes.

Everything aches. I notice it now. My consciousness is returning to my body and, with it, pain. I'm so thirsty. And *hungry.* A door opens and I hear a voice say "thank you" before it closes again. Another shuffling sound and then the scent of hot food fills my nostrils.

Someone has fries.

My eyes open slowly. A row of buildings, twinkling with an endless array of neon lights, lies on the other side of a wall of glass. I'm high above everything outside. If I focus, I can hear the din of traffic and people far below. In the distance, desert and purple mountains.

I toss my head to the other side of the pillow and take in the room around me. Everything is white.

Azure hears my movement and looks at me from her perch in an armchair at the foot of my bed. She looks over to my left.

"He's awake."

I lift my eyes and find Kamea sitting on a white couch across from me. She must've been watching over me as well.

Her cheeks rise into a small smile, and I realize it's the first time I've ever seen her show any sign of happiness. She's so beautiful. I wonder about the things in her life that led her to this moment as I drift in my semi-dreamlike state.

"Hey you," she says softly, deep brown eyes sparkling in contrast with the white-washed room around her.

Images of explosions and death flicker in my head.

I strain and use my arms to finally push myself into a sitting position in the soft white bed.

"What happened?" My throat is dry and aches.

Before anyone can answer, a door on the far side of the room opens and JB walks in, dressed in only a towel, which is wrapped around his waist. His lean, muscled body glistens like wet marble. I can't help but stare.

He notices me sitting up in the bed and stops. "You're awake."

The sight of his immaculate body sours as I start to wonder why he wasn't the one waiting by my bed, keeping vigil over me like Azure and Kamea.

"You must be thirsty," Azure says as she comes closer with a bottle. She twists the cap and hands it to me.

It's just water, but the effect on me is similar to that of the sports drinks. It must be infused with electrolytes. I feel like I'm getting a shower on the inside as the liquid immediately hits my bloodstream.

JB grabs a pile of clothes folded on the suite's dining room table and heads back into the bathroom.

I look at Azure. "I don't know what happened."

Azure takes a moment to look at my face, considering something. "None of us do."

She turns and walks over to the front door. Rows of white

bags have been placed on the floor, and she begins sifting through them. I see room service trays on the dining room table when she walks by, and my stomach groans as I take notice of the scent of fries once again.

Kamea gets up from the couch and comes to the side of the bed. She places a hand on my shoulder and looks right into my eyes. "You were very brave."

She goes to the dining room table, grabs the tray, and returns before removing the lid and setting it in front of me. It's a sandwich and fries. I don't even know what's inside, but it smells divine. I tear in, and Azure comes back with two white shopping bags in hand.

"We've been invited to dinner by our captor," she says as she lets the bags drop near the side of the bed.

Kamea shoots her a look.

"Sorry . . . our benevolent benefactor and ally."

I gulp down my bite and crane my neck over to see what's inside the bags.

"They sent someone up with new clothes for everyone. Dinner is in two hours."

A knock on yet another door, this one off to the left of the dining room table, is followed by V stepping into the room. Her eyes land on me. "Glad to see you're okay."

She looks to Azure. "You wanted to speak with me."

JB walks back into the room, now dressed in slim black trousers and a thin black sweater, pulled taut across his chest. Azure nods toward the door and starts to leave as JB approaches. Before they leave the room, Azure turns back and looks me in the eye. I can't read her face. It's as though she's looking for something behind my eyes that she can't quite find. She steps into the adjacent room with V and closes the door.

JB stands by the bed and looks at me. I can't read him either. His blue eyes bear into me, but much more than care and concern linger behind them—confusion, trepidation, reluctance all dance around in there as well. I don't understand.

"How are you feeling?"

I try in vain to stifle a burp as it rises up my throat. "Fine." The word comes out as a poorly concealed puff of gas.

He smirks, but it's halfhearted. "Good. I was worried about you."

Kamea pretends to examine something under her nail in my periphery.

I put down the last bite of the sandwich and look him right in the eye. "Were you?"

"Of course I was."

Kamea gives a small, nearly imperceptible shake of her head and sighs before standing up and excusing herself.

A silent moment passes while I wait for the door to close behind her.

"Why does she do that?" I ask him.

"Do what?"

"Anytime she catches you trying to get close to me, she gets . . . It upsets her."

He sits on the bed and places his hand on my leg over the down comforter. "Isaak, look—"

"No, you look." I knock his hand off me. "Do you have any idea how confusing all of this is for me? Any idea what my life has been like this past week? What it's been like my whole life?

"I don't know what I am, and neither do you guys. I'm supposed to be one of them, but you all look at me like I'm . . . a puzzle, a bomb, some kind of alien. I'm in a constant state of fear, and every time I try to face it and use *this*"—I hold up my hands—"I almost die."

His eyes are locked with mine. I can tell he's trying to speak, but I don't stop. I have too much to say. Too much eating me up from the inside out.

"And to make everything worse, the one person I keep getting tricked into feeling like I have a genuine connection with can't decide whether or not he wants to connect with me in return . . . and it really fucking sucks. You know, I've never even kissed anyone before, and then the other day on the cliff . . . and now you're looking at me like you're afraid to talk to me, and Kamea is huffing and shaking her head and storming out of the room. I don't need this right now, JB. I need to feel like a person. I need a friend."

His eyes turn down and several agonizing moments of silence pass. I think I've said too much, but I don't care.

"You have a friend, Isaak," he says, examining his hands. "And for what it's worth, you're not the only one who's confused."

He tries to give a faint smile, gets up from the bed, and leaves.

Alone, I pick up the last couple of fries from the plate in front of me and immediately drop them. I'm still hungry, but I don't want to eat anything more. I set the plate to the side, lie back on the pillow, and watch the sun continue to set in the reflections of the buildings across the street.

My eyes close and I silently promise myself I'll get up and start getting ready in ten minutes.

I finish getting dressed in the bathroom after I shower, choosing a new pair of black jeans, a simple white T-shirt, a black blazer that feels like it was tailored, and a pair of black leather boots with a name inside that I can't pronounce. Our host sent up much fancier stuff, but I don't feel like impressing anyone, and honestly, given the week I've had, I want to be comfortable more than anything. Who knows when I'll need to start running again.

I run my hands through my wet hair and start to examine my face in the mirror as the door opens. Kamea steps inside and closes the door behind her.

"Hey." I'm sure the puzzled look on my face isn't hidden very well.

"Keep this on you." She hands me the stick. Its silvery finish feels cool and smooth on my pruned fingertips.

"We don't know who these people are and we have to keep you safe."

The brevity in her voice gets to me. "Kamea, tell me what's

going on. Azure won't say anything, and I feel so confused and . . . lost."

She studies my face, and I can tell she's debating something in her head.

"I know I'm not normal, even by these new standards. I just want to know what's happening to me."

She looks over her shoulder to the door and then back at me. My heart starts to race at the sign of impending answers.

"The truth is, Isaak . . . we don't know."

My heart sinks again.

"What we do know is that you are special. You are different from any other Robot any of us has ever encountered. Any that we've ever heard of." She reaches for my hand and closes my fingers around the stick. "Hang in there just a little bit longer. Getting you to LA is my top priority right now. Hopefully we can find some answers then."

She goes to leave but turns back to me as she grabs the door handle. "And, Isaak, be careful with your heart. You have such a good one. I don't want to see you get hurt." She gives a faint smile and leaves.

I clutch the stick and find myself staring at the marble countertop, lost in thought.

I think I might have been looking in the wrong place for the friend I so desperately needed.

Tace closes the door behind him as he steps out into the hall-way after V. He looks effortlessly cool in a black leather jacket and a loose black shirt that exposes the top of his clavicle. V is in a long-sleeved turtleneck crop top that reveals her toned stomach. Her buzzed hair and tanned skin are accentuated by large, gold hoop earrings. She looks amazing.

She holds Tace's hand as they join the rest of us in front of the suite's doors. He gives a small nod, and it occurs to me I haven't heard him speak a single word.

I look around and notice that I'm the only one not dressed completely in black.

"We look like we're going to a funeral," I say as I turn to follow the suited guards escorting us to dinner.

No one laughs at the joke.

We move to the elevators and the guard hits the up button.

"Aren't we already on the top floor?" V whispers as the guard presses his thumb against a small square of black glass above the button panel.

The doors slide open.

"Guess not."

The elevator takes us up two more floors and opens onto a grand lobby. Jeweled mosaics are inlaid in walls that look as though they're made of solid gold. The ceiling is an elaborate fresco picturing a dark-skinned man perched upon a cloud reaching down through a twilight sky to touch the hands of earthbound mortals clamoring for the chance to touch heaven. I imagine it rivals the Sistine Chapel, but whereas that God touches the hand of a single man, this one's hand dangles just beyond the reach of hundreds. I notice the people's faces and see their desperation. It feels sadistic, in a way.

Above the Earth, written in swirling, gold script, is a phrase.

UNUS MUNDUS, UNUM SOMNIUM

The guard walks us through the marbled lobby and down a hall lined with framed pieces of art I've only ever seen in textbooks. I feel like I've stepped into the Palace of Versailles. I look to the others and notice all of them trying to conceal expressions of awe. Azure stares straight ahead, unimpressed, but I don't expect anything else from her.

"Have you met this person before?" I quietly ask V.

"Personally, no."

I look to Azure to gauge her reaction. I expect to see some sort of skepticism or doubt, but her face remains void of emotion.

"Don't worry," V says. "We were put in contact with him by someone we trust."

JB huffs. I turn and catch the end of an eye roll. I look to Kamea, but she doesn't give anything either. These people wrap themselves in mystery after mystery. I wish I had a choice other than to trust them so blindly.

We get to a pair of wide wooden doors carved from floor to ceiling with the scene of an English fox hunt. I reach out and trace the face of one of the foxes fleeing over a fallen tree, the hounds at her heels.

Our escort leaves us before the doors and walks back down the hallway.

Before we can react, a once-hidden steel panel juts from

the wall as he passes, sealing us in the hallway in front of the door, alone.

I slide my hand into my pocket to find the handle of the stick, and notice a few of the others making similar moves.

My heart starts to race as another silent moment passes.

Then the wooden doors silently begin to swing open. A perfectly groomed butler—an older man in a tux with a mustache waxed to the point of looking cartoonish—gives a small nod and gestures his hand toward a small flight of stairs.

"Welcome."

We take the stairs to a room so beautiful it takes my breath away. Thirty-foot walls of glass surround us on all sides, giving us a full panoramic view of not only the entire Strip, but the surrounding city and every star in the sky above us as well. I can only imagine what the view is like during the day. The sound of trickling water catches my ear, and I notice a man-made stream running the circumference, forming an island in the center of the square-shaped atrium. Our feet echo loudly as we make our way over the black marble floor toward a monolithic ebony table set with golden plates and crystal glasses that gleam in the light of flickering candles.

The butler directs us to our seats, leaving the chair at the head of the table empty. He offers us water, filling each crystal glass in a silence that weighs uncomfortably in the palatial room. Hopefully the sound of the stream gently trickling around us covers my audible gasps as I crane my neck to take in the sights around us from every angle.

The butler steps away, and moments later the sound of footsteps coming up the stairs fills the cavernous dining hall and a man appears.

"Forgive my tardiness," he says through a broad smile of gleaming white teeth as he makes his way to the seat at the head of the table.

We all awkwardly begin to stand.

"No, no. Please, sit. Make yourselves comfortable." He gestures for us all to remain in our seats as he pulls his chair from the table and sits down himself. "After all, you guys have had *quite* the journey today."

His smile is unwavering. His teeth are so white they kind of hurt my eyes to look at, even in the candlelight.

"Please, introduce yourselves. I'm so eager to meet all of you."

His eyes take us in rapturously as the others begin introducing themselves, starting with Azure to his left and working clockwise around the table. As I await my turn, I take in his appearance—his expertly carved face, his prominent nose and chin, and his precision-cut suit. The undone top two buttons of his crisp, white collared shirt show that he stays in shape and knows it. He looks older, but not *old*. His black hair is graying at the sides, which complements his eyes. Honestly, he'd be really attractive if he'd lose the fake smile for a second.

Finally, his eyes land on me.

"And you, young man. I've seen footage of what you did today. The news is in an uproar." He turns to address the entire table. "Don't worry; our people have planted a story about an oil tanker explosion. No one has the footage of what really happened—besides us." He beams his teeth back to me. "So tell me, what's your name, and what *are* you?"

I want to crawl under the table.

"Well," I start. Trying to maintain direct eye contact with him is like staring into the sun. His presence is intimidating. "My name is Isaak, and up until last week"—I look to the others, unsure of how much I ought to say—"I *thought* I was a human." I take a sip of the water to wet my drying throat. "But I guess that's all gone to shit now, huh?"

He laughs.

"We have a funny one!" he says through the end of his forced laughter. He looks away from me and gestures for the butler. "My boy, you are anything but a mere *human*."

The butler pops a cork from a bottle of champagne and circles the table, pouring into Azure's, Kamea's, and V's glasses first.

"I have met many of your kind, and I have never, ever, seen anything like what I saw today. It was like watching God himself come down from the sky, bringing the very future of the world itself with him in his hands."

The butler fills the man's glass last and then steps away.

The man raises the crystal flute to the table. "To your kind. To the future!" he gleefully toasts, and we all respond in kind. I take a sip, my first taste of champagne, and it lights up my tongue, singeing my throat in a way that's sweet and dry, yet refreshing, all at once. I don't mind it.

Our glasses clink to the table and Azure looks at the man. "And who are you?"

He chuckles as he swallows his drink. "My apologies. It seems I failed to introduce myself in my excitement to meet the honored guests."

He sets his glass down as well. "My name is Richard. I represent the estate of one of the wealthiest men on the planet. One of the primary members of a group of other such men who have been quietly funding the Underground for years now."

I can tell by the looks on their faces that several of the others have no idea what he's talking about. Azure and V don't seem very shocked.

"What?" He picks up his glass for another sip. "You didn't think that all those shiny toys and that sprawling, hidden fortress in Los Angeles came for free, did you?" He chuckles again. "No. You all have some incredibly powerful friends. I'm proud to say that I am here to represent those men tonight."

He gestures to the butler once more and opens his mouth to speak, but I can't keep my own mouth shut.

"What do you guys get out of it?" I ask. He looks at me, puzzled. I can tell he's not used to being interrupted and is hiding how much he's offended. I continue. "By helping us." Questions race through my mind, and I'm tired of not asking them. "Correct me if I'm wrong, but it sounds like you're funding the Underground and essentially committing treason by aiding this country's current number one enemy. That seems like an insanely huge risk to take without having something to make it incredibly worthwhile for you, in the end."

Richard takes a moment and studies my face. I can't tell if it's contempt, curiosity, or admiration I see in his eyes.

"We are investors," he says, and licks his lips. "We are the best in the world at what we do, and we believe that ensuring your survival is the best investment any of us have ever had the chance to make. We believe you are the future."

He takes another pause to let his expertly crafted politician's reply sink in, then breaks into his signature superficial smile. "Well, now that our introductions are out of the way, let's eat."

The butler leads a serving staff of six men, each carrying a silver platter, toward us from the stairs.

I look to Kamea and JB across the table. They both stifle huge grins and look down at the table to stop themselves from breaking out into laughter. V takes a sip of her champagne and raises her eyebrows at me in a look that tells me I've impressed her. Tace gives me a small nod. When my eyes go to Azure, she gives me a single, discreet admonishing shake of the head before looking away. It doesn't matter, though. I can't help but feel proud of myself.

I take another sip of champagne.

The food is exquisite and unlike anything I've ever tasted—lobster, duck, and a million other things I've never tried, can't identify, and probably can't pronounce. I feel like I'm going to explode after the fourth course, but then the servers return with dessert: banana flambé served over a hand-churned vanilla ice cream that tastes like chilled butter blended with brown sugar.

I down my third or fourth glass of champagne and scan the room for the server tending to the refills. Azure catches my eye and gives me another reprimanding glance. I don't care though. After the week I've had, I deserve this.

The server tops me off yet again, and Richard clears his throat. "Well, I truly cannot thank you all enough for your company tonight. May it be the first of many more to come."

I grin stupidly and raise my glass. I'll definitely cheers to that.

"In the morning, you will be the inaugural passengers on our group's new transit system, taking you directly from this resort to the Underground's headquarters in Los Angeles, Grand Central."

I can practically feel the jaws around me dropping. Well, maybe that's just the alcohol exaggerating things, but they're all definitely impressed. I don't really know what the hell he's talking about.

"Until then we've arranged for you all to have a carefree night of revelry in the hotel's premiere club, courtesy of the resort."

I can feel trepidation emanating from everyone. "And I personally assure you—on behalf of myself and all of my associates—that while you are inside this resort, you are as safe as you are in Grand Central itself. I guarantee it."

He raises his empty glass one more time, downs the last few bubbles, and stands from his seat. "With that, my new friends, good night."

We all follow his lead and get up from the table. As we make our way toward the door, I hear Richard ask Azure if he can speak with her a moment before she leaves. My ears perk up at this, but I follow the others down the stairs and out the wooden doors while Azure stays behind.

We stand in the bejeweled lobby for several minutes as we wait for her. My head is slightly spinning, but it's nothing I can't handle. Everything seems so fun and happy. I'm so full of good food and elated at the prospect of a night without having to worry about the Sheriffs that I don't take full notice of the look on Azure's face as she rejoins us.

The hulking guard presses his thumb to the glass square and the doors slide open for us.

"Which floor?" The man's voice sounds like a deep rumble of bass.

"We're going back to the rooms," Azure says definitively.

I can feel the others shuffle in silent disappointment, but I can't keep my mouth shut. "No way. This is our one chance to let off some steam, Azure."

My lips kind of stumble on the last part, but I'm articulating my thoughts well enough. I think.

"How much do you trust a man who wouldn't give you his last name?"

Her eyes burn into mine, and I crack a smile.

I reach over and hit the largest button on the panel—the one that reads CASINO. "You need to loosen up. We're gonna dance. We've earned it."

Her face falls into an unreadable expression. The silent grins from everyone else say everything.

She shakes her head and turns to face the doors. I notice her chin rise ever so slightly. "No more drinking," she says. "We all need to be alert, security or not."

She eyes the guard and clenches her jaw.

My eyes wander uncontrollably over to JB. He grins at me behind Kamea, and I can't help but grin back.

The effects of alcohol are apparently quadrupled on Robots when it's mixed with the electrolyte drinks they—we—love so much. Loud, pulsating music, flashing lights, and the feeling of bodies pushing against me helps elevate the experience a little as well.

I'm on my third vodka-and-whatever-this-red-stuff-is and I feel incredible. I've never been drunk before. Never felt my limbs go so loose, and all of my inhibitions just fly out the window like this. Everything is swirly and wobbly, like I'm wading through syrup, but it doesn't matter. The music feels like it's pounding inside me. I can't stop moving—and smiling.

Fuck the Sheriffs. Fuck the Underground. Fuck fear.

I am powerful and happy and free, and I am having the night of my life.

Sweat beads on my forehead, but I don't care. I raise my hands and bask in the lights flashing all around me.

I grab Kamea's hands and smile and pull her in to dance. Our bodies press into each other, my hands find the small of her back, and I pull her in to me more. She lets out a laugh, and we press our foreheads together. I feel so lucky to have her. To have everyone around me now, no matter how terrifying and confusing everything has been. We're all going through the same thing, after all. I shouldn't be so hard on them. Especially Kamea. She seems so sad. She's such a good person and deserves so much more than the life of running she's chosen for herself.

I push my chin forward and my lips lock with hers. I expect her to push me away, but she pulls me in tighter. I part her lips with my tongue and keep kissing her. I've never been attracted to girls the way I am guys, but I have so many feelings right now, and I know she can feel them all too. She's so present in the moment with me, and the sensation is more intoxicating than the liquor.

She gently pulls away and laughs. She grabs my face, kisses my cheek, and leans in to yell into my ear so that I can hear her over the blaring music.

"I'm going to get you some water."

She smiles again and lets go of my hand, leaving to make her way through the crowd toward the bar.

I watch V and Tace dance together and feel love for *their* love. They found each other in the face of all of this and cling to each other in a way that gives me hope.

Even Azure seems to be having a good time, reluctantly enough, when I notice her standing off to the side, not scowling. I feel like I should give her a hug.

A hand slides around my waist from the back.

I turn to find JB looking down on me from his tall-person perch.

His eyes light up in the polychromatic flashes, his usual smirk stretching broadly across his perfect face.

I hate him.

"How was your first kiss?" His lips barely graze the edge of my ear as he speaks and it's like liquid nitrogen dripping down my back. My body breaks out in chills.

No. I love him.

Ugh.

"It wasn't the one I was hoping for, but it was pretty fucking fantastic." I make sure to let my lips touch his ear in return.

"Oh yeah? Which one were you hoping for?" His hand slides lower down my back and pulls me in to him, hips first. He grinds against me.

"I don't know. There are so many options." This time I make sure he feels my tongue.

He leans closer and I can't hold back. My tongue and lips work in tandem, tracing his ear, down the side of his jawline—his nauseatingly perfect jawline—up his chin, and then finally to his lips. The sweet, cherry lips that I've stared at and fantasized about since the moment we walked into the bus station in Tulsa. And they're finally touching mine. He pulls me in to his chest and kisses me with reckless abandon. His tongue presses into my mouth, bringing me in and out of this swirling, heady connection with him at a ravenous pace. His left hand slides up my back as his right sneaks farther down. Soon he's holding the back of my head in one hand and pressing me in to him with a firm grasp on my ass in the other.

I've never had sex, but I can only imagine that this is what it feels like—sweaty, connected, pulsating with what feels like each other's blood, each other's energy.

A viselike grip clamps down on my forearm and pulls me away from my sweaty cocoon. My body lurches, and I feel like my shoulder has been dislocated. Anger boils up in an instant, but when I see the look of fear and I-told-you-so indignation in Azure's eyes, my stomach drops.

No.

She nods toward the front of the club and I see them: rows of Sheriffs, all wearing oversize goggles, file in on both sides of the room and move to surround the dance floor. I watch as they push drunken clubgoers aside, making their way toward the VIP table reserved for us.

V and Tace notice as well and huddle toward me, Azure, and JB.

"There's a service exit near our table," Azure yells above the din of the music. "Follow me."

Kamea.

I run away from the others, frantically scanning the crowd for any silhouette that might be hers. They all shout behind me, but I charge forward, pushing people aside, desperately trying to find her.

How could I have been so stupid?

The Sheriffs are filing farther and farther in and I still can't see her. The sweat on my body runs cold as I realize there's no sign of her and I've now been cut off from the others.

I feel a hand take mine from behind.

It's her.

"Come on!" Kamea yells, pulling me in the direction of the others.

But it's too late. They've made it to the dance floor and are coming from all sides.

Screams begin to rise up through the blasting music.

We run toward the others, and V stretches out her hand to me.

"Link!"

Kamea lets go and thrusts me toward V. I fall toward her, reach for her hand, and see she is already holding on to Azure's on the other side.

The instant our skin touches, a gleaming dome of electric yellow light springs into existence around us. All of us except Tace.

I watch in horror as the Sheriffs descend upon him.

Flashes of girls—angry girls—pummeling into my face with balled fists. Spitting on me, cursing me.

I dig through a trash can somewhere, searching for food. A boy looks at me from the other side of the shelter.

It feels like the first time anyone has ever really looked at me.

Then Richard, sliding his hand up my shirt to fondle my nipple. "But you, my dear, are not a woman." His ghastly teeth shine in the candlelight.

I can't help it. My knee arcs up into his balls, sending him into a pile, doubled over on the floor.

"And you, my dear, are no fucking man."

I turn toward the stairs and try to remember what it felt like to cry.

Azure pulls her hand from V's and the dome around us turns blue. I drop my hand to hold my forehead.

What was that?

My question is short-lived as I now see Tace, standing outside the dome. His mouth is open and everyone in the entire club is lying on the floor, shaking and vomiting. It looks like he's screaming. He closes his mouth and the dome winks out.

V grabs his hand and we follow Azure toward the back corner of the club—past our table and over bodies, moaning, writhing in agony, lying in pools of their own sick. The sound of their groans bubbling underneath the music and the overwhelming, putrid smell turn my stomach.

We race through an emergency exit and through the kitchen of the club's restaurant. Employees jump out of our way and press themselves against the walls as we careen through like a stampede. A chef shouts at us, but is halted by a crash of pots and pans as JB slips and catches himself against a rack of equipment. I yank him back to us as Azure bursts through another door up ahead.

We rush in after her, shouts echoing behind us, and I teeter on the edge of a flight of concrete stairs.

I shouldn't have had so much to drink.

I race down the stairs and hope my newfound agility hasn't totally abandoned me in my inebriation.

Where are we going?

I don't have time to think. I just follow, and run.

At the bottom of the stairwell, Azure pushes through another set of doors and leads us into a nondescript concrete hallway. We run to the end and take the only turn available. As we round the corner into another hall, we come face-to-face with a detail of Richard's guards.

I reach into my pocket for the stick as the foremost guard raises his hands.

"We're here to help you."

"Fuck you." V spits into the guard's face as she yells.

"We assure you that this attack was a security breach, and if you come with us, we will see you safely out of the resort immediately."

"Why should we trust you?" V's voice comes out as a hiss.

I can't explain why, but I believe the guy. "I don't think we have much of a choice," I say, noticing the guns the guards all hold. I might be impervious to bullets—maybe—but I know JB and Kamea most certainly are not, and I'm not willing to risk their lives to save mine.

"Richard said there was a way to get to Grand Central directly from this hotel," I say, hoping the guard will prove me right.

"Which is where we plan on taking you now, if you allow us." The guard's eyes flick from Azure's face to the back of the hallway behind us. He's worried about what might be following us as well.

Azure looks at me and then back to the main guard. "Let's go."

The guards lead us at a brisk pace through what feels like an endless labyrinth of hallways and corridors in the back areas of the hotel. I strain to hear footsteps behind us and expect the Sheriffs to pop out at every corner. We walk quickly, but it's difficult to resist the urge to run. I hope the Sheriffs won't be able to follow us in this maze, even if they are able to peel themselves out of their own puke to try.

We reach a dead end and stop cold as the main guard steps toward the smooth white wall.

He places his hand flat against it, and an invisible panel glows green. The other guards file back around and stand ready—guns drawn—down the hallway behind us. We wait like this for several minutes. It feels like hours. My pulse is still racing. We don't really know if we can trust these people. I think we can, but how can I explain the Sheriff attack just now? Either Richard's coalition of billionaires isn't as powerful as they think, or they're fully working against us. Either scenario spells terrible things for the Underground.

The white wall at the end of the hallway finally slides back, and the guard steps aside.

We file through, into a white-walled box, and the guard raises his hand once more to the wall beside him.

The door slides shut, with him on the other side.

No.

I can feel impending death pressing down on us as we sink lower into the ground. The white walls of this elevator will probably be my coffin, or at least a precursor to a very short life of dissection and grisly experiments, all while Richard and his fucking teeth smile overhead.

The elevator stops and the doors open to a cavernous chamber. Everything around us is polished, smooth stone and gleaming metal piping. Curiously, all of it is dripping wet.

We step out onto the soaking-wet concrete, and two doors set in a gleaming, chrome cylinder slide open before us.

It's a train platform.

Our feet splash over the small puddles, and we file into a luxurious car of rich, paneled woods and supple, tan leather couches. The air smells like cedar and vanilla.

The doors slide shut behind us and the train lurches forward. We slowly pull away from the platform, moving into darkness. The movement stops, and the sound of something large and metallic slams shut behind us, shaking the walls of the tunnel around us. In our still, perfect silence, I hear the sound of rushing water.

Before I can make out the source of the sound, I feel the

train lift upward and then effortlessly, frictionlessly glide forward once again.

Although the sole window in the car, the one in the door, reveals only a pitch-black tunnel, I can feel us going faster and faster.

After several minutes of silence, we all finally start to breathe.

V and Tace hold each other as Kamea drops onto one of the couches. Azure braces herself against a mahogany side table and holds her temples. I inhale sharply as I try to process everything that just happened and place my hand on the wall beside me to stop it from trembling.

JB looks to me and blinks. He doesn't know what to say. "I need to find the bathroom." He takes off farther down the train.

After a few minutes of uncomfortable silence with the others, I follow.

I walk past the bathrooms, where I assume the alcohol and adrenaline are getting the best of JB, and come upon a smooth, wooden panel. I slide it open and walk into a plush bedroom. Soft recessed lighting gently glows around a white, full-size bed, and there on the floor is Kamea's duffel and all of our new bags of clothes.

As I step into the room, a small screen lights up on the wall with a block of text.

Friends—my apologies for the unfortunate intrusion upon what was guaranteed to be a carefree night. I am horrified

to have added yet another ordeal to your already treacher-
ous journey. I sent for your things and had the train prepped
and ready for launch the moment we were alerted of the
SHRF's unwelcome presence in the resort. I can assure you
that steps will be taken to prevent such trespasses in the
future and that our only interest is one and the same: pre-
serving and protecting the lives of you and all of Robotkind.
I hope you're able to relax a bit now as you journey toward
your final destination in luxury. Best—Richard.

I finish reading the message and notice something sitting on the bed as well. My journal.

I pick it up from the bed and smell the mix of leather and paper and offer a silent thanks to whoever thought to bring it down along with the bags.

I leave the room and go back to the main car to tell the others about the note, but it's up on a set of screens out there as well, and they've already read it.

"That smarmy asshole," V says, sprawled out on one of the couches next to Tace.

I tell them about the bags and the sleeping cars farther down, but no one seems to be able to muster the energy to budge. Azure looks like she's about to pass out on the couch as it is. I have yet to actually see her sleep, come to think of it.

I turn around and make my way back to the bed in the sleeping car. The lights dim to the faintest glow as I slide the door shut behind me.

Now that the adrenaline is fading from my system, the remnants of the alcohol begin to swirl back to the surface. Everything feels like it's gently spinning, and I can't get it to stop.

I stumble to the bed, kick off my shoes, and collapse back onto it. I don't have the energy for anything else.

The bed keeps spinning faster and faster . . . or is it the train itself? I can't tell. All I know is that it's making me nauseous.

The lights dim even more, fading to darkness, and I drift away with them.

Men sneak into my room, one after the other, unbuckling their belts and unzipping their trousers.

They climb on top of me.

In the dark I see their monstrous faces, smell their acrid breath as it pours over their sharpened fangs.

They push themselves into me and it rips my body apart. I shout and cry, but they don't care.

They're demons, hungry for flesh, getting their fill. Eventually I go numb and forget how to scream.

Richard looks at me, his forked tongue flicking from behind his terrible razor teeth.

Then they get her—my baby, my everything, the only thing in this entire world I will ever care about.

They're going to come into her room next.

No.

Anything.

I will do anything.

Just tell me what to do.

The demons lock her away in a cage, dangling above a pit of flames.

Her little hand reaches out toward me as she cries my name.

The cries echo in my head as I scream for her across the flames.

The sound of my own shouts startles me awake. I try to remember the nightmares, but the harder I cling, the farther they slip away. Soon they're gone completely. My breath feels hollow and short and my skin is clammy.

Something feels different in the room. Panic begins to rise once again as I try to sort out what it is.

Then it hits me—the train is slowing down.

Shaken from the terrible dreams, I get up from the bed, slip on my sneakers, and go out to find the others. JB is sitting on one of the couches, zipping up the black duffel. It seems everyone got their things out of the room while I slept. The white bags are lined up neatly along the wall, with most of the clothes left inside. It looks like they're planning to leave them behind. I don't think designer clothes are a big priority when you spend most of your life fighting to stay alive.

"You okay?" V asks as she laces up her left boot. "You were screaming in your sleep."

My face flushes a bit, but I feel too tired and hollow to really care. "I get nightmares. Bad ones. Always have."

Azure slips her arms into her black jacket and looks at me, pondering something. She's looked at me like this one too many times.

"Azure, can I talk to you really quick?"

She rubs the back of her neck and doesn't look at me. "The train is about to stop, Isaak."

"It'll only be a second." I turn and head back toward the bathrooms.

Once I reach the doors down the corridor, I stop and wait for her to follow. She approaches with a curious expression and stands silently.

"You know more than you're letting on," I say, peering over her shoulder to make sure no one else is near.

She looks at me in feigned confusion.

"About me. About what I am."

Her face goes blank. She's not going to give me what I want, but she's not going to bullshit me either.

"I have my suspicions, yes," she says. "But I need the others to test it. Once the Assembly gives you a proper testing—"

"And that's another thing." Heat fills my cheeks as frustration gets the best of me. "'Grand Central' and 'the Assembly' and this and that and every other damn word out of your mouth is something I know *nothing* about. You've led me here—wherever the hell we're about to arrive—and haven't told me anything about where it is, *what* it is, or who I'm going to meet there. I don't know *anything*, and you keep looking at me like you know something and talking over me and—"

I stop as I realize the stress, alcohol, and nightmares have gotten to me. "I'm sorry." My head hangs and I stare at my feet. The train is slowing down to a crawl. I'm just ready for this to be over.

Unexpectedly, I feel a firm grasp on my shoulder. I look up at Azure and see something in her eyes that I never expected to see: sympathy.

"No, Isaak, I'm sorry."

Then something I never thought I would ever see happens: Her crystal-blue eyes well with tears.

The train comes to a halt.

She turns away for a moment once it stops, and by the time she turns back to me, the tears are gone. "You will be fine, I promise you." She turns on her heel and goes back to the others.

Asking questions never seems to yield any answers, only more questions—like peeling the layers of an onion with no core. Just layer after endless layer. I should be used to this by now.

After a moment I join everyone else back in the main car and stand at the door. My palms begin to sweat as we wait for it to open.

Seconds pass in silence until finally the doors part.

Everything beyond is pitch-black—no lights, no sound, just darkness.

I follow Azure out onto the platform and wait for everyone to file out. The moment Tace brings up the rear and steps onto the concrete, the doors close tight. The train comes back to life and glides away, back the way we came.

As it leaves, a small pathway, marked by tiny glowing lights set into the floor, lights up the way toward a door.

"Does this look familiar to any of you?" My voice echoes off the walls. This chamber must be huge.

"No, it doesn't," V says, the muscles in her jaw tensing and flexing.

Azure walks toward the door, and we all follow.

As we approach, the door slides open to more darkness. We march in and it seals shut behind us. Now it really is pitch-black. I can barely make out Azure in front of me, and I am supposed to be able to see in the dark.

Something is wrong.

I hear a gun cock, and my blood runs cold.

"Link, now!" V yells.

"Freeze."

A voice booms as light floods the room around us, revealing a circle of ten-foot-tall metal golems completely surrounding us. Giant machines, standing on two legs, with tanklike chests and massive arms that I assume are actually guns, given the way they're pointed toward us.

At least I got to see something genuinely cool before I die.

V's hand scrambles for Azure, and the guns lean in farther with a loud, metallic groan that reverberates throughout the room.

"Don't move," the voice says again, booming from somewhere unseen.

My eyes frantically search for a way out, but I can't see anything beyond the machines.

I stare into the barrel of one of the huge arm guns and wait for the quick, painless explosion.

"Oh my God, Malek, cut it out. You're gonna give them all heart attacks," a girl's voice says beyond the machines and the glaring lights.

Everyone besides Azure takes a deep breath and relaxes around me. V puts a hand over her mouth and shakes her head as the machines begin to step away and loosen the tight circle around us. As they part, a girl with ebony skin and long, vivid turquoise hair tied into a braid runs toward us. She practically pounces V as they embrace and laugh.

The girl stops and pulls away from V, further examining her crop top and the rest of her ensemble.

"Oh, *excuse me*," the girl says sarcastically.

"I had some gold hoops earlier, but I thought that would be a little much," V says as she flips imaginary hair from her shoulders.

They laugh and hug each other again as the machines creak and groan around us. I examine them further in the light—without the fear of imminent death—and realize they are suits and that there are faces inside. The one standing closest to us begins to open at the chest, and a boy steps out. A young man, really.

The guy walks toward us once he's free of the machine. He's tall—as tall as JB, if not taller—with broad, muscled shoulders, a chiseled face, and skin that matches the girl with the turquoise hair. He's gorgeous.

The young woman lets go of V and looks to the rest of us. "Forgive my brother, guys. He can be such a dick sometimes."

She playfully slaps him on the shoulder as others begin to climb out of the machines as well.

The gorgeous guy approaches JB. "Hey, you." He smiles, and I look to JB's face, waiting to gauge his reaction.

"Hey." JB grins in return, and they embrace.

The guy pulls out of the hug and then goes in for a long, passionate kiss.

My stomach falls to the ground, and I don't know if it's the alcohol again or what, but my head starts to spin. I look to Kamea, waiting for a stunned reaction from her that never comes. She catches my eyes and gives me a tiny, apologetic smile before mouthing, *Sorry.*

"Where is Aleister?" Azure asks the brother and sister as Tace, V, Kamea, and JB begin greeting some of the others from the suits.

"Hello, Azure," the guy replies, his arm still around JB. "Always a pleasure."

"He's upstairs with the others," the girl says, before giving her a small smile. "And hi, Azure."

Azure nods to her in reply as the brother's and sister's eyes land on me.

"I'm Arielle," she says, smiling warmly at me.

I try to catch JB's eye as the guy drops his arm from his

shoulder, but he evades. The guy catches the glance.

"And this is my brother, Malek."

He holds out his hand for me to shake.

"Isaak," I reply despondently.

His hand engulfs mine as he shakes it, squeezing hard enough to break bones, were they still human.

I try not to wince as he lets go.

"Nice to meet you, Isaak." He smiles and puts his arm back around JB.

I can't tell if I want to punch something or cry.

Arielle looks at me and smiles again. "Welcome to Grand Central."

I give a catatonic nod in response.

"Do you like the new toys?" Malek nods back to the mechanical suits as we leave the large underground hangar. Several of the others stay behind to walk them beneath metal, tentacle-like arms dangling from the ceiling on the far side of the chamber. I watch the first step into position as the tentacle comes to life and inserts itself into the head of the suit. This is a docking chamber. There must be a hundred of them.

"The charge from a Robot's body activates and operates them, so no fun for you guys, unfortunately." He looks at JB and Kamea. "They use calixarene crystals to create hydrogen fuel, so the energy toll on a Robot during a fight is much less than if you were to fight without one. Think of it as a Robot battery pack, with guns."

A steel door leading out of the hangar slides open as we approach.

"Who are we fighting?" I ask.

Arielle turns and shoots her brother a look.

"They're more of a precautionary measure," he says, before giving his sister a placating glance in return.

We step into a wide, concrete corridor. Small orange lights, recessed into the floor beneath us, glow softly along the wall, lighting our way.

"I'm assuming Aleister had something to do with them," V says as we round a corner.

"How'd you guess?" Arielle replies sarcastically.

Malek turns to see Azure's grim expression and changes the subject.

"This is all new," he says, gesturing to the walls around us. "They finished construction about three months ago. You guys have all been gone way too long." He looks back to JB and grabs hold of his hand as yet another set of steel doors slides open before us.

We step out into another large chamber—an open room three stories tall, surrounded by a balcony on all sides at each level. Rows of aluminum tables and benches line the floor. It looks like a cafeteria. The cool, white lighting overhead washes everything out in tones of bluish gray. Every surface is either metal or polished concrete.

More than anything, this place looks like a bunker and feels like a fortress.

A tall column reaches from the floor to the ceiling directly across from us—a steel elevator shaft—and staircases flank either side. Large windows line the lower level where we currently stand, looking into various large rooms. In one I can see several screens and couches, and in the other, the glass barrier of a buffet line. That must be the kitchen. I crane my neck to examine the upper levels. From my current position I can't see very much. "This is the main hall," Arielle says, looking back to me. "Where we eat, where we meet when the entire population needs to be addressed—"

"Where we party," V interrupts, grinning and pretending to dance.

Arielle rolls her eyes and laughs. "Yes," she continues. "You've made it just in time for Tribo. We're having one the day after tomorrow."

Another reference to something I know nothing about.

I look to Azure, and her face is unreadable. JB tries to stifle a surprised smile.

"Don't get too excited," Malek says, noticing the look as well.

JB rolls his eyes and gives him another kiss.

I turn away to admire a lovely concrete wall on my right.

The sound of more doors sliding apart draws my attention to the elevator opening at the center of the room. A towering scarecrow of a boy with a mop of curly, copper-orange hair teetering off to one side of his head steps out and marches toward us, flanked on either side by a pair of jet-black Doberman pinschers. Behind him is a shorter, petite girl with ivory skin and raven hair tied into intricate braids running tightly along her scalp.

"Azure," he says flatly when he stops before us. His catlike eyes, perched above sharp, severe cheekbones, land on me for a moment. It feels like ice water is pouring down my back. His gaze is heavy in a way I've never experienced before, with anyone.

"This is Isaak," Kamea says, saving me. He turns to regard her for a brief moment.

"Kamea. Always a pleasure." His tone sounds anything but pleased. "I trust you've been productive during your time away." He stops to look at the rest of our group. "V, I hear your visit with my associate was . . . tumultuous."

"I was under the impression they were *our* associates," she says as she gestures to the entire building around us.

He gives a small, hollow smile and moves on, passing over Tace dismissively. His eyes dart back to me and it's like having the wind knocked out of my chest. I don't want this person to look at me—ever.

I do my best to hold his gaze as he assesses me. A flicker of light blooms in his irises. . . .

"Aleister, we need to talk," Azure says, drawing his attention and breaking his gaze.

The glow I saw fades, and I wonder if I imagined it.

"Yuki, stay with the others," he says to the girl behind him without turning to acknowledge her.

I don't like this guy. At all.

The girl—Yuki—gives a terse nod as Azure and Aleister turn to leave. They make their way into the elevator and turn back to face us as the doors close. Both stare at me as they disappear behind the steel.

V huffs out a sigh. "Prick."

"At least he's consistent," JB replies.

Arielle takes a breath and shakes her head, then turns to face me with another one of her kind smiles. "You must be exhausted. I'll show you to the dorms."

She walks toward the staircase on the far side of the room. My feet follow on autopilot. Before placing my foot on the first step, I look back to the others just as JB's eyes flash up to meet mine. The sight of him disgusts me. I make sure he can see it in the brief moment he holds my glance, and then turn to follow Arielle up the stairs.

Exhaustion starts to creep into my body as we make it to the final landing at the top of the third flight of stairs.

"The top floor houses our dorms. New members are assigned temporary rooms and bunkmates in pairs and then given more permanent accommodations once they've been assigned."

Hallways split away from us in every direction. A wide balcony wraps around the floor that looks down into the main hall on all sides. The direction we're currently facing has three separate hallways. "The members who live here full-time stay in the larger rooms on the other side. You'll be down this way."

She walks toward the hallway on the right and looks to me.

"You lucked out though: You're the first new arrival in several weeks. You get your own room."

Lucky me.

We continue down the slate-gray hallway, dimly lit by the same orange lights embedded into the floor, and take a right at the end. Another lengthy hallway stretches out, with more hallways splitting off on either side. This place is a labyrinth. I hope they don't expect me to find my way back.

We pass door after door and eventually take the last left at the end and turn into a dead-end hall. She stops at the sixth door on our left and opens it for me. I step inside as lights—recessed into the edges of the walls along the ceiling—come to life and make the tiny room glow. A small, simple bed sits along the wall next to a nightstand with a little lamp on top. In the other corner is a sink with a mirror. To my right is a desk with another lamp and a chair. Everything is stark, utilitarian, and I can't help but notice there isn't a bathroom.

"Dorms in this wing don't come with private bathrooms," Arielle says, reading my mind, "but you'll find them at the end of the first hallway we walked down."

I take in the tiny room in silence as I begin to succumb to the exhaustion spreading over me.

She puts a hand on my shoulder. "You're safe now."

I look into her eyes and wonder if that will ever be true for me again.

"I used to be scared too. My entire life felt like a nightmare before I came here. But I made it. I found others like me.

Found out what I really am—*who* I really am—and discovered I have a purpose. You have one too. I'm not scared anymore. You won't be either."

She gives my shoulder a light squeeze. "Good night, Isaak," she says before closing the door behind her.

I collapse onto the mattress. It's firmer than I expected, but I don't care. I'm so tired, so drained, I could pass out on a slab of stone. I can't stop thinking about JB—about him kissing someone else, someone who was here, waiting for him. I feel like an idiot. Kamea kept trying to tell me, and I was too naive to take the hint. My fists ball at my sides as tears well in my eyes.

Then, for the first time in days, I think about Jonathan. I've been so caught up in this never-ending chase sequence my life has become that I completely forgot my best friend. My heart aches as I think about how hurt and confused he must be, having lost his mother and his best friend on the same day. Guilt racks my entire being as I think about what it must've been like back there since I left. Did anyone even find Patricia's and Carl's bodies? They were never warm or kind to me, but they were worth more than the end they met. They didn't deserve to be gunned down because of me. They were broken, sad people who needed more love than they were capable of accepting. Jonathan must think I died along with them. Any chance I had of contacting him was buried the moment I entered this underground fortress.

I don't even know where I am.

Tears stream down my face and I can't stop them. I feel lost, confused, and so desperately alone.

The recessed lights begin to automatically fade, and after a few seconds they go dark.

I turn onto my side and cry myself to sleep.

Out in the audience, beyond the glare of the spotlight, I catch a glimpse of my father.

The screen in his hand lights up his face and I see he's not paying attention.

The bow slips over the strings and I lose my rhythm, making a loud, harsh squeak as the music falters.

The audience gasps as I try to regain my place in the song.

My fingers fumble and I look back up to see him laughing at me.

She is laughing too, with her blond hair and obscenely inflated breasts brimming over the top of her whorish dress.

Hatred boils in me as I funnel my rage into the strings.

Something curious begins to happen: Small slivers of connection bloom in my mind, like puppet strings connecting me to everyone in the auditorium, and I am the puppet master.

I let more and more of my rage flow out of me and can feel the reaction taking hold in all of them.

They all begin to stir.

I want them afraid.

I want them to cower in fear at the mere mention of my name.

They are dirt beneath my feet—garbage—and I will trample them.

People in the first few rows begin to rise from their seats, frantically backing away from me.

No.

They will trample one another.

Chaos erupts as the entire audience bursts into screams and races toward the exits all at once.

Children cry and howl for their mothers; grown men cry out in agony as others run them over.

I continue playing.

I funnel fear into them until I feel they might break.

I push harder.

My eyes land on my father in the sixth row, frantically pulling on an arm from beneath a pile of people climbing and trampling one another like animals.

It must be her.

Too bad.

I keep pushing until he loses his footing and slips under the stampede along with her.

I watch as a hulking, beastly man uses my father's skull as a step to climb over another man.

I smile as I hear a loud crack over the screams.

My face bears into the pillow as I feel him push into me.

My hands reach back to grab his thighs and my knees take his weight as I arch my back down to let him in deeper.

I gasp in pain and pleasure all at once.

I've missed this.

His hand grabs the back of my neck and I turn to face him—JB, thrusting into me with ravenous hunger, leaning back in the dim light, jaw open, eyes closed . . . thinking of someone else.

I saw how he looked at him, that boy. The one he arrived with.

My stomach turns and I want him out of me.

A voice comes in over the speaker in the pitch-black room.

I look to the door to make sure no one is there for the third time. No one has access to this area. I shouldn't be afraid. Fear is for lesser beings.

"Can you confirm the effectiveness of the specimen?"

I lick my lips. There is no turning back now. This is what I set out to do. The only way forward.

"I can confirm. He is the one."

What is left of my heart goes still in the darkness.

"Perfect. It will happen in two days. 0100 hours. Be ready."

"Wait," I say, before he can hang up. "How is she? Can I speak to her?"

"We both know that's not possible."

I close my eyes and hold my breath.

"But I assure you, she is safe, healthy, and happy. Be ready."

I exhale and nod to a voice that can't see me as the line goes dead.

The darkness closes in as I try not to think about what I've just done.

I jolt up in the bed and the lights come to life around me.

More nightmares. I'm in the clothes I arrived in—soaked through with sweat from another restless sleep. Yet again I remember nothing. I fumble for the lamp on the nightstand and find the switch. In the increased light, I look around the room—concrete walls, smooth, concrete floor. A twelve-by-twelve-foot cube of bare-bones necessities. I have to get out of here.

A knock at the door brings me fully into consciousness. I throw my feet over the side of the bed and blearily stumble to the door and open it. A boy with fair skin and brown, wavy hair sits in a wheelchair on the other side.

"Hi, Isaak? I'm Kyle."

"Nice to meet you." My mouth feels like I've been sucking on cotton. Another gift from the alcohol last night, I assume.

I step back and let him into the room.

"I'm sorry," I say, apologizing for my appearance. "I just woke up."

"It's okay." He wheels himself inside a few feet and angles back toward me. "I wasn't supposed to be up this early either, but Malek apparently had things to do before the Assembly meeting. He sent me to wake you and take you to breakfast."

"He was supposed to come?" My brain scrambles to remember something from my dreams.

"Well, don't be too disappointed," Kyle says, shuffling in his chair slightly. He has long black eyelashes, currently cast down as he avoids my gaze.

"Don't worry. I'm not." I wait for him to look back up at me and smile once he does.

A curious expression comes into his face. "You're not," he says, surprised.

"I wouldn't have said it if I didn't mean it."

He cracks a smile now as well. "Most people say things they don't mean and don't mean most of what they say."

I try to puzzle out the statement to think of a witty response but can only muster up a yawn.

"I'm sorry," I say, halfway through. "I got drunk last night. First time. Not really feeling one hundred percent just yet."

He laughs and pushes himself past me, back toward the door. "Let's go get breakfast."

People—Robots, I assume—come and go as we make our way to the elevator. I notice that although almost everyone seems to know Kyle, they all avoid eye contact when they say hello.

We walk into the elevator and wait for the doors to close. A guy approaches, too engaged in a conversation to realize who is already inside, but turns in the other direction as soon as he sees Kyle. I look down to gauge his reaction, but he seems to be unfazed.

The doors open and we step into the main hall. The cold, cathedral-like chamber is now filled with the echoing voices of dozens of people catching up and greeting one another over breakfast, in stark contrast to how it was last night when I first saw it. We head to the kitchens on our left, where a line begins with a rack of plastic trays and continues on past a row of assorted dishes and kitchen workers serving them from behind the buffet. After the line is a small market area that looks like a miniature grocery store with rows of refrigerated glass cases housing all sorts of goods and baskets of fresh produce. It's colorful and warm and doesn't feel anything like the main hall it's attached to.

Kyle greets a few more people, who smile and avoid eye contact, as we make our way to the beginning of the food line. He hands me one of the yellow trays and then sets one for himself on the metal counter.

"Why do they do that?" I want to elaborate, but I can't think of any way of asking without being offensive. It might be offensive of me to even ask in the first place.

"I make them uncomfortable," he says, pointing to the scrambled eggs.

"I'm sorry." I don't know what else to say. I shouldn't have said anything to begin with. I look down at his wheelchair and quickly look away as soon as I realize what I've done.

He looks up at me and grins. "Wait, you think it's because of my wheelchair?"

I stammer and search for the best way to apologize.

He just laughs. "That's actually really sweet of you, but no, it has nothing to do with this." He gestures down.

I start to blush and turn to nod to the guy serving the food. He scoops some eggs onto a plate for me as well.

We make our way through the rest of the line in silence. I

grab a muffin from a large basket at the end, and Kyle hands me an electrolyte water from a small refrigerator. I follow him over to one of the long aluminum tables in the back of the room, set up near the hangar door I came in through last night. The door itself is actually quite hidden now that I'm looking for it again. There's barely any indication on the wall that there's a door there.

Kyle pulls up to the end of one of the tables, and I take a seat on the bench next to him.

"So where are you from?" he asks, before taking a bite of hash browns.

"Missouri. You?" I spread butter onto the muffin and try to keep it from crumbling.

"Florida."

We chew without speaking as more people begin to arrive and line up at the kitchen. I quickly notice that everyone here is young. There probably aren't any Robots in existence above the age of twenty-five.

"You guys had a rough trip, I hear," Kyle says through a bite of bacon.

"You could say that. How was it for you?"

"Getting here? Well, I've been here for a couple years now. It wasn't that bad, actually. I had help." Kyle's eyes get lost in his words for a split second. "But that was then," he continues. "It's gotten a lot worse out there, from what I've heard. Personally, I've never even seen a Sheriff."

I almost drop my fork. "Are you serious?"

An endless horde of men and women—clad in black, chasing after me—flashes in my head.

"Yeah. I don't get sent out into the field very often."

I'm worried I've said something wrong again, but before I can apologize, he speaks again.

"You must be something special, though. I've never seen them hold an emergency Assembly meeting like this for a testing."

"I don't know what you're talking about."

"You're getting tested this morning, after breakfast. Gonna find out what you're made of. In fact, we should go now. Finish up."

I pop the last bite of muffin in my mouth and swallow. It's so dry it scratches my throat.

Standing before the Assembly feels like standing in front of a pride of lions. My palms are slick with sweat as I wait for them to pounce.

There are seven chairs at the long, rectangular table in front of me. Aleister and Arielle flank the head chair. Aleister, in a loose, black knit sweater with a swooping neck that shows his pale clavicle, sits with both of his dogs at his feet. I wonder if they ever leave his side. Arielle, whose flowing hair is now the vibrant shade of an orange Creamsicle, gives me a small smile. On the left side, next to Aleister, sits Yuki, who has a new pattern of braids woven into her hair, and a tall, pale girl with white-blond hair whose hawklike nose and severe, almond eyes lend her an icy expression that makes Azure's look warm and inviting. On the other side, beside Arielle, sits a boy with a buzzed head; he is covered in tattoos from his hands up to his neck. A few even creep up to his scalp and face. He nods at me as my eyes meet his. Beside him is a girl with dark brown skin and long black hair. She has deep, mahogany eyes and a small, glittering gold nose ring.

Arielle leans in to the tattooed guy next to her and whispers something in his ear. Besides that, the room is silent. I look over to Kyle, sitting in his wheelchair off to the side of the table, but he doesn't look at me. The buzz of the white lighting overhead begins to fill my head as I pick at my right thumbnail and wait for whatever is going to happen.

The elevator to the main hall above us opens once again and Malek walks in. He's wearing a simple gray T-shirt that accentuates his perfectly toned chest and biceps and a pair of khakis. He looks like he should be on TV, not down here in a subterranean bunker.

He takes the empty seat at the end of the table and locks eyes with me. "Let's get started, shall we?"

Panic sets in as I realize I'm not going to get an explanation of what's about to happen, or even so much as an introduction to the others I haven't met yet.

One by one—starting with the harsh-looking blond girl to the far left—everyone at the table joins hands. A multitude of colors fills the room as light begins to emanate from each of their eyes. The girl with the nose ring to the far right gestures me toward her with a smile and an open hand.

I take a deep breath and walk toward her.

The waves of energy rippling off of them percolates into my skin as I approach, and before I have time to second-guess myself, I take her hand in mine.

Snow falls outside the grimy window.

The room is cold—almost as cold as it is out there, on the street.

I want to be thankful for the roof over my head, but I can't bring myself to feel much of anything anymore.

She lets the next one in before the last one has even finished zipping up his pants.

I watch as a child slips on the icy sidewalk below and falls face-first into a small mound of packed ice—slush from the road, turned brown from the city and frozen several times over.

His mother picks him as he cries and checks his face for a cut.

She kisses his cheek and continues down the street as he stifles his tears.

I feel a dip in the bed as the next man climbs on top of me and grabs hold of my neck.

I don't know how much longer I can keep going, but I must not stop.

He cannot be allowed to live. Not like this at least.

He will pay for what he's done to me, and I will make sure he never does it again.

I press into the deepest corners of his brain, harder and harder, until I feel him about to break.

His moans of pleasure shifted into cries of agony a while ago now, and I know I'm not far from succeeding.

The light—the burning light fueling me—is dying out.

It's all slipping through my hands and I don't know how I can sustain it any longer.

Oscar rubs his little orange head against my leg, and then I feel it.

I know what I must do.

Without breaking eye contact, I lean over and grab the loose skin behind his head.

He hisses in response, but I grip tighter.

Energy surges into me from his body, and before he can protest further, Oscar goes limp.

The stream of new energy is short-lived, though, and I desperately need more. I will need much more before this is over.

I click my tongue against the roof of my mouth, calling the other cats in the house toward me.

I hold him by his neck and look into his eyes. He has caused me so much pain—he's caused her so much pain. I can feel myself poking and prodding at every function happening inside of his body. There it is—his heart. As easily as flicking a light switch, I turn it off. He crumples to the floor, and I look to Arielle's body on the kitchen floor, lying in a pool of her own blood.

They're all here. My entire crew. These are my brothers . . . were my brothers.

Now they're standing in front of me, guns drawn, ready to erase me from the Earth.

Even Seve—the man who was my father when my real one took off and left me to fend for myself.

He orchestrated this. He must have. And for what? Money? Product?

I've moved more coke for him than all of these mother-fuckers combined.

And now he's standing with a gun pointed at my head.

They all are.

I close my eyes and think of the stories I used to create in my head.

The pictures I would draw and the stories I would write.

I was told I couldn't. Real men don't waste their time in la-la land.

These were the guys who taught me that.

Now I will drag them into my own la-la land, kicking and screaming.

I let unimaginable horrors loose inside their heads, tormenting them with images from the darkest edges of my mind. Images that aren't even there.

By the time I let the visions fade, they're all on the floor. Dead from their own bullets.

Only Seve remains standing, shaking, sweating. The dark circle around his crotch reveals he's pissed himself.

The visions are gone now, but he looks at me as though he's seen a demon come to Earth, coming to collect a debt long overdue.

His shaky hand places the gun inside his own mouth and he pulls the trigger.

The tree pushes sharply into my back as I try to calm my breath and stifle my tears.

There's nowhere else to run.

The three of them pin me back, the bark scraping the skin off my arms.

I look at the outline of the longhorn on all of their shirts and know that the devil is real.

Why did I even come here? I should've stayed at the dorm, studying.

"Raghead."

"Terrorist."

They spit in my face and repeat the words over and over.

Hot tears stream down my face.

I try to tell them I'm not a Muslim, or even an Arab, but they don't hear me through their rage.

All they see is brown. And red.

Another kind of heat prickles at my fingertips.

Terror, real terror, and anger pour out of me and coalesce into tiny stars inside my hands.

I run from their burning bodies in the woods and know I can never go back.

I snap back into the room as the others pull their hands from one another. How long was that? A second? An hour? I honestly can't tell. My mind is jelly. There is no alcohol to muddy the experience this time. I feel things, see things, when I touch other Robots. I know this now. The air in my lungs grows heavy. These flashes—they're like my nightmares, the ones I've had my entire life. This cannot be good.

What does it mean?

The others look like they've seen a ghost. Yuki turns to Aleister, alarmed. The blond girl rubs her fingers together as though she's touched something revolting, and all the others seem to exchange curious glances around the table.

"You can leave, Isaak," Malek says, leaning forward onto the table. "We need to talk."

Shakily, I nod and turn around to head back to the elevator. I want, *need,* someone to talk to me, to help me through this, but no one steps up. My trembling finger presses the button and the doors slide open. I step inside and turn to face the others, and in the brief moment before the doors close, I see that every single eye is on me.

Another group of people come in and settle on one of the couches on the other side of the room. I've been in the rec room off the main hall for what feels like hours now, waiting. Several large old couches partition off different sitting areas.

An eclectic mix of furniture styles, patterns, and colors lend the variety of tables and chairs and lamps the collective air of a gypsy tent. It's a cozy, cavernous room that I would enjoy if my stomach weren't currently tied into an insurmountable pile of knots.

Two guys play an old video game console on a TV in the corner.

"Dude, you're not allowed to connect. Controls only! Bastard."

Their banter goes back and forth, but I tune it out. I can't stop thinking about the things I've been seeing, the visions that come to me in flashes anytime I touch another Robot. I think I know what they mean, what they're all adding up to, but it doesn't make any sense, and I don't know that I'd be ready to accept it even if it did.

My mind gets lost in memories of Pacific, my old school, the woods and caves, Jonathan.

Where am I supposed to go from here?

What is all of this leading me to?

In books I used to read, the hero was always a neglected orphan who finds out he's special. He goes on a quest that leaves him broken, but ultimately saves the world with his special savior magic and returns to where it all began as a hero. I look around at all of the other Robots in the room. Everyone in here is a neglected orphan. All of us are different.

What makes you think you'll be the hero in this story?

I won't be a hero. I'm scared, and alone, and as much as I

hate feeling like no one knows me, I fear it's worse that I don't even know myself.

Kyle appears from behind a large leather sofa and nods back in the direction of the main hall.

"Apparently you're a tough cookie to crack. They're nowhere near a conclusion. Azure and your other traveling companions are heading down now to give testimonies, but as for you, looks like you have a free day."

The knots in my stomach squeeze tighter.

Guess I won't be learning about my magic powers today after all.

After lunch I spend a while exploring Grand Central.

The second floor houses all of the training facilities—myriad rooms and cavernous gymnasium-size courts where Robots train in various forms of hand-to-hand combat, weapons techniques, and hone in on their respective abilities. Members of the Underground who have clearly been here longer help those who've just arrived work with their abilities, coaching them to use these powers without burning out.

That's something I keep hearing about: burning out. Robots are not like superheroes in comics and movies—our power is finite, and easily expended. We have to pay for every single second we use them. Keeping yourself alive and functioning long enough to use your abilities in battle apparently requires a delicate balance. Every senior member in every room says the same thing:

"Save your energy. You're going to burn out. Save your energy."

I sit in on a group of telekinetics as they practice throwing rubber balls and various weights across the room. One of the girls lifts all of the objects at once and sends them flying into the wall at the far end. She gets dizzy and falls back onto the floor. The other students rush to her as the teacher grabs a bottle of electrolyte water from a cooler near the door.

"This is exactly what I'm talking about, guys," the instructor says. "You have to pace yourself. Know your limits. You will be able to push your abilities, but they grow like a muscle. They have to be properly exercised." She talks with the wisdom of experience but can't be more than year or two older than the girl, at most.

By the time I get back down to the main hall, lunch is being served. Once I've loaded up with food, I look for a place to sit. Everyone already seems to be in deep conversation, so I grab an empty table near the back and sit by myself. I haven't seen Kamea or JB, or even V or Tace for that matter. I wonder if JB has even thought about me since we arrived.

I see the group of telekinetics come down the stairs from the training floor, laughing. The girl who collapsed sees me across the room and waves before getting in line. Once they all have their trays of food, she spots me once again and heads toward my table.

"Hey, newbie. I'm Erica." She takes a seat across from me and smiles as the others take seats around us.

"Isaak." I attempt a smile in return. "You could tell I was new, huh?"

She grins. "Well, most people who've been here a while don't just walk into training sessions and sit with their mouths open in awe. Especially not at a bunch of inexperienced tele-kinetics pushing balls around a room."

The others laugh, and I smile. "Guess I wasn't being very discreet."

"It's okay. I'm the one who should be embarrassed. You saw me almost burn out trying to lift a few pathetic exercise balls."

"It looked pretty impressive to me."

Everyone chuckles.

"Ivan over here," says another girl, sitting across from me next to Erica, "he lifted three SUVs full of Sheriffs and tipped them over an overpass in Indiana before he got here."

I look down the table at a thin guy with tanned skin and jet-black hair. He smiles bashfully and looks down at his food. I get the sense that he isn't proud of what he's done.

"That must've been really difficult," I say.

He picks at the food in front of him but doesn't look up. "Yeah. Everyone always seems to be pretty impressed."

"I mean emotionally. That must've been hard."

He looks up at me and pauses. "Thank you," he says as he gives me a genuine smile.

"This is Brooke, by the way," Erica says, interrupting the moment and gesturing to the girl who spoke before. "That's Ivan, obviously. This is Bryan, Dustin, and Jessica." She points to each person as she introduces them, and we all smile and wave dorkishly at one another. Everyone keeps laughing. Thank God. I needed this.

"So what's your ability, then?" Dustin—a tall boy with sandy-blond hair, asks through a mouthful of chips.

"I don't know yet. I just got tested this morning."

"You got tested and they didn't tell you right then and there?" Brooke asks.

They all look to me in surprise.

"No. They said they needed more time to deliberate. I probably won't find anything out until tomorrow."

"Whoa." Erica looks to the others. "Pretty much everyone knows what he can do the moment he unlinks from them. Mine only took a few seconds. I don't think I even got to introduce myself to anyone beside Malek and Arielle before I was back on the elevator with my training assignment."

"That's the usual story," Dustin says.

"Somebody must be special," the girl at the far end says. Jessica. She has curly black hair and a crooked, mischievous smile.

Everyone makes sarcastic "oohs" like schoolchildren, and I roll my eyes.

"No, it's not like that. It's just"—I look around to the others; these are people who can understand what I've gone through—"confusing."

They all stop laughing and grinning and nod their heads. They get it, and I'm so glad they do.

"Well, freak, you'll be happy to know that you are no longer alone in this world. You have now officially joined the greatest freak show on Earth." Erica's voice gets loud and animated at the end, like a cartoon ringleader at a circus.

Everyone starts laughing again, and I do too.

Dinner is a lonelier affair. After falling asleep on an especially lumpy couch in the rec room, I almost miss it altogether. Most of the hot dishes have been packed up and put away, but I'm still able to get some mashed potatoes and green beans. I grab a few hard-boiled eggs from the market section and call it a meal.

I eat at a table by myself as more and more people flood into the rec room. Training sessions, and whatever else these guys do throughout the day, must all be coming to an end. I clean my plate and put the tray in the rack of dirty dishes, wishing I hadn't taken that nap. Now I'm fully awake and have no idea where to go or what to do with myself.

I make my way up to the dorms and try not to think about what it means that they still haven't called me back down to the basement.

Sometime later I hear a knock at my door. I don't know what time it is, but it feels late. I haven't heard anyone walking around in the hallway outside in at least an hour.

Maybe they're finally bringing me down.

I get up and open the door to find JB on the other side. His face lights up with a smile when he sees me.

"Hey, kid."

I hate it when he calls me that. I also hate how good it feels to hear him say it. He waits for me to say something in response, but I fold my arms across my chest and keep my silence.

"Put your shoes on. I want to show you something," he says finally.

"It's okay. I think I'm in for the night."

"Just trust me."

I pause and look into his eyes. He's giving me the same look he gave me the other night when we watched the sunset from the cliff in New Mexico. I'm not going to fall for this again.

"Isn't Malek going to wonder where you've gone?"

He wets his lips and looks back down the hallway behind him. "First off, they're going to be down there all night. Second"—he looks right at me once again—"things are a little more complicated than they seem."

This doesn't seem like a lie, but I don't know if I've ever gotten anything truthful from him at all. I have nothing to compare it to. Seeing him here though, with his wavy black hair, crystal-blue eyes, broad shoulders leaning against the doorframe, and a smile so perfect it makes me want to punch him, I have no choice but to give in.

"Fine."

Quietly, he takes me down a series of hallways until we get to a dead end. The walls here are paneled in white tiles instead of bare concrete. We pass the last door, and I look at him, confused, as nothing remains besides a fire extinguisher in a glass case. He glances behind us, then looks at me and grins.

He reaches out for the handle on the fire extinguisher's case and pulls. A portion of the wall opens, revealing a dark, closet-like room. He ushers me inside, then closes the heavy door behind us. A single red light illuminates the rungs of a ladder built into the wall. We must be in a service chute of some kind. He smiles at me again in the dim glow and nods for me to go up.

I take a rung and start up without a second thought. It occurs to me that he will have a prime view of my ass, and even after I convince myself that I don't care, I add a subtle flex to my climb here and there, just in case. After almost a minute of climbing in the dark, a second, more ominous thought arrives:

Maybe I shouldn't sneak out of the secret base it took me a week of running from deadly military killers and nearly cost me my life several times to get to?

I think about JB looking at my ass again and continue climbing.

After another minute I see a grate above me. Without waiting for JB's instruction, I push up on the grate and climb up and out of the chute into yet another dimly lit service room. There are pipes all around, and the sound of flowing water fills the room.

JB climbs out after me and leans in to my ear. "Get excited." He steps around me and walks beyond a series of pipes toward a door. He pulls a lever, pushes with his shoulder, and opens it. I follow him over and step through.

It takes me a moment to fully realize that I've just walked out into the open night air. Stars dot the inky sky, and the scent of flowers overwhelms me. I hop up a few concrete steps as my eyes adjust and then turn to fully take in my surroundings.

I'm standing in one of the center rings of a large, recessed, circular garden. Concentric circles of flower-lined pathways surround a large pool or fountain—I can't tell exactly which—with a waterfall and what looks like a small hedge maze decorating the basin.

A hand gently grazes the small of my back from behind.

"Isn't this incredible?" JB's mouth comes dangerously close to my ear as he brushes past me. "Come." He continues down the circular path, and I follow.

We wind around through the flowers until we reach a ramp that crisscrosses the circular pathways. The service room we emerged from must be hidden down on the innermost ring, behind the waterfall.

We go up the ramp and wind back around to the other side, this time on the highest level of the ring garden. Now that we are above it, I can see that we are high up on a hill, with bits of the city visible below us. Several large, blockish white buildings stand tall on the hill behind us.

JB takes a set of stairs near some ornate, flowering topiaries. My shoes echo on the first step and I realize that all of the buildings around us are made out of white marble. Under the light of an exceptionally bright moon, I watch as our shadows creep up the gleaming stone. At the top, we step out onto a long promenade, lined with various pools and fountains and dotted with trees. I've never seen anything like it. He takes me toward one of the pools and over a series of large, square stepping-stones across the water.

We take a right down the promenade between two of the large buildings and take another set of stairs down to a long, thin path of white marble that lead to a patio overlooking a circular cactus garden, and all of Los Angeles.

The view takes my breath away. I've never seen anything like it. An ocean of flickering city lights lies sprawled out over an endless span before me. Stars move through the sky in rows, and I realize that they're not stars, but in fact planes, funneling in and out of the city at a constant stream. Mist rolls up against mountains to our left, and I can make out skyscrapers dotting several different parts of the city. I can't even tell which cluster is downtown.

"Isn't this incredible?"

I don't look back at him. I can't take my eyes off of this view. "Amazing."

A glowing red and white snake of traffic winds next to the hill we're on, but everything around is perfectly silent and still, an island of tranquility in a sea of chaos. We stand silently for several minutes and absorb the sights. I think about my view back in Pacific—how it paled in comparison to this—and take a moment of gratitude. After everything I've gone through in the past week, I feel lucky to be able to see this.

"Come on," JB says, breaking the meditative silence. "There's something else I want to show you."

I tear myself away from the majestic view and follow JB back up the path, through a gate that reads EMERGENCY EXIT ONLY and around the building. We go through another gate that looks like something we shouldn't be messing with, and out onto an access road.

After a ten-minute walk down a steep hill that leaves my calves warm and my forehead sweaty, we come to another large gate. I hear cars zooming by on the other side and realize we must be by the road we saw from the top of the hill. JB looks at a security card kiosk that stands before the gate at the end of the access road and nods.

"If you would, kind sir," he says in an affected British accent.

I bow to him sarcastically and place my hand on the kiosk. A tingling sensation runs up my arm, and a series of prickling signals flow into me. I try to clear my mind and hope that I can figure out what I'm doing before I blow anything up and get us caught. I focus on the gate and what I want it to do, and a small light turns green near the card scanner. The gate begins to open.

"Nice work, kid."

He should be glad I don't have one of the KDPR sticks on me now.

We make it out to the sidewalk outside of the gates, and I look to a sign above us.

THE GETTY CENTER

When I look back to JB, he is tapping on the screen of a phone.

"What are you doing?" Panic begins to rise in my throat, remembering what Azure said about Robots and phones and what happened in Albuquerque after I touched JB's.

"It's okay. I told you to trust me."

I bite my lip and stare at the road in front of us in silence. After a few minutes a small, oddly orbicular car pulls up to us. It looks like a friendly marshmallow with wheels.

JB hands me pair of black leather gloves. "Best if you don't touch anything." I slip them on as he smiles and opens the door for me. "After you, monsieur."

I hesitate for a brief moment and get in.

It's only when JB gets in beside me and closes the door that I realize the car has no driver. I'd heard about the new automated car services before and seen videos, but they were still only available in the bigger cities. There was definitely nothing like this in Pacific, Missouri.

"Have you been in one of these before?"

I shake my head as the dome lights dim and a melodic voice chimes in over the speakers.

"Please fasten your seat belts."

I fumble for mine and click it into place.

"Thank you. Enjoy your ride."

The car glides forward and we are off, into the traffic.

I smell salt in the air as we step out of the car and onto the sidewalk. The sound of crashing waves comes to me over the grass to my right as the car glides silently away.

"This way." JB walks down the sidewalk and I follow. A little farther down, he takes a right at a stoplight and we pass under a large illuminated sign.

SANTA MONICA

YACHT HARBOR

SPORT FISHING—BOATING—CAFÉS

The sidewalk slopes rapidly downward, arching over a busy road, and spills out onto a sprawling wooden pier. Up ahead carnival rides and a massive Ferris wheel light up the night in kaleidoscopic, flickering rainbow lights. It's not as busy as I'd assume a place like this would normally be. The air has a chill that I think must be keeping most of the tourists away tonight. I wish I'd brought a jacket myself.

We take a set of stairs down toward the beach. At the bottom, JB walks ahead of me off of the sidewalk, but I pause to remove the gloves and my shoes. I step, for the first time, into cool, soft sand. Goose bumps race over my skin and I walk out to catch up to JB.

He takes a seat in the sand just before it slopes down toward the ebbing tide, and I sit next to him. Swirling mist brings the moon in and out of vision, but I can still make out the waves. I look out and take in the vast, endless black of the ocean. My eyes close and I inhale deeply.

"Now you don't have to imagine what standing at the edge of the ocean is like anymore."

I open my eyes and look at him. The lights from the buildings behind us illuminate half his face, the other half swathed in dim, misty moonlight. His eyes still sparkle at me, and all of the facade, all of the grinning, all of the endless layers seem to peel away. He feels totally bare before me.

"We're not standing," I say. I can feel myself getting sucked in.

"No. We're not."

He reaches up and gently, firmly takes the back of my neck and leans in to kiss me. Just as his lips are about to connect with mine, I pull away. "What are you doing?"

He drops his hand and looks at me, confused.

"Aren't you with someone? Does he know you're doing this right now?"

He looks back out toward the water and remains silent.

I feel my blood start to boil. I feel like such an idiot. He's with Malek, and it seems serious, from what I've gathered. I can't believe I even followed him out of my room.

What was I thinking?

I stand and start to walk away, but stop and turn back to him.

"You—" I bite my tongue and look back out to the water before I say something I know I'll regret. "You know, you haven't even asked how my testing went, how I'm feeling, if I'm okay—anything."

An exceptionally large wave crashes to thunderous effect.

"I don't know what you're trying to do, but I'm finished."

The water from the wave laps up to the edge of my toes.

"Please call a car."

I turn and trudge through the sand.

I'm halfway down the ladder by the time I hear JB set the metal grate back into place above us. After another minute I see the concrete floor below me in the darkness and drop down the last few feet. I wait for JB to catch up before I turn to go, but he grabs my wrist.

"Please. I—" He stops. I can tell he's not used to being at a loss for words. "I know you think I'm some cheating asshole, but things are . . . complicated with me and Malek." He pauses and waits for me to look up into his eyes. "I care about you, Isaak."

At any other point in my life, hearing someone like him say something like that would've made me blush uncontrollably. Now I take the words for what they are—words—and turn to leave. I push the heavy hidden door open and step out into the white-tiled hallway—

And almost run smack into Malek.

I stumble out as JB calls out after me.

"Isaak—" He follows me out and sees Malek.

Malek's eyes are cold steel, his jaw clenched.

The door closes on its own behind JB and seals shut.

We stand there, the three of us, in a moment of crushing, endless silence. I'm humiliated, embarrassed, and know that nothing I could ever say to Malek will convince him that nothing actually happened while we were out.

I am so fucking dumb.

"You guys have a good time?" he asks. I can see the breath rising in his chest.

JB squeezes the bridge of his nose between his fingers before he speaks. "Malek, it wasn't like—"

"Do you even know what he is? What his presence here means for all of us?" Malek's eyes cut into JB like daggers. He doesn't even spare me a glance.

"What are you talking about?" JB looks genuinely confused. Malek shakes his head and finally looks at me. His eyes are cold, emotionless.

"Get to your room and stay there. Any other little trips like this will result in you being placed in secure confinement. Is that clear?"

Confusion, frustration, and anger churn inside me. I am not a child and refuse to be treated like one. But before I can say anything rash, I nod to Malek and brush past them both. I refuse to look back as I walk down the hallway. I feel tears welling up in my eyes, but they're not tears of sadness. I'm so fucking sick and tired of everyone talking around me in riddles, speaking about me in codes and neglecting to clue me in. I am trapped, quite literally, in a secret bunker, under a museum, in a mountain, and every step I take toward learning something about myself only leads me deeper under the mountain that's building in my head. I refuse to let these people make me cry. I've felt what I can do. I *know* what I can do. I am free and can do whatever the fuck I want. I dare any of these assholes to try to stop me.

I feel a wave of energy surge through me, and my fingertips crackle with electricity. A thousand voices swell up in my head all at once for a single, brief moment as I step out into the balcony area above the main hall. Every light dims as power prickles on every inch of my skin. I feel bodies, minds, sources of life inside of me, everything and everyone, all at once. A million memories that aren't mine, just beyond my grasp—

I release my breath and the sensation disappears. The lights come back to full strength and everything around me swirls. I'm so dizzy.

What was that?

I stumble past the elevators and head down the hallway that leads to my room. I need sleep. Whatever is happening to me feels out of my control. Everything does. The only thing I can even think to do right now is sleep and hope that everything is better in the morning.

I make it to the small, dead-end hallway and find Kamea waiting outside my door.

"Isaak." Her eyes are filled with something I've never seen before. I can't tell if it's excitement, fear, or both.

"I have to show you something."

I don't think I'm going to get to sleep yet after all.

The elevator doors open to the basement. The long, rectangular table where the Assembly sat earlier today is empty. Kamea heads to a door on the left. Her fingers deftly spin the dial on a large combination lock built into the door until a loud *click* echoes through the room. She pushes the door aside and reveals a hallway lined with the same embedded orange lights as always. The door seals shut behind us, and we continue down the dim passage, passing several rooms until we make it to yet another set of double doors. She types a code into a keypad in the wall, and the doors slide back. The room beyond is pitch-black as we step inside.

Lights flicker to life as the door closes and Kamea steps into the center of the room. The echo of her footsteps reveal the size of this place before the lights are able to. It's huge, like an underground cathedral. The ceiling might go up higher than in the main hall, even though it isn't as large in circumference. Boards of electrical equipment, endless wires, and large generators hum as they come to life against the walls. In the center, right behind Kamea, is a large metallic pod.

I stare in awe and take everything in.

"Only a few people in the Underground know this place exists."

I stand next to her and marvel at the large steel egg before us. About twelve feet tall, it gleams and flickers as it reflects the light from various machines powering on around it.

My mind races at its purpose—*superweapon, vehicle, some form of alien spacecraft?*

"What is it?"

Kamea looks at me. "This, Isaak, is a Gate. A machine that will allow Robots to teleport." She looks back toward the egg and sighs. "Eventually."

My mind spins. I shouldn't be shocked by all of this by

now, but somehow I can't believe what I'm seeing.

"How does it work?" I approach the pod with my hand reaching out toward its smooth surface.

Kamea grabs me before I can touch it. "I think you might be able to help me figure that out." She walks over to one of the panels near the wall and flips several switches before sitting in a chair in front of a large set of adjacent monitors.

"I have been working on this project with the Underground for several years now. There's an entire team of people here devoted to projects like this, but this one . . . this is definitely the big one." She spins in her chair to press several more buttons on a panel to her right. A loud humming noise builds from the generator units on the other side of the room as the machine begins to come to life.

"Robots here designed this?" I ask.

She spins in her chair to look at me. "We don't know who created it."

Confusion spreads across my face.

"The plans were obtained during one of our most dangerous espionage missions," she says.

"Obtained? From whom?"

She takes a pause and looks at me. "From the SHRF."

My mind spins faster, but before I can respond, she turns back to the panel and continues. "I don't get to spend much time here with the equipment itself because I've been trying to crack a very big problem. One that requires me to spend most of my time in the field."

She types a sequence into the keyboard, and a large hatch opens on the metal pod, revealing a small obelisk inside. "The team here has everything figured out—except for one crucial element."

She turns in the chair to face me again. "Because of the synthetic nature of your body's cells, you can essentially be dismantled and rebuilt, exactly as you are, without losing a single molecule or memory. The Gates are able to dismantle and record the very makeup of your body and mind, transport the data instantaneously, and reassemble you from the blueprint at a new location, anywhere in the world. From what we've been able to learn, a Gate requires the energy of multiple Robots to activate and control it, and we can only send through one of you at a time. But so far, attempting a transfer while multiple Robots are connected has resulted in splicing, death, and even . . ." Her breath catches. "There was an instance in which a Robot's data completely disappeared. We never recovered it."

The room suddenly feels very small as I realize Kamea might be expecting me to go inside this death trap.

"Isaak, I'm telling you this because I need your help. The Assembly deliberated tonight after finally determining the nature of your abilities, and I don't know how else to say this— you are nothing short of a miracle."

I open my mouth to speak, but she stops me. "I can't say anything more than that right now, and I'm sorry. I know how frustrated you must be, how difficult this journey has been for you, but I promise you that I am doing every single thing I can to help you. No one wants to see you find peace and happiness more than me. I swear it."

Her eyes bear into mine. Passion and truth and something that looks a little bit like hope fill them, pouring up from the center of her being.

I take a deep breath. "What do you need me to do?"

I'm already awake and ready to go by the time I hear the knock on my door. I don't know what time it was when I finally got to bed, but I wasn't able to sleep. Not restfully at least. Not with this moment looming just a few hours ahead of me. And now here it is. I close the journal that I still haven't written in, set it on the nightstand, and go to the door to open it.

Instead of Kyle waiting for me on the other side, I find Malek.

"Are you ready?"

My mouth goes dry. If anyone could've helped buffer the weight of this long walk to the Assembly, it would've been Kyle. But here I am, with a guy who probably genuinely hates me. *Great.*

I nod, step out into the hallway, and let him lead the way.

We walk in an awkward silence to the elevator, and I count down the moments until the doors finally open. Once they do, an even heavier silent anxiety presses down on me.

All of the members of the Assembly stand behind the table at the other end of the room, waiting for me. Azure and V have joined them—Azure behind the table next to

Aleister and his dogs, V behind Arielle. They all go silent as I approach.

I sit in a chair that's been set in front of the table and notice Kyle in his same position as yesterday, off to the side, able to observe everyone. Malek nods to Azure and V as he takes his place in the center. They come around to the front of the table and stand in front of me. Azure looks into my eyes.

"When two Robots touch," she begins, "they can link." She reaches out and grabs V by the hand. "When Robots link, they become, temporarily, a symbiotic unit. Their instincts, senses, reactions, and abilities are shared. Some have claimed to have shared thoughts and emotions as well, but this is rare. I have yet to experience such things personally."

I swallow as V lifts her hand.

Azure continues. "With proper training, this connection allows us to increase our power exponentially."

V flicks her wrist and a yellow, concave shield of electrical light flicks into existence beside her.

"Sever the physical tie however"—she pulls her hand from V's and the shield disappears—"and the power is gone."

Her eyes lock with mine once again.

"When you created the shield in the desert, I was skeptical that you were actually revealing shielding abilities. It was too great, too sudden."

I feel every eye in the room bearing into me, and the sudden desire to shrink overwhelms me.

"V has an incredibly unique ability. In fact, she's the only Robot we've ever heard of with such a power."

She nods to V, who continues.

"I am able to store, metabolize, convert, and manipulate kinetic energy."

My mind is puzzled, and I wait for her to elaborate. She furrows her brow as she tries to work out the best way to explain it.

"Any physical energy exerted against me charges my body like a battery. I can then use the charge to achieve incredible feats of strength and to create powerful concussive blasts."

Something tells me that for her tough exterior and eagerness to intimidate, there is a genuine nerd inside V. It makes me wish I'd spent more time getting to know her on our journey together.

She turns to face Azure and nods, drops her arms to her sides, and broadens her chest. She closes her eyes as Azure pulls her fist back for the punch.

A lesser woman would've flown across the room and into the concrete wall at the impact of Azure's fist, but V only teeters slightly on her feet. She regains her balance and opens her eyes—they glow with a bright yellow light. She raises her fist, and it's as though she's holding rays of it inside her hand. The feeling of unbridled, rage-fueled death streaming from my fingertips on the bridge outside of Vegas comes back to me as I watch her.

Azure makes a soothing shush noise and raises her hands in surrender.

V seethes and teeters on the edge of losing control for a

moment before regaining her composure. I think the light has the same effect on her as it did with me.

She takes a few deep breaths and the light slowly begins to fade away. She shakes it off like a boxer shaking off a good punch, then goes back to her seat. Azure sits down as well.

"Isaak," the girl with the nose ring says from the far right side of the table. "I want you create fire in your hand."

A puzzled expression spreads involuntarily over my face.

I can't.

"Hold out your hand," she says. I lift my right hand, palm facing upward. "Now look into my eyes and imagine every molecule of oxygen around you flowing into the space above your palm. Feel them glide toward you—every last atom. Now ignite them with heat—heat from your surroundings, from yourself, your emotions. Spark them into flames as they gravitate toward you. You are bringing them to life. They have come to serve you. Let them live."

I stare into her deep brown eyes and try to follow her guidance. As she speaks, I remember the feeling of catching fireflies in the summer back in Missouri. Running through the grass and the trees with a mason jar, filling it, one by one, with the little, glowing insects. Marveling at my bioluminescent lantern in the dusk before letting them go. I can't make fire though. I don't know how. I don't know what I did in the desert with Azure's shield, or what happened on the bridge, but it was nothing like this. I didn't have to pretend anything, or imagine I had some power inside of me. It was defensive. I did what I had to do to protect my friends and myself. I still don't even know how I did all of that.

A small gasp from Arielle breaks my train of thought and I look down at my hand. Tiny embers of light are flowing into the air above my hand from all directions, forming a glowing orb in my palm. I don't know how I'm doing this. I can't be. This doesn't feel like me.

"Isaak," the girl says, getting me to look back up at her. "Let them live."

I let go and imagine myself pushing life into the cluster of glowing dots. A tower of flame shoots up toward the ceiling from my hand, and I stumble back. Everyone at the table lurches back at the heat, but the girl gets up and moves toward me. Her eyes glow with a deep, bronzed orange, and points of light collect in her hands as well.

"Calm yourself," she says. "The flames can't hurt you while you're wielding them, but they can hurt the others. You must control it."

The blazing inferno above me doesn't feel like something that can be controlled.

How am I doing this?

"Fire is a beast. The beast. But you can tame her, Isaak. She bends to your will and obeys your every command. You must only refuse to fear her."

I realize that the fire has yet to burn me and let her words sink in. I stand a little taller and try to bend the direction of the flame. It curves at my slightest thought, and my mouth drops in wonder.

"Radha," Malek says. "This is not a training session in pyrokinesis."

She keeps her glowing eyes on me and nods. "Now imagine all of the molecules you summoned, every particle of energy in your hand, finding peace, serenity. Let a sense of completion flow through your arm and up into your fingertips. Let them rest."

I think of myself as a child, finally taking the lid off of the mason jar, watching as the fireflies slowly began to fly back out into the night sky, free.

The flame goes out and the energy disperses. The room looks cold and sterile now, no longer bathed in the red and orange light of fire.

The girl, Radha, turns to Malek and nods before taking her seat back at the end of the table.

Every eye in the room takes me in like a sideshow attraction—an anomaly, something they can't yet figure out, a mystery that terrifies them.

Malek looks to Arielle. She bites her lip and then looks at me.

"Isaak, we believe you are a conduit," she says. "A Robot with the ability to connect to other Robots . . . without ever touching them."

The silence in the room is asphyxiating.

"The implications of your ability are unparalleled," she continues. "No one in this room ever expected to find anyone like you. I don't think any of us even imagined that a Robot could be created with such a power."

I look to Azure for some sort of reassurance, but she's staring at Kyle over by the wall.

"Your discovery has left us in a place where no one at this table is used to being—a state of confusion," Malek says, drawing my attention back to him. "We've always known who our enemies are and what they wish to achieve. Although we have very different ideals as to how to confront them, we have always known our direction forward. Your presence changes all of that."

My mouth feels like sandpaper. I try to swallow, but it's like I've forgotten how.

"A being like you could save or destroy us," Aleister says, glaring at me over his sharp nose and cheekbones. "Your abilities could lend us unimaginable power as a fighting force, but at what cost? Someone like you could also leave us vulnerable in ways we've never imagined. If you are able to connect to each of us without physical contact, who's to prevent one of our enemies from capturing you and using this ability against us? How are we to know you aren't a pet project of Asim himself, sent to collect soldiers for his private army?" He takes a pause and lets his uncomfortable gaze bear into me. "You are a domino standing at the head of an elaborate setup none of us were even aware existed until you arrived. All it takes is one push, and every single one of us will fall."

I don't think I will ever feel my heartbeat again. My entire body feels numb.

"The Assembly has much to discuss regarding your role in our society in the coming days," Arielle says, in a gentler tone than Aleister's, "but I think I can safely speak for all of us when I say that we are very lucky and very thankful that you made it to us safely."

Everyone begins to shuffle in their seats, but their eyes remain silently on me.

"You can go now, Isaak," Malek says, before turning to speak to Azure.

I stand from the chair with weak knees as I try to catch Azure's eye.

She spares me a glance, but turns to speak to Malek instead.

I pivot and head back to the elevator as their hushed voices begin to rise in conversation behind me. By the time the doors close they might as well be shouting my name as though I can't hear them.

It feels like I've been thrown off a boat to see how well I can swim and came back up to the surface to find the boat speeding away from me, off toward the horizon.

I stare at the shiny steel of the elevator doors and pray I don't drown.

"Tribo."

It's all I hear as I sit at the table by myself, dazed, staring at a breakfast I know I'm not going to eat. The word buzzes around my head like a fly—tickling my ears, annoying me out of my state of deep, anxious concentration.

What the hell is Tribo?

Erica, the telekinetic, sits down with her tray and tries to break my stare. "Hey! What's wrong with you? You okay?"

The rest of her crew follows and sits at the table, just like yesterday.

"He must be nervous," Brooke says, next to her.

The boy with the sandy hair, Dustin, speaks up near the end of the table. "Wait, is this your first Tribo?"

"I don't even know that is."

All of their jaws collectively drop, and Erica swallows her food in order to speak again. "Oh my God. Are you serious?"

"I only got here the day before yesterday. No one tells me anything."

The others all look to one another.

"When did you manifest?" Erica asks.

"A week ago. Week and a half. I can't really remember right now, to be honest."

A sly smile spreads across her face.

"He hasn't felt it yet," Brooke says.

"Felt what?"

"Robots are composed of electrically charged synthetic cells, right?" Erica says, jumping in over Brooke. "Well, about every two to three months, a buildup of excess energy causes us to get . . . aggressive. If we don't exert the energy—expend it completely—it can cause serious problems."

"Think of it like a static shock, but on a much larger scale," Brooke says. "Everything in the universe maintains a balance of protons and electrons. When a human body stores more of one than the other, the balance gets thrown off. Then, when they touch something holding an opposite charge, they get shocked—a physical reaction to the electrical charge rapidly balancing itself out. It's called the Triboelectric Effect. Electricity generated from contact."

"It's much more complicated than that, obviously," Erica says, chiming in over Brooke once again, "but basically what it means is that—"

"We need to touch," Ivan, the quiet boy with the black hair and olive skin, says from the end of the table. Everyone makes a surprised smile at his unexpected interruption. Brooke and Erica shrug and nod in agreement.

I look at them for further explanation.

"It's like a big mosh pit—dancing, for the most part," Jessica says. "Some of the super-aggro ones like to fight—"

"And others like to do *other* things," Brooke says with a grin.

Erica raises her eyebrows exaggeratedly and takes a bite of the blueberry bagel she's been holding the entire conversation.

"So it's just a dance?"

Erica swallows her bite. "It's a lot more than that. If we don't engage in vigorous physical contact with humans or other Robots—in one way or another—our bodies start to malfunction and our minds go . . . crazy."

Yet another piece of the puzzle my own body has become falls into place.

"Don't look so terrified," Erica says. "It's fun." She leans over the table with a sarcastic grin and whispers loud enough for everyone to hear, "You might even get laid."

I look down to the plate of food in front of me as everyone laughs. I'm definitely not eating it now.

Everything they said to me in the basement echoes around in my head for hours as I hide away and wait for Tribo to start—and end—without me. I'm not going down there. Dancing with and touching other Robots is the very last thing I want to do tonight. My touch leads to nightmares—visions that no one understands. That I myself don't understand. I lie on the bed in my room and stare at the ceiling while their words play over and over again.

The Assembly has much to discuss regarding your role in our society in the coming days. . . .

My role in this society, chosen for me. No choices. No options. No true friends.

Azure: She's more machine than human.

Kamea: She could've been a real friend, but after what happened last night with the Gate, how will she treat me?

JB: I don't even want to think about him right now.

The tiny room suddenly feels less like a sanctuary and more like a prison cell.

How do I have so little control over my own life?

No.

I do have control. I only need to let go of my fear and assert it.

I get up off the bed and head out into the hallway barefoot. This is my life. I will not be afraid. I will do whatever I want, be whomever I choose, and not give a damn about what anyone else has to say about it.

Bass pulses and thumps in the walls as I make my way closer to the main lobby. When I finally leave the hall and step out onto the landing in front of the elevators, I finally hear it. Music blasts from the main hall below, muddling the sound of hundreds of voices, massed together in the midst of it. I take the stairs and descend, step by step, into the fray.

I reach the very bottom and step out onto the floor. The room is lit only by the glow of orange service lights, but I can make out everything, and everyone, perfectly clearly. The entire hall is a writhing mass of bodies—dancing, jumping, bouncing wildly to the music. A circle is formed off to my right near the rec room where people are fighting. I hear the small crowd cheer over the song as a small girl with bright red hair lands a gruesome kick to the throat of a tall guy with long, wild dreadlocks. The guy recovers from the impact, dodges another blow by bending into an impossible backflip, and finally lands a roundhouse kick so powerfully into the girl's face that I can see her nose crack from where I stand near the stairs. The crowd gasps as the girl goes still. She looks back to the guy, grasps her bloody, crooked nose between her fingers, snaps it back into place, and gives a wide, scarlet grin. The crowd erupts with cheers.

My eyes drift back toward the dancing as I breathe in the crackling, electric energy in the air. Everyone appears to be shirtless—guys, girls, all of them. I guess the whole point is to establish body contact.

I take a deep breath, peel off my shirt, and toss it to the side.

A group of Robots I've yet to meet beckons me over toward a cluster they've formed near the elevator to my right. I take another breath and walk over.

Moving through this crowd is like nothing else I've ever experienced. My exposed skin begins to prickle at the energy emanating from the bodies around me. Everyone here is so beautiful, so full of exuberance and life. The fear tries to sneak back in as I wonder if I will ever fit in. Not only here, but any-where. If I will ever find anyone who knows me and accepts me. If I will ever find someone who loves me.

No more fear.

I can choose to let this be exhilarating, liberating, or I can allow it to make me feel terrified and ashamed. I'm done with having my choices made for me.

I choose liberation.

I walk right into the center of the group and begin dancing. A hand slides onto the small of my back as another rests on my shoulder. A guy and a girl take turns dancing with me, touch-ing me, and I let them. Flickers of memories—other people's memories—crest up in my mind, but I force them away. I am in control now. I am in this moment, and I will connect with these people on my own terms.

The chorus of the song kicks in and everyone throws their hands toward the sky. In the orange glow, it reminds me of the fresco in Richard's hotel—humans, reaching toward heaven, reaching to God.

Human.

That word. I think it will haunt me for the rest of my life.

"My boy, you are anything but a mere human."

Richard's words resound in my head, and I laugh at the memory of his ridiculous teeth.

My eyes come back down to look around me, and I smile. For the first time in weeks, my adrenaline is pumping over something that has nothing to do with my imminent death.

I close my eyes and bounce to the music as I move away from the group. The air is thick and steamy with sweat and an intangible electric pulse. I feel primal, like a beast. I inhale the animal scent and open my eyes.

JB, Malek, and a group of guys are together, just a few feet in front of me. JB stands, leaning back into Malek's arms while the other guys dance around them. JB and Malek's bodies are both magnificent—JB, a marble statue, and Malek, an ebony god. Their muscles glisten with perspiration as they flex and grind into each other. The other guys with them are just as tall and broad and defined.

I avert my eyes and try to pass by as though I don't see them, but one of the other guys pulls me over. He's dark and lean, with a thick layer of scruff on his face and deeply intense, dark brown eyes. At any other time I would've died to have a guy who looked like him grab me and dance with me like this, but all I can see is JB behind him.

JB's eyes catch mine and I go numb inside. A cold wave of paralysis washes over me, fighting away the heat and electricity in a single glance. I don't know what to say or do.

The guy holding my waist sees what I'm looking at and turns aside, grinning, as Malek looks back over his shoulder. His eyes land on me.

I brace myself for a punch, or a verbal assault, or some other form of well-deserved aggression, but it never comes. Instead, something else entirely blossoms in his eyes. I can't tell if it's acceptance, sadness, curiosity, arousal, or an inexplicable mix of it all, but before I can take another moment to think, he grabs my hand.

In a single fluid motion, Malek guides me toward him. The paralysis clamps down on my neck. I have no idea what's happening. The music is drowned out completely by the blood rushing in my head as Malek looks to JB, then back to me, and for the first time, he actually smiles at me. Before I can register what's happening, he leans in and begins to kiss me.

And not just any kiss—a deep, hungry, passionate kiss that sends fire through my veins and sucks the air from my lungs. His lips press into mine further, and then I feel it—the desperation of someone losing the one he loves. This isn't an act of passion, or even a cheap thrill—this is him throwing a life jacket out to something he cannot bear to let drown. The fire in my lips shifts to gentleness before I pull away.

He looks to JB expectantly, shrouding his pain in a mask of lust and appeasement, and pushes me toward him. I don't know what to do. I can't deny my desire for JB, but something in my brief moment with Malek is telling me to step aside and let whatever is running its course here play out before I act upon it. I open my mouth to speak over the music—

But JB kisses me instead.

This kiss is nothing like the one I just shared with Malek. No hunger, no desperation, just release. A dam bursting under the pressure of a burden it can no longer bear. It feels unfair at how perfect, how *right*, it is.

Flashes of another kind fill my head: a guy who doesn't look like me, but *feels* like me, holding JB's hand, kissing him, drying his tears after his family abandoned him, making him feel like he was worth more than the shame and loathing he felt inside. JB looked at this boy and discovered *hope*. A hope he thought he'd never feel again, until—

Malek grabs me from behind as I pull away from JB, reeling in my head over what just happened. Those weren't like the other visions. They were muddy, foggy, and felt more like feelings than images. Shells of emotion and fossilized dreams. But JB is a human, not a Robot. I shouldn't feel anything like that when I touch him.

Before I can process it further, Malek turns me toward him

and begins to dance with me once again. We lock eyes and begin to laugh. I can still feel his denial and his pain, but I can also feel his need to forget about all of it in this moment. Everything about this is ridiculous, but if I've learned anything over the past week, it's that life is short, bizarre, rarely takes you where you want to go, and hardly ever gives you the answers you think you deserve. Every single person in the room around me has been told he doesn't have the right to live, that he isn't human.

That word again.

I look to everyone around me, dancing wildly, shedding their pain, releasing their need to define themselves, and simply celebrating life.

Human.

This. *This* is humanity. This is acceptance and love and hope and everything I've been searching for my whole entire life. This is family.

I reach out and hold on to Malek's hand as a new song begins. I close my eyes and lose myself in it as energy ripples and crackles over my skin. My body feels connected to every single being around me. A spider, in the center of a web, acutely aware of every vibration sent down every string around her. This same energy has taken control of me several times before, but not now, not ever again. I test the boundaries of the energetic connection while my body is intertwined between Malek and JB. I push my consciousness into everyone around me and allow them all into me in return. I feel a glowing thread of light blooming between us all, even ones not here in the main hall. Several Robots are up in their rooms, on the dormitory floor. I push out farther still and feel others—others outside of this building, out on the streets, in different cities, different states. Visions flash of others even farther still—countries, lands, and peoples I've never seen, I now see for myself through their eyes. I feel their feelings, know their experiences. All I have to do is reach out and touch them. I can speak through them, control them, *be* them.

Right on the precipice, I open my eyes and take in the room around me—tendrils of electric energy pulsate from everybody. Radiant beams of light pour from their eyes. My eyes. Our eyes.

The energy builds to the breaking point. Pleasure, pain, ecstasy, sorrow, every shade of every color of the entire spectrum of the human experience boils toward an explosion—an explosion so big, so powerful, it could shake the very foundation of the Earth.

Human.

My body braces itself. It's almost here. The light swells and everything is about to burst—

Then the whizzing sound of Taserifle shots ring out above the music and someone starts to scream.

THE CREATOR

I am so sorry.

He held his daughter's tiny hand as she slept. A golden halo encircled her head as it rested against the window and light streamed in. She wouldn't let him close the shutter, not even to sleep. She'd never been on a plane before and was so excited. She'd never seen the ocean either, but that would change once they got to the island. She would see plenty of it at her new home.

Her new home.

He let his thumb trace the back of her hand. It was soft, fleshy, cherubic. He tried to burn as much of it as he could manage into his memory. A permanent image of his baby before he lost her to yet another cruel twist of fate that life had presented him with.

She was the only thing that mattered. His everything. The last little bit of his heart that existed in this world. He closed his eyes, leaned back, and remembered her mother.

He could still smell the air in the room from the first time he saw her—books, paper, the chlorinated lemon of the freshly mopped tile surrounding the professor's desk. Everything felt foreign and terrifying. The weight of a path he didn't choose for himself pressed down so heavily he couldn't breathe. Just as he got up to run from the lecture room, she came in. He took one look at her and sat back down.

Her long black hair fell down around her shoulders in waves—wild and perfectly untamed. Her skin was the color of roasted caramel, and her smile radiated like the sun. She looked like the ocean. From that moment on, she was both the ebb and flow of his entire world.

"I'm Mili."

She held out her hand after handing him the last of his books. He'd forced his way through the crowd of students after their third lecture together and had finally decided that it was going to be the day. He would finally introduce himself.

He'd tripped on the first stair and practically threw his books at the back of her ankles in the process.

She stopped and leaned down and picked them up for him as he stood and forced himself not to run and hide in horror. He took his books back and tried not to stare as the sun crept out from behind her smile and filled him with her warm, glowing light.

He told her things he'd never told anyone before, lying with his head in her lap on the lumpy old brown leather couch that he always apologized for but she loved and forbade him from getting rid of. The thick, white layers of Boston snow piled up and silenced the outside world as he told her of his childhood. About the little store his parents owned back home. How he was forbidden from having friends, from participating in things that made him happy, in order to focus all of his energy on his studies. They scraped together everything they could, toiled endlessly until they were nothing more than husks of people who once had the will to live for themselves, all to give him a life he never would've been able to have, a life they never would've been able to give him back in India.

The guilt kept him in line, kept him obedient, but now here he was, getting a graduate degree that he had no interest in. He resented his parents, yet strove to make them proud. He felt broken and his life, wasted. He wasn't even twenty-five.

She brushed his hair from his forehead and talked about other ways to look at things. Showed him different perspectives he never would've thought to take. Life seemed easier when he was with her. The world was finally a place he actually wanted to be. He'd found love.

They married while they were still in school. Their families met—a union of two peoples hailing from opposite ends of the globe. He could still close his eyes and remember the sand under his toes and the way she glowed—dressed in white—in the pink and orange and purple brilliance of the sunset. They said their vows, and in that moment, nothing had ever felt more sacred.

The day she came home with the news almost destroyed him. Little did he know back then how much the future held in store for him, and what life crumbling away from under him truly felt like. But that day was his first glimpse. He still woke up in the middle of the night, drenched in sweat, reliving it.

They were at the town house in Boston. He had a rare day off and was taking the opportunity to read a book by the kitchen window. The sky was gray and the air was getting its first salty chill of autumn. He had to shake himself from a daze and look back to the page—he'd been distracted by the simple gold wedding band on his finger and lost himself in thought, as he often did.

He heard the front door open and close softly and looked up, waiting for her to enter. She finally came into the living room and hung her coat up in the closet. Her eyes were down-turned and she avoided making eye contact.

"Mili? Are you okay?"

She sat down and held his hand and told him she'd just come from the doctor. That something had been wrong for weeks now, but that she wanted to get it checked before she said anything. She hadn't wanted to alarm him. Her hand trembled and tears filled her eyes.

"Leukemia."

The word shot through his heart like a barbed bullet, tearing every fiber, every ounce of flesh right out from his chest along with it. They held each other and cried for a time, but it felt like she was consoling him more than he was consoling her. She was always so strong. So much stronger than he was, or ever could hope to be.

She was hairless on the night of her remission party. Her oncologist had confirmed it only that afternoon, and although she could barely stand, and left the room to vomit at alarming intervals, she had insisted on throwing a party. He wasn't going to stop her. No one could. Throughout the chemo and radiation, her spirit had soared more than he ever could have imagined. Her resilience and determination were a marvel to him, and even with a bald head and a face almost unrecognizably puffy from the chemicals coursing through her, she was more beautiful than anything he could have dreamed.

It was hard to remember exactly when he'd started the project. His focus in molecular biology leant itself perfectly to the kind of research he now knew he would devote his life to. He was going to cure cancer. He would achieve the unachievable, the highest goal known to man. He would change the world, if only for her.

He was deep into his research and she had just gone back to work when they received the next bit of news that would change both of their lives forever: She was pregnant. They didn't think it was even possible. The oncologists had warned her that the full-body radiation treatments had a very high chance of rendering her sterile, but he insisted she press on. She didn't want to, at first. The notion of sacrificing her ability to create life in order to preserve her own threw her into a storm of emotional turmoil that even her diagnosis hadn't brought upon her. He didn't know what to do. It was her body. Her choice. He could only encourage her to do what would help *her* the most though, as selfish as it may have been. After all, she couldn't be a mother if she wasn't alive to bear a child in the first place. Those were the words that finally convinced her.

But now, there she sat, in the very same living room in which she'd shared with him her death sentence those few years ago, sharing with him her news of *life*.

This time, it was he who consoled her, for the first, and possibly the last time, as she openly wept. For all of their hardships, these tears of joy truly felt like treasures.

The baby was only four months old when she relapsed.

"Leukemia."

The word reared its ugly head once more in their lives. A demon, once thought to be exorcised, rose from hell and clung to both of their backs with reinvigorated determination.

"Mililani, my sweet Mililani." Her mother cried and held her when he walked in that night. He'd been at his lab. He was always at his lab. It was the only place he felt as though he could do anything to help. Sitting there, in that cursed town house with his mother-in-law, his dying wife, and a crying baby whose presence merely pressed upon him the utter urgency of his work, only drove it home further that he was needed elsewhere. He was barely around this time. This time felt so different, and it terrified him. The zest, the vigor, the sheer determination of will with which she faced cancer the first time had faded, and something horrifying had taken their place—acceptance, and a quiet, gentle admission of defeat.

He held her hand in the hospital, when things had truly

taken a turn for the worse. There was barely any life left within her veins. He thought of her wild hair, her bronzed skin, and her smile. The woman on the bed next to him had been hollowed out by this world, like his parents were before her. Everything that mattered, every reason for living, lay next to him, dying.

He handed her the baby for the last time and lifted her arms so that she could bear the weight. She leaned in and tried to sniff the scent from the baby's shock of black hair. Her little ocean spirit, brought to life from a body that could no longer hold life of its own. She kissed the baby's head and squeezed his hand with what little force she could muster.

"Be strong, my love. For her."

With that, the very last breath that she would ever breathe flowed from her lungs like a somber harbor breeze, gusting out to sea, never to return.

The next year was a blur. Memories were out of place, if they existed at all. Great spans of darkness lingered in places where major events in the timeline of his life should've stood out like beacons.

Grief has a way of clouding even the brightest sun.

It was during this time he met Evelyn. To this day he couldn't fully recall the exact details of their first encounter, or precisely how it came to be that she had his number and had called to talk about his intriguing advances in molecular biology. But she had called him, and they had met. Before long they had combined his research with her experience in nanorobotic technology and begun to forge a new path altogether, as a team. There were eight of them in total, including himself, cramped in a lab that felt tiny at the time, working tirelessly toward a cure.

They believed they had found it. After decades, if not centuries, of futile human toil against the imperishable beast that is cancer, he and Evelyn stood on the edge of cracking the code.

But they needed more money.

As they sought funding, an unexpected ally came to their aid—the United States government. He should've shut it all down, right then and there. Torched the lab, went home to his daughter, and never looked back. But that's not what happened.

Their project was to be absorbed by a classified, technically nonexistent branch of the military. This itself should've been the first indication that the deal was not one that would work in his favor and would eventually sour the fruit of his labor he'd been cultivating for years. They didn't see it that way, the others. They had funding. A bankroll that was essentially unlimited. They signed it all away and moved to Virginia.

Their progress showed no signs of slowing. Their advancements came at a rapid pace. They leaped far beyond what anyone could've dreamed of accomplishing with the human cell just a few years prior, in only a few short months. The signs began to arrive, but he chose to ignore them. At least initially.

"So these cells are impervious to disease?"

"With this sort of regenerative ability, could they be programmed to repair physical injuries?"

"Even lost limbs?"

Inquiries to the nature of the synthetic cells they were creating quickly shifted to suggestions, and soon became commands.

His protests were drowned out by reprimands, and any progress he could've slowed as a detractor was steamrolled by the dozens of new team members, all striving to earn favor from their bosses. Yearning for glory.

What began as a quest to preserve life had quickly devolved into a mission to create the ultimate death, and they had succeeded.

Glances shared with Evelyn turned into whispers. It was shortly after the first baby was born that they decided to meet in the middle of the night, in the park. They'd left their phones at home and watched for anyone who might have been following them. They were too deep into the biggest top-secret military project in the history of mankind to take any chances. They couldn't risk drawing attention to themselves, not when so much was at stake.

"What do we do?" he whispered, looking back over his shoulder, through the trees.

"End it. Before we end the world."

"How?"

"I've already started."

From that night on, a secret alliance was formed. Other members of the original team were brought on, people who could be trusted. Her plan was extreme—as precarious as setting the fuse on the first atomic bomb while it was still in the lab—but it was the only way out he could see at this point.

Under the guise of an office video game club, they met every Saturday night. "8-Bit Heart" became the name of the eight-person crew who worked together in secret to prevent the apocalypse they'd been striving toward. They even went so far as to make T-shirts, emblazoned with a small, red 8-bit video game heart as their insignia, which they would wear every Friday to work. A middle finger to General Ander, right under his nose.

She assured him the program wouldn't kill them. It would allow them to live life as normal humans, assimilate with society. All they needed to do was follow her instructions exactly. And so they did.

For months they each took turns enjoying what appeared to be a much-needed leave of absence. This was the team that had been on since the beginning. They had all earned a few weeks off.

His heart still raced when he remembered breaking into the first blood bank. He'd never done anything like it in his life. If he was caught, he would be branded a terrorist and sentenced to a life of torture in a tiny, top-secret prison the American people had never heard of, in a corner of the world no one knew existed, never to be seen again. Never to see his daughter again.

His leave was yet another link in a long chain of weeks

spent away from her. She was the source of everything for him—his love, his reason for living, his sole reason for even attempting to make this plan work. To ensure she had a world to grow up in. It killed him that she was being raised by Mili's mother.

He didn't realize at first that when she had the heart attack and died, she'd actually saved both of their lives that day. He'd had only a few days left of his leave, so everything had to be done quickly. Arrangements had been made at the hospital to get her body back to Hawaii that night, and tickets were booked for him and his daughter for that afternoon. As he buckled her in her window seat and waited for their connection in Los Angeles to take off, his phone vibrated.

New message—Samus

He unlocked it and read the text.

Luigi has forfeited to Bowser. Game over.

His thumbs slid across the keyboard, but he didn't respond. He pulled the battery from the device and slipped both into the fabric pouch on the seat in front of him. There was no going back now. With any luck, he would have a small window of time during which he could evade arrest once they landed, but even the chances of that were slim. They'd all decided to keep an emergency kit on them at all times in case they needed to disappear quickly and quietly, and he had it on him now—a passport with another name, a bank card for anonymous accounts in the Cayman Islands and Switzerland, and twenty thousand dollars in cash. He never thought he would see the day when he actually had to use them, but now here he was, on a flight to the most remote island on Earth—an island from which he would most likely never be able to leave, unless it was in handcuffs or a coffin—hoping to evade capture by the very government he had been tasked to serve. If he could make it out, it would be by the very skin of his teeth.

He looked over at his daughter once again, sleeping against the window of the plane with the little golden halo encircling her head, and tried now to memorize the features of her face.

When Leilani Kapuani received the call, she didn't know what to think. She raced to the airport and barely killed the engine before running inside. She spent three hours in interrogation before they would let her see her. They drilled into her relentlessly, trying to discern whether or not she knew anything about where he might've gone or how they might be able to find him. She didn't know anything at all, and that was the truth. The last time she'd seen her brother-in-law was at her sister's funeral, and they hadn't spoken since. Now here she was at the airport, enduring a grueling interrogation while the body of her mother was taken from a plane like luggage and shipped off to a morgue, her young niece sitting in a room somewhere with people she didn't know in a place she'd never seen before.

Once they were satisfied that she truly knew nothing, they let her go. The girl was put into her care for the time being, under the condition that she allow them to wiretap her phone and monitor her e-mail. She conceded. The only thing that mattered was getting the girl.

She left the airport in a state of shock, holding the girl's hand, trying to be strong, if only for her. They'd made it almost to the car when the little girl started crying—asking for her father, wondering where he'd gone, pleading for him. She sat on a bench beside the parking structure and held the girl to her chest and kissed her forehead.

"Oh, my baby. My sweet, sweet baby," Leilani cooed as she rocked her niece in her arms and stroked her hair.

"My poor darling Kamea."

CHAPTER 7

ISAAK

The energy of Tribo is severed instantly as everyone snaps back to reality. A sense of dread rises in the crowd between screams, and everyone around me scrambles to see what's happening. From the edge of my vision, I see a small explosion—a brilliant flash of embers floating up into the air and then blinking out of existence. I can't make out what's going on, but more of the flashes spark up near the walls. More voices scream out. Then I see them.

The main hall is being completely overtaken by Sheriffs. They're pouring in from every door, scaling down the walls, filing down the steps in numbers too great to assess in the dim light. Panic erupts around me as half-naked bodies scramble and flee.

"Everyone to the center of the room!" Malek shouts, but the din of the chaos drowns out his words. Beams of light flicker into existence from Robots around me as they stand and prepare to defend themselves. More shots ring out, and the body of a girl beside me falls to the ground.

To my right, Radha sends a column of flame over the crowd and up the stairs, incinerating a cluster of Sheriffs before they reach the floor. Behind her, Erica and her band of tele-kinetics stand shoulder to shoulder, hurling back bodies of Sheriffs as they descend. The bodies of men and women, clad in black, fly toward the walls and land with painful, reverberant cracks. Two boys hold hands and thrust electric shields like the kind Azure wields toward the encroaching horde, but it's not enough. Everyone is in a state of panic. Everything is in chaos. This is all happening too quickly.

I watch as more and more of the light bursts explode up into the air, and realize—in horror—what they are. The Sheriffs are thrusting thin, metal rods into the temples of paralyzed Robots. Once they penetrate the brain, their bodies rapidly disintegrate and explode in a flash of light.

I stand in a vacuum of silence as I watch more and more die around me. Young Robots—people—pinned to the ground, helpless, and destroyed.

I begin to reach out for the energy that has saved me before when a ringing noise fills my ears and a brilliant, blue flash erupts from the middle of the room. An almost-imperceptible ripple shoots outward from the center of the hall and, as it passes over me, my tie to the energy is severed. My body col-lapses to the floor, as does everyone around me. Everyone except the Sheriffs.

I am paralyzed, but fully conscious. No matter how my mind screams and pleads with my body, it will not comply. Nothing moves. My mouth, lips, and tongue are unable to speak.

The Sheriffs flood in, now completely undeterred, and the explosions of light fire off all around me at a rapid pace. One after another, the light of Robots dying in succession fills the hall with brilliant flashes of white.

I try to scream, but my body lies in silence.

Next to me I see Erica, Brooke, Ivan, and all of their friends. A Sheriff stoops down beside Ivan, places the rod against his temple, and drives it home. He flashes away into nothing as other Sheriffs move to Bryan, Jessica, Dustin, and Brooke. Their bodies disintegrate before me as a Sheriff finally straddles Erica. He grabs her by her wavy black hair, and I get one last glimpse of her face—one of the only faces to show me true kindness—before he places the metal stake against her temple and thrusts it in.

I try to close my eyes so I don't see her body evaporate into flecks of light, but I can't. In seconds she is gone.

In the moments before my death, something curious happens. I let go of the panic and terror inside and accept whatever is in store for me. As a sense of calm flows through me, I feel it: the energy I felt before. A tiny thread of the connective electric tissue linking me to everyone in here.

Without hesitation, I grasp it.

A deluge of blazing, golden light floods through me. Every atom of every molecule of every cell I comprise bursts with radiant power and in that instant I am one with every Robot around me. There is no me, only *we*.

The surge of energy pushes out of our skin and hurtles

every Sheriff to the walls and up toward the ceiling in a radiant explosion. Free of the paralysis, we rise to our feet and stand as one. Our skin pulses and flickers as an unimaginable amount of power flows through us. Memory, pain, experience, love, loss pass through us, and in that moment, we know one another. We are whole, and we are powerful.

The energy connecting us cannot be maintained much longer. It is finite and rapidly pouring from us. Then we feel them—tiny pinpricks of light, flickering candles to our inferno—surrounding us. There lies the energy we need. Without thinking, we reach out toward the nearest source of light and take hold of it. The body of a single Sheriff standing before us collapses as her energy flows into us, replenishes us, sustains us for another moment. But we will need more. Much more.

We will need all of them.

The bodies of each and every Sheriff in the hall rise up and glide toward us, ensnared by our unstoppable, golden light. They come to us a herd of sheep, offering their lives in tribute, and we greedily accept. One after another bodies fall to the ground as we absorb their very life force, until finally only one remains.

Ready to burst with our power, we hold the last Sheriff before our eyes, letting him wriggle in futile resistance before us.

We look into his eyes and see the very same fear we have felt for so long ourselves. But we are no longer prisoners to this fear, and never shall be again. We draw him closer to our face, so close that the heat from our glowing skin begins to sizzle his, and open our mouth to speak.

"We will live."

His body falls to the ground as we confiscate his light.

A moment passes, and within seconds the energy is racing out of us. With nothing left to sustain us, we must let go. So we release it.

The dim light of the main hall almost floors me as I am slammed back into reality. Glimpses of what just happened circle me like the nightmares I'm so used to, but this is no nightmare. This is real life.

The harsh, white lights of the main hall come to life as I look around in horror. A heaping mound of at least two hundred bodies, clad in Sheriff uniforms, lies around the remaining Robots, circling us. Lifeless limbs jut out of the pile in gruesome contortions, and blank eyes stare at us from bodies tossed haphazardly on top of one another.

Everyone is dazed, confused, trying to piece together what just took place. Several survivors begin to scream and cry, but I can't even move, paralyzed in horror at what I've done.

No. I couldn't have done this. This isn't possible.

"Isaak!"

A voice cries for me on the other side of the mound of bodies.

"Isaak!"

She cries out again, and a face pops up above the mound. It's Kamea.

"Isaak, you have to come with me. Now."

I take her hand and climb over the heap. Nausea churns in my stomach as I step over the corpses I assembled in a pile in order to save my own life. I am disgusted with myself. Everything is silent in my head, lost completely in my own despair, as Kamea rushes me toward the elevator.

As the doors close on us, I see Azure and Aleister step into the hall, fully clothed. Azure catches a glimpse of us, and just before the doors seal, I see her eyes go wide as she starts to run toward us.

As soon as the elevator opens onto the basement floor, Kamea runs with me toward the door to the left and rapidly sets the code in the lock. The door slides back and she races with me down the hall of secret projects. She punches in the next code and runs toward the control panels along the wall. Machines buzz and come to life as she nervously, frantically, steals glances back over her shoulder toward the door.

The hatch opens on the egglike Gate, and Kamea takes my hand.

"I need you to trust me, Isaak. Please trust me."

Her deep, brown eyes bear into me with a passion and ferocity I have never seen from anyone. Her spirit is wild and so full of life, and for the first time I notice something inexplicable. Standing before her, staring into her eyes, makes me feel the same way I felt standing at the top of Blackburn Park, looking out over Pacific in the early-morning light. It's like standing at the edge of the ocean.

A furious pounding at the door disrupts our gaze. I nod to her and she grasps my wrist and runs me over toward the egg.

"Just like we did last night. Both hands on the obelisk. This time, don't let go."

She's sending me away.

There's another furious pounding at the door, followed by muffled shouts.

Kamea takes me in her arms and hugs me, squeezing so hard I feel the breath expel from her lungs.

She knew.

She already knew what I was, what I could do, when she brought me here last night. She knew what the others were so afraid of, what I was so afraid of, and kept it from me. She showed me how to operate the machine and waited right until the very end—just before it dismantled me—to tell me to stop.

Please trust me.

Her words echo in my head as the sound of a powerful blast hitting the door fills the room.

I have no choice but to trust her.

She pulls back and looks into my eyes once more. "I'll see you when you wake up."

I step into the pod and place both of my hands upon the black obelisk as the hatch lowers and seals behind me. A tingling sensation rises up through my fingertips and flows through my arms into the very center of my being. I let the tendrils of my connection to the other Robots gently prod out around me and, within seconds the tingling turns into a fire.

I hold the obelisk tight and let go of everything—my body, my mind, my fear—and let the fire consume me.

Everything I have ever been or ever known burns away completely, and in a flash I cease to exist.

In death I find a quiet, all-encompassing solace that negates everything I once considered important, everything I used to value, used to *be*. Everything simply *is*. There is no pain, no wrongdoing, no judgment, only energy, flowing in and out of everything, all at once. My concept of time has been nothing more than illusion my whole life, and now, here in the void, I finally comprehend it.

At least I think I do.

The darkness envelopes me, but it doesn't frighten me. If anything, it is a comfort. I am fully a part of it all now—the nothingness, the everything. It just *is*.

A light appears on the horizon. Curious, I race toward it. I flow without fear or friction to the blooming glow. The light accepts me as I approach and absorbs me entirely. I leave the darkness as one leaves his true love—knowing, in the deepest part of his being, that they both shall meet again.

And then I wake up.

My eyes slowly open. I am naked, under a white sheet, in a white bed, in a sterile, white room. I can barely move. My body aches with a pain so deep it feels like it emanates from the center of my bones. Every nerve ending in my body is lit up, sensitive to every single touch and sound as though it might break me.

I lean my head to the left and see a series of machines connected to wires leading to small pads attached to my chest. I feel the machine operating as a phantom limb of my own body—checking me, scanning my vital signs, ensuring that I am still alive. I deactivate the machine with my thoughts and dim the lights in the room.

Within seconds I hear footsteps racing toward the door. It swings open and a man bursts in. He is somewhat short, with light brown skin and a head of thick, gray hair, cropped short. He wears glasses over his brown eyes and looks at me with what appears to be wonder.

He steps toward me, and I shake my head as much as I can. I don't want him to approach. I don't even know where I am.

"Where am I?"

My voice is raspy and weak. My own vocal chords feel foreign.

The man looks speechless. He glances at the machine to my left, powered down, then looks me up and down.

"You are somewhere quite safe, I assure you."

Safe.

The word means nothing to me anymore.

"Who are you?"

The man hesitates, then takes a step toward me. "My name is Dr. Mayur Asim."

Panic surges through me as I try to scramble out of the bed. My body refuses to comply, and I am barely able to shift more than a few inches.

"Please, please calm down."

Asim raises his hands in a peaceful gesture and moves toward me, but I refuse to let him come near me. This is the man responsible for our genocide. The terrorist attempting to use us in order to gain power. I don't know how I wound up here, but I will not let this man capture me and use me as a pawn. Gone are the days when I let others choose my path for me. I have power now, and I will use it if necessary.

I scramble for the energy inside me, but just before I find it, the door swings open once again, and Kamea walks in.

The energy dissipates before it arrives as she stands before me stunned, relieved.

"Isaak."

Nothing makes sense. Nothing feels right. The pain in my body flares up and my muscles go limp from exhaustion.

"What are you doing here?" My mouth feels so dry as I wheeze out the words.

"You're safe. Everything is fine. I promise I will explain everything, but for now you need to rest."

"I don't understand."

I glance at Asim, standing sheepishly at the side of the bed.

Kamea sighs and takes a moment before she looks into my eyes. "Isaak, this is my father."

The room swirls out of focus, and blackness creeps around the edges of my vision as her words play over and over in my head.

●─●─●

The next day, when I am finally able to stand, I take my first steps down the hallway beyond the door and try to gauge my surroundings. I appear to be in a laboratory. There are no windows, only fluorescent lights, computers, and desks cluttered with equipment. I stagger toward a flight of stairs, but Kamea runs down and intercepts me before I can make it up.

"You're up," she says as she gently wraps my arm around her shoulder for support. "Let me show you the house."

Slowly, she guides me up the steps and gives me a tour.

A few hours later we eat lunch at a large table in a dining room surrounded by glass. The house sits in the middle of what looks like a jungle—an endless, dense wall of green encloses us, hiding us from the outside world. A midday rainstorm pours down outside, and candles light the table as we eat. The food is incredible. My tongue revels in the sensations as though it's the first time it has ever tasted anything at all. Fruit and vegetables, all grown on the property, spiced with curry and cumin, served over rice. It all hits my system and nourishes me in a way I've never appreciated before.

"I can only assume you have many questions, Isaak," Asim says, breaking the silence as I clean my plate.

I put my fork down and give him my full attention.

"What you must know, first and foremost, is that I am not your enemy. Please know that."

A deep roll of thunder rumbles overhead.

"Any rumors of me being a terrorist, some mastermind bent

on using synthetic humans to achieve some sort of goal, are merely that: rumors. Planted by the SHRF, I assure you. They would not have their enemies discover common allies at any cost."

I glance to Kamea, who stares ahead in silence.

"I began work on the project that eventually led to the creation of synthetic human life many years ago, after my beloved wife, Kamea's mother, was diagnosed with cancer. I believed, foolheartedly, that I, above all other men, could find a cure. I accepted it as my destiny and sacrificed everything in order to achieve it. After my wife passed away, I met a woman who held the key to finally unlocking the door to my goal. A woman named Evelyn Adamson. Evelyn was one of the premier experts in nanorobotics at the time, and together we hypothesized that the answer to the riddle of curing the human cell lay not within the human cell itself, but in a new, healthy, synthetic version, capable of replacing it. Capable of functioning and replicating of its own accord, exactly as a healthy human cell should. But as we stood on the edge of our breakthrough, we were acquired by the United States government, with the promise of a blank check with which to fund ourselves and unbridled resources to continue our research. We were deceived."

A flash of lighting lights up the room, followed by another low rumble of thunder.

"The government had no interest in curing cancer, and very quickly we realized exactly where their true intentions lay. But it was too late. We were too far along. They had every-thing they needed to continue on without us, even if we were to pull out or attempt to halt the project. They used us to create the world's deadliest weapon, and we had succeeded."

A moment of silence passes over the room.

"The original team, including Evelyn and myself, began meeting in secret. Evelyn had already begun working on a plan to ensure that the project never came to fruition, because for all of the danger of a country wielding synthetic, impervi-ous supersoldiers, there was another even greater doom lurk-ing in the shadows that our superiors refused to acknowledge. What you may not know, Isaak, is that the cells in your body were initially created from those of an organic human. The technology that Evelyn and I developed, called the Master Cell, was meant to be capable of producing healthy, synthetic blood cells, capable of healing a human's diseased or dysfunc-tional ones. Master Cells, as they were designed, take control of a human's cell production, producing only synthetic cells henceforth, designed to help the body in which they were introduced. The government took it a step further however. They wanted synthetic life. They altered the Master Cells so that instead of targeting red and white blood cells, they took control of the germ cell production. When synthetic sperm fer-tilizes an organic egg, a being composed entirely of synthetic cells is born. The baby grows and appears to be a normal, albeit peculiarly healthy child, until the eve of his eighteenth birth-day. Like clockwork, after eighteen years, the cells inside the body fully manifest and activate to their full potential. This is when the government would have their coveted weapon: an army of synthetic soldiers, capable of feats of strength and wielding powers no human had ever dreamed of. What they didn't initially realize, though, was that what we had created behaved more like a parasite than a cure. Once the newly designed Master Cells took hold of the human host's germ cell production, the human would never again be able to produce an organic human child. In order to ensure efficiency, the government created the Master Cells to behave in a way that appeared almost ruthless in order to maximize their potential. Once the Master Cells take hold, organic men are controlled by an insatiable urge to breed, but because of the complexity of the egg itself, organic women are rendered sterile. Ultimately, the government had hurtled toward creating a synthetic cell capable of multiplying at a rapid rate, while simultaneously choking out our ability to replicate organically."

I stare openly at him while his words sink in. I can't believe what I'm hearing. The muscles in my forehead tense as I try to find the right questions to ask.

Kamea takes a deep breath and looks at me.

"Isaak, the technology used to create the Robots isn't just a weapon. It's a virus. The deadliest virus humanity has ever faced. And if we don't do something to stop it, humankind as we know it will be completely wiped out in only a few years."

My heart stops. Everything grinds to a halt as the reality of my very existence begins to finally appear clearly before me.

"There are only a handful of people left on Earth who stand a chance of stopping this from happening, and you're looking at one of them," Kamea says as she gestures to her father. "He might be the last one left, for all we know."

I rest my hands on the table and take several deep breaths. I look to Asim, then to Kamea. Her eyes are welled with tears. She reaches a hand out toward me and, gratefully, I take it.

"What do we do?"

"Fortunately, Isaak," Asim says, "I think you could be the key to everything."

I sit on the cliff and breathe deeply as the ocean crashes against the black rock below. The sky is a brilliant shade of rose gold, and the water below stretches out toward the horizon like an endless plane of blackish blue nothing. I close my eyes and try to breathe in some sort of comfort.

Kamea takes my hand and I open my eyes. She offers me a faint smile and then turns to watch the sunset. I look out as well and wonder how many of these I will be able to appreciate in my life. How many moments I'll be able to sit like this and simply be grateful that I was ever able to live in the first place.

Tomorrow we will leave this place, this hidden corner of the world, and set out to make so many wrongs right before it's all too late and no one is left alive to watch the sun set at all.

We have to get back to the others. We have to reveal to them what I now know, and unite, as a single force, to prevent catastrophe. Then we need to find her. Evelyn. She's out there somewhere and has the final piece to the giant puzzle I'm now a part of. Although Asim has no idea where she might be, he did receive one piece of communication from her during his years in hiding. A message that appeared on the screen of his computer, down in his lab.

It is functional. Find me when it is time. —Samus

The message ended with an image: a graphic of a small, red, 8-bit heart.

THE TRAITOR

She sat in the dark and checked once again that no one was behind her. He'd finally gone to bed. She thought he'd never go to sleep. Now everything was quiet, and she was sure she could make the call. She took the phone from her pocket and typed in the sequence of numbers. The momentary hold while she was patched through only seemed to amplify the silence. Her pulse quickened, as it always did when she spoke to him, and then a crackle sounded in her ear as the phone picked up on the other end.

"I've heard interesting reports."

"The invasion was a success. He's fully operational."

"And he's doing what needs to be done?"

"Don't worry. I have him completely under control. He will perform exactly as planned."

"Perfect."

"How is she?"

But before she received an answer, the line went dead.

She sat in the dark and wondered how she'd gotten here— lurking in the shadows, betraying everything and everyone she had ever known, plotting genocide.

She stepped back into the hallway and headed to her room, hoping she could sleep it all away.

ACKNOWLEDGMENTS

There are no words fit to describe the feeling of sitting down to write the acknowledgments for my very first novel. It is one of the biggest, most elusive dreams I've ever dreamed, and to think that it somehow came true is still incredibly surreal at times. In reality, dreams don't come to fruition on their own, and I'm thrilled to have the opportunity to thank those who've helped me bring this one to life.

First and foremost, I need to thank my parents, Monica and Carroll. I know that neither of you knew what to make of a child who wrote poems, refused to play outside in order to read as many books as possible, and physically needed to sing and dance in order to survive. You taught me what it means to be strong and showed me what true fortitude was when I faced cancer. You didn't understand me when you learned I was gay, but you both had the strength to seek forgiveness and to pursue the understanding that initially eluded you. I couldn't be more proud of how far our relationship has come, and cannot thank you enough for encouraging me in every single thing I've ever told you I was capable of doing.

To J. K. Rowling, for making me want to do this.

To Michael Scott, for telling me that I needed to do this.

To Alex London, for showing me that I could.

To Ernest Cline, for being so kind, warm, and thoughtful. You took the time to support me with a blurb when no one else would, and of everyone I asked, you could've easily been the one to laugh at me and simply say no. Thank you.

To Britney Spears, for existing.

To Laurie McLean, your enthusiasm, tenacity, and eagerness to say "YES! LET'S TAKE OVER THE WORLD!" to me whenever I need to hear it are so invaluable to me. I am lucky to have you as my agent.

To my publisher, Mara Anastas. I know that in publishing, the greatest support often comes from the top down, so thank you, from the bottom of my heart, for supporting this book the way that you have. I'm also so very thrilled to now have the real Liz Lemon in my life.

Mary Marotta, thank you.

To Liesa Abrams and Sarah McCabe, thank you for stepping into some huge shoes and doing everything you could to soften the blow of losing my editor. I'm so grateful to you both.

To Will Staehle, I will never be able to thank you enough for the million pieces of incredible art you created for this book, and especially for its jaw-dropping cover. I feel so lucky to have your work sitting atop a creation of my own.

Russell Gordon and Steve Scott, thank you for putting all of this together and designing it so beautifully.

Carolyn Swerdloff, Lucille Rettino, Tara Grieco, Catherine Hayden, and Chelsea Fought in marketing, THANK YOU. I have always heard horror stories about marketing a book, but you have all made me feel so supported and believed in. I am beyond honored to have your wonderful ideas and enthusiasm. Truly.

Jennifer Romanello and Jodie Hockensmith in publicity,

thank you for talking to me far earlier than any author should expect to talk to his publisher's PR team. You've made this a wonderful experience for me.

Michelle Leo and your amazing team in education/library, Christina Pecorale and your incredible team in sales, Katherine Devendorf and Mandy Veloso in managing editorial. Thank you all.

To the love of my life, Jordie Caskey. You've taught me more about what it means to be human than any person ever has. You know how real magic is and see God in everything. I am so grateful for you.

To my best friend, Corey Gibson. Thank you for believing in me more than what should be humanly possible. I'm so lucky to have you and your incredible ideas at work in spreading the message of this book, and I am more grateful than I'll ever be able to say. Thank you as well, Mary Robinson.

To everyone at the It Gets Better Project. Thank you for what you do. I am honored to align myself with your cause, and only hope that this book can help in some small way to spread your message.

Finally, most importantly, thank you, Michael Strother. Without you this book would still be an outline of ideas and fifty pages of manuscript, left waiting in various hard drives and journals scattered across my room. I can't believe the kind supporter of my music with the cupcake avatar on Twitter eventually became one of the most important people in my life, ever. I am in awe of your work ethic and your talent, and I will never be able to say thank you enough for truly making this dream come true.

I wrote this book, and the series beyond it, as a means of inspiring hope in young people. Kids who feel like outcasts, disenfranchised, like I did when I was younger. I wanted to tell a story about the power inside those things that make us different, and how capable we are of reshaping our lives once we embrace those things and harness that power. I love knowing that an organization like the It Gets Better Project is out there, working hard to share that very same message, and I'm so honored that *Boy Robot* gets to work with them to continue sharing it.

—Simon Curtis

IT GETS BETTER PROJECT.

The power of storytelling is embraced by the It Gets Better Project, not only as a vehicle for support, but also to further our mission to inspire hope and create change for LGBTQ young people around the world. Simon Curtis himself represents the It Gets Better message. He has experienced and overcome tremendous obstacles to get to where he is today. He is now endowed with the insights to weave his life lessons into a wonderfully entertaining piece of fiction. The It Gets Better Project congratulates Simon for his resiliency and perspective and is thrilled to be a part of the *Boy Robot* experience.